SEASONS
of
CHAOS

SEASONS

of

CHAOS

ELLE COSIMANO

HARPER TEEN

An imprint of HarperCollins Publishers

HarperTeen is an imprint of HarperCollins Publishers.

Seasons of Chaos
Copyright © 2021 by Elle Cosimano
www.epicreads.com

Library of Congress Control Number: 2021934340
ISBN 978-0-06-285427-8

Typography by Jenna Stempel-Lobell
21 22 23 24 25   PC/LSCH   10 9 8 7 6 5 4 3 2 1
❖
First Edition

For my readers. None of my worlds would exist without you.

PROLOGUE

The Observatory
March 2023

<u>DOUG</u>

Waking up after seventeen months in stasis is like recovering from a blunt force trauma to the head. The headache, the nausea, the shakes, the thick fog that steals all sense of place and time, leaving only the vague notion that I've been here before. Not just in this room or this place. But in this very moment.

"Douglas, are you all right?" The professor sits behind Chronos's desk, on Chronos's throne. The Staff of Time is leaning on a stand at his elbow like it belongs to him.

Daniel Lyon steeples his fingers, watching me across the desk with a wariness that could almost pass for concern.

"I'm fine." I hide my stasis tremors behind tightly clenched teeth. I want to set his chair on fire. Want to drown him, freeze him, strangle him with my bare hands, but every cell in my body feels weak, my magic spent. And he knows it. He hasn't even gone to the trouble to restrain me. A single guard—some dickhead I've never even seen before—waits outside the door.

A stasis chill takes hold. My back clings to the leather armchair, my Observatory-issued coveralls already drenched with cold sweat. All those months spent in a chamber have my senses cut sharp. The desk light's too bright, the old man's blue eyes too penetrating. The musty odors of the antique canvases and moldering books around the room are thick enough to choke me. Under it all, I swear I can taste the rot in the catacombs below us. And something else . . . a faintly fetid reek from an enclosure on a shelf on the back wall—one of Gaia's terrariums. The strange emerald serpent coiled inside isn't one of her usual pets. It's unlike any creature I've seen in the Observatory before, and I dig my nails into the armrests, wondering whose magic is trapped inside it. I hope like hell it's Jack's.

The snake's forked tongue flicks over the glass, the glittering diamondlike facets of its eyes shimmering as it watches us. It takes everything I have to drag my gaze from the tank.

"Why was I kept in stasis so long?" Three months would have been long enough to recover, even from the most violent death.

"What's the last thing you remember?" Lyon's tone is gentle, cautious. As if I'm something fragile, to be handled delicately. And I hate him all the more for it.

I massage my palm, blinking back a hot rush of emotion. I remember Denver's body crumbling to dust in my hands. Remember how I clamped ash-covered fingers around Fleur Attwell's neck, and the rage . . . the blinding rage I felt in that moment. My throat tightens painfully around the words. "I remember climbing out of the lake in time to see my best friend murdered in front of me."

"Fleur was merely defending herself and those she loved."

"And what about the ones *I* loved!" The word "loved" vaults from my mouth before I can wrestle it back. The room blurs behind a hot, bright oil slick of emotions. They're gone. Michael, Denver, my team—

"Noelle Eastman," Lyon says gently. Her name steals the air from the room. "I had hoped to be the one to tell you about her."

I shake off his sympathy with a callous shrug. "Tell me what? That my own girlfriend turned against me to defend your stupid cause? That she betrayed me to protect Jack Sommers?" I spit out his name, glad he's dead. Grateful at least for this one small victory.

"Noelle did what she felt was right. She protected you in the only way she knew how—"

"She sent me home!" I slam my fist against his desk, making the snake flinch back from the glass. "I know it was Noelle who killed me and sent me back through the ley lines! I smelled her coming." I smelled the familiar faint scent of vanilla on her skin. Felt the warmth of her whispered apology in my ear right before she slit my throat.

I can still feel the phantom pull of the ley lines as they dragged me back home into stasis, the lingering dull tug in my soul. I shove back from the desk, aching for her for reasons that make no sense. "Where is she anyway?" I growl. "If she's awake, I have a few words I'd like to say to her." Lyon just stares at me, pity in the shine of his eyes. "Where is she!"

"She's in the wind," he says, so softly I almost miss it.

I slump into the chair.

In the wind. Gone. Her soul scattered.

"Who did it?" I ask in a strangled voice. "Was it Fleur? I swear on that fucking staff, I'll—"

"Chronos struck the killing blow," he says, silencing me with a flash of white teeth. Lyon's eyes have gone hard. In them, I see a glimmer of Winter—the famed, fierce Season he used to be, not the middle-aged professor—staring back at me.

Of course he would protect her. Defend her. Lie for her. Fleur's one of the traitors who put him here.

"No!" I rise, nearly toppling my chair. "Noelle was an officer on my team. Traitor or not, she should have answered to me!"

"And if she had? If she had explained to you why she sided with Jack, would you have listened?"

I slam both palms down on his desk, ready to climb over it and rip out his throat. "You sanctimonious son of a bitch!"

Lyon's eyes darken as they slide to the staff, the twitch in his hand the only clue that he feels threatened by me. A black velvet sash is knotted around the head of the staff, covering the crystal eye at its center, as if Lyon is afraid of its power. As if he's too fucking chicken to look into it and see his own future.

I lean over the desk. "Do it, old man," I whisper. "Go ahead and kill me. That's why I'm here, isn't it? Because Jack is dead, and it was my team that killed him. And you want to make me suffer for it."

I lock eyes with him.

"Jack survived. He's alive, Douglas."

I fall back a step. "No. You're wrong. There's no way he's alive. I saw him fall through the ice. I watched him drown!"

"What you didn't see was the loyalty of those who loved him, and

4

the sacrifices they made to save him."

"That's impossible." It's not possible that Denver and Noelle are in the wind. That Chronos—*my* Chronos—is gone and Jack Sommers is still breathing. "You're lying!"

I stumble back from the desk, my heels connecting with the chair behind me as Lyon rises and reaches for the staff. The razor edge of the scythe glints as he lowers it between us and unwinds the velvet sash from the eye. It catches the light, throwing rainbows over the desktop. Flashes of my own face are captured inside them, flickering on the polished wood.

"What is that? What are you doing?"

"You wish to know what really happened. I'm showing you." Lyon turns the staff in increments, every degree revealing new images, moving backward in time until he finds the moment he's searching for. Denver's face appears, and suddenly, I can't speak.

I watch him die all over again. Watch Fleur murder him. Watch the magic and life and soul slip out of him.

"Stop," I grind out. "Make it stop."

The image rotates, the perspective shifting with dizzying speed. I don't recognize this memory. I'm not in my own head. It's as if I'm seeing myself through someone else's eyes.

Through Fleur's.

I see myself wrestle her to the ground, grappling for control of her hands. Fighting off her mind as she summons roots and vines to snare me. Noelle is there. She rushes me from behind, and I'm blinded by a quick flash of light—*my* light—as my own death plays out in front of me, and I'm pulled into the ley lines, back to the Observatory.

5

Noelle's cheeks are streaked with tears. She doesn't see Chronos approaching from behind, or the swing of his scythe. I squeeze my eyes shut as it hooks her and her magic disperses into the wind.

The vision shifts toward the shoreline, where Jack lies lifeless in the reeds. His friends hover around him, snapping arrows, compressing his chest. Fleur's a demon, savage in her vengeance, drawing more elemental power than any Season I've ever seen. Transfixed, I watch as she causes the ground to quake, commanding a dozen trees and vines to take down Chronos by his wrists and ankles. Her hair is charged with static, her eyes wild, as she presses his staff to his throat. She's merciless and terrifying and I'm disgusted by the admiration I can't help feeling as I watch her. She's a *Season* . . . a Season fueled by rage, who's managed to overpower a god. In the vision, even Lyon hesitates to stand too close to her.

Until she hands him the staff.

She falls to her knees beside Jack, just like all the others. Giving up everything for him. Fighting for *him*.

He's alive. Not in a terrarium or in an urn. Not in the wind. He's *alive*.

Sinking into the chair, I drop my head between my knees and fight the urge to be sick.

"You're not the only one to suffer a loss, Douglas. Jack survived his ordeal, and he's stronger for it. Perhaps not in the ways you imagined, but strength is about more than power and magic. It's about faith and trust and commitment. He made a choice. A choice to embrace his . . ."

Lyon's blathering abruptly dies.

I lift my head. But Lyon's not looking at me. He's frowning deep into the crystal. ". . . his future," he finishes. With a soft clear of his throat, he wraps the velvet sash back around the eye. "I hope you can move on from here as he has, Douglas. It's important that you try. The world moves on, with or without us," he says, the creases around his eyes deepening. "In one week's time, Gaia and I will be dismantling the last members of Michael's Guard. All those remaining will be awakened and relieved of their duties, as well as the magic granted to them by the former Chronos."

The damp jumpsuit chills my skin where it presses against the seat. "What does that mean? What are you saying?"

"Those who chose to serve under Michael may be swayed by conflicting values and loyalties. I cannot take any chances with the safety of the Observatory or those who choose to reside here."

"Choose?" The word tastes all wrong and I spit it back at him. "What does that even mean?"

"You may elect to retire," he continues, "in which case you will be stripped of your magic and assigned to a vacant position of service here within the school, where you may live out the remaining years of your natural life. But I will advise you that our systems have changed. Our rules are different now, Douglas. Our Seasons strive to live, both here and above ground, in peaceful coexistence. I will not allow anyone to disrupt that goal."

A cold, dry laugh escapes me. "And what if I don't want to retire?"

"Then that decision will result in Termination. As will any intimation of harm against Jack or Fleur." Lyon's eyes meet mine. There's no mistaking the unspoken threat inside them. *So that's what this is about.* This isn't about protecting the Observatory. It's about protecting Jack.

It's about keeping me powerless down here, where I can't get to him.

"You might as well just kill me now," I say through my teeth.

"It's a significant decision—"

Despite the lightness in my head, I launch to my feet. "No, it's a punishment!"

"It is also a *choice*, Mr. Lausks." Lyon doesn't rise. Doesn't reach for the staff.

"Maybe I wasn't clear, old man. I'm not giving you my magic. I'd rather die than serve you. You are not my Chronos. You never will be."

"Your Chronos would never have given you the option," he says quietly. "I will not take it from you. You will have one week to think on your decision. Extraction is taxing on the body, and you should use this time to rest and reflect. You're tired, and you have a lot of information to absorb."

One week. Long enough for me to recover the strength I'll need to survive the pain of extraction as they rip away my magic. But not long enough to gather the power to fight it. "And if my decision won't change?"

"You may use the week to put your affairs in order. Gaia and I will consider any final requests you'd like to make with regard to your personal property." His eyes lift to mine. "Death doesn't have to be the only choice. There *is* a way forward. Take time," he says pointedly, wielding that word as if it belongs to him.

"Is that all?" As far as I'm concerned, we're done here.

"Douglas," he says, stopping me before I reach the door. "I am truly sorry for your loss."

Loss, he calls it. As if it's all a game. As if he plucked a few damn chess pieces off the board and we can all just start over. I shake my head as I shove through the heavy double doors, nearly crashing into the figure cowering on the other side. Kai wraps her arms around herself, pale and shaking like she's just awoken from stasis. Kai Sampson, the best marksman in the Guard. The champion archer who shot Jack Sommers full of arrows, and for what?

For nothing.

"Doug?" Her voice cracks. She reeks like cold sweat as I shoulder past her. "Doug, what happened? What did he want?"

She has no idea. No idea Jack's alive. No idea what's happened while we've all been sleeping. I don't tell her what Lyon said. That we've lost the battle. That our enemies have taken control of our home. I don't tell her we're about to lose our lives, or our magic. Because I have no intention of letting the bastard get that far.

1

A STRANGELY ACHING HEART

FLEUR

A guitar riff screams against the walls of the villa, drowning out the morning chatter of the jays as I follow the sound through the veranda. By the time I reach the workout room, Jack's favorite '80s punk mix is reverberating in my bones. I push open the door, covering my ears against the hammering of drums.

"Jack!" I can't even hear myself over the bass. Neither can he, apparently. "Jack, you really shouldn't—"

His back rests on the weight bench, his legs spread, his bare feet pressed flat against the floor as he shakes chalk from his hands and adjusts his grip on the bar. It's loaded down with far too many plates. I open my mouth to shout again. Oblivious, he sucks in a few short breaths, gritting his teeth as he pushes the bar from its cradle. Jack's muscles tighten into distracting patterns, cords straining in the flushed column of his neck as he lowers the bar and presses it up again.

Eyes squeezed shut, he pushes out a few more reps. I hover close, my hands poised to catch the bar if it drops. His jaw strains, his breath heating my face as I help guide the bar the last few inches into the cradle.

His gray eyes flash open as the bar clatters into place with an echoing *thud*. A smile tugs on his lips. He lies there, covered in sweat, grinning at me upside down, lip-synching the words to whatever song is blaring through the speakers. I reach for his phone and shut the music off.

"I said, you shouldn't be lifting this much weight without a spotter!" My voice is too loud, the music still ringing in my ears.

"I don't need a spotter." He arcs his back a few inches off the bench, lifting his shirt to mop sweat from his face. His sly grin widens, teasing a blush out of me when he catches me staring at the taut lines of muscle underneath. We've been living together, sleeping together in the same bed, for more than a year, but the sight of him still knocks me breathless sometimes. He reaches up and tugs the end of my pink ponytail until my face hovers upside down above his. Perspiration shimmers in his dark hair and shines on his upper lip, leaving a deliciously salty taste on mine as he steals a sweaty kiss from me. Under the bright overhead lights, his eyes sparkle with mischief.

Whatever irritation I felt moments ago melts away as he swings out from under the bar and tugs me gently onto his lap. The calluses on his palms catch on the loose fabric of my skirt as he slides his hands up my hips, leaving snowy white trails of chalk on the dark cotton before settling on the small of my back.

"If you're not careful, you're going to hurt yourself," I say, the words tinged with worry. "Your physical therapist—"

"My physical therapist gave me the green light," he reminds me. It's been nearly eighteen months since Gaia brought him back from the brink of his last death with three arrow-shaped scars in his back and a hole in his heart where his magic used to be. A hole he insisted would fill with time. But some days, I'm not so sure.

My brows knit and he draws me closer.

"The doctor said you could ease your way back into a light training routine." I wipe a bead of sweat from his cheek. "Three hours a day in here isn't 'light training,' Jack. And benching two twenty—"

"Isn't going to kill me." He turns my hand over and presses a kiss against my palm. Goose bumps ripple over me as his lips travel to the crook of my arm. "My body's in excellent shape," he whispers, his dark dusting of morning stubble igniting a trail of shivers over my collarbone. "But if you want to test my endurance, I'm completely on board with that."

Laughing, I push him back by the chest with questionable effort. "I've got Spanish lessons in less than an hour." And if he keeps kissing me like this, I swear to Gaia, I'll never make it to class.

He draws me back against him by the front of my shirt. "I'll give you a very good reason to ditch."

I swat his hands away as I stand and wipe the chalk from my skirt. "You can show off your physical prowess when I get home."

"What if I want to show you now?" His fingers graze my waist as it swings out of reach. I let my gaze linger playfully on his chest. Then lower. My grin widens as I settle into a sparring stance.

"Fleur," he laughs, "this isn't exactly what I had in—"

I drop to the mat, sweeping his legs out from under him. His breath rushes out with the force of his fall, and before he can react, I'm on top of him.

"Fleur—"

Slamming his wrists against the mat, I pin him down with my knees. Something flashes in his eyes, wicked and wild. "Oh, so that's how it's going to be?" He surges under me, throwing me sideways, careful to control my fall as I crash down into the thick foam. We grapple, breathless and giggling, tumbling over each other until he's got me pinned.

"You're holding back," he says, loosening his grip, giving me an out I don't need. He may be stronger, but the windows to the villa are completely open to the garden outside. I could summon roots and vines to haul him off me and hang him from the ceiling by his toes if I wanted to.

I melt into the mat, my laughter dying as the hard angles of his hips sink to fit against the soft, warm space between mine.

"Maybe I like you like this," I whisper.

I see it then, in his almost-flinch—whatever it is he's been stacking on that weight bar and carrying alone. His dark hair falls over his eyes.

"Hey," I say, angling my face to catch his gaze. I know why he spends so many hours in here. And while I can't deny the end result is amazing, it hurts knowing why he's become so obsessed. "I love you, Jack. *You*." I didn't fall in love with him because of his magic. Nor did I fall out of love when he lost it. If anything, I fell harder, loving him more, for the strength it must have taken him to give it away. "I love you like *this*."

Lacing our fingers together, I raise our hands up over my head, bringing our faces close, the same way I held him down at the edge of the pond near the safe house, the night we shared that first earth-shattering kiss. It had started as a snowball fight, two Seasons wrestling in the marshy grass in a fit of laughter to see who would come out on top. Maybe he let me get the best of him that night, but it didn't matter. Did it? Our lips met somewhere in the middle.

"I'm making you late." His nose brushes mine, and his mouth skates over the edge of my lips. "You should probably get ready for class." The words are lost in the haze that wraps around me as he grazes my ear. His voice is deep, rough with desire, sending a delicious shiver through me, and I wonder if he knows how much power he has. How he ignites my blood and makes my body thrum, even without his Winter magic.

"Are we ever going to talk about this?" I ask.

Jack's breath stills against my neck. He pulls back a little, just enough to search my face. He presses a too-soft kiss to my lips before untangling himself from my hands. Suddenly, his warm weight is gone, and he's reaching down to help me up. "I've got my meeting with Lyon, then I'm going for a run."

"Where?"

"To the park," he says, reaching for a towel.

My hands freeze where they smooth the wrinkles from my shirt. Forcing a smile, I hitch a thumb over my shoulder, gesturing at the treadmill I bought him for Christmas. He hasn't turned it on once since I took it out of the box. The sleek black machine sprawls like a slumbering cat, positioned strategically in front of the open window. "It won't kill you to try it, you know."

"Neither will running outside alone." He tucks a loose strand of hair behind my ear. We both know why I bought it. He knows I hate running. That I only go running with him at the park every morning because I'm afraid to let him go by himself. I don't worry about myself out there. The rules of our world have changed since the rebellion. Most of the restrictions that used to keep Seasons in check have been lifted, giving us more freedom than we've ever had before. But while most Seasons seem grateful for the change, I'm not foolish enough to believe there aren't still a few out there who feel loyal to Michael and miss the old ways. Lyon assures us he rounded up as many as he could find, but it only takes one, and Jack's face is far too recognizable—he might as well be the poster boy for the whole revolution. And as much as I hate to admit it, he's vulnerable without his magic. Daniel Lyon may have granted Jack immortality as part of the benefits package for the roles we played in overthrowing Michael, but just because our bodies don't age doesn't mean we can't be injured or die. We both have to stay vigilant if we want to plant safe roots here. And running alone in the city isn't smart.

"Why won't you use it?" I ask, leaning a hip against the treadmill.

"Because . . ." He rakes up his sweat-matted hair, the jagged crown of black spikes falling back over his eyes as he paces away from me. "It makes me feel claustrophobic."

"It's in front of the window."

"I can run outside. It's perfectly safe. I don't want to be hooked up to electronic devices all the time."

I tap my ear, where my transmitter usually sits. The one Jack makes me wear whenever I leave the villa. "Aren't you being a little hypocritical?"

He shakes his head, laughing silently, his hands on his hips as he saunters toward me. He curls his arm around my waist. "I'm supposed to be *your* Handler. Not the other way around."

I lean back, raising an eyebrow. "Yeah? Well, maybe I don't need a spotter, either."

His lips chase mine, smiling against them as he steals another kiss. "Too bad. You made your choice. You're stuck with me."

I wrap my arms around his neck. "I'll never regret it."

Jack had been as good as dead, bleeding out beside a frozen lake, when I was given the choice to save one person to be my Handler and protector for the rest of my immortal life. Watching him die nearly killed me, and I have no intention of losing him again. "Treadmill, please," I say, ruffling the ends of his damp hair. I rise up on my toes to plant a last kiss on his cheek. "Or wait for me to get home and I'll go with you."

"Wear your transmitter!" he calls after me.

"I have my cell phone," I shout over my shoulder.

"Fleur?"

"I know!" My voice carries across the veranda as I stride to our bedroom. I hate that damn tracking device, probably for the same reason Jack hates the treadmill—they remind us too much of the life we fought to leave behind. But as Jack so often insists on pointing out, cell phones are difficult to locate with any degree of accuracy, and they're useless if you need both hands free to fight. And he's right—my tracker is the only reliable way he can keep tabs on me when I'm away from home. So, because it means a lot to him and I hate to see him worry, I tuck it in my ear before slipping on my sandals and packing up my textbooks for class. As I drag my backpack over my shoulder, I catch movement across the courtyard.

Through the window, across the veranda, I watch as Jack scoops up his running shoes and turns off the lights.

2

IF I SHOULD EVER COME BACK

JACK

I carry my running shoes through the villa, down the long, open-air corridor past Fleur's paintings to my office, pausing at the kitchen on the way. The jays squawk as I tear into a cinnamon roll Fleur left on a plate for me, awaiting the crumbs she always scatters over the edge of the balcony for them while she eats. Even the branches of the jacaranda seem to lean toward the villa, angled toward Fleur and her earth magic like she's their sun.

Leaning a hip against the butcher block island, I drag a finger over the puddle of hardening icing left on the plate. A paper is pinned underneath it, and I lick the last of the sugar from my fingers, careful not to leave sugary prints as I pull the torn page of a magazine from under the rim. It's an ad, featuring a glossy color photo of a streetscape in Amsterdam, a dreamy-eyed couple on a bridge, promising a week of romance. A handwritten date is circled with a heart—March 11, the day

Fleur first agreed to run away with me, which she's deemed our official anniversary.

I tack the ad for the riverboat cruise against the side of the fridge with a magnet, alongside the others: a railway tour of the Canadian Rockies, a backpacking trip through Chile, gastronomic tours of Italy and Greece. Now that we're free of the Observatory, Fleur wants to see the world. She wants to go everywhere, because I promised her we would. But as her Handler, my number one priority is to keep her safe. Nestled in our villa in Cuernavaca, the City of Eternal Spring, surrounded by Fleur's garden and a security system I've spent more than a year perfecting, I can do that.

But out there?

We barely survived our journey to get here. It took all eight of us—four Seasons, each with our own magic, and four Handlers to keep an eye on our backs—just to make it this far. We lost friends and allies along the way, pieces of ourselves. We all came away changed—me more than anyone.

I fling open the door of the fridge in search of some milk to chase away the stubborn lump in my throat. The cold air inside condenses, tumbling out in billowing smazelike clouds, and I lean into them, eyes closed, letting the chilled air roll over me. The hum of the refrigerator drowns out the birds on the terrace, until the kitchen disappears and I'm back at the frozen pond with Fleur. My fingers curl around the cool steel of the fridge door handle. I miss the crackle of frost on my skin. Miss the way Fleur looked at me when I made it snow for her. Miss the zing of magic that coursed through us when we touched.

Her willingness to give in so easily when we sparred in the training room felt like a concession. A gentle reminder that I'm not a Season anymore. No longer the one who can recharge her magic or heal her with a touch. No matter how many hours I spend fighting those weight machines, I'm just her human Handler. And there are days—my worst days—when I wonder if that's still enough for her.

With a sharp shake of my head, I snag the carton of milk and shut the refrigerator doors. Drinking straight from the container, I choke down huge gulps, but it does nothing to wash away the guilt I feel for the pathetic, selfish thoughts I've been thinking since I watched her leave the training room.

I have Fleur. We have each other and our lives. She can take Spanish classes, read romance novels with happy endings by the pool, and paint terrible paintings of every species of plant in her garden. We can make out for hours, then fall asleep in the same bed, without worrying that one of us will die.

We have a spectacular home, bursting bank accounts, and the added bonus of my immortality, all thanks to our reward for bringing about the rebellion that put Lyon in power.

We can live here, together in a paradise of our own making, forever if we want to. My magic was a small price to pay for that.

I pitch the empty milk carton into the trash can and swipe a hand-ful of crumbs from the counter into my palm, scattering them over the balcony for the birds as I leave the kitchen. They dive down to the patio below, chasing the small offering in a greedy chorus as I grab up my running shoes and pad to my office.

I can't blame Fleur for wanting to travel. Even though the house is open to acres of wildlife, it can be hard not to feel hemmed in sometimes.

Surrounded by security gates and cameras and a fortress of trees, we're completely safe here on the grounds of our villa. And for the most part, we're safe in the surrounding region and the towns within it. Daniel Lyon, the new Chronos, and his partner, Gaia, issued a protective order around our home here in Cuernavaca, including a hunting ban for a radius of a few hundred miles. But just because rules are set in place doesn't mean everyone plays by them. I should know, since I was the one who started the rebellion that got us here.

In the wake of that rebellion, freed Seasons are required to check in weekly with an assigned staff member back at the Observatory. We're supposed to report any planned trips outside our regions and submit to careful monitoring. When our friends Julio and Amber want to come visit, it's no big deal—just a few phone calls, some added security measures, and a few plane tickets. But if Fleur and I want to escape off the grid, just the two of us—a Season alone with her nonmagical Handler—things get a whole lot trickier to plan. I don't know if Lyon's just paranoid about the handful of rogue Seasons they haven't been able to round up, or if he received some kind of specific threat, but for the last few months, he's seemed more and more on edge, and not a week goes by that he doesn't offer to have a team of escorts bring us home.

But the Observatory under Greenwich Park in London isn't home anymore.

I duck into my office and settle into my chair. My state-of-the-art computer setup boasts three sprawling flat-screens and a sound system that could knock the terra-cotta tiles off the roof of the house. The walls above the monitors are decorated with old posters of classic 1980s films and obscure punk bands. An old crushed-velour couch with pink cushions lines the opposite wall. I don't know why I bought it from the flea market downtown, except that the frame sags in places that remind me of the couch Chill and I left behind in our dorm room at the Observatory, even if the color's all wrong. Above it, jammed between Dead Kennedys and *A New Hope*, hangs one of Fleur's first paintings: a lopsided evergreen capped in snow.

I wiggle the mouse, rousing the wall of monitors above my desk. The security panel beeps as the front door opens and closes again.

A moment later, Fleur appears on a black-and-white monitor in front of me. I slip on my headset as she makes her way down the cobbled driveway, the low heels of her sandals clacking and the long waves of her pink hair playing on a breeze. My chest aches every time I watch her walk out of here.

She turns and blows me a kiss. The red light linked to her transmitter moves briskly over a map on the next screen, her GPS tracker displaying every turn she makes between here and her favorite café. I'm only half listening as she enters the coffee shop and places her usual order in stilted Spanish. A new barista's working the counter. I glance up at the footage from her body cam in time to see him wink as he hands over her cappuccino. I don't know much Spanish, but I manage to pick up the gist of his question in the hopeful lift of his brow.

"Did he just ask you out?"

Fleur waves goodbye to the barista. "If you'd come to class with me once in a while, maybe you'd know." I can hear her smile. See it in the bounce of her step as she saunters from the shop. "Don't you have a meeting or something far more important to do than spying on me?"

"Nothing will ever be more important than what I'm doing right now." My attention shifts between her GPS, her vitals, and her body-cam footage. I turn to my second monitor, scrolling quickly through satellite weather images and the day's news headlines. The weather's clear a few hundred miles in every direction. Nothing to suggest any other Seasons wandering too close to our region or encroaching on Lyon's boundaries without permission.

She hauls open the door to her language school. "Did you see what I left for you in the kitchen this morning?"

"The cinnamon roll?"

"The canal cruise through Amsterdam," she says, climbing a set of winding concrete stairs. "Will you talk to Lyon about it?"

The whole idea gives me heartburn. "Fleur, I don't know if—"

"He owes us this." Fleur's red light stops moving. I lift my head to the feed from her body cam. She's standing outside her classroom door, her crossed arms reflected in the glass pane, staring back at me.

"I'll talk to him," I promise.

The corners of her mouth lift in the glass, a small smile just for me, as she reaches for the door. "I'll be home in a few hours."

"Be safe," I murmur.

I don't relax until Fleur's red light settles into the fourth seat in the second row of her classroom. I feel a stab of sympathy for Chill, my former Handler. I wonder if this was how he felt every time I walked out the doors of the Observatory during the thirty years I spent as a Winter. If he had nightmares and lost sleep worrying over me while I was out in the world alone.

An incoming video call flashes on one of my screens.

"Professor," I greet Lyon as I strap on my wrist monitor. I still haven't gotten used to the idea of calling him Chronos, but I'm not sure he's gotten used to being Chronos, either. I lean down, my voice muffled as I drag on my running shoes. "You're punctual, as usual."

I sync my wrist monitor with Fleur's tracking program, making sure the red light blinks on. Professor Lyon's weekly check-ins are usually short. If I hurry, I can make it to the park and get a few miles in before Fleur gets home. She won't even know I left the house.

"As are you, for a change." Lyon's humor is dry, his formal tone difficult to read sometimes. It's hard to tell if he's being sardonic or sincere. "It seems I've caught you on your way out. I won't keep you long."

"Sorry." I adjust the video camera, giving him my full attention. "Everything all right?"

Lyon's face is drawn. He rakes back the silvering hair at his temples and rubs his eyes, a more human gesture than I'm used to seeing from him. A smile touches his winter-blue eyes. "It's been a difficult week here at the Observatory."

"More difficult than usual? I thought you and Gaia were already past the worst of it."

After killing Michael, the former Chronos, Professor Lyon and Gaia had returned to the Observatory with a thoughtful and clear plan for liberating and reforming it—a plan they'd spent centuries secretly devising. The Guards loyal to Michael were rounded up and detained in stasis chambers within the Observatory. Awakened from their extended sleep in groups, they were subjected to hearings over the months that followed, as Lyon and Gaia replaced them with a security team of their own—a collection of Seasons and Handlers they'd been observing and quietly cultivating relationships with for years.

With the old regime out of the way, Lyon and Gaia then dismantled the old systems. New rules were established, condemning violence
between Seasons and rewarding cooperation between the previously
segregated wings. The restricted sections of the Observatory library
were declassified, and Seasons were encouraged to bridge the gaps in
our knowledge of our own history, to learn the truth about our magic—
the truth Fleur and I had discovered and exposed to the world: that in
pairs, we can survive off the complex system of ley lines Michael had
leashed us to.

Think tanks and action committees were formed, consisting entirely
of volunteers, allowing Seasons and Handlers to have a voice, paving a
gradual path to peace. With the ranking system rendered meaningless,
the barriers between wings were gradually opened, and Seasons were
slowly given opportunities to train, eat, and mingle together. According
to Lyon, there had been a handful of fights, but for the most part, the
transitions had gone smoothly. And Seasons who wanted to be liber-
ated from the Observatory, like Fleur and me, were granted the right to
leave. Subject to a period of monitoring, they were released in pairs and
permitted limited freedom of movement to preserve the environmental
balance and ensure their safety.

When Lyon and I spoke last week, everything seemed fine; Lyon
and Gaia's plan had fallen into place relatively peacefully. With all the
challenges of the initial transition behind them, it seems odd that he
should look so worn out now.

"Gaia and I have awoken the last of the members of the old Guard."

"About time," I say bitterly. That's one less threat I'll have to worry about. Michael's old regiment—a group of elite personal Guards gifted with the powers of every Season—had hunted and attacked us just miles from here, and the Guards who were left in stasis the longest had been deemed the biggest threat to me and Fleur. I don't think I'll ever forget Kai Sampson's narrowed eye in the moment before she shot me full of arrows. Or Doug Lausks's teeth as he sprinted over the frozen lake to kill me. I'm more than ready for Lyon to dole out their punishments. "What will happen to them?" I ask, remembering the bee Lyon crushed under his shoe the day he helped us escape the Observatory—a bee that had once been a Season . . . or at least the soul of one. After what Doug and the other Guards did to us, I find it hard to muster any sympathy for them.

Lyon sighs as if he's not entirely sure. "They will be stripped of their magic. Like the others, we've given them the choice to live on here, taking on service positions at the Observatory."

I raise an eyebrow. Lyon raises one in return, acknowledging my surprise. "Most are grateful for the option, given the alternative."

"Even Doug?"

A shadow passes behind Lyon's eyes. "I'm not sure he can be swayed into conceding his magic peacefully."

"Can't you just look in your magic wand and see?" The Staff of Time carries an insane amount of power: the power to grant immortality, to pause the clock, and to reveal glimpses of the future.

"I prefer not to."

"Why not? Seems like it might help you find an answer to your problem."

"Will it?" He tips his head. "Correct me if I'm wrong, but I don't believe I'm the only one who fears the consequences of my own power. Perhaps we are wise, you and I, to recognize the risks in making such decisions."

I pick at a crack in the surface of the desk, finding it hard to look at the twisting dark cloud in the glass orb atop his desk.

"Be that as it may," he continues, "I had hoped not to use the staff in the manner of my predecessor. But I fear Doug may leave me no choice. Only time will tell, I suppose." He shakes his head. "But enough of this. How are you and Fleur?"

"We're good."

He leans back in his chair, studying me over steepled fingers, his old office coming into focus behind him, the poster of Cuernavaca mounted in the same place it's hung as long as I've known him. The sudden pang of homesickness I feel surprises me. I don't miss the Observatory at all, but Lyon's office feels like a ley line to my soul. All those years, it was the one place I didn't have to speak my mind or confess my heart, because somehow, Lyon already knew what was beating around inside it.

"How is she sleeping?" he asks gravely.

"Okay. Better." It's a lie. Fleur still wakes in cold sweats most nights, screaming. Sometimes, she thrashes and calls out Doug's name, or Denver's, or Noelle's, as if she's still wrestling with them in her sleep. We're both fighting our own demons. There's no sense in worrying Lyon over it. "She's getting a little antsy. She wants to plan a trip."

"I understand. It's been a long time since you visited with your friends. Gaia and I would be happy to approve arrangements for you both to travel to California to see them."

"Actually, she wants to go somewhere for our anniversary. You

26

know . . . maybe do a little sightseeing. Just the two of us." This last part is more about me than Fleur. Fleur would probably be thrilled to have Julio and Amber tag along for a whirlwind tour of the Mediterranean or a trip to visit Poppy and Chill and check out the sights in Alaska. But ever since the battle, being around them is hard for me. I'm not a Season anymore. The last time Julio and Amber came to visit, it was like I was on the outside looking in on them all, my hands pressed against the window glass. I'd been sitting right beside Fleur, and I'd never felt so apart from her.

Lyon scratches his cheek. "Are you sure that's wise, Jack?"

"It would only be a week. The weather will be warm enough. Fleur will be fine."

"I have concerns . . ."

"Concerns about what?"

"Nothing to do with you," he assures me. "I know you and Fleur would do everything in your power to take care of one another. But the timing . . . There are still a few rogue Seasons we haven't been able to track down, and word of this final Dismantling is bound to ruffle some feathers. I'd feel better sending a security detail to shadow you, but I can't spare—"

"Never mind. You're right." I rub the glossy image from Fleur's magazine from my eyes. "It's probably a terrible idea."

"No, it's not." He sighs, scrubbing a hand over his stubble. "You and Fleur deserve this much. I'll speak with Gaia. Perhaps we can come up with a plan. Let's revisit this when we meet again for our call next week."

I give a shallow nod, unable to shake the feeling that there's something he's not telling me. "Are you sure you're okay, Professor?"

"Just tired." He forces a smile. "I'm fine."

"Still teaching?" I press him.

"Much to Gaia's dismay. She's concerned I'm trying to do too much. To *be* too much, perhaps."

"Maybe she's right." My eyes dart to the orb in the corner of the screen. The clear globe rests in its usual place on a brass pedestal on Lyon's desk. The smaze inside that orb is mine, the shadowy mist a host for my former magic, entrusted to Lyon for safekeeping when I chose to give my life for our cause. Lyon's magic had once been trapped in a globe like this one—magic he'd willingly given up in order to be closer to Gaia, then given up again to take up a much heavier mantle.

I turn away from the screen before my longing gives me away.

"I swore an oath to you, Jack. I'll keep it safe." Lyon rests a hand on the curvature of the glass. "I owe you an immeasurable debt. If you ever again wish for your magic, you need only to ask."

The gray smaze whips inside the glass, hungry to get out. But reclaiming my magic would come with a price.

My magic's not the same as it was. Gaia sensed it when it left me, that there was something wrong with it, angry and dark. She speculated that the most tortured parts of my soul—all my worst fears and resentments, the most painful bits of my deepest and most horrible memories—hitched a ride with it on its way out of me, as if it knew that was the only way I would ever survive what I'd been through. But I've always wondered if it was something more. If the darkness in that smaze isn't because of something I've gone through, but something I've *done*. And the fact that I still ache to have it back in spite of that troubles me

28

more than anything else about it.

"There is a way to make peace with it, Jack. Facing your demons may be the first step to forgiving yourself. Gaia and I said it would be painful. We never said it was impossible."

I push that thought back into a deep corner of my mind.

"It's okay to pause the world sometimes, to take the time you need to heal and think after suffering a trauma, as you and Fleur have done. But it's not too late, Jack. You can always choose another way forward. Gaia and I would be here for you, if you decided to try," he says delicately. "We won't let you go through it alone."

I bite my tongue. I made an oath, too, to keep Fleur safe. To honor her choices. And I won't throw this one in her face to save my own pride. "I'm fine."

"Very well, then," he says. "I've wired your quarterly living allowances to your accounts. And I've procured permanent visas for you and Fleur so you may remain in Mexico as long as you wish. They'll arrive by courier later this week, along with new passports in case you change your mind about returning to the Observatory—"

"Or for when Fleur and I plan our trip," I remind him.

His mouth quirks up as he continues. "Your new documents will hold up to routine airport scrutiny, but I'd advise you both to avoid any legal entanglements, to prevent any investigations into your identities. Mind the speed limit while driving, and don't get into any skirmishes involving the police." His clear eyes twinkle like the crystal in the eye of his staff, reflecting all my past decisions and every possibility in my future. I grin in spite of myself. Lyon's the closest thing I've had to a father figure in more than thirty years, and even though we don't always see eye to eye, it's comforting to know he's there looking out for me.

"I'll behave."

"I won't count on it," he says wryly. "If you speak to Amber, Julio, and the others, be sure to send my best."

"I will."

"And Jack," he says, his voice tinged with melancholy, "I know you and Fleur have no desire to return here. After all you've both been through, I suppose I've no right to expect otherwise. But you will both always have a home here. Don't ever doubt that."

If I shut my eyes right now, I could smell his office—the heavy scent of coffee and aging books, the dry pinch of his chalk in the back of my throat. I nod, swallowing a small nagging yearning to go back. To see my smaze. To see him.

"Until next time, Jack."

"See you, Professor." I hold my smile until his image flickers out.

3

THE CALLUS ON HIS SOUL

DOUG

I don't make it ten steps out of Lyon's office before I'm surrounded by four of his new Guards. I grit my teeth as they escort me down the brightly lit hall. One of them presses a phone to his ear, voicing affirmatives between extended pauses. With an abrupt jerk of his head, he indicates a change in direction, detouring us away from the gallery that should take us back to the elevator in the Crux. Back to my room.

"Where are we going?" I bite out as he slips his phone into his pocket. The sooner I get to my room, the sooner I can start planning a way out of here.

The Guard holds open a door to a familiar stairwell. An earthy, stagnant dampness rises from the passages below. My feet slow and I'm nudged from behind.

"You're being moved."

"Where?"

"To a holding cell." The team guides me down a flight of stairs.

The temperature drops, and a chill rakes up my spine. The secure cells are in the catacombs. Impossible to break out of.

This puts a fucking damper on things.

The white walls and bright overheads give way to circular steps, carved out of stone and lit with torches. They herd me through the winding tunnels of the caves below the school, into a corridor of cell doors made with heavy iron bars. A crow—one of Gaia's spies—squawks, shaking out her feathers as we brush past her perch. I'm directed into an open cell, and the locks snap closed behind me.

I turn at the sound, the stone walls closing in around me, but the Guards are gone, their footsteps already fading under the distant hum of the generators and the scratch of the crow's talons against her perch.

I pace the edges of my cell. I didn't pause to get a haircut during the weeks I spent hunting for Jack, and a stubborn piece of hair keeps falling into my eyes no matter how many times I rake it back. I'd kill someone for a pair of scissors and a razor. But Lyon's given me nothing. Clearly, he doesn't trust me to wait out the week without incident. And for good reason. I'd burn this whole place down before I'd concede to give up my magic and serve the rest of a mortal life here.

I grab the bars in the door and shake them, just to loosen some pent-up frustration. It's not like the damn things will budge. These holding cells were designed to contain Seasons. The walls are stone. The faucets and plumbing fixtures are all fitted with low-flow regulators to control the supply of water. Not a single thing in this cell will burn, and there are no roots capable of burrowing through the thick slabs of rock. I know, because for a brief time when I was a new recruit, I was tasked with guarding these cells. Back then, they were darker, colder, and far nastier than they are now. Which only goes to prove that Lyon's soft—too weak to be in charge.

A sliver of white soap is the only bright spot in the room. I unbutton the top of my jumpsuit and let it hang around my waist, washing the stink of stasis and the smell of Lyon's office from my body as best as I can with the trickle of water in the sink. I look haggard, older somehow in its steel surface, and I splash my face, wishing I could scrub away everything that's happened since I was last here.

The faucet shuts off abruptly, and my spent ration of water swirls down the drain. I lift my head, my wet skin blooming with goose bumps in the damp chill. The heat of the torches at the far end of the corridor doesn't reach my cell, but I don't need it. The cold soothes my nerves. It sparks memories of long days spent with Denver and Noelle and speaks to my oldest, most familiar magic—before we were Guards, back when we were Winters.

I keep my jumpsuit half-off, leaving the ends of my wet hair to drip down my shoulders, letting the Winter magic stir after its long hibernation. Ice pops and snaps softly as it freezes over the shells of my ears, like the crackle of a fire in a dimly lit room. I draw in a deep breath, mustering the cold to rise up until it's fully awake inside me. My breath whitens and ice laces my hands. The effort leaves me nauseated and dizzy.

Sinking onto the lower bunk, I rub the melting frost from my fingertips. A vision of Fleur comes unbidden to my mind, like a smoking car wreck in my rearview mirror I wish I could forget. I envy the way the ground ripped open for her, trembled for her. I'd kill for a fraction of that power right now. With that kind of magic, I could bring this entire place to its knees.

Metal screeches against metal as a slot opens in the cell door. A tray appears, containing a snack-size bottle of water and a paper cup full of vitamins.

I set the tray on the floor, glaring at the Guard on the other side as he slides the panel shut again. So much for eating. Despite the stasis sickness, my stomach rumbles, but I know there'll be no food coming. It'll be another few days before my body can handle anything more than bland liquids and diet supplements, and by then, Lyon will be done with his Culling.

The tablets dissolve into a chalklike paste on my tongue, but I swallow the medicine down, determined to keep my strength up. Sliding down the cold stone wall, I press the water bottle to my temple.

I have one week to find a way out of here.

And then . . . then I will hunt for Jack.

A handful of soft voices drift from the other cells. I recognize some of them, but the conversations are quickly silenced by the crow's shrill caw. I open my eyes, shaking off the heavy shroud of sleep as the echo of footsteps grows louder in the tunnels. Guards—a team of them, at least. The locks on my cell door snap and I stiffen as it swings open, wondering if the old man got smart and changed his mind about giving me a week to think.

I brace myself for a fight I can't win. If the Guards plan to haul me upstairs for Termination, I might as well spend the last of my energy giving them a reason to kill me right here. Rising to my feet, I step back from the door as a figure stumbles over the threshold. Kai Sampson wobbles on weak legs to the bunk, and the bolts clank shut behind her. She blinks at me, her dark eyes wide above pronounced cheekbones, the sharp lines of her face etched in a sickly pallor.

"What are you doing here?" I ask.

She studies me with an equally wary expression, arms folded around herself to hide the stasis tremors. "They ran out of cells. I guess we're doubling," she rasps, her voice still hoarse from disuse. She backs to the edge of the mattress, the fire-retardant plastic creaking as she sits down.

"If you believe that, you're a bigger fool than I thought." There aren't many voices coming from the other cells. Not nearly enough to fill them.

Kai's eyes pierce me through the semidarkness of the lower bunk. No. She's no fool. Lyon put her here for a reason. "How did your meeting with the professor go?" I ask in a slow drawl.

"You mean Chronos."

I choke out a disgusted laugh. "Swore your fealty so soon? I expected better from the girl who took down Jack Sommers." I sip from my water bottle.

Kai pales as she watches me drink. Arms wrapped around her waist, she lurches for the toilet.

The acrid smell of bile drifts through the cell. Kai sucks in a shuddering breath between heaves, shaking with the effort. I scrub my face and swear quietly into my hand.

"Guard!" I shout. I rattle the cell door as Kai starts heaving again. The duty guard glares through the bars.

"What do you want, Lausks?" I know him. He was an Autumn from Vermont. Denver and I knocked him around once when he stepped out of line. Figures that Lyon would restaff the Guard with a bunch of traitorous wussies.

"We need water in here."

"Sorry, *Captain*," he says through a smug smile. "I can't hear you over all the puking in there."

My hand flies between the bars in the cell door and clamps around his ear, jerking it toward me until his head slams into the iron frame.

A wave of Winter magic crackles through my fingers, cold enough to freeze his skin. "Unless you want to be stuck sweeping up this girl's ashes, I suggest you bring her some water and vitamins." I release him with a shove, holding his stare.

As soon as his back is turned, my hands begin to shake. I hold the wall, fighting back a wave of dizziness and resisting the urge to vomit.

The holding cell might be an insurmountable obstacle, but security clearly isn't. All I need to do is conserve my strength. I only need to summon enough power to overtake a single Guard. If I'm smart and don't waste any more energy, there's a chance I can get myself out of here after all.

A thin blanket flies through the slot and lands on the earthen floor, followed by a flimsy excuse for a pillow, a clean jumpsuit, and an extra towel. A tray appears with a second bottle of water and a paper cup of Kai's supplements. I snatch it from the Guard's hands.

The fire-retardant blanket is coarse and thin, but it's warm. Kai sags against the side of the toilet, and I wrap the blanket around her shoulders. When she doesn't so much as stir, I unscrew the cap of her water bottle and drop her vitamins inside. They dissolve up from the bottom in a stream of angry, foaming bubbles.

"Drink this." I hold the bottle to her lips, ignoring the smell of sweat and sick that clings to her. She takes a few small sips, watching me through slitted eyelids as if she's not entirely sure she trusts me. She's quick, this one. Sharp. That must be why Lyon chose to stick her in here with me. Probably to spy on me. Or maybe to sway my decision.

I wonder what he offered in exchange. A coveted region? A position in his new Guard? Whatever carrot he's dangling in front of her, it's a risky play. I'm not the only one in this cell with a choice to make.

Everyone has weak spots, bruises that can be prodded. And I know more than a few of Kai's. "Hell of a failed mission, huh?"

She frowns, turning away from me as if she might be sick again. "I shot Jack Sommers," she says, huddling under her blanket. "Three clean shots in the back and one in the leg before he killed me."

I scratch my jaw, unable to help the stab of sympathy I feel. She was loyal to the Guard. Faithful to Michael. She did what she was ordered to do, and this is her reward for it.

"How'd he do it?" I ask, my curiosity piqued.

"Do what?" Her eyes lift to mine, foggy and confused.

"How'd he kill you?"

A humiliated blush warms the pallor of her cheeks. "He broke the shaft of the arrow in his leg and used it to impale me." The fact that Jack was the one to kill her will only make my job easier. "They were broad-head arrows," she says, her brows knitted. "Three in the back should have taken him down. I don't know how he managed to . . ." Her eyes squeeze shut against another wave of stasis tremors.

She's right. Jack never should have walked away with those injuries. And yet thanks to Fleur, that's exactly what he did.

"You did your job. There wasn't anything you could have done to stop what happened after that."

She wipes her mouth on the back of her hand, watching me out of the corner of her eye. "You think it was inevitable?"

Do I? I wonder as I button myself back into my jumpsuit. Inevitability is dead. Ananke—Gaia's mother, wife of the late Chronos, and the embodiment of Fate—died a long time ago, killed in cold blood by her own husband. The only piece of her that's left is the crystal eye in the Staff of Time, the Eye of Inevitability that Daniel Lyon is so damn afraid to look into. But if the wielder of Time—the most powerful magic in the universe—is terrified of what he saw in that crystal, there's got to be a good reason for that. If he's worried enough to send Kai down here to spy on me, then maybe Inevitability isn't dead after all. And maybe that magic is more powerful than Lyon's willing to admit.

"Sommers got lucky," I say, spitting his name. "It wasn't fate that landed us here. It was him." Fleur may have been the one to overpower Michael and take the staff. But everything she did, she did for Jack.

"If you're right and there was nothing I could have done, then maybe it *was* inevitable." Kai takes careful sips of her water. Her skin is bronze and gold under her pallor, hinting at her former life as a Summer before she became a Guard. "What if Jack was meant to live and Daniel Lyon was meant to be Chronos? What if *we* were the ones in the wrong?"

"We were following orders."

"What if we shouldn't have?"

No. I refuse to accept that possibility. Because that would mean that my time as a Guard and all we fought for was a waste. That would mean we actually deserve the punishments we have coming. And I've worked too hard and trained too long, spent too many years proving my worthiness to Michael to become a captain of his Guard, to accept that. No, that defeat was just a ripple in our destiny.

"I said there was nothing you could have done to change the outcome of the battle. But the war isn't over yet."

I grip the edge of the sink, determined not to make the same mistakes I've made before. This time, Sommers won't walk away with his life. Because I'll make sure he has nothing left to live for.

4

WITHOUT A BREATH OF STORM

JACK

The air's thick with the smell of blooms in the park near our villa. Before the battle, I could have identified every one of them just by drawing a breath. Could have scented every grain of pollen that trailed in on Fleur's skin. But since then, my talents for tracking have been limited to a Handler's means.

Fleur's red dot is settled on the screen on my wrist monitor, safe at her desk in Spanish class for the next forty minutes. I take my first full breath of the morning, my muscles loose as I hit my first mile marker and gradually pick up speed. The nagging ache under the scar in my thigh starts to burn with my lengthened strides, and I push through the pain. I was a decent runner before I died the first time—I held my own during gym class at school—but Fleur made me fast. As a Winter, every mile I put between us meant one more day I stayed alive. But over time, every mile meant one more day I existed in the same world with her.

I may not be a Winter anymore. I can't conjure a blast of wind or make it sleet. But I'm still faster than Fleur. And maybe it's foolish to feel this way, but ever since I lost my magic, running is the only thing that makes me feel like I can hold my own beside her.

By the end of my third lap, my smaze is all but gone from my mind. I pass a flowering jacaranda. The sweet scent reminds me of Fleur, and I drag up my sleeve, veering to dodge some kids chasing ducks across the footpath as I check my wrist monitor.

Fleur's GPS signal is gone from the screen. I tap it to zoom out, my feet slowing when I can't find her anywhere.

No red light in the school.

Not in the café. Or on any of the streets leading home.

Breathing hard, I stand on the edge of the path and dial her cell. When there's no answer, I try the landline at the villa. Cold sweat rolls over me as I disconnect, calculating the minutes since I last checked my monitor. It must be a glitch with her transmitter. Fleur never misses class; she wouldn't have left early.

Swerving off the footpath, I take a shortcut through the brush, back toward Fleur's school. There's no clear trail, and I'm forced to slow down as I pick my way through the overgrown jungle around the park. The nearest side street is barely visible through the trees. Eyes glued to my wrist monitor, I search the map for a clearer route.

Snick.

I freeze at the all too familiar sound. Slowly, I lift my head until the edge of the switchblade kisses my throat.

"Dame tu billetera y tu celular." The voice comes from somewhere in my periphery. A hand shoves me from behind.

40

"*¡Hazlo ahora, cabrón!*" A different voice. There are two of them.

"I don't have my wallet on me." I keep my eyes straight ahead and my hands up where they can see them. Lyon's warning to avoid the police is still fresh on my mind. The one behind me pats down the pockets of my running shorts, but they're empty. Not even a house key, and there's no way they're getting the security code out of me. "I told you. I don't have any money."

"*Tu reloj.*" The one beside me jabs me with the blade. It's dull, but I have no doubt it'll do the job. I tip my head away from it. No way in hell am I turning my only link to Fleur's transmitter over to these assholes.

His friend grabs my wrist and I yank it away. He tries again, and I shove my elbow hard into his ribs. An icy rage takes hold of me, the desire to fight consuming every rational thought as my heel connects with his shin.

I grab the first guy's wrist, swinging the knife away from my throat. My fist crashes into his nose and he reels back, cupping it. I whirl around, kicking his friend backward into the brush. For a single bright, shining moment, it's like my magic is back. Like I'm a Winter again, fighting for my life, immune to the cold. Until a lash of white-hot pain grabs me as the knife drags against my throat.

FLEUR

The second-floor classroom is stuffy and hot, and even after drinking half my cappuccino it's impossible to concentrate. The thick odor of sweat in the room mingles with the heavy perfume of the woman sitting behind me and someone else's garlic breath from lunch.

My gaze flicks longingly to the single open window at the far side of the room, where a slight breeze carries in the faint earthiness of the park down the block. My thoughts run to Jack, to the hunch in his shoulders as he stares out the window of the training room between sets each morning, as if he wishes he were someplace else.

Or someone else.

He's been restless lately. There's a recklessness in the way he's pushing his body. As if he's testing boundaries. Testing limits. Running for hours on end sometimes, as if he can outrun this person he's become. I can almost smell the frustration building inside him. The pent-up anger he directs at himself is a growing misplaced hostility that makes me worry he'll do something foolish and hurt himself.

The teacher drones on, conjugating verbs on the blackboard. I scrape my books together and quietly excuse myself from the room. My transmitter's a hard knot inside my ear and I turn it off, dropping it into my pocket as I descend the steps. Jack's probably not sitting in front of his computer at home anyway. He was too keyed up when I left the villa. Too restless after our wrestling match. I know exactly where I'll find him.

I push through the door of the school, then cross the street and head for the park. Under the clean, fresh scent of the running creek, the air smells rich and floral. I taste the breeze for signs of Jack and catch the tang of his sweat. His human scent is one I'm still growing used to, different from the peppermint, holly berry, and pine that marked him as a Winter. The faint traces of those smells have almost entirely faded since he lost his magic, replaced by cool musk body washes and minty shaving gels. Under them, the natural human warmth of his skin is the scent I cling to. The one I lean into when I crawl under his arm at night and curl into every morning when we wake up.

Jack's scent grows stronger as I near the park. I slide off the foot-path, checking to make sure no one's looking before scaling the trunk of an oak tree and climbing to a high branch. I'm struck by a stab of déjà vu as I hide in the leaves, waiting for him. It could be two years ago. Or ten years, or even twenty. Suddenly, it feels as if I'm hunting Jack all over again, the discomfiting familiarity giving way to a nagging guilt as Jack rounds the bend in the path.

His legs and arms pump hard, the front of his shirt darkened with a deep V of sweat. I lose sight of him as he veers into the grass, his bright white sneakers leaping a fence of stacked stones.

Where the hell is he going?

Summoning an adjacent branch, I leap cautiously from tree to tree, chasing his scent until I'm near enough to catch sight of him. He's not running anymore.

Sunlight skips off the blade of a knife. Panic flares inside me as a man presses it to Jack's throat.

I reach out with my mind into the soft ground, searching for a root. Grabbing hold of the nearest one, I stretch it toward Jack and the men as they argue. Jack jerks his arm away from them, their voices rising. His elbow snaps back, and one of the men goes down with a grunt. My view is obscured by leaves and flowers. They're all moving, hard to see. Jack throws a punch, then whirls, kicking the one behind him to the ground. The knife's blade glimmers as it flashes through the branches, and the air suddenly grows redolent of blood. Blood that smells faintly of Winter.

Jack!

My root lashes toward them. A strand of ivy uncoils from a branch, snatching the blade from the man's hands and tossing it away from him.

43

Jack clutches his neck. Red trickles from under his fingers. My feet itch to run to him, but I stay hidden, using the root to jerk Jack's attackers off their feet. The first man squeals as I drag him backward into the brush. Jack turns and throws a swing, but I've already got the second man by the ankles. With a sharp pull of my thoughts, he hits the ground, a shocked breath rushing out of him.

The men cry out, scrambling to their feet as if the ground's on fire, all but forgetting whatever it was they wanted from Jack as they sprint away through the trees. Jack touches his neck as he watches them go. I release my hold on the roots and they retreat under the ground before anyone else sees.

Jack lifts his head, searching the trees for me as I swing off the branch and drop to my feet. I run to him, taking his face in my hands. He holds his body tense, reluctant to turn toward me. The wound isn't bad under all the blood, just a deep scratch, and my held breath shakes when it finally slips free.

His eyes are cold as they slide to my ear. "You turned your transmitter off."

"Just for a few minutes."

"I had no idea where you were."

"I was right here."

"Why?" he snaps, drawing the attention of an elderly couple on the path.

"Because," I say in a low voice, "I didn't want you to see I left class. I knew you would worry."

"And you didn't think I'd worry that your signal just disappeared?"

I grin tightly at the couple, hoping they'll keep walking the other

44

way. "I didn't disappear. I was right down the street, Jack. It was only a few minutes, and I was coming to find you anyway."

"Because you knew exactly where I was, right?" The sharpness of his tone catches me off guard. "You know exactly how to find me. And all it takes is one sniff, one thought . . . one snap of your magic fingers and the whole jungle is at your disposal to save me. Well, guess what? It's not the same for me anymore. The minute you slipped off that screen, I was lost!" His voice cracks, and something inside me breaks. "I can't *hunt* you anymore. I can't find you, can't *save* you if you're not wearing it!"

"I know. And I'm sorry. It was only for a few minutes—"

"Anything can happen in a few minutes."

"It's only a tracker. A communicator," I argue. Without a connection to a ley line, the transmitter can't pull me back to the Observatory. "It's not like it's connected to anything."

"Maybe it should be!" Jack swipes at the blood on his neck and looks away, guilt and anger warring on his face as I take an uncertain step back from him.

"What are you saying?"

He frowns at his bloody fingers. "Maybe we should think about going back."

"What do you mean, back? Have you forgotten why we left? We fought and risked our lives for this," I say, gesturing wildly to the open sky around me. "Woody gave his life for this. For us. You gave up your magic. You gave a piece of your soul, Jack—" My breath catches at the flash of pain in his eyes. I knew he missed it. I knew the absence of his magic must feel like a gaping hole inside him. A hole I'd hoped would heal with time, like his scars. "Is that what this is about? Is that why you want to go back? For your smaze?"

A muscle tics in his jaw.

Thunder rumbles like a low moan in the distance as rain begins to fall. Jack wipes away the blood and starts the long walk home alone.

5

CRACKED AND SPRUNG

<u>DOUG</u>

I toss a makeshift ball—two pairs of thick, Observatory-issued socks rolled tightly together—at the stone ceiling over and over again. I've been at it for fuck knows how many hours. But it gives me something to do with my hands, and it's the only way I can think.

Voices drift from the other cells. The odd laugh. The occasional swear. Listening from my bunk, I've managed to figure out who's stuck in here with us; almost all of them fought in Cuernavaca. Lixue, the last surviving member of my team, is in the cell farthest from mine—too far to communicate with her, and I'm sure that was Lyon's doing. There's no one I trust in the cells adjacent to mine . . . not enough to risk sharing my thoughts with.

Kai lies on the bunk below mine. It's been hours since either of us last spoke, sometime after breakfast. The protein shake barely took the edge off, and a hunger headache has me feeling edgy and hollow.

With the exception of the slot for the meal tray, the cell door hasn't opened since they brought Kai in here, and I'm surprised I haven't paced a canyon into the floor. I hurl the sock ball across the room and throw an arm over my face, but in the darkness and quiet, all that's left are the flickering images I saw in Lyon's office.

The lower bunk creaks. A moment later, I'm startled by a soft thump on the bed beside me. I peel my arm from my eyes and frown at the sock ball next to my leg.

"Have you decided what you're going to do yet?" Kai's disembodied voice bounces softly off the walls, and I cover my face again. I've avoided the few questions she's dared to ask since Lyon locked us up together, certain he sent her here to snoop. But she hasn't left the cell once since they shut that door, and the closed-circuit camera on the ceiling outside our cell isn't close enough to pick up much in the way of sound. Maybe I was wrong.

"Why?" I ask cautiously. "Have you?"

There's a prolonged silence from her bunk. "I was thinking I might be a good teacher. You know . . . archery. Or maybe earth science. I'd be good at that."

A dry laugh starts in the back of my throat. It builds, rolling through me until my whole body shakes with it.

"What? There's nothing wrong with being a teacher. You could teach, too, you know."

I sit up, grabbing the sock ball as I swing my legs off the bed and drop to the floor. Kai's lying on her back, fingers laced behind her head. I toss the sock ball at her and she glares at me.

Arms braced on my bunk, I lean over her, casting a shadow over her bed. "You seriously think Lyon's going to let you teach?"

"Why not? He let Nereida do it."

"Who's Nereida?"

"My Handler," she says with a frown. "She's teaching Greek. And English as a Second Language. Professor Lyon says she's happy."

I repress a twinge of something that might be guilt. In all the shock of awakening and the truths I learned during my meeting with Lyon, I never asked him about my Handler. We were never close, and truthfully, I don't give a shit what he decided to do with his life, assuming Lyon let him keep it. "Lyon told you that?" Her eyes narrow on me as I mutter, "Of course he did." I lean closer, blocking the light from reaching her bunk. "You seriously think, after what you did to Jack, that Lyon is going to let you mold impressionable young minds? That in a million years he'd ever stick a bow in your hand and cut you loose?"

She pitches the sock ball back at me. I catch it a second before it hits my face. She rolls sideways away from me as I chuckle to myself.

"Face it," I say, tossing the ball gently at the small of her back. "If you give up your magic, you're going to be stuck scrubbing floors. Maybe you'll serve the old man's Guards in the mess hall if you're lucky."

Her fists tighten around the edge of her pillow. "Since keeping our magic isn't exactly an option, what are *you* going to do? Offer yourself up for Termination? That sounds like a stellar plan."

"Better than groveling."

She whirls upright, spinning to face me. "It's not groveling. It's a second chance."

I choke out a laugh. "At what?"

"I don't know! A new life. We can start over."

"Fool yourself all you want, Sampson. This second chance he's offering you isn't an opportunity. It's a punishment."

She folds her arms over her chest. "You don't know what you're—"

"Get up!" We both jolt upright as a fist bangs on the cell door and the locks begin to open.

Four days have passed. I only know by the number of times the lights in our cell have switched off after the guards make their final rounds, and how many times they've flickered on again after the long nights I've spent staring at the ceiling.

Kai's eyes are wide in her bunk. "What do you think they want?" she whispers.

"I don't know."

I draw back as the door creaks open. A team of Guards stands in front of our cell. Like all the others who have come to check on us this week, their movements are rigid and stilted, clearly rehearsed, and I'm betting all four of them are fresh out of training. Lyon probably assumes it's the smartest thing he's done, getting rid of the old Guard and picking a brand-new squad of his own, but I'd take four seasoned officers with blood on their hands over thirty green asswipes who've never seen a fight.

A Guard—the one whose ear I pulled through the bars—sneers at me as he approaches the cell. He grins as he holds up two sets of wrist restraints and fire-retardant mitts. Since we're barely out of stasis, I guess they figure we don't pose much of a threat. Not to a whole team of them.

But one? I can handle one. It's a simple matter of getting outside this cell and separating the weakest from the herd.

"Where are we going?" I ask as he turns me to face the wall. The restraints click shut, painfully tight. He shoves me toward the door, passing me off to one of his friends, both his ego and his ear obviously still bruised. He drags Kai from her bunk, wrenching her arms back hard, not bothering to answer me.

"Chronos is giving you a little reprieve for good behavior," one of the others says, making the frostbitten Guard grimace.

The crow outside our cell flaps on her perch, watching us as we're led out of the holding area into the winding tunnels of the catacombs. My eyes rake over the Guards as we walk, but I'm unable to discern the leader. They may have been granted power over all four elements, but I'd bet my soul they can only control one—the one Gaia gave them when she made them a Season. It takes time to master the elements, to weaponize them.

We round a corner into an older wing of the Administration level. I register the subtle incline in the strain of my legs, an angle so slight I might not be bothered by it if it weren't for the stasis fatigue. The ramp-like hall widens into a brighter corridor, and Kai and I wince, our eyes slow to adjust as the torches give way to fluorescent lights in high, white ceilings.

The Guards stop in front of a pair of double doors. The placard beside them says "Restricted Access: Faculty Recreation Center—Staff Only." One of the Guards waves a key card over the scanner, and the doors slide open. The smells of soap and sweat, oiled steel and pool chemicals all blend together as the warm air inside rushes over us. I draw the scents deep into my lungs, grateful to smell anything other than the reek of the catacombs and the body odor that clings to me.

The Guards drag off our mitts and unlock our restraints, dumping towels and changes of clothes in our arms. The Guard I frosted watches me warily.

"Chronos is giving you one hour to stretch your legs and clean up," another says, checking the time on her watch. "The track and the locker rooms have been cordoned off for you to use. Sparring rooms are off-limits. So are the weight rooms. There are smazes inside and Guards stationed outside every door, so don't try anything stupid."

The door closes behind us, the slam echoing off the high walls around the indoor track. A water dispenser sweats on a table beside it, the melting ice shifting to reveal slivers of orange and lemon. Two protein packets rest beside a stack of paper cups. Kai dumps her towel and clothes on the floor, tears open a packet of powder, and shakes it into a cup of water. Not bothering to stir it, she swallows it down. Her hand shakes as she refills the cup, funneling the last of the wet powder into her mouth.

"We've only got an hour." I jut my chin toward the track. "Might as well use it."

Kai swirls the last drops on her tongue and follows me onto the rubber-coated surface, catching up to walk between the painted lines beside me. It feels good to move more than ten feet without hitting a wall.

We take the first lap slowly, in silence. There's no point talking anyway. I count smazes as we round the track: One under the water table. One hovering in the air duct high on the far wall. One dark, twisty little fucker trailing behind us, close to the floor.

"Come on," I say, veering off the track, one eye on the smazes as I test the lock on the door to the next room. I can smell it, the hot chlorine steaming through the gaps. It must be the faculty pool.

"Where are we going?" she asks.

"They told us to clean up. They didn't say where." The locks in this place are all different—a hodgepodge of hardware reflecting the time period when each particular section of the Observatory was built and the value of whatever is secured behind it. This lock isn't sophisticated, more a deterrent than a dead end. I hold the knob and summon what little magic I can to my fingers, heating the metal, before switching hands and infusing it with a blast of cold instead. The knob steams as it freezes over. With a quick press of my thumb, something pops inside and the lock breaks open. The effort leaves me woozy.

Cracking open the door, I peer inside. The pool is dimly lit, green and blue light dancing over the dark ceiling above it. No Guards. No other lights beyond those in the pool and the warm sliver that slips through the door with us.

"But the smazes . . . ," Kai says, hesitant to follow.

"Relax. They only said the sparring and weight rooms were off-limits. They never said anything about the pool." We haven't broken any rules. Not yet.

I shuck off my jumpsuit and perch on the edge of the water in my briefs. Steam rises off the surface, humid and sultry, and the smazes that followed us in shrink away from the heat.

Kai watches as they float up to hover by the vents in the ceiling.

"Relax." I jerk my chin toward the Winter wraiths. "They won't get close enough to hear us."

Warmth rushes over my head as I dive in. My blood feels thick, my bones heavy, the long years I spent as a Winter pushing back against the heat. I break the surface fast, drinking in the cooler air, letting the initial shock pass over me.

When I blink the sting of chlorine from my eyes, Kai's still standing by the door.

"You *were* a Summer once, right?" I splash water at her. "What the hell are you waiting for, Sampson?" I wade in deeper, keeping my back to her as she unfastens the buttons of her jumpsuit. The water ripples as she tests the temperature, and I wait for the splash.

There's a prolonged silence, broken only by the slosh of water against the concrete lip of the pool. "For fuck's sake," I mutter. "What's taking so long? We only have—"

I start as her head breaks the surface beside me, her short hair slicked back around her heart-shaped face.

"Not bad," I say, surprised she was able to get the jump on me. She's good. Maybe better than I gave her credit for. "Didn't see you coming."

"Maybe you're just a lousy hunter." Her chin brushes the surface as she treads water, her eyes darting up to the shadowy mist near the air ducts. "Those things creep me out."

"They're harmless," I say, turning for deeper water. "The flies are a hell of a lot worse."

I maneuver to the far side of the pool, far enough that the smazes won't hear. "We only have a few days. We should come up with a plan. I'm not going to that Dismantling. So I need to know, are you in or out?"

"I can't run." She rakes the short, dark spikes of hair from her eyes.

"You'll feel stronger in a few days. We just need to find a way past a few Guards and then lay low for a while."

"There's no time. The Dismantling is in less than a week."

"I thought you were a fighter."

"There's no sense fighting him, Doug." She lowers her voice, glancing back at the smazes. "If we do, we'll lose everything. We should just take the demotion and start our lives over."

I swipe water from my face. She's giving up far too easily. I've seen her train. I know how tough she is. I know what she's capable of. And so does she.

"You're a fool to trust him," I say under my breath. "Whatever Lyon promised to give you in exchange for spying on me, he'll turn on you."

Her eyes grow wide. "He didn't. I don't know what you're talking about."

A dark laugh rocks my shoulders. "You may be a good hunter, Sampson, but you're a shitty liar."

She shakes her head, too hard and too fast. "It wasn't like that, Doug. I swear. He's just worried about you." I raise a brow, calling her on her bullshit. "I'm serious. He's afraid you won't cooperate with the Dismantling, and he's scared someone will get hurt."

No. Not someone. *Himself.*

I remember Lyon's face when he looked into the eye of the staff. He was afraid. Not for me—he had to know I'd never give in to him, that he'd have to kill me. He was afraid for *himself.* Afraid *he* would get hurt. Probably afraid I would be the one to do it. So he sent Kai to try to soften me, to persuade me to give up my magic quietly. Fuck that.

I back her into a corner, my arms braced on the side of the pool, trapping her between them. If Lyon is afraid of what he saw in his

55

future—of something he saw happening at the *Dismantling*, something I do that *hurts* him—then that means I have a chance.

There is a way forward—interfering with the Dismantling must be mine.

"What did he offer you in exchange for talking me into surrendering?"

Her chest rises and falls faster as she darts fearful glances to the door. I get down in her face. "What do you think he must have offered Jack to inspire that kind of loyalty? More magic? Freedom? A coveted place on his Guard? And what did Jack get? Nothing, Kai. He got *nothing*. He's a Handler. A human, with no magic of his own, playing servant to a Spring." Creases of doubt furrow her brow. She stubbornly looks away. "Daniel Lyon can't be trusted," I whisper, my back shielding our conversation from the smazes. "Whatever he offered, it will disappear the moment he's done with you." Her eyes snap to mine, the truth laid bare in them. "What was it? What did he promise you, Kai?"

She swallows hard. "Clemency. For my sister."

"Who's your sister?"

She hesitates. "Her name is Ruby."

I roll the name around in my mind. Ruby's a July birthstone—a common name among Summers. There were no Rubys in Michael's Guard and the name doesn't ring any bells, but there are hundreds of Summers in the Observatory, and I only remember those I was assigned to hunt—the ones who caused problems. "What did your sister do?"

"Lyon said . . ." Her face is pained. "He said she hunted Jack and his friends. That she attacked them when they ran away from the Observatory. I told him she probably only did it for the bounty. Michael offered a huge reward, and I know my sister; she's competitive. She would have wanted it. I seriously doubt she had any ideological motives for wanting to stop Jack."

I like her sister already. "What happened to her?"

"Lyon said she's being held here in the Observatory. I assume she was rounded up with all the others who hunted for Jack. She must have had her hearing."

"What does he plan to do with her?"

"He says he can't release her. That her fate is a matter of my cooperation and Jack's willingness to forgive and let her go, and that her 'present situation'"—she puts Lyon's words in finger quotes—"is a direct result of the choice Ruby made to hunt Jack." Her sigh is shaky. She swipes a bead of water from her cheek, and I'm pretty sure it's a tear. "He said that if I choose the right path, I can free her."

"And what about you? What do you get out of it?"

She sinks down into the water, her arms crossed around her middle. "What happens to me doesn't matter. I have to know my sister will be okay." She sniffs and swats another tear from her face. "Lyon said this is my way forward. That giving up my magic is the first step toward forgiving myself."

"For what?"

"For what I've done."

The simmering anger I've felt since I woke from stasis threatens to boil over. Now that I know for a fact that she's under Lyon's thumb, I should leave her here. She made her own bed, she's tough enough to lie in it. But I can't get past the idea that Lyon's stripping away her magic from her for doing her job. For doing exactly what she was ordered to do. This isn't a choice he's giving Kai. Not if he's holding her sister's life over her head.

I lean down, forcing her to meet my eyes. "Listen to me. You did nothing wrong. *We* did nothing wrong. And we have nothing to feel guilty for. I'm not giving up my magic because Lyon decided I don't deserve it anymore. And neither are you."

Lyon made a horrible play using Kai as a pawn. If he thinks she's working for him—if he thinks she's succeeded in convincing me to give in—then that gives me an advantage. It's not like he's keeping tabs on his own future by looking in the eye. If Lyon's offering Kai her sister's life, then I'll just have to promise her more.

"There is no way out of this," she says with a resigned sniffle. "I can't run. Not if my sister is trapped here."

"We're not going to run. We're going to fight."

She laughs, ducking under my arm. "You're out of your mind. It's impossible. We're not strong enough."

"Nothing is impossible," I hiss as she wades away from me. "You said it yourself. He's afraid I won't cooperate with the Dismantling. That I'll hurt someone. And believe me, I'd love nothing more than to knock him off his throne."

"You can't. He's Chronos now."

I shadow her through the water, careful to keep my voice low. "Yes, *now*, Kai. But whoever has the staff has control." Lyon made the mistake of revealing that much to me when he showed me that vision of the battle beside the lake. Lyon only had to take Michael's staff and use it to kill him. Lyon is soft—he's a scholar, not a fighter. His Guards are new and inexperienced. All I need is a shot at disarming him. "The staff is the key to taking his power. He'll have it with him at the Dismantling. I'm going to find a way to get it."

"Lyon will know what you're up to before you've even finished planning it. He probably already does."

"He's a coward. He won't look that far." Lyon's hands had been shaking when he covered the eye. That last glance inside it cost him something. Whatever he saw in that vision threw him off his game, as if the future unnerved him. Maybe even terrified him. And I have to believe the person he saw wrecking his future was me.

Kai looks at me as if I've lost my mind. "There will be at least four Guards in that room. Maybe more. Not to mention Gaia!" She whispers Gaia's name with an almost fearful reverence. "Even if you could get close enough to take the staff, you'd never make it out of that room alive."

"So I'll break into his office and steal it before then. No one says we have to wait for the Dismantling."

She stops moving to gape at me. "Stolen magic is cursed magic."

"Who fed you that line of crap?"

"A librarian in the Hall of Records. She said stolen magic comes with a price. And if you take someone's magic without their permission, you inherit their weaknesses and faults."

"Bullshit. There's no such thing as curses."

Her laugh is dark. "Bet you didn't think there was any such thing as magic once, either."

"Whatever," I mutter, splashing her and making her duck low in the water. "I've been here a long time, and I've never heard anything like that."

"Even if you could steal the staff, you'd have to find a way out of our cell first."

I gesture loosely at the pool around us. "And?"

With a roll of her eyes, she asks, "What about the Guards?"

I pull her toward me, close enough to whisper, "All we need is a little distraction."

She looks up at me through thick, wet lashes, and I catch a glimmer of hope under them. "Even if you could manage to break into his office," she says quietly, "Gaia has a pet inside. A snake. You won't make it two steps out that door before Gaia finds out and the Guards are all over you."

The snake. I hadn't thought about it until now. I draw back from Kai, scraping trails of warm water from my face. Getting into Lyon's office wouldn't be impossible. Overtake the duty guard when he comes to our cell, steal his key card, take the staff . . . One stroke of the scythe—that's all it would take to bring an end to Daniel Lyon.

But Kai's right . . . the snake poses an obstacle. If it is one of Gaia's pets, then it could also be one of her spies. She'd sense everything that snake sees, and she would know what I'm up to the moment I breach Lyon's office.

"It's odd," I say in a low voice, almost to myself, as I watch the smazes weave through the holes in the vents. "I've never seen a snake in the Observatory before." As long as I've lived here, there have only been the crows, bees, flies, and smazes—the creatures Gaia uses as vessels for magic. If it were an ordinary pet, it wouldn't be kept in a tank inside a locked office. It would live in the menagerie with all Gaia's other creatures, until it became a host for some dead Season's soul.

No, this snake is different. Its eyes aren't ordinary at all. They remind me too much of Gaia's.

Kai's shudder ripples the surface of the pool. "I hate snakes. That one was creepy. Like the one in the painting in the gallery."

I turn sharply to face her. "Which painting?"

"The one of Chronos and Ananke."

Sweat beads on my lip and I wipe it away. I've marched past that painting a thousand times on my way to and from the Control Room. It's the only representation of Ananke that exists on the campus. In it, she's depicted as a serpent. And Kai's right. The eyes of the snake in Lyon's office are the same as the ones in the painting—the same as Gaia's. Diamondlike. Faceted, like the crystal eye in the staff.

I can't believe I didn't realize it before. Those eyes. The similarities.

"We should go," Kai says. "The Guards are going to come looking for us soon." She takes a few steps toward the other side of the pool, but I take her by the arm and drag her back through the water, keeping us out of earshot of the smazes.

"What if the snake isn't a pet?"

She frowns. "What do you mean?"

"Why else would the snake be kept in Lyon's office, apart from all Gaia's other creatures and spies, if it isn't special? If it isn't worthy of a place closer to Chronos?" As my excitement rises, so does my voice. It takes everything inside me to tamp my adrenaline down. "What if the snake is a host for Ananke's magic?"

Kai shakes free of my grip, her face paling. "Then I vote we leave it alone. There's a reason that thing is in a cage."

I corner her, forcing her to hear me out. "Don't you see? Michael must have trapped her soul when he killed her and put her magic inside that snake." She stares at me the same way I'd stared at the images projected on Lyon's desk, both mesmerized and too afraid to look away.

"So?"

"So Inevitability held power over everything—Chaos, Earth, Time . . . all of them. Chronos killed Ananke because he was *afraid* of her. Her magic outweighs them all. And if Ananke's magic can be stolen and put in a snake, then it can be stolen and put in something else." If an animal can be Ananke's host, then so can a man. All I have to do is get my hands on that snake and draw the magic out. "With that kind of power, I can do exactly what Lyon is afraid of. I can stop the Dismantling."

"And then what?" she asks warily.

"I can give you what you truly want . . . your sister *and* your magic."

6

ALONE IN THE WINTER RAIN

JACK

My lungs are still burning from the sprint home as I step out of the shower. No matter how many plates I tack onto the bar or how many miles I run, I can't work off the frustration. It's anchored deep. Not in my muscles or lungs. It's a persistent ache behind my heart, and I'm certain it's slowly killing me.

I leave the bathroom without waiting for the fog to clear from the mirror, unable to stand the sight of myself. A stubborn smear of blood stains the towel where it brushed my neck. I couldn't defend myself against two human assholes trying to steal my watch. That wrist monitor is my only means of keeping Fleur safe outside the villa, and if she hadn't shown up when she did, they would have slit my throat and taken it.

I haul open a drawer and drag a fresh T-shirt over my head. My cell phone vibrates on the dresser. I scrape it toward me, scanning the notifications on the screen. An email from Lyon.

Jack,

Your visas are in the post. I've attached a report you should see. In light of recent events, both here and abroad, Gaia and I feel it's best if you and Fleur reconsider your vacation plans.

I'm sorry, Jack. I'm here if you need to talk. And my offer stands. I've included updated passports with your visas as well as two travel vouchers, enough to cover flights from Mexico City to London, in case you change your mind about coming home.

Until our call next week,

Daniel

Professor Daniel Lyon

The Observatory, Department of Humanities

I linger on those last two lines, and a grin tugs at my lips. Lyon still hasn't gotten around to changing his title in his email signature. He's far too sharp, his attention to detail too unerring, for this to be an oversight. Lyon's new title carries significantly more weight—Father Time, Chronos, Grantor of Immortality, Ruler of Our Universe . . . Most would be thrilled to tack any one of those honorifics onto the end of their name, or over it, erasing who they were before. But not Lyon. I'm guessing he's as uncomfortable using his new title as I've been. And something about that makes that ley line to his office shine brighter.

Until I open the attachment at the bottom of the screen.

My smile fades as I skim the report, my visions of our anniversary trip to Amsterdam suddenly reduced to smoking piles of dust. Lyon and Gaia have been searching for a handful of AWOL Seasons—bounty chasers who came after Fleur and me when we were on the run from Michael. Most turned themselves in and were granted clemency. Others were caught and brought back to the Observatory for hearings. But a few slipped off the grid as soon as they heard about Michael's defeat; they haven't turned up since.

And those are the ones Lyon is worried about.

A pattern of odd and untimely storms suggests they're alive—and they aren't lying low. Lyon's restricting travel for all non-paired Seasons unless they consent to be monitored, tied by a transmitter to a ley line. Which would be an option for a Season like Fleur—whose magic could be pulled back to the Observatory through a ley line if the worst should ever happen to her—but not for a human like me.

I pitch the phone onto the bed, leaving a dent in the comforter. Arms braced against the dresser, I hang my head, struggling to figure out how I'll break the news to Fleur. We outran an army of Guards and fought off a horde of bounty-hunting Seasons as they chased us across the Atlantic and most of North America, but now that I'm human, we can't be trusted to leave the safety of our own freaking town.

A breeze lifts the sheer curtains of our bedroom. Raising my head, I catch a flash of pink through the window. Fleur's perched on the lip of the pool in the courtyard below, the hem of her peasant skirt pulled up over her knees and her feet dangling in the deep end. Ceiba and cypress trees form a pale backdrop, their branches turned down, their pale leaves wavering under the churning gray clouds behind her. Her curtain of hair is tucked behind one ear, revealing the long white wire connecting her earbuds to her cell phone. One foot draws somber patterns in the water as she talks.

The breath I draw feels heavy.

She's beautiful. Beautiful and awe-inspiring and strong; I don't deserve her.

I lurch at the sudden ring of my phone. "Cold As Ice" by Foreigner belts through the room and I rush to the bed to silence it. My former Handler's smug face fills the screen. I didn't pick the ringtone—Chill did—and no matter how many times I change it back to something that doesn't make me want to rip my skin off, he manages to hack my phone and swap it out again.

I answer with a sigh. "Hey, what's up?"

"I sensed a disturbance in the Force."

I tuck the phone under my ear and peel back the edge of the curtain. Fleur's still on the phone. And now I know who with. "Poppy told you, huh?"

"Nah. But they've been on for almost an hour, and she keeps putting my calls to voice mail. I only managed to get through once, and all she said before she hung up on me was that I should call you. Trouble in paradise?"

"No." I carry the phone down the hall, slip inside my office, and close the door. I fall backward onto the couch, an arm slung over my eyes. In the drawn-out silence, with my old roommate's voice in my ear and the sagging cushions of the ratty old couch folding around me, I can almost imagine I'm back in our dorm room.

"Because you can tell me—"

"There's nothing to tell," I grumble. When I open my eyes, Fleur's lopsided evergreen is right above my head. I sit up and swing my feet over the edge of the couch. "It's nothing. We're fine."

"Got it," he says quietly. And by the grace of Gaia, he lets it go.

"Where are you anyway? Winter's almost over. Shouldn't you be home, in stasis?"

"I've got a few days left until Jarek gets here to take over. I'm ready to get home to Poppy. I plan to Netflix and chill with my girl for the rest of the summer." Poppy—Fleur's former Handler, the girl Chill swore he couldn't stand until he was offered the chance to spend eternity with her—is Chill's Handler now. Chill became a Winter during the battle at the lake, when he was mortally wounded while trying to save me. I passed on the opportunity to take Lyon's old Winter magic so Chill would survive, and in turn, he saved Poppy by choosing her for his Handler. In a few days, his season will be over and she'll drag his matter—his soul, magic, and energy—through the ley lines, back to the home they share in Fairbanks, Alaska. After some time in stasis, they'll have the rest of the year to spend together.

"How long will you be out of commission?" I move to my desk chair and switch on my monitors.

"Only a couple of days. Why? Are you going to miss me?"

"You wish."

"I programmed my face on your phone so you won't be too sad while I'm gone."

I bark out a laugh. "I noticed. How'd you do that, anyway?"

"A hacker never reveals his secrets." A bird calls somewhere in the background. Chill's breaths come through the phone in ragged pants, as if he's climbing steep terrain. The world feels upside down, with me in front of a computer screen and Chill huffing up a mountainside.

"A couple days, huh?" A sour jealousy washes over me. When I was a Winter, I'd spend months in stasis healing from the trauma of my injuries, and waking up in my girlfriend's arms had never been an option.

"No blood will be spilled. Just need to sleep long enough to charge my magical batteries," he says, referring to the discovery that helped us figure out how to survive out in the world without running out of power. The Seasons' magic operates like a rechargeable battery. We were intended to work in groups, our opposing charges designed by nature to heal each other and replenish each other's magic. The stasis chambers were Michael's twisted solution for keeping Seasons apart—controlling us by leashing us to the Observatory by transmitters and making us dependent on those stasis chambers for power—rather than allowing us to coexist. We were too strong together, too much of a threat, capable of toppling the system that repressed us.

Those of us who left the Observatory have all come up with our own solutions. Amber and Julio can charge each other just by touching—something they never seem to *stop* doing, regardless of the weather in California. Fleur, on the other hand, doesn't need a Season to partner with, as long as we stay in a climate that favors her. But Chill, choosing to live with his human Handler in Fairbanks, with its short, warm summers, relies on a stasis chamber for a little juice once in a while.

"Huh." I fiddle absently with the mouse. The violence of the hunts, the pain of killing Amber and being killed by Fleur, the length of stasis and the sickness that followed, the loneliness and isolation of it all . . . those were the parts of being a Winter that sucked—the things I'd told myself I was glad to be done with. And now those things aren't even an issue anymore.

"You okay, Jack?" Chill spent too many winters listening to my voice through his headphones, sifting through nonverbal cues for signs that something was wrong. That I was in danger—too tired, too sick, too angry at the world . . . ready to give up.

"Yeah." I sit up in my chair and open my email, shoving aside thoughts that have been gnawing on me since the park. "I'm happy for you, Chill. No one deserves it more than you and Poppy." That's the truth. And it's the reason I passed up my chance to become a Winter again—so Chill and Poppy could have this life together.

Lyon's email appears on my screen when I refresh it. "Did you see this report Lyon sent out a few minutes ago?"

"Reading it now." Chill's breathing's steadied, as if he's finally sitting down. "What do you make of it?"

"He said they've been waking the last of Michael's Guards. They're all getting stripped. The ones who refuse will be Culled from the program."

A low whistle issues through the phone. "Those rogue Seasons who were loyal to Michael might be a little riled up about their friends being ashed. Maybe Lyon's worried about retaliation."

"Seems that way. Looks like we're all on lockdown for a while."

"So much for your anniversary plans. Is that what you all were arguing about?"

All I manage is a grunt in response.

"Hey, that's Jarek ringing through." Chill's sucking wind again, as if he's back on the move. "I've got to take this. Then Poppy and I need to coordinate my trip home. By now, the girls should be done gossiping about you. Maybe you should go talk to Fleur."

"Thanks, I will," I tell him. "Have a safe trip home, and give Poppy a hug for me."

Chill's first to disconnect. I leave the phone pressed to my ear, listening to the silence on the other end of the line.

7

OF A LOVE OR A SEASON

FLEUR

Jack steps out from under the veranda, his hands in his pockets, his bare feet pausing in the grass at the edge of the patio. I hardly hear Poppy's goodbye. My gaze is fixed on the red slash on Jack's neck as I tug the buds from my ears and rest them on my phone. He approaches slowly, his teeth digging into his bottom lip and his dark brows pulled down. The faint scent of blood reaches me before he does, and he glances up as my eyes dip to the raw wound.

"It's fine," he says, answering the question he must read on my face as I drag my feet from the pool. He sinks down beside me before I can stand, close but not touching. "How's Poppy?"

I ease my legs back into the water, careful not to splash. Afraid of disrupting the fragile surface tension between us. "She's good."

"I guess you heard about the lockdown?" He turns slightly, catching my small nod. "I just . . . I wanted you to know I did talk to Lyon this morning about us going to Amsterdam. He was supposed to talk to Gaia about it this week and let me know, but . . ." He rubs his eyes and swears under his breath. "For whatever it's worth, he says he's sorry."

"I seriously doubt that." Those bitter words are out of my mouth before I can call them back. Jack's relationship with his old professor is dysfunctional and complicated, and any time I've tried to encourage him to take a step back—to see Lyon and his actions as anything other than altruistic—Jack's instinct is to defend him. But I'm not convinced Lyon's loyalty to Jack doesn't come with a price.

"I know you don't like him. I get that. But he's not trying to make things difficult for us, Fleur. I can't just ignore everything he's done for us."

"You mean everything he's done to assuage his guilt." A breeze snaps my hair across my face. Clouds begin to gather overhead, throwing shadows over the garden. "I know you want to see the best in him. But the first time I met Daniel Lyon, he showed up late to the battle *he* made us fight for him. To claim a title *we* secured for him. He didn't so much as look at you as you bled out and died, so forgive me for not trusting him." Jack's face blurs behind the hot tears rising to my eyes, and I fight to hold them back. "As far as I'm concerned, Woody's death, your death, Poppy's death . . . Gabriel, Yukio, Noelle, and all the others . . ." I close my eyes, shuddering at the memories of them all. "Those deaths are all at Lyon's feet. And just because Gaia gave two of you back to us doesn't mean I'll ever forgive him for that. Lyon manipulated us, Jack. Don't ever forget that. And I can't for the life of me understand why you would ever want to go back to him."

"Because I can't keep you safe like this." Jack gestures to himself

71

with disgust, as if every perfectly sculpted piece of him, every curve and every angle that's perfectly fitted to mine, isn't magic enough.

"What makes you think we'd be safe back there?"

"Lyon has my smaze. He said he would help me if I wanted to try to take it back."

"You know how I feel about that. You heard what Gaia said. That smaze isn't you anymore. It's poisoned, Jack."

"They don't know that."

"They might not, but we do." We both know when it happened. During the ambush at Jack's grandfather's cabin, a group of Seasons had us surrounded. Julio and Amber had suffered mortal wounds, and my power was fading fast. The three of us were bleeding and dying, and in a final bid to save us, Jack had taken the magic from a dying Winter named Névé Onding, knowing she couldn't be saved. Even if she could have been healed, I'm not convinced she would have deserved that mercy after what she tried to do to us.

The magic Jack took from Névé gave us the strength to survive the night. Only when we woke did we realize how Jack would continue to be affected by it. That guilt rode Jack's conscience like an angry ghost. He still wonders sometimes—we all do—if a piece of Névé Onding's soul clung to him that day. If it lingers in his smaze even now.

I can't help but think that's why Gaia told him it would be dangerous to reclaim it. Because that smaze isn't truly Jack's alone anymore.

"I know it will be painful, but Lyon said—"

"Lyon's a liar and a manipulator! If that thing is broken and painful, why would he offer to give it back?"

"That *thing* was part of me!"

"It's not a part of who you are now! Do you really want to risk that?" A tear slides down my cheek as he looks at me with such yearning in his eyes, a quiet desperation I haven't seen in a long time. Suddenly, it's like I'm staring at him through a chain-link fence, our hands clasping the wire mesh, our foreheads close but never touching. He knew what he wanted that night when I tracked him to that construction site, ready to follow the rules and end his season. He knew what he was willing to risk to protect me, so we could be together. He didn't care that it was reckless and deadly; he had made his choice already.

"You want to go back anyway, don't you? That's what you want. To go back to the Observatory."

"I would never leave you alone here. Not ever." He hesitates, as if he's weighing his words. "But what if . . . what if I wanted *us* to go back? Just for a while. Just to see—"

My head shakes as I cup his cheek, turning him to face me. "There was no *us* there, Jack," I whisper. "It was you and me on opposite sides of the Crux, killing each other over and over. It was Lyon and Gaia making bets on the future of two lonely, hopeless kids as they gambled with our lives. And I love you too much to ever go back to that. We have everything we need. Right here. Don't we?"

He nods into my hand. His cheek is warm under my palm.

I press my tear-streaked lips briefly to his, then retreat inside our house.

8

THOSE WHO FAVOR FIRE

DOUG

On the morning of the Dismantling, the last fourteen members of the old Guard are led from our holding cells to the ornate double doors of the Control Room, where we are positioned in a single-file line to wait. We're restrained, our wrists bound in front of us like criminals, our hands covered in fire-suppressing mitts. Eight prisoners wait in front of me and Kai. Another four behind us.

Not as many as I had hoped, but enough.

Lixue is the last in line, shaking off the Guard as he fastens on her mitts. Our eyes catch over the heads between us, before our procession starts to move and I'm forced to turn around. Four of Lyon's new recruits accompany us, two at the front of the line and two at the rear. In front of me, sweat darkens the back of Kai's jumpsuit, her fear pungent and sharp.

I lean close to her ear. "I'll be right behind you," I murmur.

Watching her. Making sure she holds up her end of the bargain. I've been screwed over before, too many times to trust her entirely.

She gives a barely perceptible nod. When the Guards open the doors and call the first prisoner to the dais, the line's nudged forward to close the gap.

I count off seconds in my head. A full two minutes pass before the poor bastard's muffled cry breaches the doors. It isn't a wail of pain, but a high, gutting keen of loss as his magic is extracted and rehoused in one of Gaia's creatures. My stomach sours as the screams drag on. It's a good thing we're standing on this side of the door. Otherwise, I might strangle the kid with my own shackles just to shut him up.

The short dark hair on the nape of Kai's neck stands on end as the screams quiet. This will be her test. A test of her commitment, her courage, her loyalty to me.

"Now," I whisper.

Kai begins turning in circles, twisting in her restraints.

"No! No!" she protests, her voice rising to a shout. "I don't want this! You can't let them do this!" The Guards at the back of the line rush to silence her. She throws herself to the floor, kicking and thrashing against their ankles.

"Back up! Give us room!" One of Lyon's Guards shoulders me out of the way. He doesn't notice as I slip his key card from its magnetic chain in his pocket. The prisoners behind me crane their necks, crowding forward to see. Lixue's the only one watching me as I slip out of line, holding my restraints against my body so they won't rattle as I back away from the scene. She doesn't say a word as I clear the corner and break into a run.

Kai's screams fade as I reach the entrance to the gallery. Taking careful peeks around the wall, I search for crows on the high perches near the ceiling, but the branches are empty. No bees or smazes are anywhere in sight, but a lone fly circles the dome. If it sees me, Gaia will know within seconds, and this experiment will be over.

I shake off my mitts, tucking them in my pocket and snapping a plastic button off the front of my jumpsuit. Huddled against the wall, I toss the button as far as I can into the adjacent corridor. It bounces against the marble with a series of small taps.

Peering around the corner, I see the fly stall and change direction, disappearing toward the sound.

I move quickly, checking around every turn for Guards until I reach the Crux. Two shadows walk on the far side of the circular hall, momentarily obscured by the elevator at its center. I creep into the portal, matching their speed as I move through the Crux, careful to stay where they can't see me as they patrol. Hugging the walls under the security cameras, I duck into the north wing. Security is lighter than it should be, and the sight of Lyon's unguarded office is a shot of adrenaline to my confidence. He knows something's about to go down. He probably stationed all his Guards in the east wing with him because he's worried for his life. Which is exactly what I was counting on.

My restraints clank against the control panel as I wave the stolen key card over the scanner to the right of the door. The red light doesn't so much as flicker. A message scrolls across the readout: *Please scan second card*.

What second card? Lyon must have heightened security while I was in stasis. Panic ripples through me. I grab the brass knobs and pull; the heavy wooden doors don't budge.

"Hey!" a voice booms behind me. "You can't be here! What are you—?"

I turn around fast, swinging my arms high. My iron cuffs slam into the Guard's jaw, knocking him flat on his back. I straddle him, pinning his arms with my knees, my wrist restraints pressed against his throat as he thrashes. My hands are shaking by the time his head falls limp to one side. I rush to mute his transmitter, plucking it from his ear and stuffing it in my pocket.

Restraints rattling, I search his belt for his key card. Holding one in each hand, I wave both cards over the scanner. The red light flips to green and the locks click open. Grabbing the Guard's motionless body under the arms, I drag him into the office with me and close the door, shutting us inside. A faint glow glimmers under his skin, his magic preparing to leave him. He'll be dead in a matter of minutes. I won't have long before someone in the Control Room realizes he's gone.

My head snaps up as motion sensors trigger the lights. I freeze as they flicker on in quick succession—bookshelves, reading lamps, desk lamp, overheads . . .

Breath held, I wait.

The office stays quiet. No footsteps in the hall. No flashing alarms. Just the glimmer of the snake's scales in the enclosure across the room.

The serpent writhes, its flicking tongue following my movements as I creep close and kneel in front of the glass, getting a good look at the shimmering facets of its eyes. If I had any doubts before that Ananke's soul is trapped inside this snake, they're gone now.

"I've come to break you out. You're going to help me get out of this mess. But you already know that, don't you?" I run my fingers over the lid, but it's sealed on all sides. I search the room, my gaze landing on a tall, hooked reading lamp behind a leather armchair in the corner. Jerking the plug from the wall, I turn the lamp upside down and swing the base into the side of the snake's enclosure. She recoils from the splintering glass with a hiss. I swing again and again, until I've chipped out a hole big enough for the snake to slither through.

Slowly, I set down the lamp, positioning myself between the snake and the only exit. Her snout emerges, followed by six feet of shimmering scales. She drops to the floor and raises her triangular head, a warning in the cobralike sway of her body. She's bigger than I imagined, her jaws open, baring fangs like scythes.

"How the hell are we supposed to do this?" I whisper. I've seen Gaia take magic before, sucking it into her lungs like a vacuum. I knew this wasn't going to be easy, but I hadn't considered the size of those fangs. Or does it work like it did with Michael and the staff? Will I have to kill her to claim her magic?

Either way, I'll have to grab her. My hands are sweaty, and I wipe them on my jumpsuit. The snake rears back, mirroring my movements as I inch closer, forcing her into a corner.

She hisses as I feint. Sweat trails down my temple as I dart again, aiming for the slender line of muscle behind her pitted jaws.

She strikes and I cry out as her fangs sink into my wrist. My other hand closes around her as she whips her body like a tail. I try to dislodge her, but her jaws are locked tight. The bite grows hot, like fire under my skin.

A horrible, throbbing pain seizes me. My heart pounds like it's coming out of my chest and my skin burns, my desire for the magic pushed aside by the basic overwhelming need to survive this.

I squeeze, cutting off the snake's air, remembering how Lyon held the staff as the lightning passed through it. How Michael had writhed and fought against him. I remember the blinding flash of light as the magic passed from one man to the other just before Michael died.

My skin around her mouth begins to glow. The magic spreads up my arm. White-hot lines of it radiate like forks of lightning under my skin. Just when I can't hold back my scream anymore, the snake goes limp.

Her fangs retract. She falls against the floor with a heavy, dull *thud*.

I wince, blinking away tears, as the snake crumbles into a pile of ash. Breathing hard, I drop to my knees, struggling to focus on the two small punctures she left in my hand. My eyes feel strange, too sensitive to the light. It's as if they're trying to see the entire room at once.

I lunge for the floor lamp.

Dragging the base toward me, I search for my reflection in the lamp's surface. Instead, I see Lyon. I see my face reflected in his eyes. I see myself, holding his staff. I blink. Blink again. The brilliant facets of two diamondlike eyes stare back at me from the brass.

By the time I turn to leave the office, the Guard is a shapeless pile of ash on the carpet. I keep my head down, my wrists held passively in my restraints and my sleeves pulled low to conceal the bite. My bangs hang limp over my eyes as I retrace my steps to the Control Room, moving through the halls by memory.

A Guard grabs me by the shoulder as I return to the line. "Where the hell have you been?" he mutters, dragging me back toward the others.

"Aren't you supposed to know?" His sweat is sour, his eyes darting everywhere but my face. He's afraid . . . afraid he'll be held accountable for my disappearance. I fight the urge to look up and meet his eyes, curious if I'd see that fate reflected inside them.

"Consider yourself lucky. You're up next," he says, shoving me to the front of the line.

Kai's gone, already inside.

I stiffen as a sharp, sudden cry pierces the door. I keep my head down as she wails. I was supposed to get back in time. I was supposed to go first. I hadn't seen this moment, hadn't looked for it in the lamp in my hurry to get back here. Every fresh scream slices through me. *This is a test*, I remind myself. *And she's already passed*. It's not too late to fix this.

After two more excruciating minutes, her cries fall silent and the doors are drawn open.

I already know what's waiting inside. Already saw the positions of the Guards in my reflection in the lamp. Five of them, spread around the room—one team of Lyon's personal Guards, plus the one escorting me in—leaving three in the hall, along with the four remaining members of Michael's Guard . . . the ones who still have their magic.

The wall clock ticks behind us as we cut through the center aisle between the wooden pews. A crow caws from Gaia's side of the dais. The menagerie of cages behind her desk reeks like crow shit and magic. The nine dismantled Guards who've been stripped of their power form a line of sour sweat in the front pew. Kai sits at the end of the row, closest to the center aisle, curled in on herself and shaking as Lyon's Guard leads me past her to the front of the room. The air shifts, and her eyes narrow up at mine, glistening with betrayal as she lifts her head to watch me. I don't linger on them. I can't afford the distraction. I glance down the rest of the pew as I pass. None of the former Guards are wearing shackles.

The Guard pulls me to a halt when we reach the dais. Lyon stands on the short platform above me. I keep my gaze on the polished foot of the staff; my eyes shine back at me, a quick, dark reflection of what's coming. The ends of the black velvet sash covering the eye dangle between us.

"Douglas," Lyon says as the Guard removes my shackles. "There's still time to make the right choice." A crow shrieks, flapping against the bars of its cage. Gaia turns, distracted by its sudden fit.

"You left me no choice." My pulse quickens as I lift my eyes to Lyon's, and in them, I see what I'm about to do.

"I had hoped it would not come to this," he whispers.

A smile twitches on my face as Lyon raises his staff. The Guard at my side looks at me askance, stiffening as his eyes narrow on mine. He reaches for my wrists as he calls out to the other Guards, shouting a warning. With a quick sideways thrust of my arm, I catch him in the throat. The room explodes in a thunder of boots as he falls. Guards sprint toward the dais. Not to me, but to Gaia.

She whirls at the commotion, knocking over a shelf of cages as the Guards form a protective line in front of her. Her eyes skip to mine over their heads. She lunges toward us, but the Guards hold her back.

"No! Get back, Daniel!" Static crackles in her hair. Crows and insects flee their enclosures, a flurry of black wings.

I vault onto the dais, leaping out of reach as Lyon swings the scythe at my chest. I've trained in close combat for decades. I've fought and sparred in every condition, against every kind of Season, using every kind of weapon, but this . . . My limbs react with a precision and speed

I've never had before, dodging Lyon's next move as if my brain already knows what it will be. The stasis sickness is gone. Every shape and movement, even in my peripheral vision, is cut into sharp focus. My shackles are off. The room, my body, my fate . . . they finally feel like mine to control.

I kick out, catching Lyon in his abdomen between swings of the scythe. He crashes to the dais with enough force to crack the hardwood platform. The staff skitters across the floor. I dive for it, my arms a blur of speed as I grasp the handle. Rolling onto my back, I flip the scythe, raising the pointed foot like a spear. I brace myself as Lyon rushes toward me, too fast to stop what's destined to happen.

Gaia screams as Lyon plunges into it.

His mouth parts, his jaw slack with shock as a red stain blooms out from the handle. My arms shake under his weight as he sags.

Lyon stares down at me, his eyes glassy and distant. Empty.

Blood trickles between his lips. "There is still time," he says, his mouth forming words I can barely hear through Gaia's screams and the shouts of the Guards, "to make the right choices."

His chin droops. For a moment, all I can do is stare. *What the hell does that even mean?* I already made my choice—my *only* choice— didn't I?

Chaos erupts. I jolt as a pulse of electricity surges through the staff. My hands fuse around the metal, my elbows locked and trembling as Lyon's magic flows into me, too late to let go. The charred taste of smoke fills my mouth. My right eye burns like it's on fire. My head falls back and I choke on a scream.

Tears stream down my cheek with every blink. The room blurs, my perspective suddenly all wrong. The room smells like war, like blood and fear and confusion as the Guards in the hall burst through the doors. They jerk to a stop, shielding their eyes from the bright final flare of light that courses through the staff. The pulsing static dies and the room falls quiet, my hands still frozen around the frosted handle of the scythe. The last four members of the old Guard rush in, chains clanking as they grind to a halt.

I drop the smoking handle. Lyon tumbles to the floor, ash already flaking from his shoulders.

Gaia falls to her knees as he crumbles and turns to dust.

Pain throbs behind my right eye. I cup it, hand shaking as I trace the warped flesh with my fingers. Snatching up the staff, I angle the blade toward my face. A sunken black hole stares back at me from the metal.

I cover the burned socket, the words Kai said to me in the pool rattling in my head. . . .

Stolen magic is cursed magic . . . you inherit their weaknesses and faults . . .

No. That's a lie. Lyon never lost his eye. That's just a story stupid librarians preach to keep Seasons in line.

A charge pulses through the room, the air taking on the dense electric tang of an approaching storm. The Guards surrounding Gaia fall back, scrambling away on hands and knees. Her hair lifts with static, like a nest of writhing silver snakes.

"What have you done!" The ground rolls out from her like a wave and sends me reeling. I rush to my feet, backing away from the raw power coming off her. I've never seen Gaia like this. Completely unhinged. It was the same way Fleur had looked at Michael in the vision

Lyon showed me—like she would tear open the earth and unleash hell with her bare hands.

"Stay back!" I point the scythe at Gaia as she advances. When she doesn't stop, I swing. The blade hisses through the air, leaving a shallow cut in the waist of her dress. She pauses just beyond its reach, her cheeks flushed and her diamond eyes furious.

A wooden beam in the ceiling groans. The Guards, old and new, throw out their arms for balance, watching the walls and the ceiling as the ground rumbles. They turn to Gaia, as if they're waiting for some command from her.

"I have the staff!" I shout at them. "You answer to me now! Including you." I point the blade at Gaia. "And you'll stay the fuck back, if you know what's good for you!"

Gaia shakes her head, her voice pitching low enough for only me to hear as she stalks closer. "This will not end in any way you can possibly imagine, Douglas. It takes two eyes to see clearly—two *hearts*," she says, her breath hitching. "And I will never serve you." Her voice hardens as she steps over Lyon's ashes. "You are now, and will always be, alone."

Gaia leaps straight for the scythe's blade. She gasps, her body lurching to a stop as it sinks into her chest.

Our eyes catch. I didn't see this coming. Hadn't looked beyond Lyon's last breath in the lamp's surface. I never planned for this. But Gaia had. She knew. . . . So why hadn't they tried harder to stop me? I search her eyes for an answer as their lids grow heavy. A hazy vision flickers through the slits. No . . . a memory. No voices, no sound. Only an image.

Lyon sits, wrapping the sash around the eye of the staff. Gaia rests a hand on his shoulder as a smaze rolls in an orb on Lyon's desk. His lips move around the words: *I can still save him.*

The memory winks out as Gaia's eyes flutter closed. A strange peace seems to settle over her.

I swallow hard, still puzzling over the memory when I'm thrown violently off my feet. With a deafening boom, Gaia ruptures into an explosion of ash and light. The ground shakes and a shower of plaster rains from the ceiling.

The Guards retreat to the outer edges of the room, their eyes turned up as the chandelier clinks overhead. A storm of magic gathers near the apex, forming a loose funnel. The Control Room monitors flicker with static. The screens die, one by one.

"You!" I shout to one of Lyon's Guards, pointing the scythe at him. "Unlock their restraints." I jerk my chin toward the four Guards of the old regime who still have their magic. "Now!" Lyon's Guards all snap to attention, each of them rushing to free someone in a jumpsuit. When the last set of shackles hits the floor, I order Lyon's Guards to get down on their knees. "Cuff the traitors," I tell the others.

Michael's Guards—*my* Guards—don't hesitate. Lixue is first to snatch up the restraints and fire mitts. She barks out orders, and the others respond, chaining Lyon's Guards to one another as the quake shakes the floor.

"What now?" Lixue hollers.

"Kill them."

Her eyes snap to mine. The slender column of her throat bobs, her mouth falling open in protest. "But Doug. They're—"

"Now!"

Her gaze lingers on the blade of my scythe. She issues the command,

and the members of the old Guard close in on Lyon's team, summoning their magic. Light flares, dispersing through the room, until the last of Lyon's Guards is reduced to ash.

Gaia's magic roars. A howling wind whips debris around the room. Stucco crumbles from the walls and bits of fallen plaster bubble off the floor. The air grows thick with dust.

My eye rakes the room, searching for Kai. She knew about the magic's curse. Maybe she knows how to stop this. I spot her huddled beside the pews as plaster falls around her. Above her, a chunk of the ceiling creaks and breaks loose. She screams, throwing her arms over her head as the giant slab falls.

"No!" I lunge for Kai as it speeds toward her. "Stop!"

Everything goes still. Silence falls like a scythe.

My ears ring, the world outside them completely devoid of sound. Breathing hard, I look around me. It's as if the room is submerged under water. Particles of dust and plaster hover motionless in the air. The surviving members of the old Guard stand utterly still, like living mannequins posed around the room. Kai's mouth is frozen in a soundless scream, the fallen section of ceiling suspended in the air above her head.

With cautious steps, I walk out amid the debris, afraid any sudden movement might break the spell. My shoes are silent on the broken glass. Reaching out with a finger, I prod a piece of plaster where it hangs in the air, but it doesn't budge. I weave through the room, around people standing still as statues.

The second hand on the clock doesn't move.

I stare at my trembling hands. At the smoke-tarnished staff. A breathless laugh wheezes out of me.

I am Time. And Inevitability. Two of the greatest powers in the universe.

And the world is collapsing around me.

My laughter becomes panicked, almost hysterical. I turn in a circle, taking in the destruction. Gaia's soul is a motionless whorl of light above my head. It doesn't so much as blink, but I'm certain it will tear this place apart if I can't find a way to control it.

I drag my hand through the plaster dust in my hair. I don't know how to fix this. I don't know what the staff is capable of or the limitations of my new magic. How the hell am I supposed to stop this earthquake she's started? I don't know how it all works or what to do next. Or . . .

What to do next . . .

The eye.

I lower the scythe, tearing at the sash around its head, my fingernails catching on the velvet as I struggle to loosen the knot. A choked sound escapes me as the fabric pulls away, revealing a gaping hole where the crystal should be.

It's gone.

But it was here. Lyon had it.

It was *right here*, in the head of the staff, when he showed me the vision in his office last week. He looked inside it, and he saw something. . . .

I had hoped it would not come to this.

My shout echoes off the walls. I hurl the staff and it clatters over the stone.

Lyon knew! He knew this moment would happen, and he hid the crystal to punish me.

My breath billows out in angry white clouds. Ice slides into my veins, my Winter magic stirring awake as if it's responding to an unconscious thought. I pant, looking down at the frost on my hands.

Time . . . it stopped when I needed it to. When I *commanded* it to. It answered to my desires just like my Winter magic. Time is just another form of magic. If I can control the elements, I can control this, too.

I take a deep breath, assessing the room. Coming up with a plan.

Restart time. Save Kai. Together, we'll figure out what to do with Gaia's magic.

The staff sticks to my palm as I bend to retrieve it, the cold skin pulling painfully as I rise to my feet and position myself close to Kai. I raise my eye to the clock. Focusing on the long brass second hand, I envision it ticking. Imagine pushing it to the right. My blackened eye burns as the magic stirs inside me.

"Forward," I whisper.

A sudden burst of wind rips the scythe from my hand. I barrel into Kai, tackling her out of the way as the debris crashes down. Gaia's magic howls, bouncing off the ceiling and twisting against the walls. The lights flicker and die, until the only light left is the raging glow of Gaia's magic. The Guards run for cover. Kai coughs, shielding her eyes from the dust. I pull her to her feet as the storm builds around us.

"You killed them!" Her hair blows like daggers across her eyes. She jerks her hand from mine and backs away from me, her gaze locking on the scythe on the floor. "You said you would take the staff. You never said you would kill them!" Wind whips through the Control Room, hurling glass and throwing papers off the desk. "Gaia's magic is loose now. We're all going to die!"

She turns to run. I grab her and turn her chin toward me. "We're not going to die! I promised you'd be safe. That you would have your magic. We're going to fix this. You and me. Do you understand?" I'll make her more powerful than she ever imagined. I'll put her on a fuck-ing throne at my side if it means we both walk out of here alive. "*You'll* take Gaia's power. I'm going to give you her magic."

Her eyes snap to mine. The memory I see inside them stops me cold.

Her jumpsuit is clean. New. She's sitting in the armchair in Lyon's office, pale and shaking with stasis tremors. His desk calendar reveals the date—one week ago. I see his lips form the words: *When the time comes, promise me you'll protect him. That you'll make the right choice this time. It's possible to start over, Kai. We all can.*

In the memory, she nods. But it's not me I see her picturing in her mind. Not me that's driving her guilt or her need for redemption.

I drop her chin as the world falls out from under me.

I don't need magic to know what she'll do next. Kai's going to betray me.

And when she runs, it will be to Jack.

I push her away from me. The floor heaves. I duck, shielding my head as rubble crashes against my shoulder. The wind screams through the room, shattered terrariums and cages spraying glass over the floor. A crow shrieks past me. A swarm of bees rushes toward the only exit. When I look up, the heavy wooden doors are thrown wide, swinging on their hinges.

Kai's gone.

I grip the edge of Gaia's desk as another quake takes hold. I reach for the staff, using it for leverage to push myself upright. With a sharp inhale, I draw Gaia's magic toward me. It thrashes against the ceiling, fighting my control. Sparks fly as, breath after breath, I force the funnel down. It condenses into a tight ball of light as it descends toward my mouth.

Her magic burns as I breathe it in. All stingers and teeth and claws, it refuses to go down. It shreds my throat, and I fight the urge to choke it out. Groping wildly over the desk, I search for a cage. For a host. For something else to contain it before it rips me apart. The crows, bees, and flies have all escaped. But the Guards are still here. I could make one of them—

No.

I can't risk giving any of them this much power. Any one of them could turn on me, just like Kai.

My fingers close around an orb. I shake open the lid and heave into it, spitting light from my mouth. Gasping and shaking, I secure the lid in place as Gaia's magic hisses at me through the glass. Blood drips down my chin. I wipe it on my sleeve, sucking down painful gulps of air as the wind begins to die.

Dust and loose papers drift to the floor. When the last of the tremors has stilled, the four remaining members of the old Guard—*my* Guard—rise slowly to their feet. With wide eyes, they stare at the blackened hollow in my face. I avoid their gazes, afraid of what I might see inside them. Arms braced on Gaia's desk, I hang my head over the orb, wondering what the hell I'm supposed to do next.

9

PROMISES TO KEEP

◇

JACK

I'm light-headed and drenched to the bone when I finally lumber off the treadmill and head to my office for my meeting with Lyon. I ease into my rolling chair and slide to my keyboard, checking messages as I await his call. An email arrives from Poppy, complete with a selfie of Chill wearing a snow-crusted parka beside an elevation sign at the foot of an Alaskan mountain pass. My throat tightens and I close the attachment, switching to check the weather feeds instead.

Nothing but blue skies and perfect spring weather for a hundred miles in every direction, with the exception of the same small cluster of persistent heavy clouds that have hovered over our villa all week.

The front door shuts. I turn on the security feeds in time to see Fleur reach the end of the cobblestone driveway. Her GPS light flashes red on another screen as she rounds the bend, heading to her school. She wore her transmitter this morning without a reminder or an argument.

And when I went to the kitchen for coffee, all the tourism clippings she'd stuck to the fridge had been quietly taken down. Our new visas and passports came by courier a few days ago, along with the travel vouchers from Lyon. I tucked them in a drawer as soon as the delivery driver was gone.

I check the network connection as I wipe sweat from my brow. Already three songs into my playlist, I'm more than ready for a cold shower. *Where the hell is Lyon?* It's not like him to be late. I try the number for his office and listen through fifteen rings before finally giving up. Slouching back in my chair, I stare at the ceiling, thinking about all the things I yearn to talk to him about and don't know how. About the travel vouchers in the drawer. About all the reasons Fleur doesn't want us to go back, and all the reasons I feel like I need to.

A video call notification pops up on my screen. Something inside me unwinds as I sit up and click the mouse to connect.

"Hey, Professor." I pause my music, waiting for the camera to catch up and his face to appear.

"Not last time I checked." I glance up, not entirely disappointed to see Amber on the screen.

"Hey. I can't talk long. Waiting on a call from Lyon. What's up?"

"Have you been watching the headlines from London today?"

"No, why?" I'm already flipping open tabs, bringing up the world news and feeding the images to the second screen over my desk. I don't usually keep track of weather beyond a few hundred miles of Cuernavaca. But the irregular smear of green storms streaking across the radar are enough to grab my attention.

"A quake was reported there a few hours ago."

"How bad?"

"Not as bad as 2008. Barely a four on the Richter. But check out the storms."

I zoom in on the bursts of color radiating from London's center. As I watch, smaller fronts begin to appear farther out, as if one weather event is triggering the next. "Looks like someone's having a meltdown."

"Or a lot of someones." Amber's eyes dart back and forth over her screen.

"Nothing Gaia and Lyon can't handle." This must be the reason Lyon's running late. "Maybe they're finally getting this rogue situation handled. The sooner, the better." I sink back into my chair, glad for the distraction while I wait.

"Hey, speaking of Lyon," she says, turning her attention back to me, "did you and Fleur get a weird package from him? There was a strange note and three travel vouchers inside. Something about meeting up with you and going back for a visit?"

Lyon must really want me to come home if he's dragging Amber and Julio into it. "Are you going?"

"I've got two words for you, Iceman." Julio's face is a photobomb, framed by Amber's red hair and the timber walls of their bedroom behind her. "No. Fucking. Way."

"That's three words," she points out.

"What can I say? I have strong feelings on the subject. We nearly lost our lives trying to get out of that place."

"Oh, come on," she says dismissively. "It's not like we're being dragged back there by the ley lines. It'd only be for a few days."

"You know what else only lasts a few days? Food poisoning,

snowstorms, and a bad tequila hangover. I see no compelling reason to subject myself to any of them."

I rest my head in my hand, scraping the edge of my desk with a fingernail as I listen to them argue. "It's moot, anyway. Fleur already said no."

"Maybe Julio and I can convince her. We're long overdue for a visit. The four of us haven't seen each other offscreen in months."

"I have a better idea," Julio says, wrapping his arm around Amber and moving her out of the chair so he can sit in front of the camera. He drags her into his lap and talks over her shoulder. "How about you and Fleur pack a bag and fly up to our place for a long weekend? The weather's great. We can hit the beach, maybe do some camping—"

"We are not camping," Amber interjects, rolling her eyes. "We have a guest room. You're more than welcome to stay here with us, Jack. I promise we won't make you sleep in a tent."

"Can't," I say absently, watching Fleur's red light leave the coffee shop on the adjacent screen. "Lyon's set a travel ban for unpaired Seasons. We're stuck at home until it lifts."

The call goes quiet. I turn back to see Amber frowning at me. She covers the mic, says something to Julio. He glances at me, nods, and slips out from her chair, disappearing from view. The door to their bedroom clicks shut behind him.

"What happened to your neck?" Amber hasn't changed at all. Razor-sharp and never one to pull punches. I had forgotten about the healing scab until she pointed it out, and now it itches like it might open again. I give it a light scratch that doesn't quite satisfy it.

"I was out for a run. Couple of assholes with a switchblade caught me off guard and wanted my watch. That's all."

"Obviously you lived through it. So what happened? Instinct took over?"

"More like Fleur took over," I grumble. "I was doing just fine on my own. I didn't need anyone's help."

She scrutinizes me in the same piercing way she used to right before a fight, feeling out the best way to engage me without getting hit. "Talk to me, Jack. What's going on?"

"There's nothing to talk about."

"Bullshit. There are two kinds of people who know you best: those who love you and those who are determined to kill you. And I've been both."

I rub my eyes, torn between lying and spilling my guts to her. "I don't know. . . . I think maybe I'm homesick." Amber's silent for a long moment, as if this isn't the answer she was expecting. "I don't know why. I can't explain it, okay? I just . . . I miss something."

"Your magic?"

I shove the chair back from the desk, resentful of the monitors and satellites and security cameras I'm forced to depend on to do my job—a job I should be able to perform at Fleur's side, not hiding behind a screen. "Lyon's got it," I tell her. "It's right there, in a cage on his desk. He told me I can have it back. That it's mine whenever I want it."

"Do you want it?"

I shake my head, wishing I hadn't answered the call, hating the pity in her voice and the softness of her tone. I'd rather she just come out swinging at me the way she used to.

"Yes, I want it!" The confession rushes out of me with the force of a winter wind. I launch out of my chair and pace the room. "I can't describe what it's like, Amber. It's like I'm missing a limb, or—"

"Part of your soul?" she says, finishing for me.

My throat constricts. "Fleur's my soul." She's the only piece of me I can't live without. At least, that's what I've been telling myself. Only, lately, I feel like part of me is dying, and I'm not entirely sure anymore.

"Your smaze is more than just the power Gaia granted you. It lived inside of you. It became part of you. Bits of you still exist inside it—your memories, your spirit. You're feeling a void for a reason, Jack. Because there *is* one."

"Maybe there should be. I've seen my smaze. It's messed up, Amber. It's twisted and angry and dark as a hailstorm. What if I set that thing loose inside me and it tears us apart?" I sink into my chair and prop my elbows on the desk, bringing my face close to the camera. If anyone should remember what that darkness looks like, it's Amber. The first thing I did after taking Névé's magic was threaten Amber's life. But any grudges she held are long gone. Her full lips are only pursed with worry now.

"Have you talked to Fleur?"

"It came up," I say, scrubbing my face. "It didn't go well."

Amber raises an eyebrow.

"I can't blame Fleur for being upset. She chose me to be her Handler—her caretaker and her protector. I can't push that aside and say her choices don't matter." I should never have asked her to go back to the Observatory. Should never have even considered it, knowing how she'd feel about it. I rake both hands through my hair, leaving them buried in the tangled, sweaty mess of it. "I don't know, Amber. We both want the same thing—to keep each other safe—but it feels like we're doing it all wrong. We can't seem to find any balance."

Amber chews on her lip. "Maybe Julio was right. A camping trip might not be the worst idea."

I press the heels of my hands into my eyes. "You lost me."

"Maybe you and Fleur need to get off the grid for a while. You know, go back to the last place where you did feel balanced."

I think back to our time on the run, unable to put my finger on the last place where we felt balanced. Every perfect memory of us together during that time was bookended by danger or disaster. There was never a perfect moment. There was never a guarantee we'd survive. There were no safe places. Fleur and I had accepted the possibility of death. We ran headfirst into it, knowing the risks, for the chance to be together. We found our balance in *spite* of the danger, not because we were both safe from it.

"But the travel ban . . ."

She chokes out a laugh. "When have the rules ever stopped you before?"

I sit up, my mind spinning.

"Amber, you're a genius!" I bend over my keyboard, tapping out a quick email to Lyon, asking to reschedule our meeting, before leaping to my feet. "I'll call you later."

"Wait, Jack, where are you going?" she shouts.

A smile crackles like frost over my face as I grab my shoes and run for the door. "I don't know yet. We'll figure it out."

10

LET THE NIGHT BE DARK

FLEUR

The soothing notes of an acoustic guitar fill my studio. The recording is a mix Julio made for me after I told him I missed hearing him play: old folk ballads, modern pop songs, a little classic rock. Amber's clear soprano harmonizes with Julio's rich tenor, taking me back to a night we all spent sitting on the dusty floor of a rickety cabin, listening to them sing over mugs of canned stew and the crackle of a fire.

I turn my easel away from the window and pick up my brush, letting Julio's music carry me someplace else as I paint. By the midpoint of the recording, the scene on the canvas has completely changed. The hillside has darkened to a deep midnight green, and the air is dusted with chimney smoke through frost-covered branches.

I pull back to look at it, surprising myself as I recognize the imprecise and crooked outline of a pond. *Our* pond. The one near Jack's grandfather's cabin, where he took me skating under the stars.

With a pang, I wonder what Jack would think of it. If he would want to hang it in the villa, or if it would make him sad to look at it.

I pick a loose hair from the tip of the brush, struggling to remember my life before Gaia gave me my magic. My earth magic is so much a part of me. The thought of having that ripped away is viscerally painful to imagine. I don't know who I'd be without it. And even though it terrifies me to think of Jack going back to the Observatory—of entrusting him to someone as powerful and cunning as Daniel Lyon—maybe it's wrong of me to keep him from that.

My stomach growls. The sky is dark through the window above my garden, night insects singing alongside the quiet notes of Julio's guitar.

I gather my brushes and carry them to the sink, turn on the faucet, and work the paint free with soap. A hint of smoke carries on a breeze through the open window, as if conjured from the chimney in the painting itself.

I pause in front of the basin, my hand stilling around the brushes.

I shut off the tap, then the music, bristling as the smell of smoke thickens.

Slowly, I set the brushes on the counter, my thoughts leaping to Lyon's memo about the handful of rogue Seasons no one has been able to trace. A loud *click* echoes somewhere in the villa. My head snaps up, eyes darting toward the ceiling as the lights turn off, plunging my studio into darkness.

"Jack?" I call out. I reach out with my magic, into the roots of the trees surrounding the villa. I sense no pain—nothing burning.

Wiping my wet hands on my smock, I creep to the window and draw in a deep breath. The smoke doesn't taste like magic. I'm certain the smell doesn't belong to an Autumn. Maybe not even a human. There's no acrid bite of cigarettes coming from the woods.

I take off my smock and lay it across the stool. As I open the studio door, another *click* rings through the villa, and the lights in the hall extinguish. I stiffen at another *click* as the training room goes dark, then the game room beyond it. . . .

My mind reaches for a root.

"Jack?" I step tentatively out of my studio, nearly tripping over something on the floor.

My mouth parts around a fragile gasp.

A tiny white votive flickers in the hall. A lily—one single perfect lily—rests on a folded slip of paper beside it.

I bend down to pick them up. Flower held to my chest, I peek down the hall, but no one's there. I unfold the note, angling it toward the candlelight.

> *Run away with me tonight.*
> *No transmitters, no cell phones.*
> *Just you and me, off the grid . . .*

A trail of white votives lights a path to the veranda. I creep to the edge and peer over the rail. Jack stands in the darkened courtyard below, stoking a crackling campfire beside a carefully arranged ring of stones. A picnic blanket is spread on the grass, complete with a box of greasy take-out pepperoni pizza that I can smell from up here. A bag of marshmallows and two sweating bottles of beer rest beside it.

Jack's face glows in the soft orange light, and my heart flutters when he smiles up at me.

Lily in hand, I follow the trail of flickering votives, hurrying barefoot down the winding steps, then through the open patio doors and into the courtyard. More candles dot the yard, weaving through the cool grass around the moonlit swimming pool, marking a path to Jack's fire.

The night smells like jacaranda blossoms and the flame trees that decorate the garden with bright orange blooms. I lace my fingers in Jack's. He brushes a loose tendril of hair back from my face.

"Happy anniversary."

"This is amazing," I whisper, wrapping my arms around his waist.

"You're amazing." He takes the lily and tucks it behind my ear. His thumb strokes my cheek and his mouth curves into a wide grin. "And you're covered in paint," he laughs, smearing some away.

My skin flushes as I swipe my face with the back of my hand.

"Am I underdressed for our date? I could go clean up," I say, pulling out of his arms.

"Don't you dare." He tugs me back by the waist until I'm flush against his chest.

Head tipped back, I gaze up at the stars. They're brighter than usual with the villa dark behind us, and the sight of them takes my breath away. Like the night we spent lying side by side on his open sleeping bag on a mountain in Tennessee. Jack traces lazy circles over my lower back as he gazes up, too, and I wonder if he's remembering the same night I am.

"Off the grid, huh?" My heart warms at all the effort and thought he's put into this. We're stuck here until Lyon lifts the travel ban, but somehow, Jack's managed to transform our courtyard into someplace magical, an escape from the rest of the world.

"Where would you go if you could go anywhere, Fleur?" His smile is soft and vulnerable, just like it was on the sailboat when we escaped from London.

"Anywhere?"

"Anywhere." He said the same thing then. *Anywhere*, he promised me.

My eyes close, my mind wandering back to the canvas in my studio as my paint-stained fingernails trace the contours of his chest.

"Then I'd choose the pond by your grandfather's cabin." That one perfect magical night when we were careless and happy. Perfectly balanced. "I want to go back there," I tell him, aching as I realize how much I mean it.

"The pond." His smile fades. "Not Amsterdam or Chile? Not Canada?" he asks quietly. "If I could take you anywhere—anywhere in the world—that's where you'd want to go?"

My hands slide down his chest as Jack draws away from me. As I realize how that must sound. Like I want to go back there to be with the person he was before. "That night . . . it was amazing," I rush to add, struggling to put into words how that night made me feel. How *he* made me feel. "And that kiss—"

A log shifts on the fire, tossing up sparks. Jack prods it back into place with a stick. He shakes his head, not angry, I realize. Just . . . thinking. "If we went back to the cabin now, it wouldn't be the same. I can't . . ." The fire reflects in his eyes. They shimmer with regrets when he finally looks at me. "The nights would be cold. I can't keep you warm just by holding your hand. I can't freeze the pond and take you skating or make it snow or—"

I take the stick from him. When he turns to me, I press a finger to his lips. "I don't need you to take me skating, Jack." I trace the edge of his upper lip, then the lower, marveling at their softness and shape as his mouth parts.

"What do you need?" he asks.

"Just this. Just us," I say in a hushed voice. "You and me."

He smiles, his breath warm against my finger. "Is that all?"

I cock an eyebrow. "That, and maybe s'mores."

Jack's laugh is husky as he leads me to the blanket, pulling me down beside him. Lying sideways against his shoulder, I tear into a slice of pizza and offer him a bite as he loads marshmallows onto a skewer. He roasts the marshmallows slowly, careful not to burn them, his thoughts lost somewhere in the flames as he nurses his beer.

I set my slice of pizza back in the box and close the lid.

Moving behind him, I wrap my arms around his waist, my head resting in the warm dip between his shoulders. His hand closes around mine, secure and strong. He's wrong if he thinks he can't keep me safe and warm just by holding me. I press a kiss to one of his scars, my mouth slowly moving down to the next as he leans into me. Something scrapes my knee where it brushes the back of his jeans. I reach down, mouth falling open in surprise at the two small booklets protruding from his back pocket.

Passports. Two of them. I slip them from his pocket and find two travel vouchers tucked inside their covers, the destinations and dates left empty, one made out in each of our names for a generous amount. My breath catches.

Run away with me . . .

Jack wasn't kidding. His invitation wasn't a symbolic gesture. It was real.

Where would you go if you could go anywhere, Fleur?

He was serious about taking me off the grid, regardless of Lyon's wishes.

I fall back on my knees with the passports in my hands, rocked by that same thrill I felt the day I found the maps and the poems he left for me in the Library of Congress two years ago, on this exact same day, when I figured out what Jack had planned.

When I realized what he was willing to risk for us.

"Jack?" His name comes out on a shaky whisper. How could he think for one minute that he's not enough for me? That he doesn't save me with every touch. That he doesn't complete me with every breath. How could he ever mistakenly believe he's not made entirely of magic?

11

A WORLD TORN LOOSE

DOUG

Lixue watches me from across the dusky room, cupping a flame. Her face and hair are white with plaster dust. She looks at me like she's seeing a ghost. "Should we go after her?"

Spitting out a last mouthful of blood, I drag a hand through the ash and sweat on my face. My left eye burns from all the dust, and the empty right socket throbs. Gaia's magic swirls in the orb, casting a pale glow over the room. "No." My voice comes out raw. "You won't find her. Not here." By now, Kai is probably deep in the catacombs, and there aren't enough of us to split up and track her.

Lixue glances at the staff where it lies across the desk, accepting my answer as if I must have seen the future in it. But it wasn't Kai's future I saw that made everything clear to me. It was her past. That conversation she had with Lyon last week had nothing to do with me. Lyon never cared about *saving* me. Lyon's only goal was to protect Jack. That was all he wanted from Kai. He convinced her it was the right thing to do—the path to forgiving herself. Every decision Kai's made has been motivated by guilt, and he manipulated that. Her choices now will be no different.

She feels responsible for all these deaths—the Guards, Gaia, Lyon. . . . I saw it in her eyes—her horror as she watched him die, the way she looked at me. . . . I saw her remorse when he uttered his final words, as if he'd spoken them directly to her: *There's still time to make the right choice*.

In that moment, Kai made her choice. She chose Lyon. Which means she chose Jack.

And I'd bet my staff that's exactly where she's going.

"What do we do now, Chronos?"

The question shakes me from my thoughts. It takes me a moment to register what Lixue called me.

Chronos.

I straighten, scraping the staff off the desk. The handle is cold and heavy, painful and awkward in my hand. The members of the old Guard hover along the far wall. The air tastes like uncertainty and fear. Their eyes dart back and forth between me and Lixue, as if they're waiting for some directive to move.

I scoop the black sash from the floor and tie it hurriedly around the hole in the head of the staff where the crystal used to be, hoping everyone but Lixue has been too distracted to notice it's gone. I don't need anyone challenging me before I have a chance to find it. The staff is so cold, it burns to the touch, and I grit my teeth, determined not to show it.

"Lixue. You're Commander of my new Guard," I announce as I descend the dais. "I want all the wings and portals locked down. No one is to leave their dorm rooms. You have two hours to screen and deputize a new squad. Only the strongest Seasons. And none with questionable loyalties." I stop in front of her, the head of my scythe close to her face. She doesn't blink. "Anyone who declares an intent to rebel will be ashed. I assume you can handle that."

She gives a short, tight nod, her voice cracking as she says, "Yes, sir."

Her eyes are a flickering jumble of memories, moving too fast to read. I grab one fleeting image as it flashes by. All I get is the past, a moment—an image of her rushing the frozen lake in Cuernavaca alongside me. The effort I expend for that single second leaves my head splitting. Satisfied for now, I dismiss her.

My pulse slows, my mind sharpening as I focus on the logistics of operations. These are things I know. Things I'm good at. Things I can control.

"Bradwell." I point my scythe at a lanky, baby-faced kid standing closest to the Control Room. "Congratulations. You've just been promoted. I want all tracking systems back online within the hour. And check that we have power and ventilation to all the wings." Every Season we lose is a Season I have to find and replace, and I don't have time for that. The sooner I get this place stabilized, the sooner I can hunt for Jack.

"Yes, Chronos." Bradwell bolts, nearly mowing over a muscular girl with a shaved head and gauges in her ears as he rushes out the door.

The girl glares at his back as he leaves.

"Jora," I bark, startling her to attention. She uncrosses her arms, her face paling as I gesture to the sickly, sweating humans in the room. The Guards who had their magic stripped by Lyon look empty and lost, their hands shaking uselessly at their sides. "Take them to the infirmary.

After they've been treated and cleaned up, they're to report back to you. Put them in charge of the support staff . . . kitchen, custodial, and maintenance crews . . ." I pause, catching a flicker of a vision. A memory from Jora's past that leaves me unsettled; she has sticky fingers. "And send a maintenance technician to my office. I want every one of Lyon's locks re-keyed. Until I say otherwise, access to my office and apartment will be restricted."

"Restricted to whom, sir?"

"Me."

"What about your security detail? How will we—?"

I turn, fixing her with my strange new eye. She withers under it as if she knows what I'm seeing. "Was I unclear?"

"No, sir," she says weakly.

"Then what are you still doing here?" My eye trails her as she double-times it to the hall. I turn, surveying the last Guard in the room.

"Zahra." The fierce-looking girl wipes blood from her cheek. She was new to Michael's Guard before the rebellion started, but she was sharp. Good with a computer. "I want a full report on the whereabouts of every freed Season up top. I want every single one of them found and a recovery team assembled. Once that's done, you're going to find Jack Sommers and Fleur Attwell and locate their former Handlers. I want to know *exactly* where they are. And bring Kai Sampson's personnel file to me."

Kai may be gone for now. But she'll be back for the one person she cares about—her sister. And when she comes, I'll be ready for her.

But first, I have a crystal to find.

March's size is the only bright spot on his résumé, but I didn't have much of a candidate pool to pick from when Lixue found him and brought him to the Control Room, and I appointed him head of my security detail. Jora may be a dishonest thief, but she was right; I'm Chronos now, and I should have a bodyguard. There's no telling when someone—even among those closest to me—might try to slip a knife in my back.

Orb curled in one arm and staff in the other, I retrace my steps back to my new office, taking inventory of the visible damage along the way. March trods behind me, struggling to keep up. His pride radiates from him, nauseatingly sweet, and I'm already regretting my decision to hire him.

I station him outside the door, dropping the staff on the carpet the moment the locks seal behind me. My hands are blistered where they gripped the handle and I gingerly prod the angry, raw skin. I don't remember Lyon's hands being scarred when he'd reached for the staff during our meeting last week. And I never saw a single blemish on Michael's manicured fingers. So why are mine being destroyed? Is this some kind of test?

I set the orb on the desk, bracing it between a few hardback books to keep it from rolling off. Gaia's magic thrashes inside it, sparking and hissing whenever I get close to the glass. My throat starts to hurt again just looking at it.

My head pounds and a persistent pain has been spreading in my chest. Denver once confided to me that acute panic can feel like a heart attack. I dig frantically in Lyon's desk drawer for Xanax or antacids, kicking myself for my stupidity when I find absolutely nothing. This place is shrouded in magic. Heartburn and myocardial infarctions don't exist here, so why do I feel like I'm dying?

Determined to ignore the nagging burn, I rummage through Lyon's cabinets, searching every drawer and niche for the missing eye, certain I'll feel better once it's in my hands. The crystal will show me how to control Gaia's magic. It will show me where to find Jack. And how to get the staff to stop burning the crap out of me every time I touch it.

I sling open a cabinet door, muscles tensing when a prismatic rainbow dances over the wood, but it's only the light bouncing off a crystal decanter. I swirl the amber liquid inside. The pungent whiff of alcohol stings my nose before I even break the seal, and my eyes water at the burn as I greedily swallow some down. Falling into Lyon's leather chair, I tip my head back and wait for the liquor to hit my blood, begging for it to numb the pain and wrap me in a hazy layer of gauze. But it only makes the burn in my chest worse and exacerbates my headache.

I rub my sunken eye socket. Maybe Kai was right about stolen magic being cursed. But if that's the case, then why didn't Lyon lose an eye when he stole the magic from Michael? What was *his* curse? Lyon didn't even want the power of the eye. He put a blinder over the most powerful tool he'd stolen from his predecessor. Maybe that was Lyon's curse—he was too fearful of it, too weak to wield so much power. He hadn't even bothered to take Ananke's. Instead, he'd left it trapped in a cage in his office. But then, so had Michael. . . .

I pivot in the desk chair, staring at the hole I made in the snake's enclosure.

When I left this office, I had both my eyes. I had Ananke's ability to see the future. To see it clearly. But the moment I took Lyon's magic, that ability was gone. And so was my eye.

If the old stories are true, Ananke had gouged out Michael's eye to punish him for coveting her power and seeking to control her. He had stolen her eye as payback and put it in his staff. I rub the stubborn pain in my chest. Is this my curse? Is their magic fighting inside me now? Did Ananke's magic burn out my eye just to spite Michael's?

It takes two eyes to see clearly. . . .

The eye. I need to find it and put it back in the staff. Maybe then I'll get my vision back.

I tear through every corner of my new office, only pausing when a maintenance tech comes to re-key the locks. The missing crystal isn't anywhere here, but there are only so many places the old man could have hidden it. I'm just about to lift the throw rug from the floor when there's a knock on the door.

"Chronos?" Lixue steps over the threshold, a tablet under her arm. Her attention drifts to the broken terrarium and the pile of ash on the floor.

"Sit." I point to the chair in front of my desk.

She perches on the edge of the seat, as far from Gaia's magic as she can manage. The staff leans against the wall beside me, and she darts an anxious glance at it. I hesitate, trying once more to pick through Lixue's memories. The images are slippery, hard to grab. Choosing one, I chase it and focus, forcing it to slow, but I'm only able to hold it for a moment before it's lost in a tidal wave of others. But that one moment, a flicker of her in her new role over the last hour, was enough. It has to be.

I reach for the scythe. "No one else is to know about this." I wait for her small nod before tearing the sash from the staff.

A glimmer of understanding passes over her face.

"From now on, you have one job. Lyon must have hidden the eye. It has to be in the Observatory somewhere. You, and you alone, are to search for it. Jora can't be trusted with this." She nods as if she's already surmised this much. "Lyon's apartment, his old office in the Winter wing, his old staff quarters . . . I want them all turned upside down until you find it."

"Yes, Chronos. But what about Jack?"

"What about him?"

"We think we've located Jack, Fleur, and the others."

"What do you mean, you *think*?" I growl.

"Their personnel records have all been wiped from the servers. It's as if Gaia and Lyon didn't want anyone to know where they are. But Zahra pulled up all the Observatory's expense reports since the rebellion. We found some unnamed purchases in the books. The amounts matched the ones on these deeds." She holds out the tablet.

I set down the staff and snatch the device from her hand, scrolling through land title records and deeds of trust. Lyon and Gaia purchased three properties less than a month after Michael's death—one in Southern California overlooking the coast; one in Fairbanks, Alaska; and a villa in Cuernavaca, Mexico.

"Give Zahra a promotion," I say under my breath as I study a map of the layout of the villa.

"There's more. Kai's personnel records have been wiped from the servers. But we tracked down her former Handler. She's a teacher in the Summer wing. We got her to cough up an old repurposed hard drive from their dorm. We were able to recover some deleted files." Lixue reaches across the desk and taps open another folder on the tablet. I scroll through exchanges between Kai and her sister, skimming dozens of scanned handwritten letters between them. Plans and bargains, memories and arguments . . . promises made, going back nearly fifty years.

These mistakes she's atoning for—the redemption she's seeking—go back much farther than Cuernavaca. They go back to the very beginning.

Kai's been scheming all along, fighting to be with her sister since the year they first got here.

Kai's *never* been loyal to Michael. *Or* Lyon. The only person who ever mattered to Kai was Ruby.

"The sister . . . Where is she?" I ask.

"We don't know. We can't find any Summers named Ruby who have any documented connection to Kai."

"Keep looking." Lyon probably wiped all those records from the servers, too. He had no intention of making this easy for me. "I want a report the minute you find her."

Kai Sampson walked out of here with nothing. Nothing but a pack of lies and the clothes on her back, exactly like I told her she would if she put her trust in Lyon. She has no money, no passport, no food, no weapons. She'll have to stop somewhere. It's bound to slow her down. All I need to do is stay one step ahead of her.

"Any sign of Sampson?" I ask.

"Bardwell got a hit on a street cam in Peckham," Lixue offers quickly. "She got off a bus there an hour ago."

I hand the tablet back to my Commander. "How fast can you assemble a search-and-capture team?"

"Right away, sir. Should I dispatch them to Peckham?"

"No, not to Peckham." I may not be able to see the future, but I don't need a crystal to see the long game in front of me. "Have your team in my office in an hour. Before this is over, Kai Sampson will come to me."

12

SNATCH ME AWAY

JACK

The brush of Fleur's lips over my scars sends a shiver through me. Her fingers trace the tight skin, awakening a longing that erases everything else. I close my eyes, soaking up the warmth of her body behind me. Suddenly, she goes still.

"Jack?"

My throat tightens as she whispers my name. Every nagging thought I've had over the past few weeks quiets as I turn toward her.

She glances up from the passports in her hand. Tears gather in her eyes as she sets them down on the blanket. Inching up on her knees, she places her hands on my chest, bringing her face close to mine.

"I changed my mind about the s'mores." She leans into me until our foreheads are touching and my nose brushes her cheek. It's wet with tears. I follow one as it slides toward the edge of her lips. Achingly slow, she tips her head, her mouth moving softly over mine.

I toss the skewer into the fire. My hands find her waist, tracing her shape. Her mouth tastes like salt and want.

A low groan rises inside me as the kiss deepens. My hands climb up her back as we rise to our feet. Unwilling to break apart, we stagger across the grass, bodies pressed together, fingers tangled in each other's hair, all tongue and teeth and touch and breath, until her back collides with the wall of the villa and I can't get any closer to her.

My cell vibrates in my front pocket.

"Your phone," she pants.

"Don't care."

"What about the fire?" she whispers, her head thrown back against the side of the house.

"It'll burn out."

She gasps as my teeth graze her neck. Her hands slide under my shirt as we stumble into the house.

"What about the breakers?" she rasps. Her breath in my ear nearly undoes me. I can't even form a coherent thought.

"Leave them off."

We fumble through the dark, tripping into furniture as we maneuver blindly up the stairs, knocking over the burned-out votives on the landing as we slam into the wall. I'm desperate for air, but too hungry to let go. She peels my shirt over my head. Unfastens the top button of my jeans as we trip up the rest of the steps. I pull her hair free from its tie, the long pink ends tumbling down around her face, traces of her shampoo sweetening the air. I toss the lily carelessly to the floor as we reach the hall.

My fingers dig into her hips as I walk her backward into our bedroom.

"Jack . . . ?" she whispers as her heel bumps the foot of the bed.

"Did you hear something?"

My mouth is buried in her hair, kissing the soft groove where her shoulder meets her neck. "Just your foot," I murmur, snaking my arms around her waist, ready to lift her onto the bed.

"Not that. Listen." She presses me back by the chest. Her body goes rigid in my arms and her eyes shimmer in the dark. "Did you hear that?"

I pull back to listen, both of us breathing hard. A soft clatter echoes in the hall, the same sound the glass votives had made when we'd knocked them over in the stairwell.

A chill snakes up my spine as I unwind myself from Fleur.

I turn for the door. A sudden burst of sound and movement rushes in from the hall. Someone grabs my hands and jerks them behind my back. Fleur shouts as I'm dragged across the floor, the terror on her face captured in the moonlight as she's surrounded by three shadowy figures. I thrash, managing to free one arm. There's a grunt as I drive my elbow back hard. One of the shadows whirls toward me and I wind back a fist. As I swing, someone kicks my legs out from behind. My knees smack down onto the tile, and my arms are wrenched painfully behind me.

"What do you want?" I shout as two of the figures grab Fleur by her wrists, holding her immobile against the wall. I count at least four shadows in the room. They're not Seasons. Fleur would have smelled them coming. We would have known they were close. The weather would have given them away hours ago. "Take whatever you want and get out! Leave her alone!"

Fleur throws her weight forward, but one of the figures lashes an arm across her chest, holding her back. A silver scythe is embroidered on his sleeve, the familiar outline of the metallic threads sharp and clear, even in the semidarkness.

These aren't burglars or thieves. These are Guards.

A red light blinks in the periphery of my vision. A transmitter. Fleur's eyes widen as they find mine.

Panic swells inside me. I lurch against the Guard behind me, but he holds me down. "Take your hands off her!"

"Target in custody," one of them says in a rasping voice I've heard before, but my brain's too scrambled to place it.

Fleur fights, wrenching to get free of them. One of the Guards grunts and curses when her fist smacks into his jaw. Her knee swings up, connecting with a groin. The temperature in the room plummets as the Guards summon their magic to subdue her. Rime crackles over the villa walls. The warm air condenses, filling the room with cold, dense fog. A scream erupts from Fleur's mouth, streaming out in a thick white cloud as the frost creeps over her arms.

I suck in a frigid breath. The cold . . . it's going to kill her.

Surging upright, I tear myself free of the Guard. Something breaks over the back of my head, the shatter of glass ringing in my ears as my knees give out.

Fleur shouts my name, her voice distorted and far away. I shake my head as the room wavers in and out of focus.

Glass cuts into my knees as I push myself upright. A violent wind whips through the house, brushing away the fog. The smell of ozone fills the air. It crackles with static. My hair stands on end as Fleur's magic electrifies the room.

The Guards turn toward a sudden rustle outside the open windows. They lurch back as thick, ropy vines rush in over the sills. The vines slither over the floor, darting toward their ankles. One of the Guards reaches for a sheath at his waist as the plants coil to strike.

"No! Stop!" I surge forward as he draws the blade, but a vine throws me away from the fray, sending me skidding across the floor. Fleur cries out as the Guard slashes viciously at the vines. The plant falls limp, tumbling back over the ledge.

The wind dies and the curtains fall still.

The smell of blood hits me.

"Fleur!" I blink, struggling to make out her shape in the dark as I scramble toward her.

Black beads trickle down the frost on her arms, smearing the pale sleeves of the Guard's uniform as she slides down the wall. One of the Guards jerks me back by my hair.

Another Guard taps her transmitter. "Target secured," she says thickly, frowning as she wipes blood from her nose. "Ready for transport. Bring us home." A spark ignites on another Guard's palm, the hot white flame carving her features out of the dark.

"Lixue?" We were Winters together once, years ago, before she became one of Michael's Guards. I narrow my eyes, unable to understand why she's here, in my house. Why they're hurting Fleur. Lyon was supposed to have disbanded the old Guard. He was supposed to have stripped them of their magic already. Something must have gone wrong.

Goose bumps that have nothing to do with the cold rise over my flesh as I remember the storms over London. How Lyon missed our meeting. "We're under protective order," I say through clenched teeth. "Daniel Lyon will skin you alive when he finds out about this."

Lixue smothers her flame, her face inscrutable in the dark. "Sorry,

Jack. It didn't have to end like this."

Light flickers across the room. I shield my eyes against the glare as it grows. Fleur's chin rests against her chest. A red light flashes in her ear and her body begins to glow.

"No!" I shout. "No! You can't take her!" I thrash, desperate to reach her, but Lixue and her Guards only force me back down. Force me to watch as the halo around Fleur threatens to blind me. Force me to live out my worst nightmare as her light flares and burns out. And she's gone.

13

AND LEFT NO TRACE

JACK

The bedroom is dark, the curtains still.

I blink against the afterimage, choking on Fleur's name. She's gone. They *took* her.

The Guards loosen their grip as my arms go limp. I'm too stunned to fight. Lixue backs away from me as her body begins to shimmer, the halo around her brightening by the second. I hurl myself at her, soaring through the empty air where she just stood, then colliding with the dresser and crashing to the floor.

"Come back, you assholes! Bring her back!" My scream echoes off the walls of the empty villa. Not so much as a leaf stirs in Fleur's garden below.

I tear through the moonlit hall, tripping down the stairs as I take them two at a time.

My bare feet skid around corners, dodging furniture in the dark. I burst into the utility room and throw all the switches in the circuit breaker box. They snap into place, restoring power to the house room by room in gridline patterns: upper decks, main level, veranda, courtyard. . . .

The rear sconces flood the courtyard with light, trapping a dark figure against the aquamarine glow of the swimming pool. The girl's not wearing a uniform or a patch, but she stands like a fighter. Like a hunter. Odds are better than good that she's one of them.

The girl stumbles back when she spots me through the patio doors. With a burst of speed, she sprints toward the trees. I race after her, tackling her at the edge of the pool and sending us both tumbling over the lip.

Water crashes over us, the weight of my jeans and her shoes pulling us toward the bottom. She kicks my shins, scrabbling for the edge as I drag her toward me. Our heads break the surface, both of us gasping for air. Grabbing her by the collar of her sweatshirt, I twist her around, nearly dropping her when I get a look at her face.

Kai Sampson's mouth forms the same shocked expression it did when I stabbed her with the shaft of her own arrow—the one she'd shot into my leg.

I shake water from my eyes and tighten my grip. Her black hair's shorter, dripping pool water down her forehead, the chopped ends plastered in sodden spikes around her ears. There's no red light. No transmitter in either one of them. It must have come loose when we hit the water. I risk a quick glance at the bottom of the pool, then at the deck around it, still holding her above the surface by the neck of her sweatshirt.

"Where is it?" I shake her. Her eyes are wide, her nails digging into my skin. "We're leaving now! You're taking me with you!"

Her jaw clenches. She slams her foot into the scar on my thigh. I swear through my teeth as I dunk her head under the water, then let her up just long enough for her to suck in a thin breath. "Where's your transmitter?"

She coughs, eyes flaring wide with panic. "I can't take you that way," she sputters. "I'm not—"

I shove her head under again. She bucks and thrashes, but I hold her until a stream of bubbles burst from her lips. All I hear is the twang of her crossbow, the whistle of the arrows that sailed past my ear. All I see is my own blood swirling around me as the ice cracked and I sank into the lake. It was Kai's fault. She's the reason I'm human. The reason I couldn't protect Fleur. And now Kai Sampson's going to be the reason I get Fleur back.

I wrench her head up. She sucks in a desperate breath.

Her transmitter must be in a pocket, somewhere in her clothes.

"If you're planning to kill me," I warn her, "you'd better do it now." I push her back under the water, waiting for her to use her magic and fight back. But nothing happens. Her movements slow, then her thrashing stops.

The last of the bubbles rise around the floating ends of her hair. I hold on tighter, braced for what's coming. No one can play dead for this long. Her magic will either rise up and fight me, or it will fight to free itself from her dying body and her Handler will bring her home. Any minute now, it will sparkle to the surface, and I'll hitch a ride through the ley lines with her, the same way they took Fleur.

Kai's arms go limp in the water.

Her neck is loose where I hold her under. Something's wrong.

I yank her head up. Water pours from her nose and mouth, and she hangs motionless from my hand. I drag her to the edge of the pool, fighting my wet jeans and her dead weight, the rough concrete scraping my arms as I haul her over the lip. The force of her body hitting the ground knocks the water from her lungs. She rolls onto her side, coughing up the contents of my pool.

I grab the life ring from the wall and use the rope to tie her wrists and ankles behind her as she chokes. My eyes burn with chlorine as I stand over her. "Where's your transmitter?"

She coughs, sucking in ragged breaths. "I don't have one. I'm not one of them."

"Bullshit. I was here. I saw everything! Where did they take her?"

"Back to the Observatory. To Doug." She winces as the rope chafes her wrists. "They work for Doug now."

"That's not even possible. That's . . ." My protests trail away as a chill prickles my bare skin. Last week, Lyon said he'd been planning to dismantle the old Guard. To relieve them of their magic.

I'm not sure he can be swayed into conceding his magic peacefully. . . .

Doug. He must have escaped. He, Lixue, and the others who were here tonight . . . they must have fled while they still had their magic. But if Kai still has hers, why didn't she fight me?

I scrape water from my face and rake my hair back to look at her. Not a flicker of magic stirs around her. Not a flutter of wind.

"Holy shit. You're human." Lyon must have stripped her of her magic before the others escaped. But if they all made it out of the Observatory, then why are they using the ley lines to go back to it? Why not slip off the grid where Lyon can't track them? Why bother taking Fleur back to Lyon's den?

Unless they have no reason to fear Lyon anymore.

They work for Doug now.

I stumble back, remembering the professor's unanswered phone, ringing over and over again.

14

IN HIS FOOTSTEPS STRAY

DOUG

I slide the key card over the sensor. An emerald-green flash precedes the release of the locks to the suite.

My suite.

I cross the threshold, scanning the room for motion sensors and cameras, ears attuned for the telltale beeps before the blare of an alarm, but the room is silent. As lifeless as the body it formerly belonged to. I move through it, my fingers trailing over the velvety back of the sofa, then the sleek, glossy surface of the credenza. The sprawling lair is tucked deep in a corner under the Winter wing, far from the Control Room. Most of the campus sustained damage from the quake, but this room seems untouched by the chaos that went down in the east wing yesterday.

I wipe the blood and dust from my hands. They leave a stain on my jumpsuit, and I glance back at the filthy tracks my shoes have left in the plush cream-colored carpeting. I haven't slept or showered since the Dismantling yesterday. Every waking hour has been spent putting out fires as one small crisis bled into the next. The lightning storms over London started late last night, power outages and trees falling down like dominoes across the UK. By this morning, high winds had ravaged the coast of France, and the tidal surges had reached Portugal by noon. Meanwhile, some freak sandstorms buried an entire city in Tunisia. I'm too exhausted to see straight and everything hurts. I don't know what the hell to do.

An hour ago, I locked myself in my office and stopped time, just so I could steal a few hours of sleep in my desk chair, but the minute I dozed off, my grip on the magic was broken, and Lixue knocked on the door with more bad news.

We lost nine Seasons in less than twenty-four hours. Two were in the wind when their seasons ended and we couldn't get their stasis chambers back online in time to bring them home. Two others ditched their transmitters and deserted together. Another was swept off the ley lines when the power grid flickered. The sooner we can start tracking down the freed Seasons and deserters, the better. We need every region accounted for to get these storms under control.

The aftershocks of Gaia's quake have the whole Observatory rattled. We had to shut down the Wi-Fi in the dorms to keep the panic from spreading after a handful of Summers got it into their heads to bust out of their rooms. March's team got carried away when they went to quash the riot, and now I'll have to replace four dead Summers before June.

I pour myself a glass of water from a decanter on the credenza. It's warm and stagnant and does nothing to cool the burn in my chest. I sink down into the sofa. Cupping one hand, I summon a small flame, just to remind myself that I can. I've mastered new magic before. Learned to wield it without pain. I can do it again.

The flame grows, awakening the burn of the frostbite on my palm. With a hiss, I close my fist.

The cold . . . that was Michael's weapon—his affinity—and the staff had belonged to him. According to the old legends, the gods each gifted an element to Gaia. Chronos gave her the coldness of space. Ananke gave her the inevitability of the ocean and its tides. Chaos brought fire. And from those gifts, the earth was born. I can only guess that the cold magic in Michael's staff is freezing me because it's fighting Ananke's power. The staff is even colder today—almost too painful to hold. I left it leaning on the desk in my office just so I wouldn't have to carry it here with me.

A wilted plant taunts me from its pot on the end table. I stand over it, commanding it to move, but the sagging leaves don't even stir. I smack the table.

Gaia had power over all four elements. She could give them, take them, or use them herself, but *earth* magic was her essence—her strongest affinity. It was earth magic that caused that quake, and if I'm right, the key to controlling Gaia's power is in mastering that single element. I'm certain the magic in that orb will never submit to living inside me until I learn how to tame it.

As I pour the dregs of my water over the plant, something spatters against the table. Another dark drop plunks down, and I drag my sleeve across my nose, swearing when it comes away red. I set down my glass and head deeper into the suite in search of a bathroom.

I pause inside the wide double doors of the bedroom. The main living room is spare, all white walls and glass and crisp, clean lines—a place to work, to get things done.

But the bedroom feels like it belonged to someone else. The room is softly lit by incandescent lamps. Two faux windows give the illusion of being surrounded by a snow-capped forest, and a breeze from the ventilation duct overhead ruffles my hair. I swear I catch a hint of pine in the forced air. I turn from the windows toward a mahogany four-poster bed with curled, clawed feet.

I draw in a breath, surprised when I don't catch Lyon's scent on my tongue. But none of Lyon's books are on the nightstands, no ordered piles of papers or interlocking coffee rings left behind, like the ones I'd always seen in his office back when I was a Winter. A layer of dust collects on my finger as I drag it over the nightstand. Not plaster dust from the quake, but the kind that comes from abandonment, as if the room hasn't been serviced in months.

Curious, I draw open the doors to the walk-in closet, parting a sea of carefully pressed suits. Silk ties are meticulously hung. Rows of dress shoes line the shelves. I pause in front of a velvet rack displaying a collection of eye patches, neatly laid out in rows and sorted by color. I gravitate to one with a black satin band—the same one Michael wore the day he inducted me into his Guard—and feel reassured that this was, and has only ever been, *my* Chronos's room.

Lyon must have moved into Gaia's suite, hiding in his girlfriend's bed like a coward, too ashamed of what he'd done to sleep in the room that had belonged to the man he'd murdered. The same way he hid from Ananke's eye, covering it so he wouldn't have to face the ending he deserved.

I snatch a shirt off a hanger, claiming it. Grabbing a pair of slacks and a tie, I carry the suit into a vast marble bathroom. The threads of my prison jumpsuit pop, seams tearing in my hurry to strip the thing off. I avoid my reflection in the mirror as I sling open the shower door and wrench on the faucet, stepping under the spray without waiting for it to steam. Filth and blood color the water. I lather and scrub my skin raw, until the blisters on my hands soften and peel away and the last of the blood and ash swirl down the drain.

After, I stand naked in front of the mirror, my hands braced on either side of the wide marble sink. A drop of blood seeps stubbornly from my nose, and my chest feels tight. That same pain from yesterday pushes against my ribs. My gaze lifts to my reflection in the mirror. To the blackened eye socket. A memory flickers, shining back at me from my remaining eye. . . .

There's still time to make the right choice.

I start as my cell phone vibrates on the vanity. Turning from the mirror, I swipe the screen with shaking hands.

"Chronos?" Lixue asks when I don't speak. Her voice is thick, groggy, as if she's just come to.

"This had better be good news."

"We have Fleur."

"Where is she?"

"A holding cell in the catacombs. She was injured. Not badly. But she's still sleeping it off."

"Call me when she's awake." I disconnect, one hand braced on the rim of the sink. Michael's black patch rests on the fresh clothes piled beside me. I slip it over my head, brushing back my wet hair and adjusting it to cover the empty socket.

"You are Chronos now," I say, daring to look at myself again. A lump forms in my throat when I swallow. It's like I'm staring at Michael's face. I raise my voice until the facets of my eye blaze. "You are Chronos now."

I snap open the pants and step into them. Jam my arms into the shirtsleeves and cinch a knot in the tie. My jaw hardens at my reflection in the mirror. "You are Chronos now," I say, louder still, shrugging into Michael's jacket and buttoning it over my chest, surprised to find that it fits, "and you have the power to control everything."

15

CHILL AND SHIVER

JACK

Kai wriggles in the heavy wooden chair on the closed-circuit security feed from the kitchen cameras. She's been trying to slip her bindings since I left the room, but the ropes are tight enough to hold.

The hard drive in my office hums back to life as my soaked jeans drip pool water onto the floor. I wrestle my phone from my front pocket, thankful for its waterproof case as I swipe it on. Five unanswered calls and a voice mail from Poppy.

I swear, remembering the persistent buzzing in my pocket as Fleur and I were foolishly shutting out the world. This was my fault. I should never have let my guard down.

I tap on Poppy's message. There's a panicked hitch in her voice.

"Jack? It's Poppy. Something's happened. Everything was fine. Chill had handed off his season to Jarek and he texted that he was ready to transport. I locked onto his GPS, but he never made it home. I think . . ." Her voice wavers. "I think his route was hijacked. His ley line signal dead-ended in London. Jack, I have a bad feeling. No one at the Observatory is answering my calls. Not Gaia, not Lyon. I got a strange package from them a few days ago. There was a travel voucher in it. I've booked a seat on the next flight to Heathrow. I'm going to find him. When you get this message, call me."

A cold fear clamps around my chest. I dial Marie.

She picks up on the first ring.

"Jack, I've been trying to reach you." Her chewing gum snaps between her teeth. "Did you get a weird message from Poppy? I mean, Poppy's always a little weird, but this was—"

"Listen," I tell her, my voice so tight it threatens to break, "four of Michael's Guards just broke into our house under Doug Lausks's orders. They took Fleur. You need to get Amber and Julio someplace safe. Now."

Her gum quiets. "What do you mean, they took Fleur? Took her where?"

"Through the ley lines. Back to the Observatory. Chill's disappearance was no accident. I need you to track Poppy down before she gets to London. Tell her not to step foot inside the Observatory until I get there."

I disconnect and carry my cell to the kitchen. Dropping my phone on the counter, I head straight for the knife block. The thick steel blade of the cleaver sings as I pluck it from the sheath. Kai stills.

"Tell me everything you know." I slam the knife down on the island, blade facing her, letting her get a good long look at it. "Starting with why you're here. Did Doug send you?"

"No." She shakes her head. "I told you. I'm not one of them. I knew they were coming. I tried to beat them here to warn you, but I wasn't fast enough."

"Warn me about what? What's Doug planning?"

"I don't know exactly—"

I grab her by her ear and turn her to face me. "Think hard."

She grits her teeth. "All I know is he hates you."

"If he hates me so much, why didn't he just kill me?" Why take Fleur? And Chill? I would have been an easier target.

"Because he doesn't want to kill you. He wants to hurt you. He wants to make you suffer the same way he's suffered! He blames you for everything he's lost."

A horrible thought takes hold. Doug lost his best friend. And his girlfriend. But that's not all Doug lost in that fight.

My ears ring, the shrill echoes of an unanswered phone. "What has he done?"

Kai shuts her eyes.

She starts as I snatch the cleaver off the counter. "What has he done!"

"He killed Lyon and Gaia, and he took the staff."

My hand shakes around the knife's handle. "You're lying. Lyon would have seen it coming. He would have found some way to protect himself."

"Doug broke into Lyon's office and took Ananke's magic before the Dismantling."

"Ananke? That doesn't make sense. That magic is gone. All that's left of her is the eye in the staff."

Kai shakes her head. "Doug and I found it. It was strong. Doug had no problem cutting Lyon and Gaia down. It was like they weren't even trying."

I stumble away from her and set the knife on the counter. *No. This can't be happening.* I would have known, wouldn't I? Poppy, Marie, and I . . . wouldn't we have felt it when it happened? It was Lyon's magic—his control over Time—that kept us from aging and gave us our immortality so we could stay paired with our Seasons. If that magic is gone . . .

My cell phone rings. I don't recognize the number. Numb, I connect the call and hold the phone to my ear.

"Who is this?" I ask, my throat thick.

"I'm trying to reach Jack Sommers."

"You've got him."

"This is Officer Williams with the police department in Nelson County, Virginia. We were patched through by your real estate attorney in London. That was the only phone number emergency services had on file. He says you're the owner of record for a cabin out by Wintergreen?"

My grip tightens around the phone. "What about it?"

"I'm sorry to be the one to tell you, but there's been a fire . . ."

My grandfather's cabin . . . our safe house, where Chill and I first met . . . where I first kissed Fleur.

". . . still waiting on the fire marshal's report. There's not much left standing, but considering the age and condition of the place, it was likely an accident . . ." No. This fire was no accident. "Mr. Sommers? Mr. Sommers, are you there?"

I disconnect the call.

Lyon is dead. Doug has Fleur and Chill. Our safe house is gone.

He wants to make you suffer. . . .

I grip the island. The puddle of water under Kai's chair stretches toward my bare feet. Her clothes are drenched, her bruises from our fight blooming violet and gold under the harsh kitchen lights.

"Why are you here?" I ask, my knuckles white around the counter. "Did he send you to deliver a message? Did he handpick you for the job just to rub it in my face?"

"I already told you, he doesn't even know I'm here!"

"Don't bet on it," I say, struggling to contain my temper. "He has Ananke's magic and he has the staff. What were you thinking, coming here?"

"I didn't have time to think! I just ran. I couldn't trust Doug and I didn't know where else to go. I have to get back into the Observatory, and I can't do it alone. I need your help!"

I nearly choke, white-hot tears of rage threatening to spill out. "You *killed* me. You shot me in the back! What the hell did you leave down there that you could possibly think you deserve? Your *soul*? Your magic? Your goddamn immortality?"

"Ruby!" Her head snaps up. "I left my sister, Ruby! She's down there, and if Doug finds her, he'll make her suffer just to punish me because I . . ." She averts her eyes. Her cheeks flush with shame.

"Because you what?"

"Because I chose to do the right thing," she says quietly. "Lyon asked me to protect you, so I came."

A cutting laugh explodes out of me. "Bullshit. Lyon would *never* trust you with that. Not after what you did to me."

Her gaze swings to me. "I'm not proud of what I did. Lyon told me that facing you was the first step to forgiving myself. That this was my way forward. He said it's not too late to make the right choice—"

"Wait . . . what did you just say?" Those words . . . about facing our demons and forgiving ourselves . . . about it not being too late to choose a new path and find a way forward . . . Those words belong to Lyon. It was the same advice he gave me last week when we talked on the phone. "Lyon sent you? He said those exact words, and he told you to come here?"

She nods. "He said if I keep you safe, you'll help me free my sister."

I touch my back pocket, remembering the travel vouchers and passports Lyon sent right after that call. There had been two vouchers in that envelope. Three in Amber's. But only one voucher in the envelope he'd sent to Poppy.

Lyon knew. . . .

He knew what Doug would do. That Kai would come. That we would all go to the Observatory to find Fleur and Chill.

The second voucher he sent to me . . . it wasn't for Fleur.

Kai flinches as I reach for the knife and then slice through the rope between her wrists. They release with a sudden jerk.

She doesn't move. Doesn't so much as breathe as I slip the knife back in the block.

"There are dry clothes upstairs," I say. "Pack whatever you can fit in a carry-on. We leave for the airport in an hour." I feel her gaze heavy on my scars. Then I hear her shuffle out of the kitchen to the stairs. Only once I'm sure she's gone do I let go of the cleaver's handle.

16

SOMETHING SINISTER

FLEUR

My tongue sticks to the roof of my mouth and I choke myself awake. Bolting upright, I gasp in a lungful of warm, dry air. My forehead slams against some unseen barrier that knocks me flat on my back again. I blink back stars, shielding my eyes from the glare of bright lights shining through a clear plastic dome just inches from my face.

I press against it, my mind slow to process exactly where I am. Or how I got here.

I was with Jack. Kissing Jack.

No! My breath comes in rapid pants, fogging the glass of the stasis chamber as I struggle against the dome lid.

"Let me out!" My hoarse voice is muted by the thick plastic as a barrage of images assaults me: blood on the walls, on my arms. Jack on his knees, flanked by Guards. A knife, a crash, a broken lamp. Then Jack, facedown on the floor. "Jack!" I have to get to him. Have to find him before they . . .

Oh, Gaia, no. Please, no.

My fingernails scratch uselessly against the slick dome. In a fit of rage, I throw my fists against it. I twist my head from side to side, struggling to see anything beyond the stone walls that surround me. There's a door with metal bars. Through them, torches disappear down shadowy tunnels.

I'm under the Observatory. In the cells, in the catacombs.

"Let me out!" I scream. "If you lay one hand on Jack, I swear to Gaia, I'll—"

"Gaia's dead." I suck in a sharp breath. Static crackles through the speaker beside my ear. "I killed her." The gruff voice is cold and familiar, but I can't place it.

"You're lying." I don't want to believe it. Refuse to believe it. If Gaia was dead, I would know. Wouldn't I? If Gaia was dead, this place—the world and every creature in it—would be gone right along with her. My watering eyes catch on a deep, jagged crack in the stone above me. A thin film of clay dust coats the lid of the chamber, as if the earth's been rocked, its contents shaken loose. "I want to speak with Chronos."

"I am Chronos," the voice says.

"You're full of shit!"

"And you're locked in a very tiny prison."

"I demand to speak with Daniel Lyon! Where is he?" The answering silence is loud enough to shatter my soul. "Who are you? What have you done?"

The disembodied voice is barely more than a whisper. "I think you know."

Goose bumps rise over my skin. I stare through the dome, thrown suddenly back to an abandoned building, tied to a chair in a dimly lit room. Doug Lausks's iron-and-copper breath is hot on my face, the blood I've drawn dripping from his nose.

"I warned you once to be careful with me, Fleur Attwell."

"Where's Jack?" Those Guards were in our house. In our *bedroom*. The power was out, our security system shut down. The Guards outnumbered us. Without his magic—without *me*—Jack was defenseless against them.

"The world is ending, Fleur. Mother Earth and Father Time are dead, and all you care about is Sommers? I thought you were better than that." The locks beside my head snap open. I flinch back from the sudden sharp sound as cold air rushes through the broken seal.

I don't move. Don't breathe as the static dies in the speaker and the lights inside the stasis chamber flicker and go dark.

"Doug?" I smack the inside of the dome. The lid rises on its hinges. "Doug, answer me!" A minute ago, I would have given anything to be free of the chamber, but now I'd give anything just to know what's happened to Jack. I kick the lid open the rest of the way, dizzy and cold as I sit up and take in the high walls of the cell. My skin prickles. I hunch in on myself, arms crossed to conceal my bare breasts from the camera perched in the corner of the room. A single faded blanket and a pair of coveralls rest on a metal bunk on the far wall. I launch off the edge of the chamber, nearly falling on my face as my knees buckle and stasis sickness washes over me. My injuries must not have been bad—the queasiness is only mildly unpleasant—but whatever time I spent recovering in the chamber has left me drained and clumsy.

I snatch the coveralls from the bed and throw my legs into them, turning my body away from the camera, sick at the thought that Doug's probably been watching me this whole time.

Once I'm zipped inside the coarse jumpsuit, I move toward the camera's flashing red light. I stand under it, my chin high as I stare into the lens. "You thought I would care about anything else? You assumed I was *better than that?*" I spit his own words back in Doug's face. "That was your first mistake. I promise you I'm far, far worse." I press a hand against the wall, ignoring a wave of fatigue as I summon my magic. Static crackles in my hair. My fingers tingle with it as I reach out with my mind, but we're too deep below the earth for roots to grow here.

Determined and furious, I search the stone itself, seeking out the rhizomes of the mosses and algae hidden within its crevices. I've done it once before, at the border in Tecate. Only this time, I'm already so deep underground, I don't have to reach far.

I grit my teeth as the wall shivers. Chips of shale clatter past my outstretched hands. With a final push of my thoughts, the surface of the wall breaks away and slides into a heap of rubble. The camera crashes down with it, dangling upside down by its wires. I turn it upright, leaning close to the lens, certain Doug's watching me. "I'll ruin you," I promise as I rip it from the wall.

The red light winks out.

I sink to the floor, too exhausted to stay on my feet any longer. It was just a performance, a show to prove I'm not as weak as Doug wants me to be. And now that it's over, it feels even more like a farce. I drag the thin blanket around my shoulders and huddle at the foot of the bed, my tears falling silent and fast as I remember the terror on Jack's face. I swat them away.

Jack's alive. He has to be. If he was dead, I would know it. I would feel it.

But hadn't I thought the same thing about Gaia just moments ago?

The temperature in my cell drops. I lift my head as a dark gray smaze drifts through the bars in the door. It circles my cell and zips out again, leaving an icy draft in its wake. Doug probably sent it to spy on me.

No, I tell myself with a firm shake of my head, *Gaia can't be dead*. Doug couldn't possibly have overpowered them both. And yet the longer I sit, the chill of the catacombs sinking deep into my bones, the more I wonder if he was telling the truth. If Lyon and Gaia are truly dead, who's running the Observatory? Who's watching over the Seasons and guaranteeing our Handlers' health and immortality?

If Doug is free, who's watching out for Jack?

I scramble to my feet. Julio and Amber . . . I have to find a way to reach them. They can travel. They can get to him. If I can shake the door loose and get out of this cell, if I can make it to the Control Room and get a message to Marie, the three of them can find him.

My fingers curl around the bars. Static crackles as I rest my forehead against them, focusing my mind on the walls as I summon my magic.

"I know you're pretty badass and all, but are you sure that's such good idea?"

I lift my head. The hoarse voice comes from a cell farther down the tunnel. I peer through the bars to see a pair of eyes staring back at me.

"Chill?" His name comes out on a sob.

"In the flesh."

"What happened? How did you get here? Is Poppy with you?" The bars press into my forehead as I crane my neck to see into the other cells, but as far as I can tell, they're all empty.

"Honestly, I'm not sure how I got here," he rasps. "Poppy was locked onto my coordinates. I slipped into the ley lines, expecting to wake up at home. But I woke up here. Same as you, I guess." I breathe a sigh of relief that maybe Poppy is okay. That she might still be safe in Fairbanks. "What about you?" Chill leans against the bars of his cell as I sink down against mine, too tired to hold myself up anymore.

"Jack and I were at home. We were . . ." My throat swells at the memory of Jack's lips on mine, both of us oblivious to what was happening around us. "A team of Guards broke into the villa. I tried to fight them off but there were too many of them. They were wearing the old patches on their jackets. I think they're working for Doug." My eyes lift to Chill's. I wonder if he knows what happened to Lyon and Gaia, but I'm not sure I'm ready for the answer. Or what that would mean for Poppy and Jack. "The Guards must have brought me here through the ley lines. I don't know what happened to Jack after that." My voice cracks on Jack's name. I don't want to imagine what Doug's friends might have done to him.

"How many of them were there?" Chill asks.

"I counted four."

"Only one team on his home turf? My money's on Jack."

The thought of Jack fighting four Guards steals my breath. "What if he's dead, Chill?"

A dark laugh rumbles from his cell. "A better question is, what if he's not?"

My mind spins over that possibility. I hadn't stopped to consider that Jack might be strong enough or quick enough to escape the Guards on his own. If he did manage to make it out of there alive, where would he go?

"Oh no," I whisper, gripping the bars. "Jack can't come looking for us. Not here."

Chill doesn't answer. We both know exactly what Jack will do. Doug's laid a perfect trap. And we're the bait.

Silence falls over the cells. The only sound is the *whoosh* of the torches down the hall. I feel adrift in time. This far below ground, I have no sense of day or night, no idea how many days or weeks have passed since the Guards dragged me through the ley lines. Jack could have already come. Doug never answered me when I asked where Jack was.

"How long have we been in stasis?"

"No idea," Chill says. "I just woke up a few hours ago. The stasis sickness isn't so bad. Not nearly as bad as Jack used to go through. And I was fine when I got pulled into the ley lines—a little tired, maybe, but I wasn't hurt. I don't think I was out very long."

I was injured, but definitely alive, when I felt the ley lines tow me under. Maybe Chill's right, and we weren't asleep very long. Maybe there's still time to reach Amber and Julio and stop Jack from coming.

We both stiffen at the sound of boots marching in the tunnels. Two Guards pause at the entrance to the holding area, and a tall shadow stretches toward my cell. A pair of shiny black dress shoes stops in front of me. My eyes climb past them, up the carefully pressed pleat of a pair of slacks and the lapels of a crisp suit jacket. The torchlight flickering in the tunnels behind him casts strange shadows over a hard jaw and the sharp cheekbones above it. I scramble back from the bars at the sight of the black patch over his eye.

Michael's dead. I watched his ashes blow away into the wind. This . . . this is impossible.

The face moves closer to the bars, revealing a crown of blond hair. Doug's left eye twinkles with his smirk. It gleams like a diamond. Like Gaia's eyes.

"What have you done?" I stand, coming closer to the bars, searching his hands for Lyon's scythe. He holds up a finger when I open my mouth to speak.

"You're wondering if I'm telling the truth," he says smugly. "You're asking yourself, if I really did kill Daniel Lyon, then why aren't I holding his staff?"

"Was it too heavy for your conscience to carry?" I glare up at him through the bars. "Or are you too afraid to bring it within arm's reach of me after what I did to Michael?"

With shocking speed, Doug reaches into my cell and pulls me by my collar. His hands are rough, the skin cracked and scratchy where it touches my throat. I grab the bars to steady myself as he hauls me up on my toes, forcing me to meet his eye. I swallow hard against the frost and violence glittering inside it.

His whisper is cold against my cheek. "Consider yourself lucky I *didn't* bring the scythe."

He releases me with a shove, but I catch the wince he tries to hide, the barely perceptible shudder as he turns away from me. The smell of iron grows thicker in the air, and he touches his nose, avoiding the gazes of his Guards. "Bring her to the Control Room," he orders them over his shoulder.

An enormous Guard gestures to Chill's cell. "What about the other one, sir?"

Doug's voice is thick when he says, "Let him rot."

17

COIL AND HISSED

DOUG

The click of my heels on the worn stone treads echoes through the spiral stairwell. The leather dress shoes are stiff, tight in the toe and loose around the ankles, rubbing blisters into my heels, and the orb containing Gaia's magic is awkward under my arm. I wrench a finger under my tie and unfasten the top button of my shirt, drawing a deep breath of damp, stale air that does nothing to relieve the pressure in my chest.

Mossy condensation glistens on the walls, catching the torchlight. It reeks down here, and I'll be glad when we finally have the power restored to all the wings, the halls cleared of debris, and the damn elevators running.

The stairwell breaks at a stone landing, and I throw open the door. The corridor to the Control Room is pitch dark, except for a dull red glow from an emergency exit sign above me and the shine of the hissing magic in the orb. A sconce has fallen loose, dangling by its wires, and a pile of rubble has formed a dam, blocking the flow of the fountain where it spills onto the floor. I step over the dark puddles, angrier with every step I take. Every broken bulb and flooded pipe is just a reminder of my inability to control this and fix it.

When I saw Fleur in her cell, I told her she was lucky I wasn't carrying the scythe. But luck had nothing to do with it. I chose to leave the staff in my office, partly because it's too fucking painful to carry, but mostly to avoid slitting her throat with it. As tempting as it was to reach through those bars and strangle her, I wouldn't dare deprive Jack Sommers of the torture of watching her die.

But there's something I need from her first.

I push open the double doors to the Control Room. They slam into the wall, the sound echoing off the polished wood pews as I storm past them to the dais. I set the orb on the scarred surface of the desk. Gaia's magic hurls itself against the far side of the glass like a glowing swarm of pissed-off hornets. There has to be a way to harness and control it. I can't entrust it to anybody else.

The wall of screens behind the dais is shattered and dark. I lean my weight against Gaia's desk, the wood creaking under me as I look out among the rubble-covered pews where she and Michael used to hold court. This is the room where I was promoted in my first ranking ceremony. Where I was inducted into Michael's Guard.

There had been order and rules here. Everything had made sense.

The emptiness of this room—the wreckage of it—burrows under my skin. If I can't take that magic inside me and learn to create new Seasons, then the Observatory, the world, and everything in it is doomed. I will be Michael's biggest failure. Ruler of nothing. It won't matter what happens to Jack or Fleur, because no one here will live long enough to see it.

I stiffen at the approach of footsteps from the hall. A cloying, sweet scent grows stronger, like lily of the valley under a sheen of nervous sweat. I push off Gaia's desk, moving to the center of the dais as the doors open and Fleur Attwell is pushed through them.

She staggers, her toe slipping on a piece of broken glass as she sucks in a breath. Her wild gaze darts over the fallen plaster, shattered terrariums, and broken TV screens. Tears gather in her eyes when they land on the orb. The magic settles almost instantly, its light softening as it drifts toward her, bumping gently against the side of its enclosure. I tip my head, watching their odd exchange.

The Guards nudge Fleur forward, breaking the spell. Static crackles around her as she snaps to a halt in front of me.

I hold my hands behind my back, hiding my burns as I study her. "You want to kill me, but you won't. Not today."

"Did your staff tell you that?"

"Yes." I smile around the lie. I can't afford to expose any weakness. Not to my Guards. And especially not to her.

She clenches a fist. "It's been wrong before."

"The walls in here are already weak," I say, pacing the dais. "Unless you want to take down the entire Observatory, I wouldn't recommend any more impulsive displays. I've seen that ending, too, and it's not pretty."

Her eyes dart toward the fissures in the ceiling. "Why did you bring me here, then?"

"To make Jack pay for what he's done. He's going to come looking

147

for you, and when he does, he's going to suffer." I descend the dais toward her. A muscle clenches in her jaw. "I want him to sit in Lyon's empty office and mourn him the way I mourned for Michael. I want him to see his best friend murdered and watch his magic float away. I want him to know what it feels like to die at his girlfriend's hand."

Her dark eyes pierce me. "That won't ever happen."

"Are you sure about that?"

The air goes earthy and pungent as she sets her power loose. I can't see it, but I feel it. I tense as fingers of her magic reach down into the ground, creeping toward me. I back up as it speeds closer. The floor under my foot crumbles, throwing me off-balance, knocking me into the steps of the dais. Lixue strikes Fleur hard in the side of her head.

Fleur's hand flies to her temple as her magic shrinks back from me. Her knees hit the stone hard enough to make her yelp.

"Enough!" I shout. Pain and humiliation flare in my chest. I'm not sure who I'm angrier with—Fleur for trying to kill me or Lixue for acting without my order. I stand up and dust off my slacks, loosening my tie with a hard wrench of a finger.

"That!" I pant, pointing to Fleur's head. "*That's* why you're still alive. That's what I want from you."

"What?" she snaps. "You want me to strangle you with a root? I'm glad we agree on something. I can definitely arrange that. Ow!" She grabs the back of her head as Lixue cuffs her again.

"I said enough!" I shout at Lixue. I turn my glare on Fleur. Unlike Lixue, there isn't an ounce of remorse on her face. "You're going to teach me how to use the earth magic." I press the heel of my hand against my sternum as the pain subsides to a dull ache.

"Why would I do that?"

"Because your very human boyfriend is on his way here."

Her smile is cutting. "He's not here yet."

"No, but your Winter friend is. And I will make Chill's last hours a living hell if you don't cooperate."

"I thought you were saving him for some grand theatrical revenge scheme." The words drip with sarcasm, like this is some kind of joke.

My voice drops dangerously low as I get up in her face. "Jack has plenty of friends I can use for that purpose. Amber, Julio, Poppy, Marie . . . they're all on their way here. So let's get something straight. You're going to be a good little Spring and show me how to wield the earth magic. You're going to teach me to control it—the plants, the quakes, all of it—or I will cut your friends down one by one in front of you."

A spark of fear lights in her eyes. Flashes of her memories flicker inside them, the vicious, violent ways she's used that magic to protect the people she loves. It only makes me hungrier for it. Her mouth hardens into a thin line. "You aren't human enough to wield that kind of magic."

"There's nothing *human* in Gaia's magic."

Fleur's face tips up with a puzzled expression. Her eyes dart to the glowing orb on the desk, then back to me. A curious smile touches them. "You can't hold it, can you?" Blood rushes to my cheeks and she barks out a laugh. "You tried to take it from her, and her magic rejected you."

I lunge, taking Fleur by the throat, shaking with the urge to snuff out her life. Gaia's magic riots against the glass, beams of light shooting from the orb like daggers.

Frost crackles up my arms, over Fleur's chin. The ground shudders, dirt popping along the floor as she claws at my hands, starved for air. Magic glows inside her, threatening to break through her skin. I could stop time, right now. I could hold her on the brink of death indefinitely. I could watch it over and over, the way Noelle's death plays out in my dreams every time I close my eyes.

A burning pain cinches my chest, stealing my breath.

Lixue's eyes widen as a spill of warmth leaks from my nose. "Chronos, you're bleeding."

The smell of it is suddenly thick in the room. I double over, and Fleur crashes to the floor.

18

BY THE HIGHWAY HOME

JACK

Kai fidgets with the pink wig we grabbed at a costume shop on our way to the airport. The flight attendant scans her boarding pass and takes another glance at Fleur's ID. I hold my breath through what feels like an eternity, waiting to see if she'll notice that Kai's olive skin tone doesn't match the fair freckled face in the tiny picture, or that the shape of Kai's eyes is slightly more angular than Fleur's. She hands Kai the passport and returns her boarding pass, and I hurry to catch up to Kai as she takes fast strides down the jet bridge onto the plane.

"Could you have been any more obvious?" I hiss in her ear as we maneuver down the aisle.

"I can't help it. It itches. How does anyone deal with having so much hair?"

I push her toward our row. The sooner we're in the air, the better.

She wedges herself into the window seat and I leave an empty seat between us. Arms crossed, I stare at the headrest in front of me. The flight's already delayed thirty minutes, and I'm crawling out of my skin to get to Fleur.

"I don't have cooties," she says bitterly.

"Forgive me if I don't relish the idea of spending the next twelve hours sharing pretzels with the girl who attempted to murder me."

"I wasn't trying to murder you. I was——"

I turn, following the direction of her gaze. A man's standing in the aisle beside me, listening to our conversation.

"I think I'm in C," he says weakly.

Kai turns to the window as I slide into the empty middle seat. We sit in terse silence through takeoff, my leg bobbing impatiently as the plane ascends.

"So what's the plan?" Kai's tucked up in the corner, her legs drawn tightly to her chest as she flips mindlessly through a magazine. The man in the aisle seat snores softly, his head tipped away from me. No one else seems to be listening.

"I get us into the Observatory," I say in a low voice. "I find Fleur and Chill, and then I get them out."

"Wow," she says dryly, snapping a page, "sounds like you've got this whole thing figured out. I've gotta admit, I'm not sure I can handle the pressure. I mean, you may have overestimated my ability to contribute anything to the rescue mission."

"I don't need a spotter. I never asked for your help, or your protection. You came to me, remember?"

Kai slides her feet to the floor. She closes her magazine and leans close enough for me to see the sleepless shadows under her eyes. "I hate to break it to you, but this isn't Doug, Captain of the Guard, we're talking about. We're talking about Time, Inevitability, and the elemental power of all four seasons at the fingertips of a bully with a god complex. Doug's entire life goal is to use that power against you, so you'd better come up with something better than 'Relax, I've got this.'"

"I forgot you're an expert when it comes to plotting murder and acts of treason."

"I didn't murder anyone!" The person in front of me turns to peer at us through the gap between the seats. Kai glares at her until she turns away. "And I didn't commit treason," she whispers.

"No? Then why don't you tell me how Doug managed to slaughter Gaia and Lyon, take all their power, and trash the Observatory all on his own?" Back at the villa, Kai said it wasn't too late to make the right choice. Killing me might have been her first bad choice, but I'm guessing it wasn't her last. She was there in the room when Lyon and Gaia were murdered. And Doug confided at least part of his plan to her, which makes her an accomplice. Lyon might have been willing to give her a shot at redemption, but that doesn't mean I have to trust her.

She presses back against the side of the plane. "I didn't know he would kill them. I never would have helped him if I did. He told me he wanted to steal Ananke's magic so we could fight our way out and escape. He didn't tell me the rest of his plan."

"And neither will I. I'm not stupid enough to trust the girl who turned me into a walking kabob."

"You don't want my protection? Fine," she says, "face him yourself. But you shouldn't go in there without a weapon. I know someone in London who can—"

"I *have* a weapon. It's waiting for me in a glass cage in Lyon's office. And the first thing I plan to do when I get there is let it out." The only concrete goal I have is to find my smaze before Doug catches up to me. Painful, toxic, tainted . . . I don't care. I'll take it all back if it means saving—

My stomach drops. I grab the armrests, pressing back in my seat as the plane lurches through a patch of turbulence. Kai's hand clamps down on mine. I shoot her a look as the cabin shakes, and she jerks it away.

"Attention, everyone. This is the captain speaking." The passengers quiet at the garbled voice coming over the staticky PA system. "We're passing through some unexpected weather. We're going to ask everyone to please remain in their seats at this time. Please check to make sure your seat belts are fastened and secure any loose articles under the seat in front of you."

Lightning flashes outside the window. Kai shuts her eyes, her mouth moving in a silent prayer as raindrops spatter against the glass and the nose of the plain lifts.

"Is it Doug?" My knuckles tighten on the armrest, my stomach clenching as I realize how easy it would be for him to track us to this flight.

Kai shakes her head. "He hates you far too much for that. He'd never let you die that easily."

"That's reassuring."

"If it's any consolation, I don't think he can find us with the staff. I saw it after he took it from Lyon. The eye was missing."

"Missing?"

She nods, her skin turning sallow as the cabin shudders. "The head of the scythe was wrapped with a sash when I met with Lyon last week. I couldn't figure out why. But after Doug took it, the sash was gone and so was the eye."

Strange. Why would Lyon cover the staff, unless he didn't want anyone to know the eye was missing? Whatever his reasons, I should probably feel relieved that it's gone—one less weapon Doug can use against us—but considering all the other power he's managed to amass, it hardly seems important.

"If Doug has Ananke's magic, he doesn't need the staff to find us. How are we supposed to infiltrate the Observatory if Doug knows our every move before we do?"

"I'm not convinced he does. After Doug took Lyon's magic, it burned out one of his eyes," she says with a disgusted shiver. "It was probably the curse."

"Curse?"

"You know, stolen magic is cursed magic." Kai gapes at my puzzled expression. "Doug stole the magic, and the magic took his eye. See? Cursed," she says, as if our problems are solved.

"Lyon never lost an eye," I say cynically.

"Lyon never took anything from Ananke."

Another round of turbulence rocks the plane. We both press back in our seats as the plane dips violently. Lightning forks through the clouds and raindrops streak across the window.

"The storms are getting worse," Kai says. "The weather will probably kill us all before Doug gets a chance."

"What do you mean?"

"Storms mean power outages. And if power is down, then so are the connections to the ley lines. If Seasons are locked out and end up in the wind, there's no one to create new ones to restore the balance."

"Why can't Doug do it?"

She turns to me and raises an eyebrow. "Did you ever see Michael make a Season? No. Because that's not his power. That's Gaia's. And if her magic is loose, the entire world is in trouble."

The plane climbs and the cabin settles. When the captain turns off the seat belt sign, I lean on my elbows and rub my eyes, exhaustion crashing over me as I realize how much more is at stake than Chill's and Fleur's lives.

How long do we have to stop Doug before he destroys the whole damn planet?

"I'm sorry," Kai whispers. I lift my head and find her staring out the window, gnawing her lip. "It was supposed to be one clean shot," she confesses. "One clean arrow in your back so I wouldn't have to see your face when you died. But you were so determined to keep getting up, no matter how many times I shot you." She shudders. "I've never seen anyone fight like that. *That's* why."

My mouth goes dry as I remember it. "Why what?"

She turns to me. "That's why I decided to come, after everything that happened with Doug. Because I think I understand why Lyon believed in you." She settles against the wall of the plane, her head resting in the nest of pink hair. I don't say a word as her eyes drift closed.

Instead, I stay awake the whole flight worrying, wondering how many shots one person can endure, and if I'll have the strength to keep getting up.

19
PATCH OF OLD SNOW

DOUG

The faux window in Sommers's old dorm room flickers on when I step inside and switch on the light. Lixue slips in behind me and moves past me into the adjoining bedroom.

I run a finger over a low set of shelves, pausing at a vintage turntable and thumbing through a collection of old vinyl punk albums. A stack of video game cases topples over as I reach for a peeling Rubik's cube.

Jack Sommers and I lived in the same wing, walked the same halls, and ate in the same cafeteria together for decades before I became a Guard, without ever really getting to know each other. There had been the occasional Winter social event or clandestine dorm party, where Noelle would inevitably gravitate toward him and start a conversation, and that was usually about the same time I left. Something about the way she had looked at him—the way *everyone* had looked at him, as if he was some mystery everyone wanted to solve—had always pissed me off.

Lyon had been *my* faculty adviser when I first became a Winter, years before Jack. But then Jack came along, and every time I turned around, there he was. It was as if Lyon had some low-key obsession with the new kid; he was always playing favorites, devoting all his time to "help Jack acclimate" because Sommers was too much of a whining brat to realize he'd won the fucking lottery when he died and got to come here. The next year, I requested a change of advisers, just so I wouldn't have to listen to it.

When Michael invited Sommers to join the Guard, I was sure it was because Lyon had given Jack a leg up. Only later did I come to realize why Michael had tried recruiting him . . . because he had seen something in Jack's future, or maybe in his own, and was attempting to derail a runaway train before it even left the station. And yet, Jack turned him down.

I toss the cube. Dust scatters where it lands on the sunken cushions of a crappy old sofa. I move to the desk in the corner. Chill's workstation is the most impressive thing in the room—three sleek, high-end monitors, a pricey ergonomic keyboard, and a carefully dismantled hard drive. Guts and wires spill out of its shell, ensuring it's completely useless to me.

I dump out a desk drawer. Crumbs spill from an open bag of chips and a roach skitters out, disappearing under a pile of empty file folders. The trash can under the desk is mounded with shredded documents and photos. Jack and his Handler were careful when they left.

I follow the sound of Lixue's rustling to their shared bedroom and watch her tear through what little Jack and his Handler left here. Unlike Jack, his Handler seems to have amassed a few personal possessions over the years. Jack's side of the room feels stark by comparison—no framed family photos, trinkets, trophies, or hobby paraphernalia that might reveal more about him than the bits and pieces I've managed to string together from the few insignificant records Lyon didn't waste time purging from the servers. It's as if Jack Sommers never bothered to settle in. As if, from the very beginning, he'd never intended to stay.

Lixue is thorough, picking through the guts of abandoned electronic devices for anything worth saving. She overturns the beds, ripping apart pillows and cushions and checking the spaces between. Suddenly, the rhythmic sounds of her rummaging quiet. I turn to find her talking in a low voice, one hand pressed to her transmitter. Her eyes snap to mine. "It's Zahra. She says Sampson and Sommers boarded a flight out of Mexico City. They'll be landing at Heathrow in twelve hours."

Which means they'll be at our front door soon. "Then you'd better hurry and find me that damn crystal. I want it in my hands before Jack makes it down here."

"Yes, sir." Lixue disconnects and starts ransacking Jack's closets and drawers. It has to be somewhere in this room. We've searched everywhere else.

"Chronos, in here." Lixue drags a metal footlocker from the bottom of the closet, kicking aside rolled tubes of drawing paper as she hauls the box to the middle of the room.

I stoop to pick one up. The curled pages are reluctant to unroll, and the dark, sketched pencil lines smudge where I hold the edges down.

Barely legible notes fill the margins. The intersecting lines are marked with x's and question marks. I recognize the shape of the structure in the drawing before I'm able to decipher Jack's handwriting. A circular hall fills the center of the first page, the radiating spokes of each wing spreading over the next four sheets.

These are sections of a map. A map of the Observatory.

The pages are marked with dates, as details were added or erased over time. The earliest goes back to 1989. The section of the catacombs under the north wing is roughly sketched, the tunnels under Jack's dorm room meticulously labeled. Some are marked with obvious dead ends. Others are left unfinished with question marks.

He's been plotting the exits from the Winter wing—tunnels and access points, stairwells and closets—since the year he first arrived. Before Fleur even got here. As if he was itching to break free of this place since day one. But the catacombs were off-limits to Seasons and Handlers, which means Jack had help.

And I can guess who it was.

I toss the maps to the floor. "I want every tunnel under the north wing searched as soon as we're done here."

"What should I do with these?" Lixue squats in front of the open footlocker. Something clear and shiny dangles from her hand, casting rainbows over the floor. Lixue starts as I snatch the object from her hand, but it's just a Christmas ornament, a snowman bearing no resemblance to the missing crystal from the staff. One segment of the snowman's body is too small, another too large, all of them too round to be the eye.

I loop the ribbon around my finger and study the snowman. From what little I've seen of Jack's room, he doesn't strike me as the sentimental type, but the footlocker is full of keepsakes . . . ceramic, glass, and silver trinkets. There must be close to thirty of them. . . .

I kneel beside the box as I realize what I'm staring at.

"What is it?" Lixue asks.

"These aren't Jack's. They're Fleur's." These are the memorials she made for him each spring after she killed him.

In Lixue's eyes, I see a reflection of a shared memory. The day our team found one of the ornaments hanging from a pine tree in some back-woods town in Virginia. Jack's initials had been carved in the bark. That was all the evidence I'd needed to justify Fleur's Reconditioning. Lixue had been with me that day when we cornered Fleur in an alley and confronted her about her feelings for Jack. And Noelle . . . she had been the one to deliver Fleur's punishment. Clearly, she hadn't learned anything from it; she'd helped them escape anyway. And it got her killed.

"Why would he leave them here?" Lixue asks. "I mean, it's obvious why he abandoned the maps—he would have known he'd never have use for them again. But why keep these here when he was so careful to shred everything else?"

Unless he cared about them too much to destroy them.

I fish a silver angel from the box and hold it dangling from its ribbon as I read the inscription.

Love, all alike, no season knows, nor clime, nor hours, days, months, which are the rags of time . . .

The line of old poetry reads like a love note. Or a code. Regardless, if these ornaments are meaningful to Jack, all the more reason for me to hang them like bread crumbs throughout the Observatory, just to taunt him when he gets here.

"Take the box and the maps to my office."

"Yes, Chronos." Carefully, she places all the ornaments back in the footlocker and collects the maps.

I slip the silver angel into my pocket, certain I have all I need to find Jack once he gets here. He and Kai will probably hide in the catacombs under the Winter wing. Kai will break off in search of her sister while Jack forms a plan to find Fleur. With any luck, Jack won't be the only thing I'll uncover down there. The maps are all it would take to find him and smoke him out of his hole, but I won't need to. I'll have the eye. And I'll have Gaia's magic. Then all I'll have to do is dangle his shiny angel in front of him and Jack Sommers will come to me.

20

INTO THE STORM

<u>JACK</u>

Rain pours down in billowing gray sheets when we duck out of the terminal at Heathrow and jump into a waiting cab. I give the driver an address on Park Vista, a row house on the north side of Greenwich Park. The entry portal to the north wing is familiar ground, and once I'm in, the Winter wing will put me closer to Lyon's old office.

I wipe my face on my sleeve, but my jacket's just as soaked. The familiar damp cold is as bone deep as it is depressing, and every inch of me aches for our home in Cuernavaca. For Fleur.

I drag my phone from my pocket. As Kai makes small talk with the driver, I use the last of the dying battery to check my messages. My last voice mail came hours ago, right after we boarded our flight.

"Jack, it's Amber. I've been trying to reach you. We found Poppy. She's on her way to London. Please don't do anything stupid until we get there. Call me when you get this."

I try reaching each of them, but my calls go straight to voice mail, and then my battery dies.

Kai pulls back her wet hood, stripping off her wig as soon as we're clear of the airport. She shoves it inside her backpack, the zipper catching carelessly on a long pink strand as she closes the bag around it. The sight of it invites mental images that make my stomach turn.

I lean against the window, willing the cab to move faster as beads of rain slide sideways across the glass. It's nearly an hour's drive to the Observatory, and then there's the matter of figuring out how to get in without being spotted.

Kai stares straight ahead, her thoughts unreadable in the dark. I don't know what she's expecting once we get through the portal, but as far as I'm concerned, once we make it into the Winter wing, she's on her own.

I turn to read a sign as it rushes past.

"Hey," I call up to the driver, rapping on the partition as he detours toward Peckham. "Where are we going? This isn't the way to Greenwich Park."

The driver's eyes flick to Kai in the rearview mirror.

"We're making a stop first," she says.

"We don't have time for any stops."

She pitches her voice low. "You may think you have it all figured out, Lancelot, but I know what's waiting for us in there, and I'm not stepping foot in that place without a weapon. Neither should you." Brightly colored streetlights reflect off her face as we approach a part of town I'd prefer not to venture into at night.

The driver turns down a narrow alley, and the cab lurches to a stop in front of a closed steel door. Everything about the place feels like a warning. I don't even know where we are, but the security bars covering the door and the broken bulbs above it tell me enough. "It's three o'clock in the morning. The place is obviously closed. We should just—"

Kai passes a wad of bills through the partition to the driver, slings her backpack over her shoulder, and gets out. The driver glances at me in his mirror, waiting for me to do the same. With a muttered swear, I grab my own bag and follow her.

I watch the alley as Kai leans on the buzzer. A panel slides open in the door. An eye peers through it, the dark pupil bouncing to Kai, then to me, before the panel snaps closed.

Kai grabs the bars and gives them a violent shake. "Come on, Auggie! Open the damn door!"

A dead bolt screeches and the door swings open. The man's gray whiskers catch the low light as he jerks his chin toward me through the bars. "That one's not welcome."

"Great, we're all in agreement." I tug Kai by the sleeve. "Come on, let's go."

Kai shakes me off. "I just need to pick up a few things, and we'll be out of your hair, Auggie. I promise. Augustus Poole, meet Jack Sommers," Kai says, as if the guy didn't just tell me to fuck off. "Jack Sommers, meet my good friend Auggie."

Augustus Poole's name tells me everything I need to know about him. He isn't a Summer—at least not anymore—but he was probably someone's Handler once, a long time ago, if the lines around his eyes and the silver in his scruff are any indication. Some of the tension leaves my shoulders. He doesn't seem like much of a threat.

Auggie grumbles to himself as he unlocks the security door and ushers us inside. We follow him down a dark hall into some kind of shop. Two cracked glass display cases sit in the middle of the floor, the mildew-stained walls behind them piled high with boxes and loose junk. The shadows sway with the swing of a lone lightbulb, making it hard to focus.

Auggie settles himself onto a stool and leans an elbow against a display case. A huge black fly alights on a stain on his shirt. "I told you it's not safe for you to come back here, girl."

"I don't have a choice. My sister's down there, Auggie. I can't leave her."

He shakes his head. "It's suicide, whatever you're planning." The fly takes to the air and hovers around me. I wave it away, but it circles back. "There've been more quakes," Auggie says.

"Bad?" Kai asks.

"Aftershocks, mostly. I can't reach anyone in the Summer wing. Power must be down. That place is going to self-destruct, and you don't want to be anywhere near it when that happens. That Lausks boy has no idea what he's done—"

I wind back to swat the fly as it buzzes past me again. Auggie's hand shoots out, trapping my wrist. "Don't." There's a firm pressure in his grip and murder in his eyes. The fly takes one more pass around me and alights on Auggie's shoulder before I realize what it is—or rather, who it is. It must be a Summer. Maybe Auggie's.

I lift my hands to show I mean no harm as Auggie lets go. "Sorry, didn't realize."

Kai touches his sleeve, drawing his attention. "We only need a few things," she says, gesturing to a stack of boxes behind him. "Then we'll be gone."

Auggie eases off his stool and retreats behind the display cases, shoving aside a pile of boxes to reveal a panel in the wall. It opens to a dark stairwell, and Auggie motions for us to follow as he starts to descend. I duck my head, the wooden risers creaking under my weight, the low ceiling nearly brushing my head as we enter a cellar. The room is dimly lit with pull-chain lights, the walls lined with racks of wooden shelves. It's like a doomsday prepper's arsenal, every surface cluttered with collections of simple weapons.

Kai pulls a sleek black recurve bow from a rack on the far wall. Her hands pass over it, inspecting it under the light. I freeze as she draws back the string, so focused on her task, it's as if she's forgotten I'm here. Our eyes catch over the imaginary arrow she's aimed at me, and color rushes to her cheeks.

"This'll do," she says, clearing her throat as she sets it down beside her backpack. She pulls a quiver from the shelf and stuffs it full of arrows. The silver points are tipped with wicked retractable barbs, and I get a little nauseated just looking at them.

"You can't go parading through Greenwich Park carrying that," Auggie scolds her. He digs around in a cabinet and pulls out a tactical case. It could be a trombone tote, for all I know, and I'm guessing he figures most other people would assume the same. Kai packs up her bow and slings the case over her back. Pacing the long shelves, she settles on a hunting knife with jagged teeth. "How about for him?" Auggie asks as she fastens on a leg strap.

She jerks her chin at me. "Go ahead. Take whatever you want." To

Auggie, she says, "Put it on my tab."

"You won't live long enough to pay it," he grumbles, teasing a smile out of her. She reaches into her pocket and presses something into his hand. "What's this?" he asks, the color draining from his face.

"Your money." She pats his shoulder. "I won't live long enough to need it, right?" She slips another knife from the display and tucks it in her pocket.

Auggie's eyes well, but his expression's stony when he turns to me. "Go on, boy. You heard the lady. Find something you like."

Kai stuffs her backpack with gear as I strip off my coat and slip my arms through a leather shoulder holster. Two hunting knives hang snugly against my ribs, their leather grips within easy reach. Their shape reminds me of a knife Amber once gave to Woody, and I feel the familiar pang of his loss as I secure the knives back in their sheaths.

Exploring the racks and displays, I step through a beaded curtain into another room. The tight rows of shelves are stocked with survival gear: canned food, jugs of water, batteries and generators, lanterns, medical kits, compasses, fire spits. I pause in front of an empty glass display case, eyes widening as I realize what I'm looking at: the domed lid of a stasis chamber. It looks like some kind of Frankensteinian junkyard creation, cobbled together from the parts of models I haven't seen in the Observatory since before the turn of the millennium.

"It's a beauty, isn't it?" Auggie says, coming up behind me. "I hear the new ones have all kinds of fancy bells and whistles. But this one's really something. Found all the parts and built it myself."

"Does it work?" I ask, tracing the surface with a finger.

"The chamber itself powers up just fine. Without a transmitter, it's hard to know if it actually works." He shrugs. "I'm good with a pair of pliers and a screwdriver, but I'm no expert in computers. Never have been able to get the thing online. When you all are done with whatever nonsense you're up to, maybe you can come back and show an old man how it's done." He turns to leave with a plaintive nod, and the beaded curtain rustles in his wake.

I load my jacket down with matches, a flashlight, a roll of electrical tape, a handful of smoke grenades, and a small utility knife. Patting my pockets, I still feel ill-equipped.

A flicker of movement catches my attention. I turn in time to catch a black leather case against my chest. "I heard you're good with these," Kai says.

The case rattles softly as I turn it over and unzip it, revealing a set of the most beautiful lockpicks I've ever seen. "Who told you that?"

"Lyon might have mentioned it once," she says, looking down at the floor. "Let's go," she says with a pained smile. "Don't want to keep Doug waiting."

I close the case and slip it into my pocket. I'm not about to thank Kai for anything, but for the first time since I boarded the plane last night, I feel almost ready for the impossible task in front of me.

I thank Auggie and start up the steps, giving Kai a moment to settle up. Behind me, I hear their murmured goodbyes, the slap of hands on shoulders as they embrace, and a sniffle that must be Auggie's.

Kai runs to catch up as I push through the door into the foggy blackness of the alley. "There's a park a few blocks north," she says. "We can catch a taxi there."

The rain has slowed to an icy drizzle, and I jam my hands deep in my pockets for warmth, keeping my pace brisk to put as much distance as possible between us and Auggie's place, hoping it wasn't a mistake to stop. Ahead, the trees bordering the park rustle, their branches stirred by a wind that seems to whip and change direction too often, too quickly. Lightning flickers in the distance, and a handful of scattered snowflakes swirl on the breeze. Kai's feet splash in the puddles behind me.

"How do you and Auggie know each other?" I ask Kai over my shoulder, not entirely sure I trust him.

"He was a Handler when I first came to the Observatory," she explains, trotting to catch up. "He and his Summer lived in the room next to mine. I had a difficult transition. He and Daisy helped me adjust."

"The fly?"

Kai nods, confirming my suspicion. "Daisy was like a sister to him. He adored her. But she was outspoken. Reckless. She had strong opinions and refused to keep her head down. Michael made an example of her and had her Culled." Kai winces, as if the memory still stings. "Auggie was allowed to stay in the Observatory. He worked in maintenance for a while, laid low and kept an eye on Daisy's fly for a decade or so, until a faculty member helped them escape."

"Who?" I ask eagerly. "If this staff member's still down there, maybe they can help us."

"He's not there anymore," Kai says, her expression shuttering, the grief in her eyes telling me everything I need to know. Whoever helped Auggie was probably Terminated for it. We're on our own. "What now?" she asks, scrambling to keep up with me.

"We get to the north portal and find a way down to the Observatory."

"How?"

"I'll know it when I see it."

"So you're just going to wing it?"

"Pretty much." I stop at the edge of the park, pacing the sidewalk, searching for a taxi, but it's oh-dark-thirty out here and there's no one except a cluster of homeless people huddled around a trash barrel. Fire licks up the side of it, throwing sparks and orange light over their faces. A deep rattling cough comes from under a blanket on the ground.

Kai's eyes leap to mine as tiny flickers of light, like lost sparks from the fire, swirl into the air with the girl's next bout of coughing. As we come closer, the girl presses the end of a threadbare quilt over her mouth, trapping the bits of magic before anyone else notices. Her skin is a sickly sweat-slicked gray, her eyes glassy and distant in the firelight.

I kneel beside her. "Summer or Spring?" I ask in a low voice.

Her eyes flutter, heavy-lidded and confused. Her lips crack around her whispered reply. "Summer. How did you . . . ?" Her dark eyes narrow on my face. They slide to Kai and relief washes over her. The thin wheeze she expels sets off another fit of coughing. Kai drops down beside her, rubbing slow circles on the Summer's back until the fit calms.

"You know her?" I ask quietly.

Kai shakes her head. "Not well. I was a Summer in the Southern Hemisphere. I think she's north." Kai draws the Summer's tangled hair back from her ear. A transmitter light blinks, a steady red pulse, and Kai covers it up again. "Can you get home?"

The girl shakes her head. "I haven't heard from my Handler in six days. Last time we talked, she said there was some kind of coup. That the Guards were locking everyone in their rooms. She sounded scared. And then she just stopped answering. I didn't know what to do, so I caught a flight here, but I can't get through to her, and I was too afraid to turn myself in at the portal."

Kai and I exchange a worried glance. Auggie said he couldn't get through to the Summer wing. That the power was probably down. This girl has hours, a day at most, before this weather devours her. At this time of year, we're not likely to find a stray Autumn or Winter wandering the streets of London to help her.

Kai tucks the quilt around the girl's shoulders and smooths her hair. She draws me aside so the girl won't hear. "There's nothing either of us can do for her, except get down there fast and try to restore power to the Summer wing."

We both look up as headlights approach. A taxi. "Come on. The sooner we get to a portal, the better." I jump off the curb, flagging it down. Kai gives the dying Summer one last look, and we sprint through the freezing rain to the cab.

21

SMOTHERED IN THEIR LAIRS

<u>FLEUR</u>

My stiff limbs groan as I shift against the cold stone floor. Slowly, I turn my head, twisting to see my surroundings, orienting myself against the iron bars. I touch the sore muscles in my neck, testing the bruised flesh and swallowing fire. My knees scream as I sit up against the wall, struggling to remember what happened right before I passed out.

A red light winks at me from a new camera mounted by the ceiling.

A clump of fallen stone sits beside my hand, and I consider pitching it at the camera's lens. But then Doug would only send someone to replace it. Maybe he'd even come himself. And I'm not ready to face him again.

I rub my temple where Lixue cuffed me, listening to the soft snores coming from the direction of Chill's cell, praying that he was wrong. That Jack's not coming. Praying that Doug was lying about the others.

A shadow moves in the corridor. A cold draft ruffles my hair as a filmy gray smaze darts between the bars into my cell. It tumbles like an angry cloud, as if it's aggravated or impatient, circling my head and then doubling back. I hurl a handful of rubble at it, rubbing the warmth back into my arms as it zips away.

A steady march of boots echoes from the catacombs. I push myself to my feet as Lixue stops in front of my cell. Her hands are empty. No water. No food. The same huge Guard I saw before stands behind her.

"What do you want?" It hurts to speak, and the words come out hoarse. Unease sets in as she works a key into the lock.

"Chronos wants to see you." She slings open the door, and I back away from the huge Guard as he steps inside my cell. He smiles, a little sheepish as he snaps a set of shackles around my wrists before gently escorting me out.

I try to pay attention to our route as I'm marched through the winding tunnels, but after two or three turns, they all look the same. The passageways are dark, the torchlight casting shadows that make it hard to see. Bits of broken shale dig into my bare feet as the Guards follow me up a narrow spiral stairway.

At the top, Lixue pushes open a metal door. Bright white light streams through the gap, and I narrow my eyes like some kind of surfacing mole. A long hall runs to my left. Another to my right. After the trip through the dim tunnels, the shiny floor tiles and pristine white walls are almost blinding, but I'm sure I've never been in this part of the Observatory before.

Something cold brushes my left ankle. I pause, startled to see a smaze zipping around it. It darts back and forth, frantic and restless, and I wonder if it's the same one that wandered into my cell.

Lixue propels me forward with a shove, nudging me toward a door at the end of the hall. She scans a key card and the locks snap open. Lixue pops her head in, talking in a low voice as the huge Guard watches me.

"Leave us," comes a familiar voice from inside.

Lixue swings the door wide, nudging me through it when I refuse to enter.

Doug sits on a crisp white sofa inside, his elbows resting on his knees and his fingers threaded together, watching a TV. He doesn't look up. The rest of the room is spacious and spare—clean angles, no frills, all white and glass and chrome. My eyes dart to every corner, but there's no sign of the Staff of Time anywhere.

"Close the door." Doug's voice is gravelly and deep, as if he's been here alone for a while.

"Are you sure, Chronos?" Lixue asks, her eyes flicking to me.

"The Spring won't be a problem. Will you, Fleur?" Snowy black-and-white footage plays on the TV screen. Two Guards enter the frame. They lean against the wall outside Chill's cell.

I stiffen as the door clicks shut behind me.

Doug rises and moves to the sideboard. He pours water from a crystal decanter into a short glass and holds it toward me. His shirtsleeves are rolled up, his forearms tensed, waiting for me to take it. I clench my fists, forcing myself to look away.

"Suit yourself." He swirls the glass, turning to watch me as he takes a deep gulp. My swallow is painful and dry, loud in my own ears. His eye dips to the bruises on my neck as if he's reading my thoughts. I haven't had anything to eat or drink since I was yanked from the villa. Doug sips the rest of his water luxuriously, every slow swallow taunting me.

He steps closer, his hair falling over the patch covering his right eye. The cold diamond of his left eye rakes down my sweat-stained coveralls, all the way to my filthy, bleeding feet. He gestures with his glass toward the sofa. I give him a wide berth, pausing midstride in front of it.

A glazed pot rests in the center of the glass coffee table. The waxy green leaves spilling over the edge of the pot are the only splash of color in the room.

My mind lunges for them, sliding into their moist, cool roots, clutching the houseplant like a found weapon as I ease down onto the sofa.

Doug watches me over the rim of his glass. "I've been staring at that pot for days, and I can't budge a single leaf. Why?" he demands.

His tone earns him a contemptuous smile.

In a flash of movement, he reaches for a leaf, pinching it between his thumb and forefinger. My right arm bends at an odd angle in response. I cry out, yanking my mind from the plant a second before the stem snaps.

Doug sits on the sofa across from me, twirling the broken leaf between his fingers. He sets down his glass with a sharp *clink* against the tabletop and stares at me with that horrible gleaming eye.

I leap for his glass and slam it against the table. It shatters with a deafening crash, and I back away from the sofa, clutching a thick, gleaming shard in my hand. I bolt for the door, braced for Doug to pounce, but he makes no attempt to stop me. The doorknob slips in my blood-slicked palm. I rattle it, but it's locked, the security panel beside it blinking red. Whirling around, I search the room for another exit, but there's no way out. Doug rises from the couch. He feints as I swing at him, grabbing my wrist as it flashes past his neck. The shard slips from my fingers as he wrenches my arm behind my back. "Don't make this harder than it has to be."

"You're an idiot if you think I'm going to make this easy for you. Why should I?" I snap. "You're only going to kill me anyway."

Doug yanks me toward the TV. He reaches for the remote with his free hand and turns the channel to the satellite feeds. An explosion of color bursts onto the screen. My eyes dart back and forth over the weather maps, my mouth falling open as I follow the path of the deadly storms spreading across Europe and Africa. News headlines cut across the bottom of the screen. Devastated cities. Trade routes interrupted. Markets in panic. The death tolls are staggering, and I turn away.

Doug hurls the remote across the room and spins me around by the arm, forcing me to look at him.

"This isn't only about you and your boyfriend anymore. It never was, but you and Jack were too selfish to see it. Gaia's magic is loose, and if I can't control it, every living creature on this godforsaken planet is going to suffer and die. The destruction of the world will be on you!"

"*You* killed them!" I say, fighting back tears. "Everything was fine. Everything was *better* under Lyon and Gaia. *You* did this."

"I only finished what you and Sommers started. And now you and I are going to fix it." His voice is strained. He presses a palm to his breastbone and shoves me away from him. Drawing thin breaths, he claws at his tie, dragging down the knot as he lumbers to the decanter. Clutching his chest, he turns over a glass, filling it to the brim with a shaking hand and sucking down the water in huge, greedy gulps.

"What's wrong?" I ask, darting a hopeful glance at the door.

"Nothing. So don't get any stupid ideas about leaving." His voice is hoarse. He sets down the glass and wipes his mouth on his sleeve.

My own mouth is too dry to even salivate. I lick my lips, trying to remember the last time I had any water, and my stomach growls. Doug turns at the sound, dragging his tie over his head and tossing it over the arm of the sofa. He juts his chin to a set of double doors behind him.

"You're bleeding on my carpet. There's a first-aid kit in the bathroom. Clean that mess up. Then we'll get started."

I open my mouth to protest, but he gestures to the broken leaf wilting on the table in front of him. "You'll stay here with me and we'll work round the clock. You have until Jack gets here to show me how to control the earth magic. I suggest you make your last moments on this earth count."

He turns his back on me, letting me know this conversation is over.

I stare at him, unable to move. How long until Jack comes looking for me? How many days until Doug kills us both?

"You've tied my hands before," I remind him. He turns, and when his eye meets mine, I dredge up a memory—the day of my Reconditioning when he tied me to a chair, the satisfying snap of my head against his nose. "How well did that work out for you?"

A muscle tightens in his jaw.

I storm into the bedroom and close the doors behind me, falling back against them and holding them shut.

22

NIGHT FALLING FAST

JACK

The portal to the Summer wing is just south of Greenwich Park. Kai and I duck behind a row of hedges beside the two-story house in Blackheath. The windows are dark and the porch lights are out. A low brick wall shields us from passing traffic as Kai readies her bow. I grip my flashlight and lockpick set, searching for signs of movement in the house.

"You think they'll bother posting Guards in a house with no power?"

Kai nods. "They'd be foolish not to guard a portal, *especially* one without power."

"How long will I have to get through the locks?"

"Once they hear you, you'll have about five seconds to open that door before they're all over us." She stows her backpack within reach of the window beside us. Then she rolls out her shoulders and shakes out her hands. "Ready?"

"Not really." My own hands are so cold, I can barely feel my fingers.

"Don't worry. I've got your back."

The darkness hides my grimace. Last time I showed Kai my back, she put three arrows in it. But as she rises to her feet and stalks toward the door with her bow raised, I don't have much of a choice but to go along with her.

I creep up the porch steps. My hands feel clumsy as I kneel in front of the door, less sensitive to the feel of the pins than they should be. I listen, breath held, watching for Kai's single sharp nod before turning the knob.

The hinge creaks as I crack the door open. Through the narrow gap, I have a clean line of sight straight into the darkened parlor.

Into the face of a Guard as she looks up from behind a desk.

I shove the door open. It swings a full four inches before it bounces to a halt, a chain lock stretched across the opening.

"Shit!" I croak.

The Guard leaps from her chair. My flashlight shines off the barrel of her gun.

I jump to my feet and hurl my shoulder into the door. "You didn't tell me there was a chain!" The wood around the chain splinters, the sound of it drowned under the Guard's shout as she calls out for her team. I recoil as a bullet lodges in the doorframe. I ram the door again. It flies open, and I stumble in with it.

Kai's foot smacks into the back of my knee. I crash to the floor as something hisses over my head. There's a *thwack* and the Guard holding the gun goes down, an arrow protruding from her throat.

Another *thwack*. A Guard at the end of the hall falls.

Kai stalks around me, bow raised, arrow nocked. She jerks her head to the side, instructing me to stay behind her as we tiptoe around the body into the kitchen. The floor shakes with the thunder of heavy boots and the cellar door flies open—

Thwack. A Guard falls through it. Kai kicks him, making sure he's down.

She nocks another arrow and steps over him, disappearing down the cellar stairs. I pause to fish a key card from his pocket before remembering we left Kai's backpack outside. I retrace my steps to the window, ducking as the dead Guard's magic soars over my head. Shouldering Kai's pack, I blink away the glare, unsure what I'm seeing as I spot a shadow moving down the hall.

A Guard creeps into the kitchen. On silent feet, she stalks to the cellar door. I draw my knife and follow her, reaching the top of the stairs just as she sneaks up behind Kai.

I hurl the blade. Kai spins, bow raised, as the Guard tumbles down the last few steps, landing facedown at the bottom with my knife in her back.

Kai blinks up at me and lowers her bow. Neither of us speaks as I bend to retrieve my knife and grab the Guard's key card from her pocket. We shield our eyes as her magic flares and soars away. When the light fades, I hand over Kai's backpack and one of the key cards, keeping the other for myself.

I snap on my flashlight, swinging the beam around the cellar. The elevator to the Summer wing sits in the far corner of the room. Resting the flashlight on the floor, I pry the elevator doors open and peer into the shaft. Dank, musty air whips up from below. It smells strongly of minerals and moss, the same closed-in smells that fill the catacombs under the Observatory. An open Coke can sits on a rectangular folding table beside me. I pour the remaining contents onto the floor and pitch the empty can into the shaft.

Kai tiptoes up behind me, both of us listening as the can falls. After a long, long time, I hear a faint echo of it rattling at the bottom.

I scrub my face with a muffled swear. Getting up an elevator shaft as a Season was one thing. Getting down an elevator shaft as a human feels like stepping out of a plane without a parachute. I stare at the heavy cables that disappear into the blackness below. We could slide down them for a story or two . . . but thirty? It'd be far too easy to lose our grip and fall.

Kai hauls a length of rope from her pack. Without warning, she grabs me by the front of my shirt and pulls me toward her, working the rope into a series of knots.

"What are you doing?" I swat at her hands as she runs the rope around my backside and cinches a knot at my groin.

"Making you a harness. I'm strapping you to the cables."

"No," I tell her, wishing we had infiltrated the Winter portal instead. "This is a very bad idea."

"You have a better plan? This is the only way down." She repeats the process with a second length of rope, creating a sling around her own midsection. Satisfied, she moves to the folding table beside the door. With a sweep of her arm, she clears the clutter from its surface. "Help me with this," she says as she flips the table and collapses its legs.

I grab the other side. Together, we position it inside the open doors of the elevator. Kai slides it across one side of the shaft, avoiding the cables. Resting it on the thin lip on the opposite side, she forms a shelf across the opening. She slings her pack on her back and shrugs her bow over her shoulder. Putting one foot out onto this makeshift bridge, she tests her weight. I feel sick as she takes another cautious step. Then a third. Until she's standing beyond reach of the shaft's walls, clutching the cables for balance.

"Come on," she says in a shaky voice, "before I lose my nerve." She ties the free end of her rope around the cable.

I point my flashlight down into the dark hole below her.

"Don't," she says, swallowing hard. "Don't look down."

"This is nuts." I slip my flashlight into my front pocket, shining it upward toward the ceiling. Breath held, I take a tentative step out onto the table.

We both freeze when it creaks, bowing slightly under our weight. I take another cautious step, trying not to think about the thirty stories of open air below me.

Kai works fast, tying the free end of my rope to the cable above hers. "This is a friction knot. It should be secure enough to hold your sling in place—"

"Should be?" She ignores the crack in my voice.

"You loosen it like this," she says, demonstrating the release technique. "Slide a few feet down and it will tighten again. We'll take it slow. If you slide too fast, you'll burn through your cord." She waits for my nod. Panic grips me as I realize what I've just agreed to. "I'll go first," she says. "Wait for me to call up to you, then come down behind me. Slowly," she emphasizes.

Kai swings off the platform and leans back into her sling. She slides a few feet. Then her knot cinches around the cable, stopping her descent. She nods up at me, flashing me an exhilarated smile as she tugs her rope and starts down the shaft. I glance back into the cellar, listening to Kai's knot cinch and release, cinch and release, as the slide of her rope fades into the darkness. The cone of my flashlight casts eerie shadows around me.

A faint voice reaches me. I tip my head over the ledge, but the voice isn't coming from below. It's coming from the floor above me. The voice grows louder as boots storm down the cellar stairs. I grab my flashlight from my pocket, fumbling for the power switch with both hands.

"He's in the elevator shaft!" A gun discharges. I duck as a bullet whizzes past my head. It lodges in the stone wall, pelting me with shards. My flashlight slips. I lunge for it as it tumbles down the shaft. Another gun fires. Pain rips through my upper arm, and I leap off the table into the darkness below before I realize what I've done.

I fall, grasping thin air. My harness slides a few gut-twisting yards before jerking to a stop at the same moment my hand closes around the rope. The force of my momentum triggers the release, and suddenly I'm falling again. Cold air whips over me. The rope whines, burning against the cable as I plummet through the blackness.

Bullets ping the walls of the shaft above my head. Kai shouts instructions, but I can't hear them past the pop of guns and the scream of the rope. I reach for the cable to slow my fall, jerking my hands back when it tears the skin from my palms.

The smell of burning nylon fills the shaft, and Kai shouts my name as the ground rushes up to meet me.

23

FIRST TO YIELD

DOUG

My eyes fly open at the jarring knock on the door of my apartment.

"Food service." The muffled voice on the other side is gruff and familiar. I rub my face and push myself upright on the couch, groggy and unrested, then get up to let Boreas in. The retired Winter wheels a meal cart over the threshold, his cheeks ruddy from the walk from the north kitchen. "Where do you want it?"

I gesture loosely around the room, the universal sign for *I don't fucking care*. "Put it anywhere," I mutter.

The doors to the bedroom swing open. Fleur blows through them in a clean jumpsuit, scowling as she scrubs a towel over her damp hair.

"There's only one toothbrush in there, and I'm not using . . ." Her rant trails off, and Boreas glances up from his cart. With a polite nod, he lowers his head back to his task, locking the wheels of the cart in place and removing the silver domes from the serving plates.

The dining hall manager clears his throat. "Call the kitchen when you've finished your meal, Douglas. I'll return to pick up the cart." Fleur's breath quickens as the old man turns to go.

"Chronos," I correct him, blocking his exit. "You'll address me as Chronos if you want to keep your job."

Eyes downcast, he dips his head. "My apologies, Chronos. It won't happen again."

I stand aside. Fleur clutches her damp towel to her chest as she watches him shuffle out.

She starts when I slam the door.

I steal a peek at her eyes as I return to the couch, sifting clumsily through flashes of jumbled memories, but Boreas's face doesn't appear in any of them.

"Eat," I tell her, jerking my chin at the plates. We've already wasted too much time, and I won't be summoning him back anyway. His offer to return for the cart was clearly a message for her.

Her stomach growls. She drops the towel on the arm of the sofa and lunges for the cart, grabbing a glass of orange juice and downing it in four huge gulps. It spills down her chin. She doesn't bother to wipe it away before piling vegan sausage, fruit, and pancakes onto a plate and drowning it all in syrup. She folds a dripping pancake into her mouth with her hands before she makes it to the sofa.

It hurts just watching her. I haven't eaten a real meal in days, and the constant burn in my chest isn't helping my appetite. "You just came out of stasis two days ago. I don't have time to wait while you make yourself sick."

Fleur's chewing slows. Her eyes move back and forth as if she's calculating in her head.

"You were in stasis for eighteen hours," I say, answering the unasked question in the crease of her brow. She frowns, shoving another bite into her mouth, her eyes closing with her greedy swallow.

I yank her plate away, dropping it onto the cart. "Now," I tell her, shoving the potted plant toward her and sitting opposite her. "Show me."

She glares at me over a napkin as she wipes the syrup from her chin. "I can't show you," she says sharply. "It's not something you can learn that way."

I slam my palm against the coffee table. "Then tell me!"

Her expression's hard to read—anger, hostility, impatience maybe, but not fear. Never that.

I drag my hands through my hair, reining in my temper. The angrier she becomes, the harder she'll fight me. "Tell me how to command the plant," I insist with forced calmness.

She shakes her head at me, as if I'm some kind of idiot. "That's just it. You can't *command* it. Plants aren't human. They don't care who you are or how much power you have or what crown you think you're wearing. You can't boss them around like they're members of your kitchen staff."

I leap off the couch, jerking her up by her arm as I summon a flame and hold it close to her face. "Fire's not human, either, but it comes when I call it."

She watches it, clenching her teeth. "That's just it. You strong-arm your way through the world, taking what you want and shoving people around, threatening and yelling and demanding they obey you. . . . That's not how earth magic works. You can't just barrel your way into a living thing, exert control through brute force, and expect it to cooperate with you." She reaches for my arm to push away the

187

flame, but I hold it closer, tightening my grip.

"I'm running out of patience."

"Plants are living things," she says through a wince, her cheek flushed from the heat. "They breathe, they eat, they reproduce, and they suffer, just like we do. And the best way to understand how to move them is to make yourself feel what they feel!"

"Stop fucking with me and tell me how to control the goddamn—"

The plant stirs in its pot.

I turn toward the sound, going still as Fleur's eyes take on a faraway look. No visions. No memories. Just the dark void of her irises, as if her mind has left and gone someplace else. My fire gutters out.

The plant stretches awake. A vinelike stem slithers toward me, reaching up for my free hand as I lower my arm to my side. I don't move as it creeps over my wrist, coiling slowly around it, dragging its pot over the table inch by inch. It's nothing I haven't seen before. Nothing as impressive as the video footage of the earthquake Fleur started in Tecate or the entire grove of cedars she commanded to take down Michael. But as the pot scrapes toward me, a shiver crawls up my neck, and I'm careful to check my grip on her.

The vine climbs higher in a serpentine pattern, the pot sliding closer in small, predatory movements.

"This is *Epipremnum aureum*," Fleur says as the plant circles my forearm, "commonly known as devil's ivy. It's nearly impossible to kill." Her vacant gaze slides to my throat as the plant winds around the crook of my elbow. "Its heart-shaped leaves stay green, growing to surprising lengths, even when it's kept in the dark. This species climbs by clinging to surfaces," she explains. "It's been known to cover entire forest floors, suffocating entire ecosystems. And its leaves, deceptively harmless in appearance, are deadly to weaker species. So you see," she says with a menacing smile, "she doesn't need you to *command* her. She's perfectly capable of hanging you, suffocating you, or sickening you all on her own, with or without your consent or participation."

The pot scrapes over the edge of the table. I turn in time to see it tip, then crack against the floor, scattering soil over the carpet. The roots of the plant dangle stubbornly from my arm. Tightening its hold, it drags itself to the crest of my shoulder, dangerously close to my throat.

I drop Fleur's arm, a section of her hair catching on my wristwatch as I scrabble to fend off the vine. She yelps as a pink lock of it tears from her scalp.

Ripping away the ivy, I toss it, roots and all, onto the table. "That stupid performance of yours just cost us a lot of time. I don't have any more plants down here. Now I'll have to send Lixue to the gallery for another one."

"You don't need another one." With an exasperated sigh, she kneels, gathering the dirt into the cracked pot.

"What are you doing?"

"Fixing it."

"You can't fix it. It's dead."

"It's not dead," she snaps, delicately setting the sagging vine back in the soil. "If you could feel it, you'd know."

"You keep saying that like I know what it means!"

"It's empathy, Doug!" She shoots to her feet, her voice rising. "The basic human ability to share someone else's feelings! But clearly the ability to feel is beneath you, since you're too busy playing god and renouncing your own humanity!"

"I'm not *playing* anything!"

"No? Prove it!" She points at the broken pot, a challenge in the lift of her chin. "Fix something."

I get up in her face, resisting the urge to throttle her. "If I could do that, we wouldn't be having this conversation."

"You can," she says, shoving a finger at my chest. "Gaia gave you that power when she made you a Guard. It's inside you, whether you choose to use it or not."

"I did choose it! It didn't choose me!"

I turn and pace to the other side of the room, disgusted by the flash of curiosity in her eyes. Massaging the flare of pain where she poked me, I drag my phone from my pocket to call Lixue.

"You can have a thousand plants delivered to this room, but you're only going to kill them all," Fleur says irritably. "You'll never learn how to control the magic that way. The nature of earth magic is creative, not destructive. It's different than fire. It doesn't respond the same way water and wind do. Learning earth magic isn't the same as learning to fight."

She draws a deep breath through her nose and stares at the broken pot. Her arms fall loose at her sides, and her eyes take on that faraway look again as they slowly drift closed.

Magic crackles through the room. I lower my phone, cautiously returning to the couch as the plant begins to stir. Fleur gasps. Her eyes pinch with pain, then deep concentration, as the plant pulls itself upright in its pot. Its roots dig into the soil, tiny nubs appearing on the stem and unfurling into bright new spades that spill over the edge of the pot. I grab Fleur's arm as the stems creep toward me.

"That's close enough."

The plant stills. Fleur's eyes open. Her lids are heavy and her arm slides from my grip as she sinks onto the couch, drained and shaken.

"Why did you do that?" That plant had been ripped from its pot. I tore its stem when I threw it. Why would anyone subject themselves to the effort of trying to fix that?

She shakes out her hands, massaging some phantom ache from her muscles. "You can't fix something if you can't acknowledge that it's broken. Before you can heal pain, you have to be willing to feel it, whether it's your own or someone else's." She raises an eyebrow at my blank expression. "Gaia's power wasn't rooted in conflict and dominance. Her magic was rooted in synergy . . . in *connection*. That was how she achieved balance. Until you come to terms with that, her magic isn't going to work for you."

Her gaze drops to my chest. I hadn't even realized I've been rubbing it and I quickly drop my hand.

"The pain you're feeling—"

"I'm not in pain," I snap.

"I've seen it before. It happened to Lyon." My hands curl into fists at the mention of Lyon's name, but she presses on. "After he took Michael's power, he grabbed his chest the same way you did earlier. Gaia said the magic of the Seasons is incompatible with the magic of Time. Their natures are too different. That's why Gaia had to take Lyon's Winter magic from him; he couldn't have both. Eventually, they would have killed him."

"That's a lie!"

"It's advice, Doug! Maybe you should consider that you're in over your head!" She points to the muted satellite images on the TV.

"And why would I listen to any advice from you? You think I'm that much of a fool that I'd give up a single element in my arsenal because you tell me I should?" I choke out a laugh. "You just want me weak when your boyfriend comes. You want to give him a fighting chance. But guess what? He doesn't have one. Jack is fragile. He's *powerless*. I will destroy his weak mortal body from the inside out. And then I'll destroy everyone he's ever cared about, beginning with you."

Static crackles between us. Fleur's eyes lower to my lip as warmth trickles over it. I touch it, my face heating when my fingers come away red.

"You go on believing that," she says. "Go ahead and hold on to all that magic. We'll see who you manage to destroy first."

24

LIKE GHOSTS BY NIGHT

JACK

Ears ringing, I lie on the wavering top of the elevator car, palms resting against the cool metal, blinking up at the faint swing of flashlight beams cutting through the dusty shaft. Kai works fast, jerking the harness from my legs and cutting me free of the rope. "Get up. We have to go."

My head feels foggy, disconnected from the rest of me. I cry out, pain ripping through my arm as she latches on to it and hauls me up. She hefts open the access hatch. It falls against the elevator car with a rattling *smash*. Fragments of stone and dust shower around me, and a bullet plinks down beside my foot.

"Come on," she urges, shoving me toward the hatch as another bullet pings beside us. I drop into the elevator car, hitting the floor with a *thud*. The compartment shakes as Kai drops in beside me and the hatch slams closed.

The darkness inside the elevator car is disorienting. My arm's wet, the sleeve of my jacket sticky and warm. I reach out to steady myself as Kai shuffles away from me.

Her hands slide over the walls. With a grunt, she pries open the elevator doors. Dim red light from an emergency exit sign spills into the car. Broken glass glitters like rubies in the hall. The floor is littered with plaster and debris, and the air is thin and heavy with dust.

Kai crouches beside me. "You okay?"

I manage a shallow nod. She slings my good arm over her shoulder, easing me upright. My head pounds as I follow her to a set of double doors at the end of the hall.

"Spooky down here, isn't it?" she says in a hushed voice. Hairline cracks branch like spiderwebs over the walls, and the steel doors are bent in their gnarled frame. It looks like we parachuted into a war zone.

"Did Fleur do this?" I ask.

"Gaia," Kai says, testing the latch on the door. "When Doug killed her, her magic went apeshit. I was certain it would bring the entire place down. The Observatory was still quaking when I left." She throws her shoulder into the door, but it doesn't budge.

"How'd you get out?"

"Through the catacombs."

"Wait." I take her arm, steadying myself against a wave of vertigo. "You know your way through the catacombs? All of them?"

Kai nods, her eyes reflecting the eerie light from the exit sign above us. There's no power in the catacombs. No cameras. No Guards. If there's a way to pass from wing to wing through the tunnels, we can move through the Observatory undetected.

"Can you show me?"

Kai stiffens. Her head cocks toward a muffled noise on the other side of the broken door. Our eyes catch as the voices grow louder.

"I heard it on the shortwave radio," says a female voice. "A Guard in the Control Room said there was a disturbance in the south portal."

Kai and I back away from the door as footsteps stop in front of it.

"They have to be in here." Another female voice. "It's the only way they could have gotten in."

Kai readies her bow. Drawing an arrow from her quiver, she kneels in the middle of the hall. I palm a knife and press back against the wall.

The door rattles on its hinges. The metal groans, reluctant to open.

"Help me brace it." The male voice is familiar. Probably one of the Guards who attacked us at the villa.

A section of loose rebar slides through the opening. Kai lines up her shot as the gap in the door widens. A shoulder wedges through, the Guard's biceps bulging and the muscles in his forearm straining as he forces it open, holding it for the others.

A long leg in tactical pants stretches through the gap. Kai draws back her bowstring, taking aim as a slender arm and two long auburn braids slip sideways through the opening.

"Wait!" I shout, shoving Kai's bow as the string slides from her fingertips. The arrow flies wide, ricocheting off the wall and skidding to a stop at Amber's feet.

"What the hell are you doing here?" The rush of adrenaline makes me sway on my feet.

"Thank Gaia we found you!" Amber throws her arms around me. My arm throbs as she squeezes the breath from me. "We got a direct flight out of San Diego. Did you seriously think we would let you go after Fleur and Chill alone?"

I pry her away as Julio, Marie, and Poppy slither through the gap in the door. "Sorry, I tried to call, but the battery on my phone died, and I—"

The hall flares with light as Amber conjures a flame. Kai peels another arrow from her quiver, shielding herself behind me as Amber's firelight finds her. "What the hell is *she* doing here?" Amber's flame kicks up sparks. "Stand clear, Jack. I am going to roast her."

"Wait . . ." I raise my hands, nearly falling as I back into Kai's bow. The tip of an arrow slides into my peripheral vision, and I shove it to the side. "It's not what you think. She came to help."

Julio stalks closer. "You'd better explain fast, Jack, because I'm about ready to drown someone." I can't exactly blame him. Julio was the one who yanked three arrows from my back and got stuck performing CPR on my bleeding corpse after Kai skewered me.

Amber's flame roars and Kai ducks behind my shoulder.

Poppy pushes her way to the front of their group. "Knock it off, all of you! And put that fire out. The air's thin enough down here already." Poppy turns her attention to me, her big blue eyes softening when they find me. "It's good to see you, Jack." She plants a kiss on my cheek.

"How'd you get down here?" I ask. Obviously, they didn't come the same way we did.

Julio snatches Kai's bow from her hands. The look she gives him could burn the place down. "We staked out the Winter freight elevator and got a message to Boreas," Julio says, passing the bow to Amber. "He smuggled us down. We've been hiding out in my old room since we got here a few hours ago, but we can't stay there. The whole wing is operating on reserve power. A team of Guards just escorted all the Seasons and Handlers from Amber's old hall and relocated them somewhere else, probably to conserve power. All the systems running to the vacant rooms have been shut down, including ventilation. We can't risk turning on the air. Someone is bound to notice."

Marie checks the hall outside the door. The wheel of her lighter rasps in her pocket as she inclines her head toward Kai. "If we're going to kill Robin Hood, let's get it over with already. We don't have much time before the Guards come to the same conclusion we did and start looking for Jack."

Kai backs away from them, using me as a shield as she pulls me by the shoulder toward the dead end. "I just want to find my sister."

"No one's killing anyone," I say, holding out my arms. Amber and Julio stare at Kai as if they're actually considering it. Sweat soaks through my shirt. The room spins and I shake my head to clear it. The movement sends shock waves of pain through my skull, and I'm pretty sure I'm going to vomit. The tension between Kai and the others feels like it's the only thing holding me up. "Kai knows a way through the catacombs," I say, taking Julio by the arm as he tries to sidestep around me.

Julio and Amber exchange a look. I loosen my grip, dangerously light-headed, as the tension dissolves.

Marie juts her chin at me. "Whatever we do, we'd better do it fast before lover boy over here bleeds out."

Confused, I follow the line of her gaze down my arm. My sleeve's dripping, a steady patter of blood. A pool of it spreads over the floor, almost black under the dim red light.

The room swims. Kai sucks in a sharp breath and Amber swears. Julio surges toward me. The floor drops out from under me as I sink into his arms.

25

ONE STEP BACKWARD TAKEN

FLEUR

Doug stares at me, his hands flexing at his sides. I can't tell if he wants to strangle me or he's resisting the urge to wipe the blood from his nose.

His phone lights up in his hand and he paces away from me, wedging it in the crook of his shoulder. "I told you I didn't want to be disturbed," he snaps, tearing at the loose pink hairs dangling from his watch and stuffing them in his pocket. "How long ago? . . . Where are they now?" His jaw hardens. "You had one job, Lixue. I want this handled. What about the storms? . . . How many more?" He swears quietly, pinching the bridge of his nose. "Get an escort team ready. The Spring and I are leaving, and I want the situation in the south portal under control before we return." He starts to disconnect, then changes his mind. "And bring a toothbrush and some clothes. I can't take her out of here looking like this." He disconnects and drops his phone on the side table.

"Where are we going?" I ask.

"Above ground," he says, dabbing at his nose.

I resist the urge to look at the door. If I can get close to a park or a forest, I can overpower him and escape. I can find Jack before Jack finds me, and get him someplace safe. If Amber and Julio are already on their way here, we can come up with a plan to rescue Chill and figure out what to do with Gaia's magic.

"Don't get any stupid ideas," Doug warns me.

"What are you going to do? Put me in time-out in your big scary bedroom with your ginormous, intimidating four-poster bed and your traumatizing room service? You and I both know you don't want to hurt me."

A few tense minutes pass before there's a loud knock on the door. The taut wire between us snaps as he turns to answer it.

He comes back with a stack of clothes and drops them in my hands.

"Get dressed," he says.

The clothes smell like Gaia. The thought of putting them on makes me ill. When I don't move, Doug pushes me toward the bedroom. I stumble into the breakfast cart, dropping a blouse. As I kneel to pick it up, my gaze catches on the side of the cart. A sticker says it belongs to the north kitchen.

I stand slowly, clutching Gaia's clothes.

The dining hall manager had smelled faintly of Winter. When I lived in the Observatory, I never met Boreas, the retired Winter who helped Jack and I escape through the freight elevator behind the north kitchen, but Jack had described him to me once. The man who delivered the cart fit Jack's description, and he had looked at me strangely when he offered to come back for the cart, as if maybe he knew who I was.

If I passed him a message, could he find a way to get it to Jack?

Doug and Lixue whisper in urgent tones, arguing over some incident in the south portal. I slip quietly into the bedroom and shut the doors. Dumping the clothes on the bed, I tear open the drawers of an antique secretary, rummaging through them for a notepad and a pen.

I write a hurried note to Boreas and fold it into a tight square. Then I change into the slacks and blouse Lixue brought for me and shrug on Gaia's overcoat. The clothes all fit me, even the low heels, and suddenly I want to tear them off.

I turn away from the mirror, tucking the note in my palm before I open the bedroom doors.

Doug's back is to me, his voice clipped as he quietly tears into Lixue for whatever security slip her team must be responsible for. My hand brushes the cart as I pass, sliding the paper under the fruit plate a moment before Lixue comes to retrieve it.

My eyes trail after the cart as she pushes it into the hall.

Doug snatches his jacket off the couch and tucks the cracked potted plant under his arm. "You wait here," he says, not bothering to look at me as he strides to the door.

I rush after him. "You said I was going with you."

"I have something I need to take care of first."

He slams the door behind him, and I kick it, fingers itching at my side. This is the first time he's left me alone in this apartment, and I turn, taking inventory of anything I can use to my advantage. No phone. No computer. No way to communicate with anyone outside. Just a faux window and a stupid . . . TV.

I grab the remote, remembering the black-and-white images of

Chill's holding cell. I don't know as much about technology as Poppy does, but if the TV is connected to a network, there must be a way to get a message out. I flip channels . . . weather, global news, closed-circuit feeds of the Control Room, the Crux, the gallery, and there—Chill's cell.

I click on the menu button and scroll through the options, pausing on the word "camera." The arrow keys seem to control the camera's angle. But there's no audio. No speaker or way to communicate with . . .

Three figures enter the holding area and approach Chill's cell. Doug leads the way, carrying his scythe, and my breath punches out of me as I move closer to the screen. There's something strange about the staff—something wrapped around the head, like a scarf or a sash. Doug glances up at the camera as he talks into his phone. It's as if he's staring right at me.

The image flickers and static fills the screen.

"No," I whisper, frantically pushing buttons. "No!" I race through every channel, but the only ones that work are the weather feeds and the news.

I sink into the couch, the bright blooming splashes of color on the radar images still bursting inside my closed eyelids. I take a slow, deep breath. *Doug won't kill him. Not yet.* Doug's plans are bigger than that; he told me that much. He's just using Chill to get to me. The same way he'll use them all to get to me. Every person I love in this world is on their way here, stumbling into his trap to save us.

There has to be some other way to send a message. Or a way out of this room.

I pitch the useless remote against the wall. The radar maps on the screen are awash in storms. Tidal surges, power outages, fires. My eyes well with tears as I read the news tickers. There are already hundreds of victims. Within weeks, there will be thousands, millions, maybe even billions more.

Soon, what Doug has planned for Jack and our friends won't matter. If I can't find a way to stop him and fix what he's done, we're all going to die—every last one of us.

26

SNOW FOR COLD

◇

DOUG

The Guards in the hall part for me. Their fear is palpable as I stride past them. I gesture for Jora and March to follow me to my office. They stand guard outside as I deposit the plant and retrieve my staff. My burns are still raw, and I slip on a pair of gloves before grasping it. Even through the leather, the staff sends cold flickers of agony through my joints, and I double over at the sudden fire in my chest.

You can't fix something if you can't acknowledge that it's broken. Before you can heal pain, you have to be willing to feel it. . . .

With a barely contained scream, I slash my arm across the desk, narrowly missing the potted plant as I send pens, folders, and a stapler flying.

I'm not broken. There's nothing wrong with me or the magic. I just need time. Time to master it.

Braced against the desk, I focus on my breathing. The pain is nearly intolerable. But pain is an inextricable part of my life now. Power can only come from pain—from conquering it. I can master this magic—all of it.

Jaw clenched against the throbbing ache, I storm from the office with my scythe. My Guards fall in behind me. The pointed heel of the staff taps the floor as I lead the way to the Crux, the blade reflecting their wary expressions as the elevator doors slide closed around us.

Jora and March keep their heads down, refusing to meet my eye in the mirrored walls. Along with the clothes Lixue brought to my apartment earlier, she delivered the kind of news that should result in a mass Culling. If my mood were any worse, I'd have every Guard in the south wing lined up for Termination, but Kai and Jack managed to dispatch four of them before disappearing into the south portal, and I need every remaining, conscious Guard in this place ready at my disposal.

I can't afford any more mistakes. I won't risk underestimating Jack and Kai, who are probably scampering like roaches through the tunnels under my feet. They were never supposed to make it this far. The portals were all manned and armed. Jack and Kai should have been intercepted and captured coming in. And yet one of the few functioning cameras in the south wing captured an image of them ninety-seven minutes ago. And they weren't alone.

I don't know how Amber Chase or Julio Verano managed to penetrate the portals, but I'm damn sure going to find out.

The elevator doors glide open. The Guards follow close enough for me to feel their heartbeats as I storm toward the catacombs. The tunnels to the holding cells narrow around us. A torch roars as I stride past. Fleur's cell door hangs open, and I kick it shut, the loud *clang* reverberating off the walls as I march past it toward Chill's cell.

A camera whines behind me. I turn, watching the lens move clumsily back and forth, as if someone is messing with the remote. I glare into it as I drag my phone from my pocket and dial the Control Room. Bradwell answers. "Disable all the closed-circuit feeds to the TV in my suite." Pocketing my phone, I turn toward Chill's cell.

"Get up," I growl into the shadows inside. I can smell him, his unwashed body and stagnant breath. I snatch a torch off the wall and pitch it between the bars. It lands beside him with a hiss, and he jerks his leg back to keep his jumpsuit from catching fire. "I said, get up!"

Torchlight glimmers in his eyes as he kicks it away from him. He rises slowly, bringing his face close to the bars. This isn't the same timid Handler Denver and I once dragged from the mess hall. Not the same pathetic loser who hid behind a pair of phony glasses and used his Season's reputation as currency to buy a seat at the cool kids' table. Chill's eyes swirl white, his magic building like a storm, waiting for a chance to bury me.

He stares at my eyepatch with blatant disgust. "Where's Fleur?"

"I'm not here to talk about Fleur. You and I are going to have a talk about Poppy."

There's a lengthy pause between his fogging breaths. "What about Poppy?"

"You're going to tell me how the hell she and her friends made it down here."

His knuckles tighten around the bars. "She's here?"

"With Chase, Verano, and their Handler. And you're going to tell me how they got in."

"How would I know? I was asleep when you and your friends snatched me off the ley lines. If Poppy and the others *are* here, I wasn't along for the ride."

"No, but you were instrumental in planning their escape from here, so I'm betting the key to solving this mystery is locked away in your skull, and if you won't tell me how they got down here, I'm willing to crack it just to see what spills out."

Chill takes a step away from the bars. "Do what you need to do, asshole. I'm not telling you shit."

I call over my shoulder for Jora to unlock the cell. Chill fights as the Guards haul him out and Jora cuffs his wrists behind him. She kicks his legs apart and secures each one to the bars.

"Open his eyes," I bark as Chill turns his cheek.

March holds the Winter's head, turning him to face me. Jora pries open his eyelids.

His memories rush me, disorienting and chaotic. I struggle to grasp a single image before the next one starts. A house in Alaska . . . the lake in Cuernavaca . . . a fire in the desert . . . the earthquake in Tecate . . . a beach by a cliffside . . . the back seat of an SUV with his Handler . . . a subway underground . . . a cabin in the woods . . . a boat . . . an elevator . . .

"There." By sheer will, I seize the image. My head pounds as I wrestle to hold it.

A wooden crate rests on a dolly, wheeled by a man with a familiar ruddy face. Money exchanges hands. A set of keys is pulled from the pocket of a kitchen smock. . . .

I bend over my knees, hand pressed to my eye as the sharp pain begins to dull.

Michael never figured out how Jack and his friends escaped. The footage from the cameras around Jack's dorm room had been wiped, leaving mysterious gaps in the recordings on the servers, and the van we'd tracked had been purchased under a fake name. By the time we were able to pin down their location, Michael was more concerned with ending Jack's little adventure than figuring out where it began.

If Michael had seen this moment—this face—in the eye of his staff, he could have put an end to Jack's rebellion before it ever happened. Jack and his friends would all be in the wind.

"When you see Jack," I growl at Chill, "you tell him I have Fleur. And you tell him I'll be waiting for him."

27

THE HEART ACHING TO SEEK

JACK

A cold hand cups my face. My mouth tastes like dust. "Wake up." The sound of snapping. A splash of tepid water, then a sharp, cold slap.

I suck in a startled breath, my eyes flashing open as I struggle to sit up.

Someone holds me upright. Someone else presses a water bottle to my lips. I swat at the arms around me, my left triceps stretching painfully as I shield my eyes from the bright light of a torch. "Get that thing out of my face!"

The torch makes a whooshing sound as Marie wedges it into a hole in the rough stone wall. Stalactites drip from the ceiling, each *plink* bouncing off the high cavern walls. I'm sitting on a stone slab . . . some kind of raised coffin, by the look of it. Rows of them surround me, and more of them are carved into columns in the rock. A giant iron stove— an incinerator with a huge iron door and a tall silver vent—takes up the center of one wall, disappearing into the ceiling above it.

We're in the catacombs.

"What time is it?" I ask, my thoughts becoming frantic. I reach across my chest, fingertips prickling over coarse stitches just below my left shoulder. "How long was I out?"

"Drink." Poppy holds a water bottle in front of me. "The bullet just grazed you, but you lost a ton of blood. You need to hydrate." I open my mouth to argue, but she silences me with a finger. "Drink!"

I take the bottle, scowling around a few cautious sips. Once I'm sure the water won't come back up, I greedily drink the whole thing down. My head spins as I tip my head to get the last few drops, and I lose my balance, slipping off the coffin.

Amber grabs me around the waist, her cold fingers gripping me in place. She lets out a low whistle as she prods my abs. "Holy crap, Jack! When did you get so ripped?"

I shake her off.

"Seriously, Sommers," Julio says. "You've put on a few pounds since I last saw you." He leans shirtless against the rough stone walls, gnawing on a piece of bread. The shredded, bloody remains of his turquoise button-down are still tied around my arm.

"Free weights." I work the knot loose on the tourniquet and shake out my numb fingers.

"Finally got off your ass and stopped feeling sorry for yourself, or were you just tired of suffering by comparison?" he teases.

I arch my back, clenching my teeth against a wince. Amber eases away slowly, as if she's not sure I'm competent to sit up on my own. Marie snaps a first-aid kit closed and sets it down on a flat of bottled waters. A piece of bread hangs between her teeth. She tears off a chunk and holds it out to me. I take it, only because my stomach seems to have a direct line to the nerves in my fingers.

"Where'd we get all this stuff?" I ask.

Julio answers between bites, hitching a thumb at Kai. "The goddess of the hunt snuck some supplies from the kitchen."

Kai flips him off from the dark corner where she's sitting, alone. "You said I could have my weapons back."

"I said you could have your *bow* back. And that's exactly what I gave you!"

"I want my arrows, too."

"Fat chance."

Kai stares at her quiver where it rests on the far side of the cavern. She's the only one *not* staring at me. The air is still wrought with a fragile tension as my friends hover protectively around me.

"I'm fine. See?" I gesture to myself as I stand up. "Totally fine. Let's go." No one moves. "What the hell are we waiting for? By now, Doug already knows we're here. The faster we get moving, the faster we get to Fleur and Chill. Right, Poppy?"

She gnaws her lip. "We were talking on the way down here, Jack. We think . . ." She looks over her shoulder at the others. "We think maybe it's better if Julio and Amber take point on this."

I give a reluctant nod. "Okay, sure. That makes sense." Julio and Amber are the strongest of us. And if anything happens to them, they can heal each other. It's a smart move to put them out front. "Fine. Julio and Amber take point, and Kai and I lead from behind. Got it." Amber and Julio exchange a glance. Marie raises a brow. "What?" I ask, looking between them.

"It's just . . . we thought the Handlers should stay back and support in other ways."

"What other ways?"

"You know, monitoring Julio and Amber's progress from a safe distance."

My narrowed eyes dart from Poppy to Julio to Amber to Marie. They're serious.

"Kai told us everything," Amber says softly. "Doug's looking for *you*, Jack. Not us."

Julio jams his hands in the pockets of his jeans. "The minute he finds you, that's it. It's game over for Chill and Fleur."

Poppy rests a hand on my shoulder. "If the rest of us stay hidden while Julio and Amber look for them, we can buy them more time."

"What?" I step out from under her. "No! There's no way I'm staying back. Kai knows the way. And I know how Doug operates. All I have to do is make it to my smaze."

Amber's mouth falls open. "Yeah, no. That's definitely not a smart plan, Jack. That smaze is a wild card. We have no idea how it will react if you try to take it back—or how *you* will react, for that matter. It's a risk we can't afford right now."

"So that's it?" I shout. "You're just going to stick me in a room and make me watch from the sidelines while you rescue my girlfriend?"

Amber folds her arms around herself, her brows pulled low. "I'm sorry, Jack."

Julio doesn't even have the balls to look at me.

"I told them," Kai says in a low voice, "we were doing just fine on our own. We have weapons, and we have a plan. You're going to find Fleur, and I'm going to find my sister. We don't need anybody else's help."

Julio rolls his eyes. The others ignore her.

"I need to take a leak," I mutter. I don't. I'm just tired and frustrated and I need a minute to think.

Julio inclines his head toward a tunnel at the end of the chamber. "Need me to go with you?"

"Thanks," I bite out, "but I can piss by myself." I touch the knot on the back of my head, careful not to pull my stitches as I limp between the coffins. Kai's eyes flick up to mine as I pass where she sits. There's an urgency in them, or maybe it's rage. But no sympathy. And I'm surprised by how grateful I am for that.

I melt into the darkness of the tunnel and slump back against the wall, listening to the others argue in hushed whispers.

"If Sampson's not screwing with us, then the Autumn wing isn't far," Julio says. "The northwest tunnel should take us close to Amber's room. We can leave the Handlers there."

"Jack lost a lot of blood. We should let him rest here for a while first." *Dammit, Poppy. No.*

"I agree," Amber chimes in. "He's in no shape to be navigating the catacombs. What if he has a concussion?" Like she ever worried about my head injuries before. *She* was the one who gave me most of them.

"We can wait here another hour, then take him to Amber's room," Julio says. "He'll be safe there with the two of you while Amber and I search for Chill and Fleur."

The hell you will, Verano.

I push off the wall, ready to storm out of the tunnel and start a fight, when I catch Kai staring right at me, her eyes burning a hole through the dark.

Her knuckles whiten around her bow. She nods once, the faintest dip of her chin, as if she knows I'm watching. Her mouth moves, her lips forming a single silent word: *Go.*

She juts her chin once toward the tunnel. Her hand slides from the bow to the neck of a water bottle, prying it open as the others continue talking between bites of bread. She sets the bottle down beside her and reaches into her pocket.

What is she doing?

Without a sound, she withdraws a spool of fishing line. She glances up at me as she ties the end of the clear filament to an arrow hidden under her outstretched leg.

Understanding burns the last of the fog from my head. I start backing down the tunnel. That's all the cue Kai needs.

She rolls onto one knee, lifting her bow and taking aim at the torch. Poppy shrieks, ducking her head as the arrow finds its mark. Kai jerks hard on the string, yanking the torch from its hole. The others recoil from the spray of sparks as Kai pulls the torch across the ground, dragging it hand over hand toward herself. There's a shout and a hiss as she empties her water bottle over the flame, plunging the cavern into darkness.

I turn, feeling my way through the tunnel. Kai plows into my back, pushing me deeper into the cave.

"Faster!" She takes my hand, pulling me behind her. Arrows rattle in the quiver under her arm. There's scuffling in the chamber as the others scramble after us. Amber calls my name and Julio swears as the catacombs swallow us whole.

28

A DEEPER ROAR

<u>FLEUR</u>

I've been drifting in and out of sleep for an hour, probably more, my heels hanging over the end of the sofa in Doug's apartment. The security alarm chimes, and I sit up fast as the door flies open.

Doug storms into the room. He strips off a pair of black leather gloves and tosses them on the arm of the sofa as he drops into it, releasing an angry sigh. One of the gloves slips over the edge and falls on the floor, leaving a smear of red on the fabric. I kneel and pick it up.

"Why is there blood on your hands?" I ask. The leather is soaked, staining my fingers. I catch a hint of peppermint and pine. Winter magic.

My breath comes quick when I remember the feed on the TV screen. Doug was carrying his scythe when he visited Chill's cell.

But this blood isn't Chill's. Only faintly tinged with residual hints of magic, it smells too human, as if it belonged to a Winter once.

My mind reels back to Doug's argument with Lixue. The incident at the south portal. Something about a breach . . . "Whose blood is on your hands?"

Doug laughs under his breath, and my knees threaten to buckle.

"What have you done?" The question comes out on a choked sob. The lamp flickers, and I feel the ends of my hair rise. Doug shoots to his feet as I stalk toward him, until I'm standing eye level with the red sprays blending into the patterns on his tie. Tears stream down my cheeks as I kick and throw punches at him.

There's too much blood. Everything about it smells like Jack's.

Doug stumbles back, tripping against the sofa as I shove him. He reaches out, catching my fist as it swings. With a sudden sharp wrench of my arm, he spins me around, trapping me against him, pinning my hands as I try to claw and scratch him.

"Stop it!" I feel the blood soaking into the back of my shirt, and a scream explodes from me.

The floor begins to shake, making the crystal decanter rattle on its tray. Doug grips me tighter as I thrash to get free. The chandelier above us swings, threatening to break loose, but I don't care. I want to bury him under it.

"Calm down!" he shouts, watching the ceiling. I bite down on his arm, tasting the blood on his sleeve and the tang of his magic as my teeth break skin. He barks out a curse.

There's a sudden, dizzying whirl of motion as Doug picks me up and throws me down onto the couch, his face livid. "The blood isn't Jack's, dammit! I said stop!"

The tremors still. He stands over me, his chest heaving, his one eye glittering and wild. His eyepatch has slipped off, and the sight of what remains where his other eye should be steals my breath. The empty socket is black, the burnt flesh surrounding it withered and sunken. I swallow, fighting the urge to be sick. Doug turns away from me, letting his hair fall over it as he snatches his eyepatch from the floor and slips it over his head. He adjusts it to cover his missing eye before brushing back his hair and watching the slowing swing of the chandelier.

"Believe me," he says through his teeth, "when I find Jack, I have no intention of killing him quickly."

"Then whose blood is it?"

"None of your business." He unbuttons his shirt cuffs, tugging up his sleeve. Blood trickles from the bite in his arm, and he frowns at it, then at me, before stripping off the shirt and tossing it in the trash can. "Get your coat. We're leaving as soon as you've pulled yourself together."

I swipe at my lips, surprised by the smear of red on them but not guilty enough to acknowledge any remorse. If he's looking for an apology, he won't get one from me. I stalk to the bathroom and splash water over my face, spitting out the vile taste of him as I rinse my mouth in the sink.

Whatever Doug has planned, our little field trip will get me outside that door. And that means an opportunity to run. To find Jack and the others before they make it here.

29

THE TREE THE TEMPEST

DOUG

The elevator to the surface is slow. Halfway up, the power flickers and the car lurches.

Fleur grips the railing. Her eyes dart skyward as the lights flash on and off, and the car resumes its climb to the east portal. I didn't dare take her through the Winter wing, where Lixue just dispatched four teams of Guards to hunt for Jack. Jack may have come down through the Summer portal, but the Winter halls were his stomping ground. Every map in his footlocker was of the catacombs below the north wing—below my office and my apartment. I'm not ready for that confrontation. Not yet. When I face off with Jack, I will have the eye, and I will have Gaia's magic. Jack may be human, but his friends are not. I won't underestimate them the way Michael did.

The elevator doors open, and the Guard inside the townhouse leaps to her feet. She dips her head. "Chronos."

"Where's my team?"

She gestures to the door. "Already in position."

Lightning flickers through the windows. The wind howls, branches scraping like nails over the siding. I don't relish the idea of going out in this weather, but I have no choice. According to Lixue, we've lost seventeen Seasons on two more continents, and that number will only climb as the storms spiral out of control.

Fleur recoils as I throw open the door and an icy mist blows in. I shove her out into the night, drawing up my collar against the rain as I direct her by the arm toward Greenwich Park.

"I thought Gaia's magic protected the weather here," she says through a shiver, "or did you manage to screw that up, too?"

She's talking about the magic that insulates this region from the constant passage of Seasons through the portals. If I hadn't managed to cage Gaia's magic in that orb, the city would probably be leveled by now.

"I didn't screw up anything," I say, spitting cold rain as it slices down my face. "We are protected. You think it's bad in London? You should see the rest of Europe right now. This," I say, gesturing to the violent sky, "is what happens when you have windstorms in Germany, torrential flooding in Spain, and hailstorms in France. Welcome to the shitshow you and your boyfriend started." Fleur pulls ahead, her intent gaze illuminated by a quick flash of lightning as she cuts through the rain toward the empty park. There's not a soul in sight, no one else crazy enough to brave the storm that's hovered over our region for days. I give her enough rein to cross the street and vault the brick wall onto the grassy knoll. Not far in the distance, I catch the flash of four red transmitter lights. I tap my own, confirming my connection to the Control

Room and ordering everyone to conceal their locations.

A surge of static bites the air as Fleur reaches the oak on the other side of the wall.

"Just so we're clear, I have a team of Guards positioned around us. They're watching everything you do. If you so much as step one toe out of line, your friend Chill will pay the price. And if you even attempt to run, they will hunt you down and end you." The blood on my hands could just as easily have been Chill's, and she knows it.

Her eyes narrow against the rain. The air sizzles as lightning shatters the sky over the park. "What are we doing out here?"

"Resuming class." I gesture to the tree, a grin stretching across my face. "The faster you show me how to control the earth magic, the sooner we go inside."

She scrapes her hair back from her eyes, darting glances into the shadows. Static crackles around her as she flexes her fingers. "Fine," she says, staring at the oak behind me. "Why don't we start with a demonstration?"

Her magic vibrates like a ley line, singing a path under my feet. She jerks her fist. A branch hisses through the air like a whip and slices across my cheek. My hand shoots out to grab it. Fleur cries out as I snap it between my fingers.

She leaps back, clutching her hand. Blood streams between her knuckles, mixing with the rain. Her face contorts with pain as she stares at the misshapen bone in her pinkie.

"I told you not to do that!" My cheek stings.

She drops to her knees, pain and the cold stealing her strength.

"Damn it, we don't have time for this." I summon my Winter magic.

She reels back from me, shrieking as I grab her broken finger with a freezing hand. Pain like a heart attack grips my chest, and she gasps, doubling over as my magic pours into her. Her wound knits together as the bones in her finger straighten and fuse. When it's over, I shove her away from me with a groan.

Fleur clutches her ribs, both of us panting as the pain of the magic ebbs. "That magic . . ." she breathes. "It's going to kill you. No amount of practice is going to save you from that!"

"Only if you don't kill us both first." The park swims as I rub my chest, willing the pain to subside. I've seen some of the scant video footage of Jack and his friends while they were on the run from the Observatory. I know, in theory, how one weak Season and one strong Season can touch and share magic . . . how they can share power and heal each other. But nothing could have prepared me for this. The sudden loss of energy's left me woozy and weak. Fleur, on the other hand, looks like she could summon every tree in this park to level me.

Her eyes dart to a branch above my head.

"Buckle up, *Chronos*," she says, as I reach for my transmitter. "It's going to be a very long night."

30

AGAINST US IN THE DARK

<u>JACK</u>

Kai runs, dragging me behind her, her bow jostling on her shoulder as she whips through the tunnel. Julio's swearing, hollering for Amber to give them some light. A flame roars, and we break right at a fork, out of reach of the fire, my friends' voices fading behind us. The blackness ahead is suffocating, disorienting. I can't tell if my eyes are open or shut.

"How did you do that?" I pant.

"Humans can make magic, too. Sleight of hand. Rabbit out of a hat. Trick of the light. Anyone can do it," she says, pulling me around another corner.

"But—"

"Keep your voice down. They'll hear you."

Kai hangs a sharp left. My shoulder scrapes the wall, the fresh stitches snagging on the rough stone as we change direction. I bark out a swear and jerk her to a stop.

"Do you even know where we're going?"

She claps a hand over my mouth. I don't hear Julio, Amber, Marie, or Poppy anymore, and a ripple of panic washes through me. I tear her hand away and hiss, "We can't just leave them in the dark like that!"

I shield my eyes from the glare as her flashlight flicks on. The soft yellow cone shines up from her pocket, casting creepy shadows over her face.

"If you wanted to go back, you wouldn't be whispering. You don't want to be stuck in some dorm room any more than I do. We'd just be twiddling our thumbs while Amber and Julio get lost down here, looking for your girlfriend."

I grit my teeth, glancing back the way we came.

"Don't worry about your friends. Doug won't be looking for them. He'll be too busy looking for us. They're safer this way anyway."

Torn, I give the tunnel behind me one last look. It all but disappears beyond the glow of the flashlight.

"I'm doing you a favor," she says with a shrug, "but if you don't want to come, don't let me stop you." She slides her bow over her shoulder and starts walking, taking her flashlight with her. I follow, still feeling the pull to go back. But she's right. If they're all busy worrying about me, I'll only slow them down.

"Where are we going?" I ask as the tunnel narrows, forcing me to walk behind her. I duck my head to avoid smacking it on the stalactites hanging from the low ceiling.

"The Winter wing should be about a quarter mile north of us."

My chest feels tight, the walls too close around me, as I consider how easy it would be to get lost down here. To wander through the maze of tunnels until the battery in her flashlight dies and this place becomes one big tomb.

Kai pauses, shining her light at her compass when we come to a fork in the cave. "There's an incinerator duct behind the kitchens under each wing," she explains. "We can climb up and hide in the Winter dorms until we figure out where they're holding Fleur."

"I thought you wanted to find your sister. Isn't her wing directly above us?"

"My sister's a Winter," she says, picking a tunnel and disappearing ahead of me.

"A Winter?" I jog to keep up, stubbing my toe on a rock. "How?" It's rare for siblings to come to the Observatory as Seasons. I've only ever known of one set, twins who came together after an accident when their car skidded off a bridge and plunged into an icy creek. Gaia made them both Winters, assigning them to adjoining regions so they could stay close.

"My sister and I died together. A house fire," Kai explains. "When Gaia found us, we agreed to go with her, but we didn't understand the cost. That we would be different, separated forever. She even put us in different hemispheres. I haven't seen her since." Kai picks up her pace as the tunnel widens.

"When was that?"

"Christmas Eve, 1973."

I pull ahead to walk beside her, but I don't know what to say. "That sucks. I know Gaia was all about balance and everything, but that seems pretty heartless, even for her."

"Yeah, well . . . she and Lyon had their reasons," she mutters.

223

"Why would Lyon have had anything to do with your placement?"

Kai looks at me askance. "It's not important. Water under the bridge, right?"

Maybe. But I can't shake the feeling that something is odd about it. "What's the deal with your sister's name? Not that I'm one to talk, but I thought Ruby was a Summer name. You know, like the birthstone."

"Ruby's her *real* name," Kai says curtly. "And that's how I remember her."

"Believe me, I get it." If anyone understands the significance of a name here, it's me. "What does she go by now? I know most of the Winters in my hemisphere. Maybe I can find out which room she's in." There are only a few hundred Winters on campus. She shouldn't be hard to find.

"Professor Lyon said she goes by the name Névé. Névé Onding."

My breath leaves me. Kai plods ahead, turning over her shoulder to see why I've stopped. My eyes dart over her face . . . her cheeks, her nose, the dip in her chin. I swallow hard, my mind pushing away all the small resemblances that seem so obvious now. This can't be Névé's sister. Not the same Névé that Amber killed at the cabin.

My throat's tight as I remember the feel of Névé's limp mouth against mine, the magic on her breath when I took it as she died.

I look away. At the wall. At the floor. Anywhere but at Kai's face, so I won't have to see traces of her sister in it. "You talked to the professor about her?"

"In secret. He helped us exchange letters for a while."

It sounds like something Lyon would have done for one of his favorite students. Like something he would have done for *me*. That knowledge stirs a fresh wave of guilt inside me. Lyon knew Kai and Névé before I even got here. Not just in passing, but closely. Maybe as closely as he knew me. Yet when I'd called him from the pay phone behind the bar in Oklahoma—when I'd confessed that Névé was dead and I had taken her magic—he hadn't said a word. Not to me *or* to Kai. Why didn't Lyon break the news to her when she came out of stasis? Unless he was just trying to protect me. . . .

He said if I keep you safe, you'll help me free my sister.

Her sister. My *smaʒe*.

Did Lyon send Kai to find me—to *help* me—because he knew we'd be searching for the same thing?

"When was the last time you heard from her?" I hear myself ask.

"A long time ago. We had an argument." Kai glances up, mistaking my stunned silence for curiosity. "Ruby blamed me for what happened to us. The fire was my fault. I left a candle burning in our room and the window was cracked, and the curtain . . ." She closes her eyes with a shudder. "Ruby could always hold a grudge, but after that . . . well, she never really forgave me for that. She never wanted to be here, but I thought maybe . . ." Kai's sigh is heavy. "I thought maybe we could get past it, but Ruby stopped writing back, and after a while, Lyon stopped offering to pass letters for me anyway."

I swallow back the sick taste in my mouth. Kai thought her sister stopped writing because she was angry. But what if she stopped writing and Lyon stopped offering to be their go-between because her sister was dead?

Kai's gaze drops to her hands. "When I was promoted to the Guard, I thought I'd get a chance to see her. Guards have so much more freedom of movement, down here and up top, but I was thrown into training so fast and there wasn't any time. Before they'd even issued me a key to the Crux, I was sent to Cuernavaca to find you. Next thing I knew, I woke up in a cell. And then, when everything blew up with Doug, I had no choice but to run. But I'm here now," she says defensively, as if she's afraid I'm judging her for her choices. Only it's not her I'm judging. I'm judging myself for things she doesn't know I've done. And I'm judging Lyon for keeping them from her. "I came back for my sister," she says with a stubborn lift of her chin. "And we're going to find her."

The hope in her voice is an arrow to my heart. She walks on ahead of me, oblivious to the fact that the person she trusted to bring her here, to help her save her sister, is the very same person who watched her sister die and stole her sister's magic. No matter how long I've spent wanting to jam knives into Kai's back and make her suffer the way I have, how do I tell her that a piece of her sister's soul was once tangled up with mine? That it was inside me, staring back at her on that mountain in Cuernavaca?

"How can you be sure she's still alive?" I call after her.

Kai stops. She turns over her shoulder. "How do you know Fleur's alive? Or Chill?"

"I don't."

"Neither do I," she says quietly, waiting for me to catch up.

31

HOW THE COLD CREEPS

◇

<u>JACK</u>

The walls of the tunnel widen suddenly, opening into a cavern laced with icicles of stone. Kai stops just inside, her flashlight sweeping over the room. She digs in her pocket for a packet of matches. With a snap and a *whoosh*, she lights a torch and nests it back in its hole in the wall.

I turn in a slow circle. More stone coffins, just like the others. "Where are we?"

"Under the Winter kitchen," she says, sliding off her backpack and bow.

For all the years I spent poking around down here, piecing together sections of hand-drawn maps, I can't believe I never found this room. "Who do you think are in these things?" I ask, trailing a finger over the cold stone.

"Where do you think the faculty and staff are buried when they die? Apparently, if you make it through retirement without pissing anyone off, you get to choose." She gestures from the coffins to an incinerator on the far wall. The furnace is identical to the one we just left under the Summer wing, with a wide silver duct rising up from the top.

Kai points to my arm. "Can you climb?"

"Do I have a choice?"

She yanks open the incinerator's iron grate and pokes her head inside, aiming her flashlight up the duct. She tucks the light in the front pocket of her jacket, the beam pointed up. "I'll go first," she says, shrugging on her gear. "Once I'm sure the coast is clear, we'll make a break for the dorms. You'll need to move fast. We'll only have a few seconds to make it past the cameras before someone sees us. Where do you think we'll find Boreas?"

When Kai had asked me where we would start our search once we made it down here, Boreas's name had spilled from my mouth like contraband. He's the go-to guy of the north wing. He hears everything that happens down here, and he's got contacts everywhere, both above and below ground. He'll know where Doug's holding Fleur and Chill.

He'll also know which room was Névé's.

And I'm betting he knows what happened to her.

"We should check the kitchen."

Kai ducks into the incinerator. I peer inside. A ladder runs up one side of the duct, disappearing into the blackness above it. Every word I haven't said rises like bile as she starts to climb. "Kai, wait . . ." She hangs from a rung by one hand, twisting back to look down at me. "Before we talk to Boreas, there's something you should know."

"I already know how Boreas operates, if that's what you're worried about. His reputation wasn't limited to the Winter wing, you know.

Don't worry," she says, turning back to the ladder and scurrying up a few rungs, "Auggie refused to keep the cash I gave him. There should be more than enough to convince Boreas to tell us where Doug's holding Fleur."

"It's not just that, there's something else." I climb inside and grab the first rung, hissing as a stitch in my shoulder pops. A warm trickle of blood slides down my arm.

Kai pauses. "Sure you don't need any help?" she asks, frowning down at me. "It's a long way up. Maybe you should go first."

"Thanks, I'm okay." I let her climb a few more rungs before I follow, careful not to put too much strain on my arm. It feels good to be moving. To be doing something. To have the beginnings of a plan: find Boreas, figure out where Doug's keeping Fleur and Chill, reclaim my magic from the orb in Lyon's office, and then get us all out of here. But what happens once I tell Kai about her sister?

I climb faster to keep up, determined not to think about the pain, or the possible alternative endings to this story. I'll tell Kai everything. Just . . . not now. There's nothing I can do to change what happened to Névé. But if we hurry and stay focused, there's still a chance we can save Chill and Fleur.

We climb two stories, passing through the administration floor to the cardinal wings above it. I nearly collide with the sole of Kai's shoe when she stops.

She presses her ear to the duct before wedging a pocketknife into a seam. With a grunt, she pries a panel loose. Dim light pours in, illuminating a swath of her face as she eases the panel to the floor.

I climb out after her into some kind of storage closet. The shelves are packed with cleaning supplies and kitchen uniforms. Mop buckets and brooms line the walls.

Kai cracks the closet door and peeks down the hall. "The cameras are going to be hard to dodge," she whispers.

"Hold on. I have an idea." I grab a couple of white kitchen smocks and elastic caps from the shelf, just like the ones Boreas gave Julio and me the day he helped break us out of here. Kai and I drag them on over our clothes. I hand her a gauzy germ mask with an elastic band and draw a second one around my head.

Kai's petite frame swims in the smock. An obvious lump protrudes from her back.

"Ditch the bow," I tell her.

She angles away from me. "No way," she says, narrowing her eyes at my arm. A red stain is already seeping through my smock. "You're not perfectly disguised, either."

I grab an apron off the shelf and sling it over my arm.

She rolls her eyes, grumbling to herself as she strips off her bow and tucks it behind a stack of brooms.

We slip out of the closet and head toward the kitchen. The hall is quiet. Too quiet. No clatter of steam trays. No buzzing timers. No hum of exhaust fans sucking up the food smells wafting from the serving stations. A line of abandoned meal carts is parked against one wall, piled high with sandwiches and fruit cups. "Where the hell is everyone?"

"I don't know," she says warily.

The kitchen is dark. Kai tucks herself close behind me, as if she senses it, too—the wrongness of it.

"Boreas?" I call out. His name echoes off the stainless-steel ovens.

The door of the walk-in freezer hangs slightly ajar. A sliver of light spills out of it, stretching toward our feet. I turn toward the high-pitched whine of a camera on the wall. It rotates slowly toward us. Before it catches up to us, I sling the freezer door farther open and usher Kai inside. She sucks in a sharp breath.

"Relax," I say, ducking into the freezer behind her, "it's not that cold in . . ."

Kai's rigid, a hand clamped over her mouth.

"Shit. No!" I rush past her and kneel in the swirling fog around Boreas's feet. He's propped upright on a vegetable crate, his chin resting against his motionless chest. The bald crown of his head is a strange shade of gray, and the chilled air reeks of blood. I press two fingers to the soft, cold flesh at his throat. Boreas's eyes are open, wide and unblinking. A slow trickle of blood leaks from a gash in his throat, trailing into a drain in the floor.

A note is pinned to the front of his shirt.

WELCOME HOME, JACK. I'VE BEEN WAITING FOR YOU.

My hands clench into fists. Boreas and I weren't exactly close, but this . . . this death is on me. Doug literally *pinned* my name to it, killing the one person—the *only* person—left here who could help me and leaving his body in a freezer to taunt me, just to make a point. That even in the coldest room, I'm powerless. Completely vulnerable without my magic. And Doug knows it.

Boreas's head lolls as I tear the note from its safety pin. A lock of bloodred hair falls from the creased page to the floor. The ends are pink.

"No," I whisper. My hands shake as I stoop to touch it. "Fleur?"

Kai drags me back by the elbows. "We have to go, Jack. We have to go now!"

"Where the hell is she?" I croak. "What has he done to her?" I jerk free of Kai and bend to pick up the lock of hair. To clean it off. I can't catch my breath. Can't drag my eyes from that small stained piece of Fleur as Kai takes me firmly by the arm. My stitches pull as she drags me out of the freezer and up against the wall, directly under the camera where Doug can't see us. But it doesn't matter. He's seen enough. He saw that Boreas helped us. He saw that we were coming. Kai said it herself. He's Inevitability. *My* inevitability.

I've been waiting for you.

Kai leads me back down the hall into the closet. She rips off her smock and slips on her bow. "Where do we go, Jack?" she asks, her movements quick, her voice frantic.

I shake my head and drag my fingers through my hair. Doug knows exactly where we are. What we'll do next. He's waiting for me to find him, like this is some kind of game.

"I have to find Fleur and Chill." It's what I've been telling myself since we got on that plane. And now we're here. So close, I'd be able to smell them if I had any magic. But I have no idea where the hell they are. "We have to find them. We have to hunt them."

"How?" She shakes me, leaning into my field of vision. "Think, Jack. Where do we go? Who else would know where to find them?"

"Lyon's office," I say, the closet coming into sudden sharp focus. "There's something in Lyon's office I need to pick up."

32

LET LOOSE BY THE DEVIL

<u>FLEUR</u>

Doug wants a lesson, so that's exactly what I give him. With razor-sharp focus, I summon two roots from the oak. They surge toward his feet, but he rolls to avoid them. While his head's down, I run. The Guards shout, boots pounding the grass from all sides. A red light flashes to my right. The second I'm within reach of a root, I call it to the surface, ensnaring the Guard. There's a sickening *snap* and a brilliant flash as her magic is sucked into the ley lines below us.

A second red light blinks to my left, closing fast. I sling out my arm. The branches of a chestnut whip out as the Guard rushes past it. The Guard screams, and the sky brightens with the flare of her magic.

Another set of boots thunders behind me. My mind grabs a root, and a third flare ignites the park. In the fading glow, I spot the last Guard. He stands in the open clearing ahead, waiting to intercept me. My magic spirals through the earth ahead of me. The ground collapses under his feet, and the sinkhole devours him.

I sprint toward a cluster of trees, slipping behind a wide trunk and pressing my back against the bark. Trying to quiet my ragged breaths, I listen for Doug's footsteps behind me.

"Fleur!" he roars. "You can't run from me!" His feet slow, as if he knows he's close. "There is no escape from this. Not if you want your friends to survive."

Chill . . . I tip my head against the trunk, eyes squeezed shut against the cold rain that spatters my cheeks. Chill would want me to run if it meant saving Jack and Poppy.

A twig snaps. I reach my mind into the soil, searching for his soles against the wet ground.

"I can smell you," he says, his voice low enough to send a shiver up my spine.

My thoughts surge into the branches of the sycamore at Doug's back. With a loud groan, its huge limbs lash around him, dragging him off his feet and slamming him into its trunk. Doug screams at me as the tree forces him to his knees. I swing out from my hiding place, grabbing roots with my mind, coiling them around his wrists and jerking his arms out wide. A vine curls around his head, tipping it back, exposing his throat to me. Another slithers down from the tree, plucking the transmitter from his ear and slinging it into the grass. The red light pulses like a heartbeat between us.

Doug's eye is wide, the rain carving rivers down his face. "What are you waiting for?" he shouts.

I summon a branch and aim it like a spear at his chest.

His breath hitches. All it would take to end his life is a single command from me.

And if he dies, then what? What happens to Time if that magic is lost? What happens to all of us? The transmitter blinks in the grass. If I send Doug back through the ley lines with the rest of his Guards, how long will he sleep? And what happens to the earth while he does?

My spear shrinks away from him. Doug watches me back away as if he has no idea who I am. I can't end this alone. I need to think. I need a plan. I need Jack.

"Fleur, don't do this!" Doug's voice rises to a shout as I turn and break into a run.

City lights flicker through the trees ahead. I sprint toward them, keeping the wind at my back, no idea which direction I'm heading. I'll find a pub or a tavern. Someplace with a phone or a computer I can use. Somehow, I'll get through to Jack.

Doug's scream becomes muffled and distant. In a faint corner of my mind, I feel him hurl himself against the tree's roots. I strain to hold on as long as I can, only letting go when I reach the fence at the farthest corner of the park. I'll be hard to track by scent in the rain. Doug doesn't have the staff with him—he can't see where I'm going.

I cross the road at Crooms Hill, orienting myself by the street signs as the rain blows sideways. Sleet pelts my face, and the wind is nearly intolerable. It must be late. Every store window is dark, and I have no money for a cab. I don't know how long I manage to walk before I spot the orange peaks of a flame ahead.

Teeth chattering, I wander toward it. The smoke billowing from the fire in the barrel smells like burning trash, but I'm drawn to the promise of its warmth.

Other smells reach my nose, and I stop short.

Charred wood . . . dead leaves . . . damp hay.

Autumn.

I take a cautious step backward . . . right into him.

The Autumn's hand snakes around my throat, his gloved fingers digging in. I can't get any air. I grasp out for a root, but there's pavement below me and brick walls tower above me on either side of the street.

"Nasty night for a stroll, Spring." I choke, seeing stars as he pushes aside my hair. "Where's your transmitter, girl? Or are you one of those free-range Seasons we've all been hearing about?"

He shouldn't be here. Not in this region. Not at this time of year.

He must be a rogue. And if he was on the run because he was loyal to Michael, that doesn't bode well for me.

I rake my heel down the Autumn's shin, cutting off his scream when I throw my elbow into his ribs. I scramble out of his grip, but he catches me by the hair and holds me over the edge of the barrel, my face dangerously close to the fire. "I recognize you. You're the Spring who started the rebellion. Guess you haven't heard the news. Gaia is gone. No more natural law. No more boundaries. No more regions or territories. Nothing to keep us from taking what we want." The flame whooshes up with a show of sparks.

"I don't want your magic or your territory." My eyes water and I choke on a lungful of smoke. "Let me go." I reach back for his hand where it's buried in my hair. This cold weather favors him, but if I can just touch him . . .

The Autumn laughs. "You're forgetting who holds the power here."

"*I* hold the power. Apparently, you've *both* forgotten." Doug's cold, rasping voice comes from somewhere behind us. The Autumn goes still, his grip firm as I cough. "Let the Spring go, and maybe I'll overlook it."

The Autumn draws in a breath, scenting the air. "Who the hell are you?" he snaps over his shoulder.

"I'm your new Chronos."

"What if I don't believe you?"

"Then I strongly suggest you turn around."

The Autumn jerks me upright and swings me around. I blink away smoke and see Doug standing in the mouth of the alley, his hands jammed into his pockets and his wet hair dripping in his eye. The facets catch the flames, reflecting them back at us.

The Autumn drops me where I stand, sidestepping away from me. "I'm sorry, Chronos. I didn't realize. Take her. She's—"

I reach for the Autumn, grabbing him by the throat and maneuvering him between me and Doug. The second my bare hands make contact with his neck, his power surges through me, seeking balance with mine.

"Stay away!" I warn Doug as I drag the Autumn backward, stalling for time, starved for strength. The power I took from Doug in the park is already exhausted after fighting and running in the cold. "You stay away from me."

Doug saunters closer, his hands shuffling in his pockets, until he's standing right in front of us.

"If you're going to barter with a life, Fleur, you'd better be sure that life is worth something." The Autumn gasps as Doug plunges a knife into his gut. His body sags, a sudden dead weight in my arms as the prickling pulse of his power fades.

The Autumn drops to the pavement. Doug watches me through the rising sparks of the dying Season's magic, their glow reflected in the hard surface of his eye. When the last spark is in the wind, all that remains is a pile of ash.

The fire in the barrel crackles in the silence.

"I won't teach you," I say, taking a step back from him. "Kill me if you want. I'm not going back with you."

His jaw rocks back and forth as if he's actually considering it. After a moment, he tosses me his phone. I catch it against my chest, the screen coming to life when it falls into my wet hands. A video plays. The image is grainy, a five-second loop of monochromatic snow. But there's no mistaking who I'm seeing, or where they are.

My knees splash into an ash-gray puddle as I watch Poppy and Marie hurry down a hall. Amber and Julio follow them with Jack between their arms. His feet drag along the floor tiles. A dark stain spreads down his sleeve. They're moving fast, past familiar doorways and signs. A dark-haired girl with a pixie cut follows behind them, her face cast in shadows, as they slip off the screen.

I'm too late. They're already here.

I watch the recording loop. Watch them drag Jack's limp body over and over again. He's down there, hurt. They're *all* down there. And I'm up here. And the only way to get back to them is through Doug.

33

TILL THE TREE COULD BEAR NO MORE

<u>DOUG</u>

The Spring and I have been at this for hours, and if it weren't for the pouring rain, I'd burn every tree in Greenwich Park to the ground.

"Show me again!" Rain pours down the neck of my coat. The cold wind sinks in its teeth. No matter how many times I try to grab hold of the branch with my mind and make it do something useful, it won't answer to me.

"There's no point!" Her cheeks are flushed and her teeth won't stop chattering. "I told you already, it's not something you do. It's something you feel!" All I feel is utter exhaustion and a persistent nagging pain that seems to worsen the more I attempt to use the very magic I'm expecting her to teach me. It's as infuriating as my ability to stop time. I can occupy space, but I can't affect anything.

"I was close last time. I was inside the damn tree, and I felt myself pushing!"

"You only felt *yourself*, Doug."

"The branch moved. You saw it! All I need to do is learn how to——"

"This isn't working! I want to go inside."

I grab her by the front of her jacket. "I said, show me!"

"I'm tired." Her voice breaks, and she wavers on her feet. "It's too cold out here. I can't . . ." She teeters, sways. Her eyes roll back into her head and her body falls sideways, collapsing into the muddy grass.

I kneel beside her, swearing under my breath. Her skin's cold to the touch, her slack eyelids unresponsive when I slap her cheek. I could summon my Winter magic and try to bring her around, but last time I gave her an ounce of power, she took down all four of my Guards and handed my ass to me. It's nearly three in the morning. We're both soaked to the bone, frozen and hungry and raw, and this is getting me nowhere. I slide an arm under her knee and haul her against me.

Her head swings loose on her neck, rain pooling in the dip between her collarbones and trailing down the neck of her shirt. Her eyes roll under her lids, flickers of her memories appearing to me in distracting flashes through the narrow slits as I stumble through the park gate. Thunder rumbles in the distance. My soaked boots tread through puddles in the street. By the time we make it back to the townhouse, Fleur's shivering violently.

I kick the front door. A hand peels back the curtain over the sidelight. The face of the same nervous Guard from before appears through the glass. As soon as the door cracks open, I shoulder through it. Fleur's lips are blue in the dim light of the foyer, and I curse myself for missing the signs. She's not Gaia. Not a Guard or a god. She's a Spring, and this weather isn't warm enough to sustain her.

The Guard locks the door and rushes after us toward the stairs to the cellar. "Is everything okay, Chronos? Can I do something?"

"Stay out of my way." I shift Fleur upright and sling her over my shoulder. Her dead weight swings against my back as I descend the narrow stairs and pound the button for the elevator. The doors slide open and I heft her inside. Rainwater drips from her hair, spattering the floor, as we make the long trip down.

The Guards in the Crux back away as I emerge from the elevator with Fleur on my shoulder.

"Get Commander Lixue on the phone," I snap as they part for me. "I want fresh towels, extra blankets, and a change of clothes delivered to my suite. And a meal cart with something hot to drink."

"Yes, Chronos." They lower their heads as I brush by. I've grown used to it, their aversion to my eye, as if they're unsure how much I can see in theirs and they're not willing to take any chances. If I thought they were bowing their heads out of respect for my position, maybe I'd be happier about it. But most of them are doing it because they're hiding something and terrified of the consequences. The more of my own people I'm surrounded by, the fewer of them I trust. Loyalty motivated by fear is easily won, but those bonds are just as easily broken. Any one of them would turn on me to save their own skin. At least Fleur has the guts to fight me.

One arm around her knees, I use the other to unlock the door with my key card and swing it open. Plaster dust and broken glass still litter the carpets in my suite. It crunches under my boots as I carry Fleur into the bathroom and crank the shower as hot as it will go.

She slides from my shoulder like a limp rag, refusing to be held upright. Needles of hot water seep through my clothes as I brace her against the shower wall and she slumps to the floor. Her skin's rippled with goose bumps, and a pink flush creeps over her neck.

I squat beside her, tapping her cheek. "Fleur, wake up." Her heavy lids pry open, her dark eyes slow to focus on me.

I wait for her to push me away. To lash out.

"I'm hungry," she rasps.

I get to my feet and stand out of the spray. "I've already ordered food."

Fleur watches me, hands braced on the shower basin beside her, as I back out of the shower. When I'm sure she's not going to drown, I grab a towel from a stack on the counter, mopping my face as I leave her alone in the bathroom. I shut the bedroom doors behind me, trailing water over the carpet as I head to the living room. There's a meal cart in the middle of the room and a pile of extra blankets and fresh clothes stacked on the arm of the couch.

As I peel off my jacket, something falls to the carpet—a broken twig with four pathetic buds that must have gotten stuck inside my clothes.

I rub my chest, twirling the torn stem, thinking back to the things Fleur said about feeling pain.

My thoughts reach out toward the plant, bouncing off its membrane when I push too hard too fast. I try again, a careful, curious brush of my thoughts this time, and I'm rewarded with a sharp sting. I breathe through it, sliding deeper inside the plant's skin, conforming to its shape. I imagine my lungs expanding. Imagine my fists uncurling. The buds shiver, then slowly open, their leaves unfurling right in front of me.

The bedroom doors snap open. Fleur stands in the gap between them, her hair wrapped in a towel, clutching the collar of a long bathrobe tightly closed. Her eyes dip to the plant, then lift to my face. A flash of fear passes over them.

I jerk my head toward the cart, tossing the branch in the waste bin. She rushes to turn over the silver domes, her hands moving furtively around the edges of the tray as if she's looking for something. "What did the kitchen send for dinner?" she asks, lifting a plate and brushing her fingers under it.

"If you're referring to Boreas, he's dead." The plate clanks quietly against the tray as it slides from her hand. "You asked me whose blood I was wearing. Now you know."

She moves away from the cart. Face paling, she takes the pile of Gaia's clothes in her arms and holds it to her chest. Then she disappears into my bedroom and locks the doors.

34
HEAPS OF BROKEN GLASS

JACK

The rec rooms in the Winter wing are conspicuously vacant, the training rooms silent, the hallways dark. Usually, Kai leads the way, but since we left the kitchen, she's trailed behind me, her eyes darting to every doorway we pass as if she expects her sister to be standing in it. Dorm room after dorm room . . . every door is shut. The Observatory feels abandoned, dead inside, eyes closed, fists clenched. But as we move through the halls on silent feet, listening to the murmurs of tense voices through the walls, it feels like we're being watched, as if every Season and Handler trapped in these halls is holding their collective breath, waiting for something.

The hum of an urgent conversation quiets as Kai passes close to one of the doors. She raises a fist to knock, her mouth parting to call out to whoever's inside. I reach for her hand to stop her, mouthing the word *no*.

"Shouldn't we let them out? They're trapped."

"They're safer if they don't see us," I whisper. I move away from the door, towing Kai behind me as the girls inside start banging and calling out to us. There are hundreds of Seasons and Handlers down here, trapped in their rooms. We can't possibly save them all. As we pass Gabriel's and Yukio's old rooms, I have to remind myself they're gone. In the wind. I could try knocking on a few other doors of Seasons I knew, but anyone who knew me well enough to help me is probably under surveillance. I can't risk drawing attention to this wing. Not until I've found what I came for.

Lyon's old office is tucked deep in the Winter wing. I never thought much about it before, but in hindsight, its remote location makes sense. Gaia would have wanted to keep Lyon far from Michael's sight, well off his radar. I only hope the cramped, dusty office—and the orb Lyon was keeping inside it—is off Doug's radar, too.

Kai stalls in front of every bulletin board we pass, skimming the posted announcements with her flashlight, probably searching for her sister's name. I maneuver through the halls quickly, sticking to the darker corridors without power, forcing her to keep up. Her shoes splash in puddles left behind by broken pipes, the clack of her bow against her quiver letting me know she's still behind me.

I jerk to a stop.

Kai slams into my back, and I hold up a hand to silence her. The door to Lyon's old office hangs open. Instinct makes me draw a breath, desperate for any clue to what might wait for us inside. But all I smell is plaster dust and my own sweat.

I creep closer. Kai's bow no longer rattles, and I glance back to see she has her weapon already drawn. Hugging the wall, I peer inside. The hinges whine as I nudge the door open wider.

Kai lowers her bow. My breath punches out of me as the red light of the hall washes over the room.

I step into the smell of chalk dust and the faint remnants of Lyon's cologne. The orb and its bronze pedestal are gone. His desk lies on its side, the drawers emptied and their contents strewn. The spines of his favorite books are splayed wide, their pages torn, tossed in piles on the floor.

I turn his chair upright. Broken glass crackles under my feet. The shards are curved and thick, and I sink down into the chair with my head in my hands, staring at the remains of the shattered orb.

My smaze is gone.

How much had Doug seen in Lyon's and Gaia's eyes before he killed them? Did Doug break the orb while they were ransacking the room searching for something else, or did he know the smaze in the orb was mine? I rock back in the chair, my throat thick, as I imagine all the things Doug could have done with it.

"We should go," Kai says gently, her tone less urgent than before, as if she knows how close I am to breaking. As if she understands a piece of me died the minute I walked into this room. "We can go back and hide in the catacombs until we figure out what to do." She touches my shoulder.

I lift my head, giving myself one last look at the room. A reflection above Lyon's desk catches my eye, the wink of light on glass over the faded poster of Cuernavaca that always reminded me of Fleur. I spent countless hours sitting in this chair staring at it over the past three decades. It's always hung in the same spot, the adhesive so old, it may as well have been cemented to the wall. Strange that Lyon suddenly decided to frame it.

The leather groans as I rise to my feet, remnants of the orb crunching beneath them as I cross the room and pluck the frame from the wall. I hold it in both hands, my eyes tracing its edges. Kai gasps as I smash it against the wall.

Glass rains over my shoes. Shaking the loose shards from the frame, I lay it facedown across the arms of the chair, peeling back the edges of the poster inside. A folded piece of paper is taped to the matting. I set the frame on the floor, unfolding Lyon's letter as I drop into his chair.

> *Jack,*
>
> *If you're reading this, then the worst has come to pass. I've always tried not to put too much stake in fate. I had hoped things might work out differently, and yet if you're here, it seems my efforts to shift the tide were unsuccessful, making this moment inevitable. My only regret was not having the chance to see you one last time, to tell you how much you've come to mean to me. There are so many things I wish I could have explained. Letting you go hasn't been easy. I can only hope, in the end, it was the right thing to do.*
>
> *Do not mourn Gaia or me. Remember, we are only matter in a closed system, incapable of being created or destroyed. We are simply changed, from one form to another. Believe me when I tell you I am still here, in every lesson and every conversation we've ever shared. Hold fast to those talks, as I have while I sit before the empty chair you occupied on so many occasions, your energy so very much alive in this room as I write this final farewell to you.*

Not long ago, I made you an oath. I swore I would protect you. That I would keep you safe should you ever feel a need to return here and find yourself. I've done all I can to honor that promise.

A piece of each of us lives on here in the Observatory, Jack.

Go back to your beginnings for the answers you seek. Find those missing pieces. Breathe deeply and remember the lion that you are, but be mindful: broken teeth can be sharper than we realize. Take care not to harm those closest to you.

With gratitude for all you've given me and hope for all I've seen in you,

Professor Daniel Lyon

"Jack, the Guards could patrol this hall any minute. We have to go." Kai peers through a crack in the door, bouncing on her heels, but I can't stop staring at Lyon's note.

The note. The travel vouchers. The request he made of Kai . . .

Lyon knew. He knew this exact moment might happen. Had known long enough that he had tried to change it, all the while making contingency plans in case he failed. He knew that I would come here. That I would sit in this very chair, ankle deep in broken glass, mourning his loss, searching for Fleur while Doug ransacks the Observatory, taking lives and stealing souls, probably wearing my smaze like a goddamn trophy.

Lyon knew, and he planned, and he never told me.

I read the note again, my brow crumpling over his words.

Breathe deeply, he tells me, *and remember the lion that you are*. But I've never felt more powerless than I do right now.

I swore I would protect you. That I would keep you safe . . . I've done all I can to honor that promise.

How the hell has he honored that? How could he possibly think it was safe to leave a piece of my soul vulnerable in this room? I crumple the note and pitch it at his toppled desk. He knew the havoc Doug would wreak on this place. So why did he leave the orb here, my soul and magic trapped and exposed, where Doug was sure to find it? Why not hide my smaze, too?

I bury my head in my hands, elbows on my knees, staring at the chaos on the floor. The room looks like a tornado rolled through it.

I lift my head.

Bending to retrieve a curved shard, I hold the piece of the orb in front of me.

Letting you go hasn't been easy. I can only hope, in the end, it was the right thing to do.

Ignoring the sting, I drop to my knees in the glass and sift through the debris.

"Jack," Kai whispers, "what are you doing?"

I turn over books and papers, shove aside a fallen lamp. "It's not here." Hope swells inside me as Lyon's message begins to make sense.

"Whatever you're looking for, Doug probably destroyed it. And if any of his Guards find us in here, we're definitely going to be next!"

I push aside empty drawers and Lyon's scattered files. "Not the orb. The pedestal. The pedestal is missing." The bronze stand that held up my orb . . . I don't see it anywhere. If Doug had shattered the orb, the stand would be here.

With an impatient huff, Kai peels herself from the doorframe and gets down on her knees a few feet away from me. Glass tinkles and papers shuffle. "Please tell me why we're risking our lives searching for a glorified cake stand."

"Because I don't think it's here."

Kai stops rummaging. She crouches on the other side of the desk, gaping at me as she brushes her sweaty hair back with her sleeve. "And this makes sense how?"

"I don't think Doug shattered the orb. I think Lyon did." Even if Lyon couldn't see beyond his own death in the staff, he had to know the Observatory would crumble under Doug—that the entire place would fall into chaos. It's easy to conceal something in a mess. "I think he shattered the orb and set my smaze free, then hid the stand so Doug wouldn't know what he was looking at when he got around to searching in here. If my smaze is free, I can still find it."

And once I do, I'll be strong enough to get Fleur and Chill out of here.

Kai disappears behind the desk. A soft creak is followed by a hollow thud. "Whoa," she whispers.

"What is it?" I round the desk. Kai's bent over a square cut into the floor, the hinged wooden panel resting open beside her.

"A hidden passage." She turns on her flashlight and shines it into the hole. "This must connect to Gaia's suite."

"Why would you think that?"

She stills, her mouth opening and closing again as she shrugs. "Just . . . you know . . . rumors. After Gaia and Lyon fled the Observatory during the rebellion, people talked. If they really were secretly in love, plotting to be together for years, they must have had a way to be together without Michael knowing, right? I bet this was it." She turns back to the passage too quickly, as if she's uncomfortable meeting my eyes. She leans down into the hole, one hand braced on the lip, the other holding her light. Her hand slips off the edge, and I grab the back of her jeans before she goes tumbling through the opening. Papers crunch under my fist as I haul her upright.

"What's this?" I ask, catching the thick stack of folded sheets as they slip from her back pocket.

"Nothing." She reaches around me, desperate to get it back. But she's too short and my arms are too long, and in a second, I have the folded papers peeled open. At first, I can't make sense of the sketch—a cross cuts through the middle of the page, each cardinal point snaking off the edge of the paper. The perfectly straight lines bisect a labyrinth of softer curving, forking ones. Tunnels. Dozens of them. Swirled with narrow sets of hidden circular stairs, all labeled in Lyon's handwriting.

"This is a map of the catacombs." My eyes dart over Lyon's neatly printed markings. The paper is thin, the ink faded with age and the creases worn. "Where did you get this?"

"It's mine," she says, still reaching for it. "Lyon gave it to me."

"When?"

"A long time ago. Give it back!"

I hold it higher, out of her reach, the light from the hallway shining through the paper, revealing other faint markings. A second piece of paper clings to its folds, and I peel the pages apart. This second map is familiar, full of landmarks I recognize. The Crux at its center, the Control Room below the east wing. The Hall of Records below the west. And to the north and northeast, two expansive apartments, one labeled

"Chronos's Suite" and the other "Gaia's."

A thin dotted line connects Gaia's apartment to a space below the Winter wing, close to where we're standing. I hold the two maps together against the light, overlapping their creases until they're perfectly aligned. Four lines disappear off each end of the page, one in each wing, marked "emergency escape routes."

"This is how you found your way out when you ran from Doug," I say, tracing the exits. These were the tunnels I spent years searching for—the ones Lyon caught me looking for and knew I was desperate to find. "Why didn't you tell me you had a map?" For that matter, why hadn't Lyon?

I tip the page, angling it to read Lyon's markings and notations. Directly under the Control Room, a stairwell opens into a corridor flanked with nearly a dozen small square rooms. Holding cells.

I turn to face her, keenly aware of the bow at her back. "You told me you had no idea where Doug was keeping Fleur. Why would you keep this from me?"

She eases away from me, one hand poised to reach for her quiver. Her eyes are wide, her cheeks streaked with cavern filth. Lyon trusted Kai. Trusted her enough to give her a map he hadn't even shared with me. Why? What else were they hiding from me?

"Who were you to him?"

"Someone who could help you."

"Before or after you shot me?" She flinches as I back her into a corner. "Who were you to him when he gave you this map?"

Her heel connects with the wall. "I was lost, like you! I was alone and scared, and I just wanted to be with my sister. Lyon gave me the map, and I thought he could help us, but I was wrong."

Her admission feels thin, like she's hiding something. "What aren't you telling me?"

"Nothing." Her sigh is shaky, like she's trying not to cry. "I screwed up. Lyon gave me this map because he trusted me. I broke that trust when I joined the Guard. And now I'm trying to fix it. I'm trying to help you. That's all."

"If you were trying to help me, why didn't you tell me about the map?"

"Because I didn't trust you not to take it and ditch me. And I need you to help me find my sister."

She didn't tell me about the holding cells because she wanted me to take her to Boreas, so she could find her sister first. Her sister, who tried to murder my friends for a bounty. "Good luck with that." I fold the map into my pocket and turn for the door. Lyon kept things from me. Kai kept things from me. The only person I trust right now is myself.

"Wait," she cries, rushing after me. "You still need me. I can still help you."

"Thanks, but I think I can navigate this place on my own."

"You're a fool if you think you can take Doug down by yourself."

"Believe me, you're the last person I want watching my back."

"Because you don't need a spotter, right?"

"Right."

"That's bullshit. If you really believed all that, you'd be forced to admit that Fleur doesn't need *you*." I jolt to a stop as those words slide deep under my skin. "Everyone needs someone to look out for them, Jack. Even you. I can help you find her. And if your magic is down here,

I can help you find that, too."

My fists flex at my sides. Maybe it's this room. The smell of it. Maybe it's that hole in the floor or his damn leather chair. Maybe it's his letter in my pocket, all those carefully chosen words so fresh in my mind. But I can practically feel Lyon's presence here. I know exactly what he would say. He'd tell me to take help where I can find it, to take others' strength when it's offered. That there's a reason he gave her this map all those years ago and never gave it to me. That there's a reason he never told Kai what happened to Névé. I just haven't figured it out yet.

Glancing up at the empty space on the wall where Lyon's poster used to hang, I whisper, "You'd better be right about this," hoping a part of him is still here. That a part of *me* is still here. And that somehow, we'll be able to find it in time.

35

TRUSTING FEATHERS AND INWARD FIRE

FLEUR

I dress quickly, zipping on a fresh jumpsuit and dragging one of Gaia's wool sweaters over my head, uncertain how much time I have left alone. I remove the key card from the pocket of the bathrobe without looking at it and tuck it inside my sock, concealing it against the sole of my foot. I slipped it from Doug's coat pocket as he knelt beside me in the shower. All I have to do is find a way out of his suite and come up with a plan.

Doug's mastered the basics—feeling his way past boundaries, stretching his mind inside a plant as deeply as it will go until the connection to the host is deep and stable. Like sliding his fingers into a snug leather driving glove, any movement the hand makes, the glove is sure to follow.

I didn't think he'd learn so fast. I thought I'd have more time. Now that he's had a chance to practice, it won't be long before he tries to take Gaia's magic again. If he fails like he did before, he's likely to bring the entire Observatory down on our heads. And if he succeeds? Assuming the magic doesn't tear him apart first, the next thing he'll do is go after Jack. I can't let that happen.

A door slams in the living room. I pause, hand braced on the foot of the bed, the other sock pulled halfway over my foot, listening for voices outside. I drag up the sock, cracking open the door to find the living room empty. Doug's jacket is gone from the arm of the couch.

I nearly trip in my hurry to fish the key card from my sock as I race to the door. I wave it over the sensor, but the light doesn't turn green. I swipe again. Not even a blink. I tear through the apartment, searching drawers and cabinets, behind picture frames and TV monitors, unsure what I'm looking for. *How would Jack get out?*

I stand on a chair and rattle a vent on the wall, but even if I could get it open, it's too small to fit through.

A shiver crawls over the back of my neck. Another creeps up my pant leg.

I yelp as I whirl around. A smaze hovers in the air right in front of me.

"You," I whisper. "What are you doing here?"

The little dark cloud twists and rolls, spinning in circles as if it's trying to get my attention. It flies past me into the living room, then doubles back, only to zip away again, as if it wants me to follow.

It hovers beside the credenza.

"What? I don't understand."

The smaze stretches itself thin, diving behind the cabinet and popping out again. It lingers there, watching me. Then it slides back between the cabinet and the wall until it feels like we're playing a game of charades.

"Look, I don't have time for hide-and-go . . ." *Seek.*

It wants me to find something.

I lean over the credenza, but it's snug against the wall and I can't see anything through the narrow space behind it. Grabbing one side, I heft it a few inches. A large metal grate is screwed to the wall—an intake vent, big enough to fit through. When I turn around, the smaze is gone.

Heart racing, I lean my shoulder against the cabinet and push. The plush carpet fights me, but I manage to shove it out far enough to wedge myself into the gap.

Screwdriver. I need a flathead screwdriver. Or a knife. Or a letter opener.

I run to the antique secretary in the bedroom, but it's been emptied of anything sharp. I try the bathroom, flinging open cabinets and drawers, frantically unzipping a small leather grooming kit. The scissors are conspicuously gone, but the dull metal nail file might do the trick.

My hands shake as I fit the file into the groove in the head of one of the screws. The file slips and my knuckles graze the edge of the grate. I try again, managing to loosen all four screws until the grate slides away from the wall. The air inside the duct is musty and cold. I crawl in on hands and knees, wondering how I'll navigate the ventilation system once I'm deeper inside, when the light trickling in from the apartment finally fades behind me. I'd give anything for a transmitter right now—to hear Jack's voice in my ear, telling me where to go and how to find him.

My startled yelp echoes when I come face-to-face with a ghostly shadow.

The smaze darts ahead, waiting for me at the end of the first turn.

"Hang on, Jack. I'm coming," I whisper as I crawl through the air duct after it.

36

BEFORE I SLEEP

JACK

Two years ago, the prospect of hunting wouldn't have been so daunting. It would have been as simple as drawing a breath. Now I don't even know where to start.

"Where are we going?" Kai's voice echoes through the tunnel, the toes of her shoes catching on my heels as I walk. I glare over my shoulder and she hangs back a bit. Just enough so she won't keep tripping me.

"We're going to my room." In his letter, Lyon said I should go back to my beginning to find what I seek. My old dorm room was the first and only home I ever knew here.

"Are you crazy?" Kai squeezes alongside me, forcing me close to the wall. "Doug knows we're here! He's probably got Guards staking out your room. What makes you think he won't be waiting for us inside?"

"You have a better suggestion?" I pause at a fork in the tunnel. Flashlight clamped between my teeth, I peel open Lyon's hand-drawn map and hold it in front of me, comparing it against the two paths ahead. I turn left. After a few paces, the tunnel ends abruptly.

Kai huffs. "Give me the map."

"Not on your life."

"Clearly, we're lost."

"*You're* lost. I know exactly where I am." I shine the light at the wall in front of me, turning slowly in the confined space. The walls are solid, but there's supposed to be some kind of stairwell here. Or at least, there was once. I run my fingers over the grooves in the stone, wondering if Chronos cemented over the whole thing years ago. That would be just my luck. I bring Lyon's drawing close to my face, squinting to read the tiny lines.

"For Chronos's sake, would you give me the damn map already? Why are men so reluctant to ask for help?"

"I'd as soon let you take my smaze as let you take this map."

"I'd *never* take someone else's magic."

I'm grateful she can't see my wince in the dark. "You'd be surprised what you might do if you thought someone you loved was going to die."

"What you're doing isn't the same, Jack. That smaze belonged to you. Reclaiming something isn't the same as stealing it," she says thoughtfully. "Besides, I can't take anyone's magic. I'm human."

"So am I."

"But your magic is part of you. It has a connection to you. It should be drawn to you. And Lyon already said it was possible for you to reclaim it."

"He never said it would be easy." I scratch the back of my neck, finding it hard to look her in the eyes. "What about yours? It must be in the Observatory somewhere."

She shakes her head, resting her weight against the tunnel wall. "The orbs were all smashed in the quake. It was lost during the Dismantling."

"I'm sorry."

"It's okay," she says with a tight smile. "I've made my peace with it."

"How do you make your peace with something like that? Doug promised you he'd help you and he lied through his teeth. Because of him, you'll never have it back."

"Maybe I don't deserve it," she says quietly. "I didn't have to help him. I made that choice. And now I have to live with the consequences. It's too late to save my magic. The only part of me left here that matters now is Ruby." She pushes off the wall and shifts her bow higher on her shoulder. "I guess we're kind of like you and your smaze. . . . Ruby and I haven't been together in a long time, but we'll always be connected. I have to believe I'll find her. That when I do, she'll come with me."

Guilt lodges in the back of my throat as she turns to walk back the way we came.

"Kai, wait. There's something I need to tell you—"

A low rumble starts under my feet. The ground begins to shake. I brace my hands against the sides of the tunnel as dust and pebbles clatter over us. Kai ducks, her eyes wide with panic.

"What's happening?" she asks. The ground shudders once more, then goes eerily still.

"Pretty sure that's Fleur." An awed smile tugs at my lips. "And I'm guessing she's pissed."

Kai watches the ceiling, swallowing hard. "Maybe when you find her, you can ask her not to do that again."

We wait, listening for an aftershock. The cave whistles softly. The edge of the map flutters as a cool draft hisses through a new crack in the wall. I trace it with my light to a hole in the ceiling. Kicking aside a pile of fallen stones, I stand underneath the hole and shine my light up. The beam reflects off a short metal rail.

Those weren't stairs on the map. It was a ladder.

"Give me your bow," I say, tucking the flashlight in my shirt pocket so the beam points up. Reluctantly, Kai shrugs out of her bow and hands it over. I lift it high, catching the bottom rung with the hooked end. The ladder slides down with a shriek.

Dropping to a crouch, I lace my hands together and boost Kai up. She scales the rungs ahead of me, as eager to be out of the dusty, claustrophobic space as I am. I jump, and the ladder trembles as I snag a rung and haul myself up after her. My shoulder aches, and with a pang, I wonder where Amber, Julio, Poppy, and Marie are. If they felt Fleur's quake and experienced the same relief I—

An aftershock rocks the ladder, raining loose shale over our heads. Kai shrieks, losing her grip. She grasps a rung as she slides, her foot catching on my shoulder as she scrambles for leverage. We hold fast, waiting for the tremor to still.

"Hurry," I tell her. "Before the next one."

We clamber up the last few feet to an opening in the floor above us. Kai wriggles out of the tunnel, then reaches down and helps me through. My light bounces off walls of metal shelving.

"Where are we?" Kai asks.

"If Lyon's map is right, we're in a maintenance closet close to the Crux." I dust myself off and crack the door. The overhead lights in the hall flicker like strobes. I duck back from the opening as a team of Guards ushers a group of Seasons and Handlers out of their rooms toward the Crux. The Winters' arms are weighed down with backpacks and luggage, as if they're being moved to another hall. I recognize a few of them. Kai peeks over my shoulder through the crack, hoping for a glimpse of her sister. Guards holler to each other on the other side of the plexiglass port at the end of the corridor. One of them points to his computer monitor, smacking its side. I glance up at the nearest camera, but there's no blinking red light.

"The quake must have taken down the network. Come on." Once the group has cleared the Crux, I lead Kai through the corridor, away from the Guards. Voices bark down the hall. My hands shake with adrenaline as I kneel in front of the door to my old dorm room and slip a set of picks into the lock. Kai draws her bow, aiming it toward the sound of approaching boots.

"Jack?" she whispers.

"I'm hurrying."

"They're coming!"

A flashlight beam rounds the bend as the final pin slides home. I turn the knob, dragging Kai inside and shutting the door behind us. I fall back against it as the Guards thunder past, only flipping on my flashlight once I'm certain they're gone.

The sight of my old dorm room brings a rush of memories. I do a quick pass through each room, tearing open the shower curtain, swinging open every door and checking under the beds, trailing a string of soft curses when there's no sign of my smaze anywhere.

Kai's sprawled on the floor, staring at the ceiling as she recovers her breath.

"Looks like someone beat us here," she says. Piles of loose papers and files are scattered around her. Our ratty old couch is flipped upside down, the hard drive's dismantled, and the glass top of Chill's desk is cracked. My stasis chamber is gone, its wiry guts dangling from the wall.

I kick aside Chill's keyboard, a sudden heaviness settling in my chest. The room still smells faintly like him. Like Dorito cheese and contraband beef jerky. With a pang, I bend to pick up the remains of his plush polar bear. Its seams are ripped open, the stuffing spilling out. I carry it into our old bunk room and set it back on his bed. My closet doors hang open and my old rolled-up sketches of the Observatory are gone. And the footlocker where I kept Fleur's ornaments . . .

I slam the closet door and drag my hands through my hair. I should have paid Boreas to pack them up and store them. Should have asked Lyon to ship it all to our home in Cuernavaca. And now Doug's taken them. I can guess why he'd want the maps, but why her ornaments?

Rubbing my eyes, I lumber back to the front room. Kai's righted Chill's desk chair. She plops down into it, tearing open a bag of chips. She holds one out to me. "I found them in a drawer. Candy bars, too," she says. "And there are some bottled waters in the mini-fridge under the window—"

"I know where my own mini-fridge is," I say irritably, ripping the bag from her hand. "These are Chill's."

With a scowl, she snatches it back, tucking a chip forcefully into her mouth. "In case you haven't noticed, we haven't had anything to eat besides bread and water since we got to London. I don't care *whose* chips they are. I'm hungry. And you should eat, too." She pitches a Twix at me, and my stomach grumbles like a damn traitor for it. With an infuriated sigh, I tear into the wrapper, jamming a whole candy bar in my mouth.

"We should stay and rest for a while," she suggests. "Maybe your smaze will come."

I answer around a mouthful of chocolate. "We've been down here for more than a day already, and it hasn't bothered to show itself."

"Maybe we're moving too fast. Like, remember when you were little and your mom would tell you if you ever got lost, just stay put so it'd be easier for her to find you?"

I choke on a dry laugh. "I stayed put for years waiting for my mother. I promise, she never came looking for me."

"Oh," Kai says quietly. I hate the undercurrent of pity in it. The last thing I need or deserve is Kai's sympathy. "Either way, it wouldn't hurt to rest," she suggests. "Aside from that nap in the catacombs, you haven't slept since we left Cuernavaca. And you lost a lot of blood."

I pace the room. If I sit down, I might not get up again. "We don't have time to rest. We need to find my smaze. And then I need to find Fleur and Chill."

She stares into the bag of chips, searching for a whole one in the crumbs. "Relax. He won't kill them. Not yet, anyway," she amends. "He'll wait until he finds you."

I watch her face, wondering what kind of relationship she and Doug had for the short time they were here, planning their escape. She talks as if she knows him intimately. And I can't reconcile that with the person Lyon trusted with those maps.

I pluck the second Twix from the wrapper and chase it with a bottled water. Thirst slaked and hunger momentarily sated, fatigue finally digs in its claws. I slip off my jacket and holster, the air too thin and warm in the powerless room.

The sleeve of my jacket sticks to the crusting blood on my shirt. I peel aside the tear in the fabric, unsurprised to find two popped stitches and a hell of a bruise.

"How are you feeling?" Kai asks.

"Like I got shot and fell down an elevator shaft." My stitches pull as I flip the sofa right-side up and drop into the sagging cushions. It sucks me deep into its familiar embrace and I breathe in the smell of it. Kai crunches the last of Chill's chips, shaking the bag upside down over her mouth. I throw an arm over my face, pretending she's not here, pretending it's Chill sitting across from me, reeking like Doritos and trying my patience.

They're alive. They have to be, I tell myself as I fall asleep. Because I can't picture a world without them in it.

37

WASTE THEM ALL

FLEUR

The light at the end of the duct grows brighter. I crawl toward it faster on aching hands and knees, following the smaze around a final turn before tumbling into a cavern somewhere in the catacombs.

A single torch lights the chamber, casting eerie shadows over the archways carved into the stone. I'm surrounded by a maze of cold, damp options, each pathway darker and more uninviting than the next. The smaze brushes my ankle, nudging me into one of the narrow tunnels. I pluck the torch from the wall, uttering a swear when the flame begins to shrink and the tunnel ahead dissolves into a drafty black hole.

"You've got to be kidding." The air smells like moldering bodies. A steady *drip, drip, drip* bounces off the floor, and an animal skitters somewhere close. I move slowly through the tight passage, my fingers trailing over the mossy surface of the walls. I can hardly see my hands in front of my face, and I drag my feet to avoid tripping or plunging into a hole.

The smaze zooms around me, making the last of the torch fire waver. "I'm going as fast as I can. I can't see. It's too dark." This has to be Jack's smaze. It's too impatient to be anyone else's. It swerves back through the tunnel, chilling the air as it whips past me.

Abruptly, the smaze stops. It hovers perfectly still, alert for something I can't sense. I draw in a breath, smelling nothing but the musty foulness of the catacombs.

"What is it?" I lower my voice to a whisper as it occurs to me that the things I should fear most in this place aren't easily tracked by scent. The Guards could be anywhere. Or Doug.

The smaze surges past me, back the way we came, the breeze strong enough to lift my hair as the tiny flame at the end of my torch blows out. Breath held, I wait for my eyes to adjust to the darkness. But there's no light here. None at all. As the silence stretches out indefinitely, my other senses sharpen to compensate.

"Come back here!" I whisper, groping at the walls, taking a few cautious steps forward. The temperature in the tunnels grows warmer, and I panic as I realize the smaze must really be gone. "Wait! You can't leave me alone in here! Where are you?" My voice echoes differently here, as if I've entered a larger space. I reach out, taking tiny steps. A low hum vibrates in the distance. A dim glow burns through the blackness ahead, and I head toward it, desperate for light.

Slowly, the glow begins to brighten and the hum grows louder. After a few more steps, I can clearly see the outline of an arched opening into another room.

At first glance, the room seems empty, and I step cautiously toward the hulking shadowy shapes inside. The hum is almost deafening now.

Stasis chambers.

Dozens of them. Lined up in rows. Most of them dark. A handful of them are plugged into generators. The room's thick with the smell of exhaust that's being sucked by huge fans into a hole in the cavern's ceiling.

I move toward a row of lighted chambers. The faces of sleeping Seasons are silhouetted inside, their control panels blinking. I recognize one of them—a Spring who lived across the hall from Poppy and me. Poppy had heard rumors that she'd met a girl and moved to France. That she'd been freed by Lyon and Gaia. If the rumors were true, why is she here, in the belly of the Observatory? If she did decide to come back, why isn't she sleeping in her dorm?

Voices and laughter carry through the chamber, along with the squeak of a rolling cart. I duck down, scurrying on hands and knees between two unlit stasis chambers. Breath held, I press back against a stone slab as the voices grow louder.

"How many more chambers does Chronos want us to bring down?"

"As many as we can fit." I can hear their grunts as they heft a chamber off a cart. It scrapes against the stone as they ease it onto a slab. "We lost another six Seasons yesterday. Control Room says they're all in the wind. He's dispatching another hunting party tonight."

"I don't understand why he's going to all the trouble of rounding them up and bringing them back. Why not just make more?"

"Commander Lixue says he's not ready yet. Besides," he adds over the hum of the fans, "Chronos says they're the property of the Observatory and they belong here. He wants them all brought in for Reconditioning and Reassignment. Here's a list of the ones he's bringing in tonight and the chambers he wants on standby."

I crouch low as a switch flips and a soft halo of light washes around the slab. I draw my knees tight against my chest, pulling the toes of my sneakers out of the light.

"Do you smell that?" one of them asks.

"Smell what?"

"Something sweet."

I breathe shallowly, reaching into my pocket for the nail file.

"Can't smell anything over the fumes." The Guard flips on a few more switches.

"Hey," another one says. I catch the reflection of his transmitter light in the chrome frame of the stasis chamber across from me. I don't dare move. "Control Room's calling. Commander needs us upstairs. She says it's urgent."

The Guards' boots move away from me. My held breath pours out of me as their voices disappear. Lifting my head, I peer over the stasis chambers. A few are still dark, but several more are lit, the blinking yellow lights on their control panels set to standby.

My stomach turns. This room . . . it's just a giant holding cell.

Doug's Guards are hunting freed Seasons, forcing them back, abducting them through the ley lines and tearing them from their new lives, as if he could ever put this place back the way it was. As if any amount of Reconditioning could ever make a freed Season forget what they had.

Enraged, I look around at the dozens of chambers waiting to be occupied. How many, like Jack and me, like Chill and Poppy, will be ripped out of each other's arms tonight?

I grab a heavy fire extinguisher from its mount on the wall. Careful to avoid the occupied chambers, I swing it into the closest empty one, shattering the dome and smashing the control panel. If the stasis chambers aren't online when the hunting party sets out, they'll have no way to bring those Seasons back. I ruin every empty chamber in the cavern, one by one.

When I'm done, I stare at my bleeding hands. I won't let Doug turn this place into the prison it was. We worked too hard and gave up too much for that.

I will not let him use me. I will not let him hurt Jack, or Chill, or anyone else.

If Doug wants to experience the power of Gaia's magic, if he wants to know what kind of destruction it's capable of, then *I* will find Gaia's magic, and I will show him myself.

38

BUT NOT A GHOST

JACK

My eyes fly open. I reach across the bed for Fleur, but my arm hits the back of a couch. My leg flings over the side as I struggle to sit up and remember where I am.

A thin band of light seeps through the gap under the door of my dorm room. Shadows move on the other side of it. There's a metallic shake as someone tests the knob.

I ease off the couch. A key scrapes into the lock.

A muffled voice. "Doug wants two Guards posted in here around the clock until we have a lead on Sommers. Jora got held up in the Control Room. I told her I'd cover until she shows up."

"Why doesn't he just check the eye in his staff and see where Sampson and Sommers went?"

"If he could do that, we'd have found them already. They're not like us anymore." The keys clatter against the floor. "Would you open

271

the damn door, already? You have one job, for Chronos's sake, March."

I slip silently into the bunk room, grateful that Lyon never got around to upgrading the locks in the wings to key cards. Kai's a dark lump against the pale sheets of my bed. I kneel beside it and press a palm over her mouth. The whites of her eyes flash wide. Her hands clamp around my wrist, and her breath stills as I stifle her gasp. I hold a finger to my lips as the door rattles and the Guards argue outside.

"Keep your voice down," the first Guard says.

"No point sneaking around," the other answers. "Sommers would have to be an idiot to hide in his own room."

I slide my hand from Kai's mouth, touching my ear where a transmitter would be. She nods.

The bedsprings creak softly, her movements catlike in the dark as she searches for her bow. She pats the surface of the bed, then reaches deep into the gap between the mattress and the wall. Her hands come up empty. She turns to me, drawing a panicked breath. She must have left it in the front room.

I reach for my knives, but my holster's out there, too, lying on the arm of the sofa with my jacket.

The door swings open a few inches. A flashlight cuts across the floor, making a slow pass over the furniture as a first Guard enters the room. A second Guard follows.

"March, look at this," the first says, lifting my jacket off the couch. "This wasn't here earlier."

I slip behind them and toe the door closed, cutting off the light from the hall.

The Guard shouts, and her flashlight beam sweeps toward me.

Kai rushes in from the bunk room, smashing my skateboard into the back of March's head with a deafening *crack*. She grabs his transmitter as he drops. I've got the other Guard in a choke hold from behind. I mute her transmitter before pitching it to Kai.

The Guard's elbow slams into my ribs. She swings the butt of her flashlight into my knee, pivoting out of my arms and shining the beam in my eyes.

A Kai-size shape emerges behind her, my skateboard poised to strike.

"No!" I shout to Kai, dodging the Guard's next blow and using her momentum to slip between them. "We need her alive."

The Guard drops her flashlight. She whirls on me, throwing punches with both hands. My stitches pull with every block, and I miss a few in the dark. Her fist connects with the side of my head. I swing and miss twice before nailing one solid hit to her face. Cartilage snaps.

"Oh, you're going to pay for that," she says. The air grows thick with the smell of blood. Magic crackles in the room as a flame lights in her hand.

Lixue.

I duck, tackling her around the waist. Her breath rushes out of her as she crashes to the floor. I straddle her, pinning her hands flat.

Kai grabs the flashlight. She shines it over my shoulder.

Lixue glares up at me, her eyes watery and her upper lip glistening red.

"Where's Fleur?" I demand.

"Why should I help you?" she growls. "You and your girlfriend were content to take a nice, long vacation in Mexico while my team was stuck in a cell, waiting to die."

"Lyon would never have killed you."

"He was going to strip our magic. You know as well as anyone, that's the same damn thing! As far as I'm concerned, Doug saved my life. To hell with yours." She spits blood at my face.

I tighten my grip. "Where is she? Where'd Doug take her?"

Lixue's snow-white eyes roll back in her head, and her breath thickens like fog. Frost crackles over her face, and for the first time I understand why Amber used to get so freaked out by my Winter magic. Her skin burns my hands, blistering cold. I grip her tighter through the layer of ice.

A low groan starts in the bathroom walls. Tile cracks and a pipe bursts, shooting a plume of water into the bunk room. The stream spirals through the air toward Kai. She drops the flashlight as the water attacks her, forcing itself into her nostrils and between her lips.

"Call it off!" I shout at Lixue. Water rushes over the floor of my bunk room, splashing across the threshold toward me.

Blood stains Lixue's smile. "Or you'll what?"

Kai gags, water slithering in and out of her nose and mouth. Her knees give out.

"Tell me where he's holding Fleur!"

Lixue laughs. "The one place you wish you could, Jack."

"Where!"

She twists, throwing me off-balance. Twin sparks ignite her palms, and I roll away from the heat. Lixue rolls with me, reaching for my face as the water soaks my clothes. I clamp down on her wrist, shaking with the effort of holding her back, her skin suddenly hot enough to sear me. I shut my eyes, turning away as her fire licks my cheek.

Across the room, Kai gags and sputters.

This is it. We're both going to die.

A wave of cold suddenly envelops my arm. I blink open my eyes, unable to believe what I'm seeing. A smaze clings to my forearm like a sleeve, insulating me in a pocket of cold mist. Lixue's fire hisses, rearing back at it. A triumphant cry erupts from me as the smaze binds itself to my burned skin.

I want to roar in Lixue's face. I want to tear this whole place apart. My smaze. It's here. It came for me.

Breathe deeply . . . remember the lion that you are.

I part my lips and draw a breath. I open my mouth, my lungs, my soul to it. The cold fills me, carrying with it a strange pain. It sinks in its teeth, spreading through my chest as flashes of memories gust through me like a hailstorm—some of them familiar, but not all of them mine.

My hand reaches for Lixue's throat like it's possessed. Her eyes go wide with panic as I choke her. She clutches my wrist, her long nails digging into the skin. I breathe, fighting to let go, as conflicting needs seem to wrestle for control of my body. I want to kill her. I want to end her life for what she's doing to Kai. But I want . . . no, I *need* her alive if I'm going to find Fleur.

Lixue's lips turn blue and lifeless. My own hand fights me as I forcefully shove her away from me.

I shake off the last tendrils of my smaze as Lixue collapses, and I'm relieved when the color starts to return to her cheeks.

Kai pushes herself up on all fours, a river of water erupting from her mouth. The flashlight drips as I swing the beam around the room.

My smaze is gone.

I sit back on my heels, my shirt drenched in melting frost and a dull ache throbbing inside me. I felt it the second the magic left my body, like a barbed hook had been yanked from my heart.

Water sprays from the broken pipe, and I stagger to the main shutoff valve in the bathroom to turn it off. A puddle sloshes under me as I sink to the floor, listening to Kai cough in the next room.

My smaze is here. It knows me. It came to me and protected me. But instead of working with me, it felt like we were fighting for control.

Kai sags against the doorframe to the bunk room. She holds out my holster and knives. "Was that your smaze?" she rasps.

I didn't think she'd seen it. I'd assumed the water had blinded her. "I think so."

"Why didn't you take it?" she asks. "All you've talked about is finding your smaze. Why'd you let it go?"

I get up and throw open my closet door, digging around for dry clothes. "I don't know. It felt wrong." I jam sweatshirts and jeans into my backpack, along with the last of the bottled waters and some jerky from Chill's drawer.

"Wrong? It's yours, how can it feel wrong? It came for you, Jack. It knew you were in danger and it came to you. It practically jumped up your—"

I throw my pack on the bed. "It just felt wrong, okay? I don't know why I didn't take it. I can't explain it. My smaze is broken! It's damaged goods, and apparently there's no coming back from that!"

Her brow furrows. "What do you mean, broken?"

I pinch the bridge of my nose, pushing back memories I'd rather forget. "It doesn't feel like my magic anymore. It doesn't listen to me. It feels . . . angry." I think about what Kai said on the plane, about stolen magic being cursed. Is this my curse? A pissed-off smaze that refuses to forgive me?

"A little rage might be exactly what we need right now."

I shake my head. "Even Lyon said it was dangerous. That I could hurt someone. I can't control it."

"And you'll never control it if you keep pushing it away. Like it or not, that smaze is part of you. And if you want your magic back, then at some point, you're going to have to face whatever it is inside it that's bothering you."

"I know. And I will." I rub my eyes, weary and empty. Lyon and Gaia were supposed to be here, to help me piece myself back together. To help me figure out who I am now. But they're gone. And Fleur's missing. And the truth is, I'm not sure I can face what's hiding in that dark fog alone. "My smaze won't go far. I'll try again." I still feel it, hovering over me like a cold shadow.

"You blame me, don't you?" At my puzzled look, she says, "For what happened with your smaze."

"No," I mutter. I blame myself, but I can't tell her that. Not now. I've already stared into that abyss once tonight. I can't stand the thought of taking Névé's sister in there with me.

"Then when are you going to start trusting me?" Kai's question catches me off guard. "No more kabob cracks," she says. "No more jokes about keeping my arrows where you can see them. I didn't bring you all this way to screw you over. And I don't plan to start now."

I try to wrap my mind around how I feel about that. The fact that we both did something terrible to each other, knowingly or not, doesn't cancel out the damage we've done.

I grab my jacket off the arm of the couch and pull the map from the inside pocket, holding it out to her. She reaches for it with dripping sleeves, then pauses.

"Maybe you should keep it," she says, gesturing to her wet pockets. She slings on her bow as March and Lixue begin to stir. "We'd better get out of here before they come to."

I tuck the map back in my jacket, along with the two transmitters we took from the Guards. Slinging my backpack over my shoulder, I glance back one last time, thinking about what Kai said, about how I won't be able to control my magic until I'm able to face it without pushing it away. I look for signs of my smaze in this place that I used to share with Chill—before we ran, before Fleur, before all the choices that led us to where we are now—and wonder if it will ever feel the same again.

39

NOT CEASE TO GLOW

❖

DOUG

Gaia's magic stirs awake as I enter my office, the glowing sparks edging away from me as I sit behind my desk. The air inside the orb hums with static, the magic throwing tiny bolts of electricity at the glass as it watches me shuffle through the box of Fleur's ornaments.

I set down the silver angel and lean closer to the enclosure, resisting the urge to smash it when the light recoils from me.

Gaia's magic didn't act this way when Fleur came to the Control Room. The sparks had calmed when she'd walked in, dimming to a soft glow, the magic reaching toward Fleur like the nose of a curious pet, eager to sniff her. Not at all like it looks at me now.

You aren't human enough to wield that kind of magic.

I shove myself back in my chair, glaring at the orb as the magic settles. *Human.* Fleur had hurled that word at me as if it had power. As if being *human* was something to aspire to. As if any Handler or broom pusher in this place could reach inside that orb and take Gaia's magic. But not me.

The thought of swallowing that bees' nest again makes me shudder. But there's no other way around what has to be done. I squeeze my eye shut, remembering the way Fleur's face had pinched with pain when she'd slid her magic into the broken plant. I'd felt something—not so much a pain as a deep discomfort—when I'd healed the branch in my suite. It hadn't been unbearable. Nothing like the fire spreading through my chest now. Fleur had said the first step to fixing something was being willing to acknowledge the pain. To suffer through it.

I massage my chest as I watch the magic swim in the glass. If I succeed, I'll have the power to fix everything Lyon broke—to restore the systems of balance Michael put in place. Jack is here. Fleur is my prisoner. As soon as I do this, I can eliminate them both. So what the hell is stopping me?

I lean toward the desk. The magic leans away.

This will not end in any way you can possibly imagine, Douglas. It takes two eyes to see clearly. . . . You are now, and will always be, alone.

I rest my head in my hands. I should be searching for the eye.

A knock at the door pulls me from my thoughts. I push aside the angel ornament and call out, "Come in." Lixue cracks open the door and peeks around it. The smell of shame wafts in with her, and I grit my teeth. "I thought you were setting up a surveillance team in Sommers's room."

"I was, Chronos. I mean . . . I did." She steps inside my office. Her nose is swollen and her eyes are blackened. A ring of dark bruises circles her throat. "March and I . . . we were ambushed," she says hoarsely. "By the time we got to Sommers's room, he and Kai were already inside."

I rest my knuckles on the surface of the desk and lean toward her. "Jack Sommers is injured. Kai Sampson's been stripped of all four of her elements. There's not a drop of magic left between them. Are you telling me two of my most senior Guards had their asses handed to them by a couple of powerless humans?"

"Not exactly, sir." She clears her throat. "There was a smaze with them."

I search her eyes for signs that she's lying. But the memories of her fight with Jack are chaotic, the images of his dorm room too dark to see clearly. "Tell me."

"It . . . it came out of nowhere. It . . . seemed to bind itself to Jack. It appeared to be . . ."

"Spit it out, Commander!"

"It appeared to be letting Sommers use its magic."

My thoughts run back to the memory Lyon showed me of the moments leading up to Michael's death. There had been a smaze in an orb, like the one Gaia always kept as a pet on her desk—Daniel Lyon's smaze. Is it possible that this same smaze is the one helping Sommers?

No . . . no, I saw what happened to that smaze in Lyon's visions. Gaia had given that smaze to Jack's Handler when she made him a Winter. But what happened to Jack's?

I can still save him. That's what Lyon had said to Gaia. In the memory I'd seen in his eyes before I killed him, there had been another smaze. Another orb. It had been sitting on a desk. But not this desk.

I capture Lixue's chin with my hand, sifting clumsily through her memories until I stumble on the one I'm looking for—the day she searched Lyon's old office. The cramped room is destroyed, as if it had been damaged by the quake. The orb isn't there. Papers, books, and glass are strewn everywhere.

Glass . . . The orb.

Damn Lyon to hell. He broke it.

I slam my fist against the desk. "Did Sommers claim the smaze? Is he a Winter again?"

Lixue blinks, flustered. "I . . . I don't think so."

"I would think that answer would be obvious."

"By the time March and I came to, they were already gone. But I didn't catch a scent in the room." She fidgets, one hand discreetly moving to her ear.

"Where's your transmitter?"

She lowers her hand, her pause longer than the question warrants. "It was damaged during the fight. I've asked the Control Room to find me a new one."

I sink back into my chair. If Sommers's smaze was so eager to help him, why didn't he claim it? Why not arm himself to the teeth with magic and come after me?

"Sir?" Lixue's voice is a distant nagging tug on the end of my patience. "There's something else. It's about the stasis chambers in the catacombs." The air around her seems to quiver. "Someone's destroyed them."

"How many?" I bark.

Lixue shrugs. "At least a dozen."

That's twelve free Seasons my Guards won't be able to recover. If I can't get the Seasons under control, there will be no chance of restoring what we've lost.

"Sommers and his friends," I growl. "How did they get past the Guards?"

"The Guards were all dispatched to find the Spring." She shrinks back from me. "The two stationed outside your apartment went to check on her—like you said—every hour." She swallows, clearly afraid to say the rest. "They found an open vent behind a cabinet. She's gone, sir."

"No," I say through my teeth, jerking on my gloves. "Sommers is here, along with everyone she cares about. She won't leave this place without them."

"I have the Control Room searching the engineering diagrams for a map of the ventilation—"

"Don't bother. I'll find her." I grab the scythe on my way to the door.

"But sir, I can—"

"I said I'll hunt her myself!"

40

A CAREFUL VOICE

<u>JACK</u>

Every hour that passes squeezes the fear closer to my heart. Kai was reluctant to leave the Winter wing. If it wasn't for the problem of Lixue and March, she would have thrown caution to the wind and knocked on every door in that hall, intent on finding her sister. But she knew as well as I did that it was only a matter of time before the Guards came looking for their missing commander. Soon, they would swarm the Winter dorm hunting for us, leaving us no choice but to retreat back into the catacombs.

Lyon's map is burning a hole in my pocket. My need to find Fleur and Chill and make sure they're alive is so intense, I'm ready to explode.

"Your friend Chill?" Kai asks as we near the holding cells. "He's good with computers?"

"The best." I'm seized by a fierce longing. I haven't seen Chill in person since we all parted ways after the battle in Cuernavaca, when

Lyon and Gaia escorted him and Poppy to Fairbanks and settled them in their new home. Every time he called, I promised I'd visit. I kept coming up with lame excuses not to—Fleur had class, contractors were booked to install new security systems in the villa, the weather wasn't right to leave Fleur alone—but the truth was, it pained me to look at Chill. It hurt to look in his eyes and see the magic glittering in them—magic that could have been mine if I'd accepted it when Gaia offered it to me rather than letting Chill take it. In moments I'm not proud of, sometimes I resent the choice I made at the lake. But ever since Poppy told me Chill disappeared, I'd give anything—make the same choice all over again—to see that magic alive in him right now. "Chill's the only person I know who's capable of hacking the Control Room servers. He's your best chance at finding out which room belonged to your sister." I press my lips tight, realizing my mistake after the words are already out.

"You think they've moved everyone?" she asks curiously.

"Don't know," I mutter. I don't like lying to her, but talking about her sister in the past tense is a quick way to end up with an arrow in my back. Our partnership feels fragile at best, and I can't risk losing the only ally I have right now. I try to shrug off the guilt, but it clings, and the longer I hold it, the heavier it feels. "Lyon and Gaia were making a lot of changes down here," I explain. "They were desegregating the dorms, but I don't know how far they got."

"As soon as we figure out which room is Névé's, I'm going to find her."

I nod. Wishing her luck feels like a shitty thing to say, so I don't say anything at all.

The tunnel widens ahead. Torchlight flickers through an archway at the end. I pause and hold up a hand, listening. Kai switches off her flashlight. I don't see any Guards standing sentry at the entrance to the holding cells.

I toss a small pebble through the archway. It clatters across the stone floor and pings off one of the cells. Kai stands ready with her bow as someone stirs. A cool breeze brushes over us.

"There's a camera to your left, above the door to the first cell." Chill's hoarse voice finds me like an answered prayer. I glance back at Kai. She ducks low, peering around the corner, her eyes roving the length of the wall until she spots the blinking red target. She lines up her shot. Her arrow flies true, slicing through the wires. The red light winks out.

I throw myself past Kai into the corridor, rushing past the empty cells, searching for Fleur, my pulse climbing when I don't see her. A set of bloodied knuckles grips the iron bars at the end of the hall. I reach into Chill's cell, dragging his face toward the bars until our foreheads are touching.

"Took you long enough." He smiles, his chapped lips cracked from thirst. I want to rip Doug to pieces for keeping my best friend in a cage.

"Where's Fleur?"

"I overheard one of the Guards on his radio. Sounds like she got loose and slipped off their radar a few hours ago."

My held breath rushes out of me. "You okay?" His skin's clammy but cold. He looks too pale, too thin. If it weren't for the temperatures down here, I doubt Chill would be able to stand. "Are you hurt?"

"I'm fine. Have you talked to Poppy? Is she okay?"

"She's safe." I kneel in front of the lock on his cell, tucking two picks between my teeth. "She's with Julio, Amber, and Marie," I say around them, hoping it's the truth.

He sags with relief. "Where are they?"

"We split up," I mutter. "Amber and Julio were going to look for you and Fleur. The Handlers should be hiding out in Amber's old room."

As I wedge a brace into the keyhole, the temperature plummets. Frost crackles over the lock, sticking my skin to the metal. I yank my hands back and shake out my fingers. Chill's eyes are white, swirling with magic. "Get down, Jack," he says in an icy voice.

I spin on my knees, expecting to face off with a team of Guards, but it's only Kai, her bow half raised behind me.

"Relax, she's with me." My heart rate slows as I frown over the lock.

Chill looks like he's ready to hurl an icicle into her eye. "What the hell is she doing here?"

"Helping me."

"A little less chatting and a little more lockpicking, please?" she growls.

"I'm trying, but these locks are older than . . ." Lyon's name jams in my throat, and I push that thought away. "The locks are old. It may take me a while." I fight back a shiver. "Lighten up, Chill. This is going to take a lot longer if my hands are cold."

He glares at Kai over my head. "No one's coming. The Guards tore out of here a while ago. They're all out looking for Fleur. She can't have gone far. As soon as you get this cell open, we can go find her and the others and get the hell out of—"

The ground heaves under me, throwing me backward and tossing my picks. Chill's grip on the bars is the only thing holding him upright as the cavern shakes. Dust billows through the corridor as the walls splinter around us. Kai wobbles left, then right, staggering into a cell door and holding herself up against the bars. I rush to recover my spilled picks, bracing myself against another wave of tremors.

"That doesn't bode well," Chill says when the ground finally stills. "They must have found her. Doug's probably taking her back."

"Back here?" My heart leaps as I realize how close she is. How soon I might see her.

Chill's eyes meet mine, apologies swirling inside them.

"Back where? Where's he keeping her, Chill?"

"In his suite in the north wing."

His suite. Michael's apartment.

I plunge a pick back into the lock, surprised frost isn't crackling over my fingers. "When I open this door, you're going to take Kai to the Winter wing and find a computer. Hack the Control Room servers and find the number of Névé Onding's room—"

"Névé Onding?" Chill asks. "But Névé Onding is—"

"Kai's sister." I glance up sharply from the lock. His mouth falls open and his eyebrows rise. "Kai helped me get down here on the condition that we help her find her sister," I explain. "After you find Névé's room number, you'll split up. She'll go looking for her sister while you go to the Autumn wing to find Poppy and the others. I'll meet you by the incinerator under the Winter wing in three hours. That should give us both plenty of time." I pop the lock and press Lyon's map and my flashlight into Chill's hands.

"Where are you going?" he asks.

"I'm going to find Fleur."

Kai doesn't argue. If anything, she seems as eager as I am to get out of here and start hunting. I turn and start running down the hall, back toward the Winter wing.

"Are you crazy?" Chill hisses, catching up with me as we pass the rows of empty cells. "You can't go to that suite alone. You'll be walking into a trap."

"I've walked into worse."

He grabs my elbow and drags me to a stop. "You can't go after Doug like this. Not while you're . . ."

I round on Chill. "Not while I'm what? While I'm her Handler? Because last time I checked, keeping her alive was my job."

Chill backs off. He'd be a hypocrite to argue, and he knows it.

"I screwed up once. I won't do it again." My teeth clench around the memory of the night I last saw her. "I'm going to find her. And I'm going to bring her back."

Chill nods. His eyes skip to Kai, where she waits at the mouth of the tunnel. He takes me by the ear—the same ear where my transmitter used to sit, where his voice kept me company, watching over me through every winter, every hunt—and shakes it gently. "Don't do anything stupid. Stay low. Keep your back to the wall and keep your exits in sight. If anything feels wrong, get out of there. Three hours. Then I'm coming after you."

He holds out his knuckles. I bump them gently with mine.

"Three hours," I promise.

"Jack!" Kai's voice stops me as I turn for the north tunnel. "Thank you. For everything," she says quietly. "I hope you find Fleur."

I nod. Guilt thickens my throat. I can't wish her the same. But she deserves to know the truth. I pull a set of lockpicks from the case she gave me and hold them out between us. "I'm sorry for anything I might have done to hurt you before."

A sad smile touches her lips as she takes them. "Water under the bridge, right? Be safe, Jack."

I watch until she and Chill disappear from sight.

41

A FEW MIGHT TANGLE

FLEUR

The smaze zips around me, agitated and urgent as it circles my leg. The key card I swiped from Doug's pocket in the shower slips from my hand. I bend to pick it up, shaking so badly it takes me two more tries to slide it over the sensor. A huge unit of Guards tore through the catacombs as I was sneaking out, their boots thundering through the walls of an adjacent tunnel, searching for me. Doug's voice had boomed over their radios, confirming that he was down there, too. It won't take them long to pick up my scent and track it here. This office used to be Michael's. Then it had been Lyon's. I can only assume it's Doug's now, and I hope it wasn't a mistake to follow the smaze here.

I slide the key card over the sensor again.

Please let this work. Please let this work. Please let this work.

The locks snap free. The door creaks on its hinges as I scurry inside. Suddenly, the room floods with light, and I press back against the door as the smaze drifts around the perimeter of the room.

The office is empty. Just motion sensors. I release a held breath.

Sitting on top of the huge ironwood desk, propped between the spines of a few leather-bound books, is an orb.

Gaia's magic casts a warm glow over the wood. As I approach the desk, a soft hum penetrates the glass. Tiny sparks hover like fireflies inside it, drifting up to meet my fingers when they graze the lid.

The plant from Doug's suite rests in its broken pot beside it. Its long stems lean toward Gaia's light. One bright, waxy leaf seems to be caught on something. I untangle it, gasping as I pull a loop of red satin free of the vine and a small silver angel comes away with it.

I hold the tarnished ornament out in front of me, the inscription on the back becoming visible as it spins.

This is *my* angel. The one I left for Jack in the woods.

A footlocker lies open beside the desk, loaded with ornaments. Twenty-nine of them . . . a number I know without having to count. I withdraw a tiny snow globe. Cherry blossoms drift around the tree inside.

"How did these get here?" I murmur through a shaky breath.

"I could ask the same about you."

I spin toward the door, clutching the snow globe in my fist. Doug looks smug as the door closes behind him. He rests the staff against the wall. It's the first time I've seen him carry it. It's exactly the way I remember it, cold and glittering sharp, with the exception of the strange black sash around its head.

He steps closer, blocking my view of it as he strips off a pair of gloves. "I spent all night looking for you."

"Isn't that a little hyperbolic? I only left your room a few hours ago."

"Oh, that's funny," he says, shaking his head and dropping his gloves on the desk. His hair's matted to his forehead with sweat. There's a streak of dirt on his cheek and cavern filth on his dress shoes. A trickle of dried blood trails over his lip. "Nice trick, using the exhaust from the generators to mask your scent." My hand clenches around the snow globe as he stalks closer. I move away from the desk, but he only backs me deeper into his office. "It was dumb luck when I caught you coming up the back stairs to the gallery."

"You followed me here?" How? I'd been so careful. I was sure no one was behind me as I followed the smaze.

Doug pries the ornament from my fingers, tossing it in the air and catching it in his palm before pitching it at the bookshelf. I flinch as it shatters and a shard of glass skims my arm.

"I've been following you for an hour, waiting to see if your boyfriend would show up. He's been making a hell of a mess looking for you." He reaches into the box for another ornament. Then another. Smashing them against the wall, raining glass and porcelain over me.

"Stop it! Those are mine!"

He reaches for another ornament. It's the first one I ever left for Jack.

My mind lunges for the plant. The leaves shudder as I slide into its roots. I grab hold, surprised when the plant draws back from me. Not as if it's resisting, but as if it's being pulled by someone else. With a violent jerk, the plant is yanked from my thoughts.

My eyes snap to Doug's.

A smile curls his lips as a vine surges toward me. I grab my temples, forcing my mind back in, pushing up against Doug's as we wrestle for control of the plant. Doug and I circle each other beside the desk, our minds feinting and lunging at each other. The ceramic pot rattles on the desk. Soil and shards explode over us as the roots burst free and the vines extend. His mind grabs hold of mine. My thoughts push his back. A sickening sense of déjà vu washes over me, like we've done this before.

A sharp pain shoots through my temple, and I kick out with my thoughts in one final push, gasping as Doug's mind is thrown from the plant.

My body flies backward, slamming onto the carpet with bruising force as Doug crashes into the desk.

"You're an asshole," I groan, my thoughts scattered.

"And you're a good teacher," he says through a pant.

I feel Doug's mind rush for a root at the same time mine does, but I'm faster. I push my mind inside it, taking control and staking my claim to it. Doug reaches behind him, groping for the remains of the shattered pot. With a savage grin, he digs his fingers into the soil. My ribs clench with a suffocating pain as his fist closes around the plant's root ball.

Panic seizes me. I try to withdraw my mind from the plant, but it's stuck, as if Doug's holding me there. He squeezes the roots harder. My lungs contract. I can't get any air.

Doug grabs his chest, a sudden pain streaking over his face. He drops the plant with a startled cry, and I reel back, sucking in a starved breath.

"How did you do that?" he rasps, his hand pressed to his sternum, mirroring mine.

We're both bent over our knees, pale and shaking. I don't know what's happening. I've never felt so out of control of my magic. It feels like it's fighting itself. Like it's fighting *me*.

Static crackles as I stand upright. The room begins to shake. Doug maneuvers closer to his staff.

"Are you insane?" His eyes jump to the ceiling, where the brass candelabra is starting to sway. "Stop it, before you kill everyone in this place, including your friends!"

He stumbles as the ground heaves.

My heart slams against my ribs, the rising pressure inside me too wild to control. "I can't. Something's wrong."

Magic swells inside me. It's like there's suddenly too much. I can't wrap my arms around it. I breathe deep, reaching out with my mind, following the hot, electrified ends of it. I try to take hold of them, but they're flailing. Fighting me. Digging deeper into the earth.

A map in a thick glass frame lurches off the wall. Leather-bound books wobble off the ends of their shelves. The scythe slides from its corner and smacks against the carpet. Lightbulbs pop and the room goes dark.

"Get this under control, Fleur!"

There's a violent rattle behind me. Glass shatters as something heavy hits the floor. I shield my eyes from a flare of light. Like a swarm of angry fireflies, Gaia's magic is loose.

Wind hurls papers, blowing books open and whipping broken glass around the room. Doug swears as the magic begins to organize into a funnel, raining plaster on our heads.

Our eyes catch under it. He shoves me, throwing me backward into the bookcase and positioning himself between me and the magic. His head tips back as if he's drawing a breath.

"No!" I scrabble upright and kick out the backs of his knees. My only chance of getting free is to beat him to the magic.

Doug pushes onto all fours, reaching for the head of his staff. His fingers catch the sash, the knot coming loose as he pulls it closer.

The blunt handle of the staff sings through the air, striking me across the chest. The force of it sends me flying. Doug kneels over me, pinning my arms at my sides with his knees, his hand pressed to my mouth, the lights swirling behind him.

"It's mine," he says. "All of it."

I can't breathe. Can't open my mouth to warn him that he's making a mistake. Doug throws his head back and his lips part. I thrash as the magic descends toward him. My throat stings with the heat of a thousand suns as he breathes in the sparks. I cry out into his hand, certain we're both dying, as he takes the magic completely inside him.

His chest glows like amber fire as he collapses. Lightning flashes. Ice and snow whip my skin. I cover my ears against a deafening roar. Then everything goes black.

I awaken sprawled on the floor, gasping and coughing as the tremors quiet. Glass tinkles as I push myself upright, brushing shards of porcelain and plaster from my shirt. My throat burns. I ache everywhere, and there's an acute, pulsing pain under my breastbone that's hard to breathe through. I blink, but there's not a speck of light in the room.

My leg brushes against a shoe. I scoot away from it, bumping into the desk. I hear Doug's slow, steady breaths, and I hold perfectly still as they become irregular and shallow.

He groans. I grope around me for his staff, my hands moving wildly over the carpet. Doug sucks in a sharp breath as a shard of glass catches my palm. Ignoring the sting, I feel around me on hands and knees. My fingers close around a cold metal pole as Doug's clamp down next to mine.

"Don't be stupid, Fleur." His voice is gravelly and tight, his grip on the staff unbreakable. I throw my weight backward, but Doug rips the staff from my grasp, leaving me dizzy and unmoored in the dark. I back away from the direction of his voice. My heel connects with the desk. Feeling along its edges, I trace my way to the leather chair. Then to the wall.

"Where are you going?" He grunts, glass crackling as if he's sitting up.

The door is right behind me. I reach for the knob. As my hand closes around it, a tight fist seems to grab my mind. I cry out as the muscles in my legs contract and my backside hits the floor. My head smacks against the desk as I fall back on my elbows. Stunned, I rub the throbbing ache at the base of my skull, struggling to figure out what just happened.

Doug goes very still.

I roll onto my side and push myself upright. I reach out with my magic, but it feels caught on something, like a loose thread of a sweater that's snagged on a nail. The more I try to reel it back to me, the harder it pulls.

Closing my eyes, I trace the magic to the point where it's stuck. It's like chasing a string through a dark tunnel. Nothing about this place feels familiar. I'm not inside a root. Or a rhizome. But this place is alive. Breathing. A rhythmic *thump* beats inside the walls.

A dim light glimmers at the far reaches of my consciousness, and my mind follows it into a glowing chamber. My thoughts jolt to a stop. My magic is coiled in the middle of a vast space, surrounded by glittering stars.

No. Not stars. . . .

Twinkling lights drift around my magic like fireflies. The way they move reminds me of the magic in Gaia's orb. I tug the thread of my magic, backing my mind slowly out of the cavernous room. I don't know where this place is, but I know I shouldn't be here. As I retreat, the lights swarm me, agitated and buzzing. I pull, but my magic doesn't budge.

"What are you doing?" Doug's voice seems to reach me in stereo, both inside and outside my head. I give my magic a hard jerk, and Doug roars. "Knock it off!"

My thoughts slam back into my body. I recoil against the side of the desk, shielding my eyes as a flame ignites in Doug's palm. He shines it over me. "What are you doing in my head?" he yells.

"Your head?" *Oh, Gaia, no!* I cast out my thoughts, feeling for the place where my magic ends and Doug's begins, but I can't untangle the two.

"Get out!" he snaps.

"Believe me, I would love nothing more than to be anywhere other than trapped inside your screwed-up, sadistic mind, but I can't. I'm stuck. Stop messing around and let me go!" I yank hard on my magic.

Doug lurches and swears, clapping a hand over his forehead. My knees buckle and I drop like a stone, as if a cold hand is holding me down by my head. I kneel, frozen, unable to move. "What the hell did you do to me?" he roars.

"What did *I* do? This isn't *my* fault." My heart hammers. It's like my knees are glued to the carpet.

"This is *your* affinity! *Your* magic. You taught me, remember?"

"I never taught you this. I can't even do this! This isn't . . ." My breath stills as all the pieces come together. My magic is trapped inside Doug, but those lights I saw were Gaia's magic. Doug's using it to manipulate *me*. "This is *your* fault. You took Gaia's magic. You're holding on to too much power. You can't control it. Neither could Lyon."

Suddenly he's in my face, his glittering eye wild. "Don't you ever compare me to him." His magic releases its hold on me with a shove. But no matter how hard I pull it back, my magic can't break free.

My hand closes around a thick shard of glass. I swing it into the side of Doug's leg. Pain rips through my thigh as we both scream, and he drops to one knee in front of me.

Matching red stains seep through our clothes. Teeth clenched, Doug jerks the shard free. I gasp, pressing my hand to my wound as his murderous eye lifts to mine. He rubs his chest. A dark smear stains the front of his shirt. Frowning, he stares at the slash across his palm. My mouth thins as I register the matching cut on mine.

I'm stuck. Shackled to him by our magic. "This was all part of your stupid plan, wasn't it?"

"This was definitely not the plan! How am I supposed to kill you if I can't hurt you without hurting myself?" His face reddens in the warm glow of his fire. He bends to pick up the overturned lamp, setting it on the desk and resting his flame in the cradle of the broken bulb. Hands on his hips, he paces the demolished room, his staff abandoned on the floor.

"We can fix this," I say with a forced calm. "We just have to figure out how we became connected in the first place and back our way out of it. It must have happened while we were fighting. Our magic has touched before, when we fought in Cuernavaca." In a fit of rage, Doug had attacked me during the battle. I summoned a root to hold him back, and he pushed it away. Not with his hands, but with his mind. Overwhelmed by grief, he probably hadn't even realized he'd been using his earth magic. I'm sure we weren't connected then, but this time, I felt it when his will wrestled with mine for control of the plant. "We must have crossed some kind of barrier this time. Opened some kind of pathway between each other's magic."

He paces like a caged tiger. "I've never heard of that happening before."

I think back to all my years of training. "It's possible for the minds of two Springs to occupy a physical space at the same time, but I've never heard of anyone getting stuck like this."

I massage my sternum, wondering which one of us the dull ache belongs to. Doug stops pacing, surprise coloring his cheeks.

"The pain, it's not as bad as it was," he says, leaning back against the wall, watching me with a curious expression.

"How is that even possible? If anything, you should feel worse. I saw Lyon after he took Michael's magic."

"I'm stronger than Lyon," he says, practically spitting Lyon's name. "I wasn't just a Season. I was a Guard. I had far more magic."

"You *took* far more than anyone should be able to handle. You should be writhing in agony. The magic should be clawing and fighting its way out of you. How is it even possible that you're holding Gaia's magic, too?"

I feel a shove against my mind, as if he's trying to push me out. His gaze snags on a piece of the shattered orb. An emotion flusters my thoughts, and it takes me a moment to realize it isn't mine. It flickers through his mind, almost too quickly for me to identify it. Resentment? Jealousy? With a sudden shock, I realize I can *feel* him. Not just his physical pain, but his mood.

"Gaia's magic," he says bitterly. "It . . . responded differently that day you came to the Control Room. It seemed . . . drawn to you."

"So?"

"So maybe *I'm* not the one holding on to you."

I think back to the way Gaia's light had surrounded me in Doug's mind. How it had seemed to cling to me when I tried to back myself out of it. Doug had been the one who breathed Gaia's magic in, but we'd both been fighting for it right up until he took that breath. Could Gaia's magic have followed that connection to mine? Could it have bonded to me and trapped me with it inside him? Is my presence inside Doug keeping the fragile peace, making it possible for him to contain so much magic? And if so, which one of us controls it?

Reaching out with my thoughts, I prod the magic that connects us, attempting to manipulate it, but it doesn't respond. Doug's head snaps up, as if he knows what I'm up to. His thoughts slide into his new power like a cold hand into a glove. Doug's mind is clearly the vessel, and it seems to have control over both me and Gaia's magic.

His head tips toward the door as I hear a soft knock. Distracted, he loosens his grip on my mind.

"Leave us," Doug barks.

"But sir," Lixue says, her voice muffled through the ironwood, "you asked me to report in as soon as we found something."

An emotion washes over me—hope. Not my own. Doug's. His mind prickles with it as he yanks open the door. "You found the eye? Where is it?" My gaze flicks to the staff on the floor, surprised to see the sash is gone. And so is the eye. There's a hole in its place.

Lixue's brows pull down as she looks past him to the shattered orb on the floor. "No, Chronos. I haven't found it yet. We found the sister."

He snatches her tablet from her hands. As his eye skims it, I feel a flash of surprise.

"What's going on?" I ask as he angles the tablet away from me. "Whose sister?"

"Take the Spring to my suite." Doug talks about me to his Guard as if I'm not even in the room. "Make sure that air vent is sealed and every inch of the place has been checked for other possible escape routes. No one is to lay a hand on her. If a single hair on her head is harmed, there will be hell to pay. Am I understood?"

"Yes, sir."

He bends to pick the black sash off the floor. I bristle at the sudden, dark urgency I feel inside him as he reaches for his staff. I wedge myself in front of the door, blocking his path. "Where are you going?"

He shoves me into Lixue's arms and walks past me out the door.

42

SNOW FOR DUST

DOUG

Flame in hand, I move through Névé Onding's darkened dorm room. According to the personnel records Bradwell uncovered, Névé's been dead for more than a year and a half, killed by Amber Chase while Jack and his friends were on the run. Névé's Handler, detained along with all the others who had hunted for Jack, was given a custodial job after the hearings, and was moved to a room in the staff quarters, leaving this one abandoned.

I trail a finger through the dust on Névé's desk. Oddly, nothing on Névé's side of the bunk room has been removed. Either Lyon was too busy to bother with it, or he wanted someone to find it like this. Messy. Lived in. Warm, even though the room still smells stubbornly like Winter. The blue paint on the walls feels distantly familiar, from hall parties when I was a Season in the same wing.

I drop into the fuzzy blue reading chair in the corner and rest the staff across my lap, grateful not to be holding it. The damn thing feels heavier every time I touch it, and in my rush to get here, I forgot all about my gloves. I wince as I rub the chill from my palm. The cut Fleur gave me is still angry and raw. When I left her in my office, her shouts had given way to a persistent pounding against the walls of my mind that I'd felt all the way to the Crux. I still feel her there, seething in a remote corner of my thoughts, but the farther away she is, the easier it is to think, and the weaker my ability to sense her seems to be. Still, I find myself checking to make sure she's there.

There's a strange static hum inside my chest. Head tipped back against the chair, I rub it, thinking about what Fleur said back in my office. Gaia's magic doesn't sting—not like it did before—and the persistent pain that's haunted me since I took the staff has dulled, as if a sharp corner's been broken off and given to someone else.

Somehow, I have to get Fleur out of my head and end this. As the host, my mind might be in control of Gaia's magic, but clearly that magic feels connected to Fleur. The possibility that Gaia's magic is holding on to her like a security blanket poses a problem. How do I untangle us and still hold on to the power? And if I do manage to push Fleur out, will Gaia's magic fight me once she's gone?

I sit up with a sigh. A dead plant sags over the edges of a pot on a bookshelf beside me. The brown leaves are rigid and brittle, the soil so dry it's sunken and cracked. I prod its edges with my mind, feeling for signs of life. When I touch it with the tip of a finger, a dried leaf breaks away from the stem and drifts to the floor. I've seen Gaia breathe life into things a million times. Watched Fleur revive a frozen butterfly on an old video feed. Leaning close to the plant, I blow a gentle breath. The dead leaves rattle, and two more fall.

If I'm truly in command of Gaia's magic, I should be able to breathe life into something. Me, not Fleur. If I can't bring back something as small as a houseplant, what hope do I have of creating new Seasons?

Soft footsteps pause in the hall, just outside Névé's room. Fingers on the doorknob. A tentative knock.

I snuff out the flame as metal scratches against metal. A key—no—a lockpick slips into the lock. I take up the scythe, listening to a series of scrapes and clicks. After a few failed attempts, the knob turns, and a dim cone of hallway light stretches across the floor.

The door shuts quietly.

"Ruby?" Kai's voice cracks. The narrow beam of a flashlight shines out in front of her, catching on the furniture in the sitting room. She follows the light into her sister's bunk room, completely unaware of me, pausing when it reaches the Handler's stripped mattress and empty shelves. "Ruby?" she whispers, her voice trembling as the beam moves over the line I drew in the dust on her sister's desk.

The light swings toward me.

I stop time before our eyes can catch.

Dust particles hang suspended in the beam of her flashlight. A thin cobweb dangles, frozen, in the corner of the ceiling above her head. Kai's completely still, as if she's made of wax. I rise from Névé's chair and circle around her, my movements reflected off the dark surface of her eyes.

"You lied to me," I whisper. "You betrayed me. And for what? Because you made a deal with Lyon? Lyon was dead! There was nothing he could give you! Nothing he could promise you that I wouldn't have offered you, and you chose him anyway." Deep in my head, I feel Fleur's mind go still. Her pacing has stopped, her consciousness listening, as if she senses something is wrong. I lower my voice. Whisper in Kai's ear, "I came back. I honored my promise. I offered you her magic. We could have fixed all of this together. But instead, you ran to Jack." I come around her, putting my face close to hers. "You thought you could trust him. But the joke is on you."

Easing upright, I push time forward. Kai sucks in a sharp breath. She drops her flashlight. I grab her by the wrist as she reaches for her bow.

Her eyes dart to the scythe. She knows better than to ask what I'm doing here.

"You never should have killed them," she says, as if that justifies her betrayal.

"Someone had to stop them. You've seen the storms. The disasters. The fires and floods. They're only getting worse."

"Because of what you've done!" In her eyes, I see the flash of a memory—a sick girl, huddled under a thin blanket on a sidewalk, sleet bouncing off her shoulders as she coughs.

I shake my head. "You know as well as I do that Lyon put all this in motion a long time ago." She turns away from me, a guilty flush sweeping across her cheeks. "If it weren't for Sommers's rebellion, everything would be like it was. Lyon is ultimately responsible for this."

"Lyon was only trying to free us!"

"Really?" I ask. "Who was it who put you in that holding cell with me? I was the one who let you go!" She glances sharply at her wrist, and I drop it with a shove. I wander to her sister's bookshelf, trailing a finger over Névé's trophies and figurines. "I see you and Jack made an alliance. Does he know who you are?"

Her pause is too long. "Of course he knows."

"Not who you were when you shot him in Cuernavaca. Does he know who you were supposed to be? You and your sister?" I circle behind her as she holds a breath. "Does he know about your secret alliance with Lyon all those years ago?" I lean in and whisper, "I do."

I come around to face her. "All that time, it was supposed to be you. Before Sommers arrived. Before Fleur came along. It was supposed to be you and your sister breaking the system to be together. Lyon saw something in you, didn't he?" Kai's unwillingness to look at me is answer enough. "So Gaia turned you and Névé into Seasons, but she made you both different. She split you into different wings, knowing how much you'd fight to be with your sister. Lyon groomed you for years. He played off your guilt about the fire, making you feel like you had to redeem yourself for it, delivering those stupid letters for you and planting thoughts in your head, hoping you'd convince your sister to run, expecting you'd be the pair who'd start his rebellion. But Névé was the weak link, wasn't she? She didn't care enough about you to risk what she had."

"She loves me," she says, her voice quivering. "She was just scared."

"Or maybe she was just too angry at you." Kai flinches, staring at the floor. "Then Sommers and Fleur came along, and Lyon had new puppets to play with. And suddenly, you weren't the professor's pet project anymore. So what happened? You were bitter and jealous and joined the Guard out of spite?"

"No! I joined the Guard because it was the only way I could think of to see Ruby."

"Because Lyon had given up on you, and you'd lost your chance. And when you had an opportunity to bring down Lyon's star pupil—the person who'd accomplished what you couldn't—you took it."

"I didn't want to!"

"Does Jack know? Did you grovel on the doorstep of Jack's villa and confess that it was *your* failure that brought him here?" A bead of sweat trails down her temple. "Did you tell Sommers that you shot him for doing what you couldn't? That the only reason you joined the Guard was to be closer to your sister, and that's the only reason you're helping him now?"

"Shut up!"

"You and Sommers haven't been very honest with each other. What makes you think you can trust him?"

"He brought me this far."

"So you could find your sister and save her?" I shake my head as I slowly pace the room. If I didn't hate her so much, I might feel sorry for her. "He could have saved you so much time. Not to mention the plane ticket." I pluck a dead leaf from Névé's plant and hold it up where Kai can see it. "Jack should have told you what happened to her."

Her voice shakes. "What did you do to her?"

I laugh. "I didn't touch her."

"Then where is she?"

"Maybe you should ask Jack and his friends, since they were the last ones to see her alive."

"You're lying," she says in a strained voice.

"What would be the point?" I lean my hip against the desk. "I'm curious . . . did Jack forgive you for shooting him before or after you told him who your sister was?"

"Stop saying that."

"Saying what?"

"You're talking about my sister like she's dead."

"You really don't know, do you?" I push myself off the desk and come closer, the staff tucked in the crook of my arm as I twirl the dead leaf between my fingers. I crush the leaf and let the pieces fall. "Névé's in the wind. Jack and his friends killed her eighteen months ago. A week before you failed to kill him in Cuernavaca. And Lyon never told you."

Her throat bobs, and her eyes well with tears. "I don't believe you."

She turns and sprints for the door. I snag her by the hood, dragging her backward, the blade of the scythe dropping like a guillotine in front of her face. Her wide eyes reflect back at me in the blade, her staggering breaths fogging the steel.

"Amber Chase murdered Névé. She destroyed your sister's transmitter, then snapped her neck. But do you want to know the real kicker?" A tear slides down Kai's cheek. "Jack Sommers took her magic. He stole it as it left her body. He's a liar and a thief. Why do you think he gave you those picks for the lock? He knew she wouldn't answer the door."

She sags against me, chest heaving, as her knees give out. I hold her upright, whispering against the cold, shocked shell of her ear, "That smaze you've been hunting . . . do you think it's only Jack's soul inside it? Weren't you the one who said stolen magic is cursed? That it comes with weaknesses? What if Jack's weakness is Névé?" Kai goes deathly still. "Jack stole your sister's magic. And now he's here, faced with the possibility of reclaiming it. But maybe that smaze has a connection to someone else." She lifts her head, understanding dawning. "Who do you think that smaze was protecting when Lixue attacked you?"

Her breath hitches. She jerks free of my arms and staggers away from me. "The smaze . . . You think a piece of Ruby is inside it?"

I kick her quiver toward her, spilling arrows over the floor. "There's only one way to find out."

43

FIRE FOR FORM

◆

<u>JACK</u>

The torch roars, throwing shadows over Lyon's map as I dart down the final tunnel to the spiral stairwell leading to Doug's apartment. By now, Chill should be deep in the catacombs with Kai. With any luck, they'll find a computer and Kai can go her own way to search for Névé's old room. Then Chill can track down Amber, Julio, and the others and make it back to our rendezvous point by the time I break Fleur out of Doug's room.

I prop my torch against the wall at the base of the stairs. It catches a rust-colored stain on the pale gray slab by my feet. The bloody footprint is small, roughly the same size as Fleur's.

My heart gallops, and I take the stairs two at a time, mentally preparing myself for whatever condition I might find her in, painfully aware that I won't have the power to heal her.

My injured arm is throbbing and hot, and my clothes are soaked in sweat. Doug and his Guards will probably smell me coming, but there's nothing I can do about that now. I've lost too much time already.

The metal door at the top of the stairs squeaks as I crack it open. A bright sliver of light slices across the landing as I peek out into the hall. Two Guards stand watch beside Doug's apartment door. I reach into my pocket, my fingers closing around one of the smoke grenades I picked up at Auggie's house. Silently, I pull the pin, setting the grenade beside me on the floor. Knife drawn, I press my back against the wall, breathing into my sleeve as clouds of white smoke spill into the corridor.

"Do you smell that?" one of the Guards asks.

"Something's burning," the other answers.

Suddenly, they're running, their boots squeaking on the marble tile.

"It's coming from the stairwell!"

The door swings open. Light from the torch I left burning at the foot of the stairs flickers through the smoke. "Down there!" one of them shouts between coughs.

The two Guards descend the steps. I blend into the smoke behind them, plunging my blade into the nearest Guard's back and snagging his key card from the hook at his waist as he drops. The second Guard turns, eyes watering from the smoke. I drag the blade across his throat before he can make a sound.

Two quick flashes of light soar down the stairwell into the tunnel. I cover my mouth, coughing into my sleeve as I wade back through the smoke to the hallway.

An emergency light tinges the thick haze red. I break the glass to the fire alarm and snap down the lever. Sirens wail, and the sprinklers sputter on. Drenched and dripping, I duck back into the stairwell and crouch behind the door.

Doug's apartment door swings open.

"What's going on out here?" A Guard rushes out, slamming the door behind him. His boots storm in my direction, but the smoke and water mask my scent, and his feet splash past me toward the Crux.

I wait a beat . . . two, checking to make sure the camera on the ceiling is turned away from me before sprinting through the thick smoke toward Doug's apartment. I wave the key card in front of the scanner, throwing myself over the threshold and slamming the door closed behind me as I draw my knife.

My eyes burn, and I wipe my face on my sleeve. I'm in a dimly lit room. There's a sofa and a bar, and a glass-topped oval coffee table. I start at a flash of movement. A shadow passes behind the thin gap under a set of double doors at the far end of the room. Adjusting my grip on the knife, I start toward the doors. They're bolted and padlocked from the outside.

"Who's there?" My pulse races at the sound of Fleur's voice.

I'm reaching for my lockpicks when I spot a set of keys on the glass coffee table. Frantic, I thumb through them until I find the right one. I strip away the padlock, throw the bolt, and swing open the doors.

Fleur's breath hitches when she sees me.

"Jack?"

I'm across the room, my hands around her face, in her hair, my breath ragged, my throat thick with smoke and exaltation and fear. I cup her head, drinking in her face, her eyes, her body. "You're okay? You're okay?" She's wrapped in a chunky sweater that hangs to her thighs. A dark red stain peeks out from the torn leg of the jumpsuit she wears under it. I reach for it at the same time she reaches for the tear in my sleeve. Our fingers lace together and she pulls me closer.

"I'm okay," she whispers, choking on a laugh. Then a sob. A tear slides down her face, both of us shaking and grinning like idiots.

I take her gently by the face, framing her smile with my hands, leaving smears of blood and smoke on her cheeks. The kiss I steal feels hurried and desperate. "I thought I lost you."

Her arms loop around my neck, holding me to her. "You're too damn stubborn. I knew you'd find me." Our breath comes faster, our kisses becoming frantic and deeper, full of need and disbelief, as if we're each expecting the other to disappear.

I need to feel every part of her, to know she's really here. I wrap my arms around her waist and lift her, a hiss of pain escaping when my stitches pull under her weight. My hand curls under her injured leg and she sucks in a sharp breath as I hook it around me.

"Sorry," I say, pulling back to make sure she's okay.

"Don't be." She grabs a fistful of my shirt and brings my mouth back to hers, kissing me hard, her legs looping around my hips as I back her against the wall, our chests heaving.

"He'll be back soon," she says, tipping her head back to catch her breath. I kiss her jaw, the side of her neck, behind her ear, her throat. She lets out an agonized whimper that might break me. "You have to go," she pants. "The smoke alarm . . . He'll know you're in here."

"It's okay," I say between our shared breaths. "By the time Doug realizes you're gone, we'll be deep in the catacombs."

"But Jack—"

"I already found Chill." I smooth her hair back from her face, my fingers lingering on her cheeks as I kiss her again. "Amber, Julio, Poppy, and Marie . . . they're all here. I've found a way out. Lyon left a

314

map. There are tunnels to the surface. Exits Doug doesn't know about under the—"

Her hand covers my mouth. I pull back, searching her face, the sudden absence of her warmth jarring. Her lips are swollen, her neck flushed, her dark eyes focused on me. She shakes her head. "I can't leave."

I let her slide to her feet. "If you're afraid for me, Fleur, don't be. I made it this far. I can handle Doug. My smaze . . . it's here. Lyon freed it, and I—"

"I know." She sniffs. "I've seen it. It found me. I think it's been trying to help me find a way out." A sad smile tugs at her lips. "But I can't go. No matter where I run, Doug will know where I am. If I leave with you, I'll be putting you all in danger."

"No." I brush a loose strand of her hair behind her ear. "He can't see you in the staff. The eye is missing. Lyon knew what was coming. He must have hidden it. I don't have time to explain. You just have to trust me. If we run, Doug won't be able to find you." I pull her toward the door. "But you're right. We should get out of here. I sent the Guards back through the ley lines. We don't have much time before another team shows up."

"I know the crystal is gone," she says, digging her heels into the carpet and pulling us to a stop. "That's not it. I can't leave."

I study her face, but it's not fear I see in her eyes. It's resignation. "I don't understand. What are you saying?"

"Something happened when Doug and I were fighting. I don't know how, exactly, but our magic got tangled. We're . . . connected by it."

"What do you mean, connected?"

"Doug and I were both using our earth magic inside the same plant. We were grappling for control of it, and I think we got tied together somehow. It all happened so fast," she says, the words tumbling out in a rush. "There was a quake. Gaia's orb fell on the floor and broke, her magic was free, and we were fighting for it. Doug got to it first, but when he breathed it in, it must have latched on to me instead. It's holding on, Jack, and it won't let go, and now a piece of my magic is trapped inside him." She shakes out her hands. Her breath flutters.

"What happens if you leave?"

She throws back her head, as if she's struggling to find the words to explain. "You know how when I use my earth magic, I can sense someone coming through the grass? How even if they're far away, I feel their vibration through the ground? It's like that. The farther away Doug is, the harder he is to feel. I feel him now," she says, putting a hand to her chest. "He's far away, but we're connected through the magic, and if I wanted to, I could trace that line back to him, like following a string through a tunnel. Eventually, I would find him." Her mouth turns down. "And he'll find me, too, Jack. No matter where I go, he'll be able to track me."

A million nightmares claw their way into my mind. "No! I'm not leaving you with him! That's never going to happen, Fleur. He wants to kill you!"

"He won't hurt me."

"How do you know that?"

"Because he can't!" She bites her lip and turns away.

I cup her cheek, making her look at me. "What do you mean, he can't hurt you? How do you know?"

"Because I'm stuck inside his head and I just . . . know." She slides my hand from her cheek and paces away from me, as if she needs to move. Or think. "Gaia's magic is clinging to mine. For some reason, it's drawn to me. Maybe because it feels some affinity with my earth magic."

"Can you control it?"

"No, I tried. Doug's body is definitely the host. I think my magic is just acting as some kind of buffer between them." She paces, pushing her hair back as she thinks. "Right now, he seems able to control it. But if we do manage to untangle our magic, Gaia's power—on top of all the power he's already taken—would probably kill him. Chronos's and Ananke's magic don't seem capable of coexisting peacefully within one host. It's like they're fighting inside him. Gaia's magic is . . . calm when it's attached to mine. The presence of my earth magic seems to have disrupted some of the tension between them. But all that power should be wreaking havoc inside him. If part of me wasn't in there, he'd probably explode," she says, rubbing her forehead.

It feels like there's something she's not saying.

"So what now?" I ask in a strained voice as she comes to stand in front of me. She takes my hands and holds them between us.

"He won't hurt me, Jack," she says quietly. "He can't. But that doesn't mean he won't hurt you."

"So, what . . . ," I sputter, "I'm just supposed to walk away and leave you here with him?"

"What choice do we have? Do you think I want this, Jack?" she cries, the words breaking. "Do you think for one minute that if I could come up with a way out of this, I wouldn't run out that door with you right now?"

I take her face in my hands. They're shaking with the need to pick her up and carry her out of here. "That's a good plan. A *great* plan. Run with me. We'll keep moving. If we move far enough, fast enough, he won't find you. I won't let him."

"This isn't like before, Jack! It's not just our lives we're putting at risk anymore. Gaia's magic, Lyon's, Ananke's . . . Doug has taken *all* of it. And he can't control it, not alone! The world has fallen into chaos since he killed Lyon and Gaia, and it's only getting worse. If I leave, he'll come after me. You know he will. And what then? What about the hundreds of other Seasons who are lost out there right now? What about the hundreds who are trapped in here, waiting for the ceilings to cave in? This is as much our fault as it is Doug's. We started this! And now we have to face the consequences of our choices!"

"We'll find a way! *I'll* find a way! I'll come up with some other plan. You know I will."

"There's no time!"

"I'm not leaving!"

"Neither am I!" I know this tone. This set of her jaw when she's made up her mind about something.

"Please," I beg, resting my forehead against hers as I whisper, "Please don't . . ."

Fleur clasps my wrist. Her face pales. Her eyes go blank and distant, focused somewhere behind me. It's the same vacant look she gets when she's using her magic in her garden or in the jungle around the villa, as if her mind has slipped away someplace else.

"What is it? What's wrong?" I ask.

"He's on his way back."

"How long?"

"Minutes . . . maybe less."

"Fleur, listen to me," I say, taking her by the shoulders. She blinks, her pupils narrowing as she reclaims her focus. "You said you're inside his head? Is he inside yours?"

She thinks for a moment. Shakes her head.

"Can he hear your thoughts? Can he see what you're thinking?"

"I don't think so. Not like that." She frowns. "But his eye . . . he has one like Chronos. It seems like all he can see is the past. Without the crystal, he doesn't seem able to see much else."

"Because the Eye of Ananke sees the future." I remember the chalk drawing Lyon had sketched when he explained how the Staff of Time worked. Michael could look in someone's eyes and see their memories— critical moments from their past and the choices they made that had led to that moment. But the crystal in the staff projected all the paths ahead of them, revealing a potential road map to every possible future outcome. "Without the crystal, he can't be certain of his future. Or anyone else's."

"That must be why he's so desperate to find it," she says. "He keeps the head of the staff covered with a sash. Probably because he doesn't want anyone to know he has a weakness."

"A weakness that can be exploited," I murmur, the rough edges of a plan already beginning to take shape. If I'm right, Lyon hid that crystal to weaken Doug and protect me, to make sure I could get to my smaze and Fleur. He would have hidden the eye someplace he knew I would find it. "I'm going to find it. And then I'm going to use it to draw him out. If Doug wants to see his future that badly, he's going to have to trade for it."

"Trade what?"

319

"You."

Her brow furrows. "He can't. I told you, we're stuck."

"No, *you're* stuck. He's in control. You said as much. And if he controls the magic, then he has the power to release you. He just needs a little motivation." I draw Fleur's head against my chest so Doug won't catch any visions of what I'm about to tell her. "I'm going to find that crystal and come up with a plan to get you out of here. I swear on my life. Me, Julio, Amber, Chill, all of us . . . we're going to find a way to free you. Do you trust me?"

She nods against me.

"Listen carefully. There's a tunnel between Lyon's old office and Gaia's apartment. That's how they spent time together without Chronos finding out. If anything happens and you feel unsafe, get to Gaia's apartment. You find that tunnel, and you run. There are exits to the surface from the catacombs, one at each cardinal end. Run and don't look back. No matter what happens, I swear I'll find you." I press the hilt of my knife to her palm. Her warm hand closes over mine. "If you can hold on until tonight, I'll leave you a message at the entrance to the tunnel as soon as I've found the crystal, letting you know where to meet me. When Doug comes after you, we'll face him together. And we'll have the eye."

"Tonight? Jack, he's been searching for it for days. How will you—?"

I press a kiss to her forehead, whispering against it, "He doesn't know Lyon the way I do. I know how Lyon thinks. It shouldn't take me long to find it."

She pulls my face down to hers as she folds a key card into my hand.

"I stole this from Doug. It'll open any door on the administration level and the portals to the Crux, but be careful, Jack. He's going to be pissed when he finds out Chill is gone. He already killed Boreas. If he catches you—"

"He won't find me." I steal another deep kiss as I consider throwing her over my shoulder and dragging her with me into the catacombs. We're both breathless when we finally break apart. I wipe a tear from her cheek. "I'm going to get you out of here, I promise." Even if I have to kill him to do it.

She whispers for me to be careful. But I don't want to be careful anymore. I want to be dangerous. I want to be cold and deadly. I want to find my smaze, rip Doug's magic from his body, and jam the Staff of Time down his throat.

44

LETS DEATH DESCEND

FLEUR

There's no point in locking myself back in Doug's bedroom after Jack's gone. The closer Doug gets to his apartment, the clearer his emotions become. His suspicion snakes through me, its long tongue sniffing around the edges of my magic. He knows something is wrong.

The light on the security panel blinks green a second before the door swings open. "Where are the Guards I stationed outside? And what are you doing out of your . . ." His head tips curiously and his lips part, a deadly flash of recognition flickering in his eye. It jumps to the bedroom behind me.

He licks his lips, as if he can still taste Jack's scent in the room. "Sommers was here." He saunters closer. His shirt is soured with the smoke from the hallway outside. "And he left without you."

"Because I asked him to."

"How honorable," he says, brushing past me into the bedroom.

"It takes courage to walk away. You should try it sometime."

"I was talking about you." He inspects the room as if he's expecting Jack to leap out from behind a door. I feel his thoughts probing, searching for an opening into my head.

"It's endearing how you think he's safer out there, hiding like a mole in the catacombs." He drops onto the couch, loosening the top button of his shirt, less wary of me now that he knows there's nothing I can do to hurt him. "But I'm not the only deadly thing lurking in the dark." He raises an eyebrow, inviting a question. But I'm not sure I want to know what he's talking about.

Doug watches me. I feel his magic circling mine, pacing, taunting. "Tell me, what did you and Sommers talk about while I was gone? Did you tell him about our little predicament?" he asks smugly.

"None of your business."

"You must have told him. Otherwise, he never would have left. He's far too heroic for that. But you didn't tell him everything, did you?" He tips his head, watching me curiously. "Let me guess . . . you didn't tell him how you got that stab wound in your leg. Because if he knew how vulnerable you are, he might be reluctant to defend himself. See? Like I said . . . you're too honorable for your own good. He didn't deserve you."

His use of the past tense makes me want to put him through the faux window. "He deserves a hell of a lot more than you."

Doug drags his phone from his pocket and scrolls absently through his messages, his voice falling low. So low, I almost can't hear it when he mutters, "He's a dead man, anyway."

Static crackles in my hair. "What do you mean?"

"None of your business," he says, mocking me, as he tosses his cell phone onto the coffee table. A pulse of pain flares inside him. Not the persistent physical pain I've felt since our magic became tangled. This is sharper, more acute. Betrayal.

An image flickers through my thoughts . . . no, through our connection. The picture is hazy at first. Hard to grasp. All I'm getting is a girl. The contrast of short, dark hair against a blurry face. I chase it deeper into his mind, concentrating hard as the girl's features slide in and out of focus.

I know her. I've seen her before. The short pixie cut. Her petite frame. This is the same girl I saw trailing behind Jack and our friends in the video footage on Doug's phone. But as the image grows clearer, so does my certainty that I've seen her somewhere else.

I'm not the only deadly thing lurking in the dark.

I grab Doug's phone off the table before he can stop me and click open his photos app, scrolling through his videos as he scrambles after me.

It's her. Kai Sampson, one of Michael's Guards. I only saw her for a moment on the mountain before Jack and I were separated and she went after him. But her name is burned into me like a brand. Jack still screams it sometimes, bolting upright in bed in a blind panic, grabbing at invisible arrows in his back.

Doug snatches away his phone.

"No!" The word rattles the room. "You call off that Guard right this minute!"

"I would, but she's not mine. Sommers brought her here. Come on," he says, taking me roughly by the arm. "We're leaving. There's something we need to handle up top."

Jerking free, I step out of his reach. Kai's face is suddenly clear in Doug's mind, his feelings for her glaring under a painfully bright light. He resents her. Doesn't trust her. And what does he mean, Jack brought her here? "Why? Why would Jack do that?"

"Because they both wanted the same thing. He wanted to find his smaze so he could swoop in and rescue you, and she wanted to find her sister." Another face appears in his mind. A blue streak in her hair. Frost on her skin, a white swirl in her eyes.

"Névé," I whisper, finding it suddenly hard to breathe. "Névé was her sister?" They're both looking for Jack's smaze. "I don't understand. Why would they come here together?" Jack couldn't have known. Névé's death has haunted him. He never would have used that kind of secret for leverage. But Doug . . .

"You," I say, struggling to stay grounded as his mind becomes agitated and violent, "you *told* her. That's where you were going when you left the office before."

"Kai Sampson's not my problem!" Doug rounds on me. "Do you want to know what my problem is? My problem is this." He pulls a dead leaf from his pocket and crushes it in his hand. "Sixty-eight Seasons are in the wind, this place is falling apart, and people are beginning to question my ability to fix it! That's my problem!" He bangs his pointer finger into his temple. "And as long as you're along for the ride, it's your problem, too! So when you're finished worrying about whatever bullshit scavenger hunt for your boyfriend's magic is going on in the catacombs, maybe you could help me figure out how to restore the world to its proper working condition!" His mind is a storm of emotion.

I have to find Jack. I have to get a message to him. And I can't do that while Doug's watching me. I have to keep calm. Hold my emotions in check. I don't know how much of my mind Doug can see, or if he's even figured out that he can, but if he suspects I'm up to something, he's sure to try.

"Fine," I say with a forced calm. "But I'm not going out there in a bloody prison jumpsuit. I want real clothes. Warm ones. And a coat."

He eases away from me. "I'll call Lixue—"

"No," I say, careful not to think of Jack as I slip my recalcitrant hands into my pockets. My fingers curl around the wooden ornament I took from the floor of Doug's office earlier. "Last time she picked my clothes, I nearly froze to death. I'll choose the clothes myself, or I'm not going."

"Fine," he grumbles. "We'll stop in Gaia's room on the way."

45

THE EDGE OF DOOM

JACK

I turn Lyon's desk chair upright and fall into it, reading his letter again, certain I must be missing some clue inside it. I've been through all of his scattered files. I've checked the underside of every tossed desk drawer and the margins of every poetry book. Elbows on my knees, I stare at the secret panel in the floor. Leaving Fleur in Doug's apartment feels like a mistake, but I know better than to try to force her to go. All I can do is find the eye, come up with a plan, and wait.

The worst part—the worst fucking part, worse than knowing she'll spend another day trapped in there with him—is that she's doing it because she thinks she's protecting *me*. Because she's afraid for *me*. I'm supposed to be her protector, her Handler, the one who guides her out of impossible situations like this one. And instead of following me out of that suite, she's determined to stand her ground and be my personal tornado, to shield me from Doug. But she's forgotten the most important lesson we've learned.

You can't make the perfect storm alone.

I rub my eyes, replaying our conversation, reminding myself she's not entirely alone. Knowing my smaze has come to visit her heartens my resolve to find it. If my smaze knows her—if it has any desire to protect her the way I do—then maybe it really is mine after all. Maybe Kai's right, and the only thing holding me back from claiming it is my fear of actually *facing* it.

I pull my head from my hands and check the clock on the wall. I have a few hours before I'm scheduled to rendezvous with the others. Enough time to find the eye and hunt down my . . .

My gaze locks on the whiteboard. On the last notes Lyon wrote on it before he died.

ENTROPY: <u>chaos</u>, disorganization, the degree of disorder or uncertainty in a system.
"Entropy is the general trend of the universe toward death and disorder."—James R. Newman

I walk to the board and wipe the word *entropy* with a finger. It doesn't smudge away. Below it, a permanent marker rests on the tray.

Lyon didn't want this message erased.

I read it again. My mind hooks like a scythe around the single underlined word.

Chaos. It was what Chronos feared most. What he couldn't predict. It was his reason for seeking balance and control. To keep chaos at bay. And then Fleur and I came along and toppled his entire world. We invited chaos. Unleashed it. And from the ashes of it all, Lyon and

Gaia re-created our world. They made it better. Peaceful. They gave everyone here a reason to hope.

Everyone except Doug.

So he lost a war. We all lost something that day. Pieces of ourselves. People we loved. Fleur and I were no exception, but we moved on with our lives.

Doug didn't. . . . He couldn't stand the thought of losing anything— not his position, not his friends, and definitely not his magic. And then he had to go and take more. Gaia warned Lyon about holding on to too much power, that it was dangerous. That all that magic would eventually tear him apart. Lyon had traded one magic for another. But Doug . . . he had to have it all—Time and Inevitability, Earth and all four of her elements. If it weren't for Fleur, Doug would probably self-destruct and take the whole world with him.

Doug isn't just Chronos anymore. He's the embodiment of entropy. A damn vessel for chaos.

Lyon's chair topples behind me as I spring to my feet. "A vessel for chaos. That's it. That's what you're trying to tell me," I whisper.

We are only matter in a closed system, Lyon had written, *incapable of being created or destroyed. . . . Go back to your beginnings . . .*

I run for the door, my footsteps muffled by the hum of generators as I use the key card Fleur gave me to maneuver through the Observatory, following Lyon's map back to the east wing. Steps away from the Control Room, I freeze at the sound of wheels on glass. I duck into a side hall and crouch in the shadows. A crow blinks from her perch, head tipped, as two custodians amble past me, pushing mop buckets toward the Control Room. I watch the bird with wide, pleading eyes, waiting for it to call me out. But the crow stays mercifully quiet until they're gone.

Glass crackles under my feet as I pass Gaia's menagerie. The wall is framed by jagged shards, the habitats destroyed and all the cages empty. A gigantic bulbous beehive lies abandoned on the ground, crushed from the force of its fall. Tiny piles of ash—the souls of dead Springs—dust the floor around it.

The crow swoops over my head, her wings brushing the branches of the ancient fig tree shadowing the archway ahead. The gallery beyond the arbor is dark. I pluck a torch from the wall and strike a match. I can just make out the crow ahead, resting on a hunk of fallen ceiling under the dome. As I enter the gallery, I lift the torch toward the quake-damaged fresco. The fire licks at the brilliant colors, making the missing sections of the painting seem darker in contrast.

Most of the story is there—the painted history of the origins of the world. *My beginnings* . . . the birth of the Seasons.

The legend starts at one end of the hall, with an image of Chronos and Ananke joining together—just water and wind in a cold, stark universe. Their union was full of conflict. Time and Inevitability couldn't seem to get along, and the universe eventually erupted in fire, giving birth to Chaos. The painting moves through time as it crosses the dome, to the birth of our world. Gaia's image hovers over the highest point in the room. Dressed only in leaves and flowers, she's standing in the ashes of Chronos and Ananke's fiery union. Our elemental magic exploded from Chaos, and Gaia harnessed that magic to create the first Seasons.

I stand under the final image of Chronos and Ananke. Parts of the painting have broken away, but the end of the story is there, exactly the way I remember it. Their outstretched arms encircle Gaia and her offspring, controlling Chaos, their balance keeping it in check. But had they really ever been the ones controlling it? Or had Gaia been the one to bring balance to the universe—to keep the fragile peace between them?

. . . all that power should be wreaking havoc inside him. If part of me wasn't in there, he'd probably explode. . . .

Chronos's painted scythe curves toward me. He holds Ananke's hand, but the expanse of dark matter between them—the chaotic cosmic soup that was the origin of the Seasons—is gone, the plaster cracked and smashed on the floor.

"I'm here, Professor," I whisper. "I'm at the beginning, seeking answers. What are you trying to tell me?" I nudge aside a piece of rubble with my foot. "Is this it? Is this what we've started? The end of the world?" Doug took Time and Inevitability and trapped them together inside him. He's the very embodiment of their union. Is he the harbinger of Chaos? The beginning and the end of the universe? Is it only a matter of time before he explodes? If I do manage to free Fleur, what happens to the world? How do we save the magic and start over?

The crow, perched on a mound of rubble, caws and flaps her wings. I shush her, but she squawks violently and pecks at a brightly colored piece of plaster. The flame dances as I move toward her. She settles as I rest the torch against the wall and begin pulling chunks of the fresco from the debris. A painted arm. Gaia's hands. Earth, water, wind, and fire.

A huge slab slides to the floor, revealing a face when the dust settles. A snake curls around Ananke's neck. Her two diamond eyes gaze up at me, one of them dull and flat. The other seems to wink in the torchlight.

I drop to my knees in the debris, tracing the shimmering edge of the gem with my fingers. Then I work the crystal free of the slab and blow off the dust. The Eye of Ananke stares back at me.

Lyon's missing piece . . . It's been hidden in plain sight all along. The eye . . . our future and all the answers . . . the scythe and the crystal . . . the earth and the Seasons . . . all the magic . . .

They were all right here, at the very beginning.

Suddenly, I understand what Lyon wants from me. I see the plan he envisioned before Doug took his life. I know why Lyon brought all of us back here. I told Fleur I'd come back for her as soon as I figured out how to free her. But it isn't just Fleur Lyon wanted me to save. Lyon expected me to save everyone.

46

THE ROAD NOT TAKEN

❧⬥☙

FLEUR

"Five minutes," Doug says.

Gaia's scent is overwhelming in the enclosed space: forests and oceans and desert flowers. And other things . . . rancid odors that shatter the illusion that she might still be here. A loaf of bread is beginning to mold in a bag on the kitchen counter, and the sour reek of spoiled milk drifts from a cereal bowl left in the sink. The potted plants scattered around the rooms sag in their pots. I don't have the heart to revive them only to leave them to suffer again.

Doug leads me through Gaia's apartment. Gaia's dining room table is littered with files and reports, as if she expected to come back to them. He pauses, shuffling through the pages, picking up a hastily scribbled note. The looping script matches Lyon's signatures on the memos in Jack's office back at the villa.

It's time, my love.

Doug crushes the note and tosses it away as he moves to the next room. I linger there, seeing the apartment differently. All the small clues that hint at the hurried, careless manner in which she must have left. All the loose odds and ends she left unfinished. How long had Gaia and Lyon known they were walking to their final deaths?

As I follow Doug, I slide a pen off the table and slip it inside the sleeve of my jumpsuit. Doug opens a set of doors in the hallway, revealing Gaia's home office.

"Her bedroom must be in there," he says, gesturing loosely to the only other pair of doors at the end of the hall. "Find some clothes and let's go."

His mind trails me as I go, but he seems more interested in snooping through Gaia's office than following me. Gaia's bedroom door is cracked, and I push it open, feeling like an intruder as I step inside. A long fissure streaks across the drywall over a four-poster bed, probably a remnant of my breakdown earlier. A trickle of water seeps through the crack, soaking the floral pillow shams.

I move quickly through the room, scanning the walls and peering behind furniture, searching for the secret panel Jack mentioned.

When I don't see it, I throw open the closet door, shoving hangers across the rack hard enough to make them screech. My hand stills as a rectangular panel appears in the wall. I grab the ornament from my pocket and the pen from my sleeve, using the open closet door to shield myself from view as I scratch out a note to Jack.

KAI IS HERE.
SHE KNOWS.

BE CAREFUL.
—F

The ballpoint pen cuts into the soft wood, clumsy and barely legible, but it's the best I can do. I dress hurriedly, stripping off the torn, bloody jumpsuit. The cut in my leg stings as I free the fabric from the healing wound. I layer on warm clothes and choose a long, heavy coat from the closet. Slipping the ornament over the hanger in its place, I position it just over the opening, where Jack's certain to find it. I leave the pen on the floor, tucked between a pair of shoes.

Doug's mind scratches impatiently against mine. I take a pair of gloves, a scarf, and a hat from the shelf and slam the closet shut, then meet him at the threshold as he reaches for the door. He gives me a distrusting once-over. I try not to think about Jack.

"What?" I snap, sliding my arms into Gaia's coat. "So it doesn't match. What do you expect? You told me to hurry."

His thoughts circle suspiciously around mine. I look him straight in his eye as I remember him on his knees, trapped in the arms of a tree, shouting as I ran from him when I dispatched his Guards in Greenwich Park.

Doug snags me by the collar and shoves me out the door.

47

"COME OUT! COME OUT!"

JACK

I sit in the tunnel beside the panel to Gaia's room, the walls of this place closing in around me as I read the message from Fleur.

This is all I have, the only information Fleur left me. She used her one shot to communicate with me to warn me about Kai. But how did Fleur figure out Kai is here? And more importantly, what does Kai know?

I tuck the ornament in my pocket. I can't worry about Kai right now. It was only a matter of time before she learned the truth about Névé anyway. She's probably got an arrow nocked with my name on it already. And if she knows the secrets I kept from her, I guess I really can't blame her.

Ananke's eye is heavy in my pocket. I pull it out and study it under the torchlight, but no matter how many times I've looked into it for an answer, all I see are the lines on my palm through the glass.

A piece of each of us lives on here in the Observatory. . . . Find those missing pieces.

Pieces. Plural. I found Lyon's missing piece, but my smaze is still roaming loose in this place. In the hands of a human, the eye is just a useless chunk of crystal. If Lyon's plan is ever going to work, I'll have to reclaim my magic first.

Exhausted and sore, I force myself up, ducking to avoid the low ceiling of the tunnel as I head back toward the catacombs. The tunnels are eerily quiet, creepier now that I'm navigating them alone.

The torchlight jumps, jostled by a sudden breeze. A chill crawls over me, and I pause, listening. This deep in the belly of the north wing, there shouldn't be any wind.

"Come on," I say in a low voice, certain my smaze is close. "I'm sorry about what happened before. But we can try again. Right?"

Pain pitches me forward, blinding and white-hot. I cry out, dropping the torch as my knees smack down on the stone. My left arm burns, refusing to move. I twist to see over my shoulder. An arrow is buried deep in the muscle.

A warning shot.

I throw myself forward on my torch, using my jacket to smother it. Darkness floods the tunnel and I crawl forward, trying not to shuffle as I squeeze into a recess in the wall. The arrow's shaft brushes the stone, sending a lightning bolt of pain through me. I grit my teeth, stifling the urge to scream.

A flashlight beam clicks on. Pale yellow light streams past me.

"You should have told me." Kai's voice shakes. Her foot splashes softly through shallow water. "I know what you did to my sister. I know what you took from her. Doug told me everything."

Arm clutched to my side, I will myself to stay upright. I don't want to speak, don't want to risk giving my location away, but she deserves an answer. "You have to believe me," I say through an exhalation of pure pain. "We had no choice."

Her flashlight swings toward the sound of my voice. "If we have no choice, then the war you started was based on a lie. That's what your stupid rebellion was all about, wasn't it? Choices?" The cone of her light grows brighter. A loose stone crunches under her shoe. "Amber made a choice when she broke my sister's neck. *You* made one when you stole her magic for yourself."

"I didn't do it for myself. I did it to save my friends. Whatever Doug told you, it wasn't the whole story."

"Part of the story is better than none of it." Her light snaps off, the sudden darkness disorienting.

"I know you're angry," I call out. "And you have every right to be. I'm not proud of what happened."

"Then you should have no problems giving it back."

"Giving what back? What do you mean?"

"My sister's magic." Her voice is close, but I can't tell where it's coming from. "I came here for Ruby, and I'm not leaving without her."

"You can't take the smaze. It's mine. It's part of me."

"And my sister was part of *me*."

The tunnel goes deathly quiet, the silence only broken by my rasping breaths and the soft spatter of blood dripping from my arm.

A fist slams into my leg. Pain explodes through my thigh as Kai jams the head of an arrow into the skin. Her breath is hot against my face as she pushes it deeper.

"Call it!" she says, grabbing me by the hair as I scream. "Call my sister's smaze. Make it come to you!" She knees me in the ribs. I double over, unable to breathe. With a ruthless jerk, Kai tears the arrow from my shoulder. A roar of pain rips through me. She knots her fingers in the front of my shirt, slamming me backward into the wall. "Do it!"

"I can't!" I gasp. "I don't know how—"

"It came for you before!"

I can't think. In the pitch blackness, all I see is the mountain in Cuernavaca, the blinding pain as I tumbled over ledges, her arrows buried in my back. All I taste is blood and dirt. All I hear is the *thwack* of her bowstring releasing and the ice cracking, the roar of bloody water in my ears as the lake swallows me.

Cold. Suddenly, I'm cold all over.

A draft stirs the air between us and Kai goes still, her breath heavy with condensation as the temperature in the tunnel plummets.

My smaze. It's here.

Kai eases her grip. I feel her retreat a step. Hear the rustle of her arrows in their quiver as her head whips around, searching for the smaze.

I bolt, staggering through the dark, left arm pressed tightly to my side, certain she's right behind me. I throw my right elbow back. Cartilage snaps. She gasps, and I hear her shoes skidding, followed by a thump. Her arrows rattle as they scatter.

My leg screams with every lurching step, my right arm braced against the darkness as I run. Kai's flashlight clicks on. The beam jumps off the walls, skipping over me, then doubling back as her feet pound the ground. Air rushes from my lungs as she slams into my back and my body hits the stone.

I buck under her, throwing her into the tunnel wall. Her flashlight rolls, the weak beam glowing a few feet away. I scrabble forward on hands and knees toward it as she gropes for the shaft of the arrow in my leg. A scream shreds my throat as she rips it out of me.

Before I open my eyes, she's on top of me. Blood drips off her chin, her flashlight casting shadows over her red-smeared teeth.

A frigid wind gusts between us, ruffling her hair.

We both freeze, breathing hard, each of us trying to catch sight of the smaze as it swoops over us.

One of us. Only one of us can take the magic.

I empty my lungs. Draw in a deep breath. Kai's hand clamps over my mouth, her head whipping to keep sight of the smaze as it dashes around us.

"Ruby?" she whispers. "Ruby! Is it you?"

The smaze tumbles in the air, dark and frantic. I don't know whose magic it is. Mine? Néve's? Both of ours, tangled up like Doug's and Fleur's? All I know is that if Kai takes it, there's only one way I'll ever get it back. And I need that smaze to rescue Fleur.

I bite down hard on her fingers. With a swear, she jerks her hand from my mouth. I kick out with my good leg and roll out from under her. Using the wall, I pull myself to my feet.

A cold gust of wind rushes between us. I suck in another breath, willing the smaze to come to me. Kai leaps at me, throwing me into the wall. She punches my injured shoulder. Kicks the wound in my thigh. I drop and cry out, unable to stay upright, as she draws in a breath and I watch my smaze disappear into her mouth.

Electricity crackles in the air. The temperature drops as the wind builds, spinning dirt devils through the tunnel. I shield my eyes from the flying dust, listening to the familiar snap of frost as it crackles over the walls. With a final violent gust, the air goes still.

I lower my arm. Through the thick white clouds of my breath, I see Kai kneeling, staring at her hands. Frost covers her forearms in lace-like patterns. Her short dark hair shimmers with ice, the frozen strands clinking softly in the silence. A tear slides free, freezing halfway down her cheek, and a hysterical laugh bursts out of her.

She looks up at me, her eyes swirling white.

She walks toward me and bends to pick up her flashlight. Then with a sudden whiplike crack, she backhands it across my jaw. I fall facedown in the dirt. She leans close, and her cold hand pats my side. "You don't deserve my forgiveness. Or my trust."

I wait for another arrow to sink in its claws. Instead, the temperature in the cave warms. I lift my head as the crunch of her retreating steps grows softer, moving farther and farther east. The direction we came from.

The direction I was headed when she shot me.

Toward the incinerator, where Chill and the others are waiting for me.

I stumble through the dark, no idea how far I've gone. My pulse pounds painfully against the swath of torn shirt I've tied into a tourniquet around my thigh. I focus on the roughness of the walls, on the sound of the tunnels, every other sense heightened by the absence of light. I have to find Amber before Kai hunts her down.

A dim light shines around a bend in the tunnel ahead of me. I stagger toward it, tripping through a familiar arched opening. Voices trail softly from the other side. Julio and Chill bickering. Poppy's half-hearted admonishments. Marie's dry laughter.

The cavern swims around me, their faces coming in and out of focus as I grab the edge of the archway to hold myself up.

"Jack!" Poppy cries out.

Three other sets of eyes swing my way. Chill rushes toward me. "Jack! What happened?"

"Where's Amber?" I manage between breaths.

Julio and the others exchange an odd look. "She smelled someone coming—a Winter. She said it smelled like you—that you must have found your magic. She was too excited to wait, so she went to find you." He pales. Like a shot, Julio grabs a torch from the wall and sprints down an adjacent tunnel. I stumble after him through the narrow opening. Behind me, I hear Chill and the others following.

I chase the torchlight. The glow expands as the tunnel widens, illuminating a cavern ahead. Amber's on her knees in the middle of it, her body limp and her chin sagging against her chest. Kai stands behind her, holding her upright by an arrow in her back. Kai's white eyes swirl with frost as she lets go.

Amber collapses facedown.

Julio's scream echoes through the cavern. Kai's bow snaps under her weight as he tackles her to the ground. She holds him back with icy hands as he reaches for her throat.

Too late. I was too late to stop her. Too late to save Amber.

A faint glow bleeds from the center of the cavern. Chill rushes to Amber's side as needles of light pierce her skin. Pulling her into his lap, he rolls her on her side, sharing his energy as he yanks the arrow from her back. She gasps awake. Marie and Poppy run to help him keep pressure on the wound.

Julio is a storm of rage. His arms shake as he holds Kai by her throat. A faint light flickers under her skin.

"Take it, Jack," Julio says through gritted teeth. "Take the magic!"

Kai's eyes fly wide. Her knee slams into his thigh, throwing him off-balance. She scrambles away from him, her chest heaving as Julio grabs her from behind. He takes her in a choke hold and turns her toward me like an offering. "Take it now, Jack!"

My magic brightens inside her, dangerously close to the surface.

I reach for the last knife in my holster. Kai struggles in Julio's grip. My leg throbs under the tourniquet and the ground wavers beneath me. I could take my magic back. It would heal me. I'd be strong again. I could go after Doug and try to save Fleur. But I can't do it. Not this way.

Breathe deeply and remember the lion that you are.

My hand pauses inside my jacket, the fabric heavy where the last smoke grenade and the transmitters we stole from Lixue and March are still tucked inside the pocket. Kai's frost-obscured eyes find mine. Her hand slides into her own pocket as if she's reaching for a weapon.

My fingers slip from the knife. Before I can talk myself out of it, I reach for the grenade, pulling the pin as I toss it at Julio's feet. If he sees what I'm about to do, he'll only try to stop me.

Julio leaps back as it rolls toward him. I dart for Kai before I lose sight of her in the thick white cloud of smoke. Her head snaps up as my arms come around her and I press my knife to her side. With a firm push, the blade sinks between her ribs.

Her back arches. My magic glows through her skin.

"I'm sorry," I whisper, slipping March's transmitter around her ear. The red light blinks as Kai goes limp in my arms. Then she's gone.

I drop to my knees, nothing left to hold me up as her magic—*my* magic—coalesces into a ball of light and soars away through the tunnels, hopefully making its way to March's chamber, somewhere safe.

As the smoke settles, I see everyone hovering over Amber. Julio's hands are on her face, his lips pressed to her forehead. She stirs, her eyelids heavy, but her wound is already healing.

Julio lifts his head, gaping at my bloody tourniquet and the jagged edges of my red-soaked shirt as if I've lost my mind.

"Anybody got a first-aid kit?" I ask raggedly, breaking the taut silence.

Chill, Poppy, and Marie all look up at me, their foreheads crushed with worry lines, as if they're mourning my loss. And maybe they are. Maybe part of me is, too. But I don't have time for that. I've got a plan to get Fleur back, and it's going to take more than magic to pull it off.

48
SEND MORE SPARKS UP

<u>DOUG</u>

The sleet sprays sideways, the sidewalks outside the portal covered in a thick layer of slush. Lightning flashes close. Thunder echoes off the brick buildings on either side of us as I direct Fleur toward Crowley's Wharf. I can feel her rising discomfort as we near the shearing, icy wind coming off the Thames. She found a heavy wool coat and hat, a long cashmere scarf, and lined leather gloves in Gaia's apartment. The base layers under her jeans and heavy sweater make her look stronger, more solid, but under it all, her magic is already shivering. I'll have to be careful not to keep her out here too long.

The storms have been getting worse as rumors of Lyon's and Gaia's deaths are spreading. According to Lixue, Seasons have been pairing off, forming small groups and fleeing their regions rather than risking a trip back through the ley lines. For every freed Season we manage to hunt down and bring home, two more disappear from our system, creating new storms. Power grids have collapsed in dozens of cities, making it even harder to bring the connected Seasons home. My Guards are putting out fires everywhere, but no matter what we do, the sparks keep jumping.

There's no more time for useless lessons with potted plants and battles of will in the park. No more time to waste searching for the eye. It's time to come up with my own answers. I have control over Gaia's magic; that's all I need to create new Seasons—my *own* Seasons. If I can make enough of them, I can indoctrinate them myself and restore the balance Lyon ruined. Kai is certain to keep Jack occupied for a while, which means Fleur and I can get to the business of fixing this mess. If anyone is stubborn and altruistic enough to bring back the dead, it's Fleur.

The magic inside me stirs as I follow the Prime Meridian north, responding to the low thrum of the massive ley line's power under my feet. Through it, I feel connected to the entire universe. If I close my eyes, I can almost see the mesh of the world—a map of time and space—every electromagnetically charged line glowing under the surface of the earth.

The Trinity Hospital bell tolls from the chapel ahead, the low *bong* muted by the gusting wind. Somewhere close, a lock snaps open and the smell of trash blows from the next street. I cut east, following the scent into a parking lot near Highbridge Wharf. A teenage boy exits an apartment, hunched into his coat, sleet pelting his shaggy hair. A trash bag swings from his hand as he crosses the parking lot to a waste receptacle.

Fleur bristles beside me. "What are you doing?"

"I'm doing all of us a favor." Fleur grabs my sleeve as I break stride with her to follow him, her grasp slipping as I lunge for the boy's collar.

The boy drops his bag, tin and glass clattering inside it as I take him around the neck and hold a knife to his side.

"Relax," I tell him, "this will all be over soon."

"Doug! No! What are you doing!"

The boy arcs forward as I plunge the blade in. He clutches his coat, the thick wool concealing the blood. Fleur's panic sets the magic inside me buzzing. Her wide eyes leap from the windows of the boy's apartment to the empty street behind us. The last toll of the church bell rings and dies.

"The world needs Seasons, Fleur. He's dying. Show me how to save him."

"I don't know how! I can't!"

"I've seen you do it."

I search her eyes. See her mind search and grasp the same memory. She's sitting in a glade of wildflowers. A butterfly's perched on her face. Sommers freezes it, killing the thing in some stupid display of his magic, or maybe just to piss her off, payback after she'd hurt him. Fleur cups the butterfly in her hand. Blows into her fingers. The butterfly flies away.

"You know how to do this," I say, holding the kid up by his coat. "You can bring him back. It's the same damn thing."

"That was an insect! That was small magic! It took me years to figure out how!" she cries, clutching her head. "He's a human. A person. I'm not strong enough for that!"

"Then he dies."

"You're a monster!"

"Maybe I am. But I'm a monster with a destiny, and you've become part of it, like it or not." She'll do this. She feels too much. Cares too deeply for life to let this boy bleed out in the street. I chose this spot, in the shadow of a hospital, its steeple visible behind me, reminding her where she came from. How she got here. That she's only here because she was saved.

Her choice is easy. Because I haven't left her one.

FLEUR

The boy's eyes are wide on me as blood seeps between his fingers. The church bell clangs in my head.

I drop beside the boy, taking his hand as his eyes close. My touch won't do anything to stop his death, but it seems wrong to let him suffer without offering any comfort.

Doug paces through the slush in tight lines in front of me. "He's out of time, Fleur!"

"I can't do it," I shout up at him, blinking away sleet. "*You* control Gaia's magic! Not me."

An angry muscle works in his jaw. With a grunt of impatience, he sinks to his knees across from me, glaring at me over the boy as he rolls him onto his back. Doug takes him roughly by the neck of his coat, tipping up his airway and pressing his open mouth to the boy's slack lips. Doug blows two quick rescue breaths, pausing to glance uncertainly at me before dipping his head and blowing two more. A thin stream of gold light passes between them, and I feel the boy's cold wrist for a pulse. Doug's cheeks flame as he draws another breath and tries again. Over and over. The boy's face only grows paler. His bleeding slows. Then his heart stops.

Chest heaving, Doug breaks the seal. The boy's neck sags against the ground. Doug reels to his feet, watching the dim glow fade in the boy's throat.

"You have Gaia's magic! Do something!" I shout at him, angry that he's giving up. That he would start something like this without any certainty that he could finish it. "We can't just leave him here!"

Doug's lip curls with a callous smile. "You're right. We can't."

A cold hand grabs the back of my mind. A chill crawls down my spine as Doug's magic slides into my muscles. My body arcs forward, my palms slapping on the icy ground, bracing me over the boy.

"What are you—?" Heat roars through my body like fire over a fuse. I feel Gaia's power pass from Doug's body to mine, crossing the tangled bridge between us like magic over a ley line. There's a buzzing in my head. My lungs are on fire. Stars creep into my peripheral vision as the magic fills my lungs.

Light flickers, low in my field of vision. Brilliant beams of amber light radiate through the gap in my coat. I gasp, a tendril of magic puffing out on my breath. "What did you do to me?"

"I rid you of your pathetic excuses. What the hell are you waiting for! My permission?"

Doug's mind forces me forward until I'm hovering over the boy's lips. Static crackles in my hair. I focus my thoughts and feel Gaia's magic rise up and respond, as if it already knows me. Doug thrusts my mouth against the boy's.

"Breathe!" he shouts at me.

Magic gushes from my lungs into the boy, a flood of amber fire. A soft glow kindles in his chest. I feel Doug's mind hovering, watching the light brighten with a sick curiosity as my lungs empty completely.

The cold hand releases me. I jolt upright and cough, breathing hard. A few stray sparks slip between my lips, and I wipe them on my sleeve. The boy's cheeks fill with color and his chest expands. I fall back on my hands, light-headed, as Doug calls the earth magic back to him.

The boy stirs. Doug reaches down and opens the boy's jacket. The wound is gone, leaving behind a faint scar and the musky-sweet scent of fallen leaves. With a smug smile, Doug snaps a transmitter around the boy's ear.

"Lixue," he says, reaching into the boy's pocket and withdrawing a ring of keys, "bring the Autumn home."

Needles of light begin to pierce through the boy's skin. I shield my eyes from the flare as his body dematerializes, and with a static hiss, his magic soars toward Greenwich Park.

I shake the red slush from my trembling hands. "You're sick! You just ripped that boy's life out from under him! What about his family? And his friends? He had his whole life ahead of him, and you took it!"

He hauls me up by the back of my coat. "I don't know why you're so upset about it. I was the one who killed him. You just saved his life."

"You could have revived him yourself. You didn't need me."

He leans down into my face. "You're wrong. You were the one who said you have to *feel* something for the magic to work! You have to *want* to save someone. And I didn't give a shit about that kid," he says, throwing a finger toward the bloody slush he left in the street.

Doug's jaw rocks back and forth as he fidgets with the boy's keys, his mind holding tightly to some emotion he doesn't want to reveal to me.

"Let's go," he says, turning back for the parking lot. "It's too cold for you out here."

49

AND GOES DOWN BURNING

JACK

Amber shakes her head, frowning over Poppy's shoulder as Poppy ties off the last of my stitches. "I don't know, Jack. This plan feels like a long shot. You're trusting an untested theory. We could be risking Fleur's life. We have zero assurances this will work."

"My theories have held up before." I tense my leg, testing Poppy's handiwork as the muscle flexes under the stitches. Our escape from the Observatory—hell, our very survival off the ley lines—was based on a theory. We've made it this far. Lyon believed in me. Enough that he and Gaia sacrificed themselves to make sure Fleur and I survived. He prepared for his death, knowing I would come. He left me the letter, the eye, and my smaze for a reason. I have to believe this is the right path. "There's no undoing what Doug's done. Doug *is* Chaos. He's entropy in action. Eventually, he's going to break. We have to find a way to untangle his magic from Fleur's."

"Then I say we do it." Julio's arms loop around Amber so their skin touches. He presses a kiss to her temple and the color returns to her cheeks. She leans back against him, letting him hold some of her weight. "No way are we letting that power-tripping asshole take Fleur down with him."

Chill admires the wicked retractable barbs on the arrowhead he pulled from my leg. He slaps the bloody thing into my palm like it's some kind of souvenir. "I'm in. What about you?" he asks Poppy, ruffling her hair as she leans over my thigh, surveying her work.

She offers me a grim smile as she bites down on the thread, snapping it off the spool. "We're not letting Fleur go through this alone. Of course I'm in."

"So how do we do it?" Marie asks, leaning against the wall, destroying a piece of spearmint gum with her teeth.

I drag my pant leg down and ease gingerly to my feet. I fish the second transmitter from my pocket and toss it to Chill. "We need a working stasis chamber."

Marie raises an eyebrow. "You said Fleur demolished the chambers you found in the cavern."

"The power is still running in the Autumn wing. If Julio and Amber can sniff out an empty dorm room, I can get us in. Chill shouldn't have any problems getting a stasis chamber online."

"How do we get the transmitter to Fleur?" Chill asks.

"We find a way to get a message to Doug and use the eye to draw him out. We tell him we'll only bring the eye if he brings Fleur. That we want to negotiate her release. Then we find a way to pass her the transmitter and haul her out through the ley lines."

Julio glances down at Amber. She nods against his back. "Amber and I can get the transmitter to Fleur. We should be able to distract Doug long enough for Chill to get Fleur out of there. Between the two of us, we can probably take him down."

Poppy frowns as she closes her first-aid kit. "Whoever kills Doug will just take the brunt of all that power. We'll be in the same boat Doug is in now. No," Poppy says, rubbing blood from her hands with a wet wipe as she thinks, "we already know how this works. The magic is anchored to the objects. Chronos's magic was tied to his scythe. Ananke's was tied to the crystal eye. If Amber or Julio strike Doug down, the magic will be free. Time will jump straight to whoever's in possession of the staff, and Inevitability will find whoever's in possession of the eye, but if Fleur's gone, Gaia's magic will be lost all over again. It needs someone to jump into. And I think that someone has to be tied to the earth."

They all look to me, each of us silently answering the question. Fleur is probably the strongest Spring in this place. Had Gaia and Lyon seen this moment coming all along? Is that why Lyon never told us what he knew about our future—that Fleur would be kidnapped and brought here—because he knew this was the only way she'd come? Did they let it happen, knowing the role Fleur was destined to play in all this? If so, that only makes *my* role in Lyon's overarching plan clearer.

"It has to be me. I have to be the one to meet with Doug." I fight back a wince as I shrug on what's left of my blood-stiffened shirt. "Doug won't see me as a threat because I can't take his magic the way you can. I'll meet with him alone and get the transmitter to Fleur."

"Then what?" Marie asks around her gum.

"Then I take the staff."

She stops chewing to stare at me. "But you already said you can't take the magic for yourself."

"No, but I can steal his toy for a while." I think back to what Kai said. About how we all have the ability to wield a little magic. All this plan needs is a little sleight of hand. "We'll use Fleur's disappearance as a diversion. Fleur's flash should be all the chaos we need to pull this off. While Doug's distracted, I'll steal the staff and run. Poppy will ensure Fleur makes it through the ley lines. Chill will be my eyes and ears, making sure I have a clear path of escape with the staff."

Chill grins, holding his knuckles out to me like he always did before I left for a hunt. "Just like old times."

I tap my knuckles to his, wishing this was a hunt I could finish on my own. "I'll try to keep Doug away long enough for you to wake Fleur. How long will she need, Poppy?"

Everyone turns to Poppy as she thinks. "If she's conscious and strong when I pull her through, I can open her chamber and wake her right away."

Julio shudders. "Better give her a barf bag for that flight."

"She'll be fine," Poppy assures me. I look to Chill, satisfied when he nods.

"I'll buy her as much time as I can. As soon as I make it back to you, one of you will have to take the staff and finish Doug. Once you cut him down, the magic will be loose. It'll be up to us to harness it. We already know Gaia's magic will be drawn to Fleur. Ananke's magic should be drawn to whoever has the eye. And Chronos's magic will be drawn to whoever has the staff."

Amber and Julio exchange grave looks. Whoever takes the magic will be bound to this place, responsible for all of it—time, natural order, inevitability—indefinitely. It feels like too much to ask. We only just got free of this place. But I already know what Fleur would do. The same thing I would do, if only I could. She'd sacrifice anything to save the rest of us.

"I'll take the staff." Julio squeezes Amber's hand. She nods tightly.

"I'll take the eye," she says. Amber glances at Marie. For once, Marie doesn't argue. What choice do we have? Amber holds out her hand for the crystal. I reach inside my pocket and freeze.

"What's wrong?" she asks.

"The crystal. It was here, zipped inside my pocket." I take the torch from the wall and wave it over the ground. I get down on all fours, scraping aside loose dirt and pebbles, eyes peeled for a glimmer, but it's not here. My hand stills as I retrace my steps. I'd been facedown in the dirt after Kai hit me with the flashlight. She leaned over me and patted my side. No, the side of my *jacket*. Then here, right before I put the transmitter in her ear and sent her into stasis, she'd reached inside her pocket.

"Damn it, Kai!" I throw down the torch, pacing the chamber. "Kai. She took it. She has it with her. It's in her hand. We have to find it." It's the only bait I have.

I sling on my pack and run, limping back through the tunnel toward the incinerator, the fresh stitches stinging with every step. Kai had a Guard's transmitter. She would have materialized somewhere in the dormitory level, not down here with the captured Seasons. The Guards' stasis chambers would be kept somewhere more comfortable and secure. Someplace with power.

The Autumn wing.

The footsteps of the others are close behind me. When I make it back to the incinerator, the heavy iron grate creaks as I swing it open and climb in. Shoes scrape metal as the others scale the rungs of the ladder after me. I'm almost level with the Administration floor when a rush of hot air rolls up from below.

I look down. The heads of the others are silhouetted by a bright orange glow. Black smoke billows up from the bottom of the shaft, choking and thick. Someone's lit the incinerator.

"Climb! Hurry!" Poppy shouts.

I scramble up the rungs, stitches pulling. The ladder shakes under our combined weight. Steam hisses up through the cylinder as Julio wrangles the moisture from the caves. The thin cool mist settles over us, insulating us from the heat, but it's not enough to quench the fire. The metal bars are getting hotter by the second.

I look up, gauging the distance to the Admin level, just as Lixue's head stretches through an opening in the shaft. A flame ignites in her hand. It grows, stretching downward until I feel its heat on my face. Guards above us. A fire below. We're trapped between floors.

"Hurry!" Marie shrieks. "The bars are too hot! I can't hold on!"

"Holy crap, Chill! Your hand is cold! Let go of my ankle," Julio snaps.

"Sorry, buddy. I need a little juice for this. Everybody hold on!" Chill's voice echoes up the shaft, carried by a howl of icy wind. The blast chases Lixue's flame back. The metal rungs groan with the rapid change in temperature.

"I can't hold it for long," Chill shouts. "Move it, Jack!"

I start to climb, propelled by the wind. A screw cracks loose from the ladder, nicking my cheek as it flies past. The metal rung under my foot creaks.

We'll never make it to the dormitory level. The others have too far to climb, and the fire below us is blazing hotter. The access panel to the Admin level is only a few feet above me. I already know Lixue (and probably her team) is waiting on the other side, but it's our only way out.

I climb the last rung and crawl through the opening. Lathered in sweat and soot, I tumble into the thick haze of the hall. Smoke pours from the access panel. Marie coughs as I haul her, then Poppy, through it.

Lixue's voice comes from behind me. "You and I have a score to settle."

I turn, positioning myself in front of the opening. Lixue plays with a fireball, tossing it between her hands, staring at me down the length of the hall as if she'd like to skewer me and roast me for dinner. Two Guards flank her. Behind me, Marie shouts down to Chill, Amber, and Julio, screaming at them to climb faster.

"Where's your smaze?" Lixue asks me with a cutting smile. "Oh, wait. I'm pretty sure your guard dog—*and* your magic—just turned up in a stasis chamber in the gymnasium in the north wing. I guess Sampson turned on you, too. Too bad," she says with a careless shrug. "You two defectors deserved each other."

I hold up my hands. Keep my voice calm. "Kai Sampson left because she knew this place was spiraling out of control. Doug's going to bring this entire place down. All we want to do is put things back the way they were. To restore the balance. There's still time to do the right thing and let us go."

"Put things back the way they were?" She barks out a laugh. Her eyes slide to Chill, Amber, and Julio as they climb out of the shaft behind me. "What do you think we've been trying to do? Do you have any idea how many Seasons are loose up top? Do you have any idea what happens when they can't survive out there alone? They're in the wind, Jack! Their territories are deserted! And these storms and quakes and fires and floods are the result. People are dying! They're dying everywhere! And it's supposed to be our job to keep the world balanced! To keep control of it!" Her eyes well with tears, all casual pretenses abandoned to rage. "This is all your fault! This all started when you and your girlfriend decided you were too good for this place. Your selfishness started the rebellion that got us here. All Doug wants to do is restore order to chaos."

"He *is* Chaos!" I shout. "Don't you see what's happening to him? He can't control that much magic. It's going to rip him apart. And when it does, everyone in this place is going to be in the wind right along with him."

Her twisted scowl is full of contempt. "Then how about you go first?"

Her flame roars as she advances toward us. The other Guards follow, one wielding a lance of ice, the other a sphere of churning water. Julio, Amber, and Chill take up positions beside me. There's a hiss of fire, a crackle of ice, and a rush of water as they prepare to counter the attack.

Suddenly, the ground shakes, throwing Lixue to her knees. We all reach to steady ourselves as the tremor takes hold. Plaster splinters, falling in chunks from the ceiling. A crack splits the marble floor with a deafening *snap*.

Lixue backs away from it, touching her transmitter.

"Chronos, do you read me?" she shouts. A squawk. Chatter over the radio. A Guard's voice is broken by static, the words too garbled to catch. "*Chronos and the Spring . . . up top . . . not answering his . . .*"

A torch rattles and falls from its sconce, throwing sparks over the floor. A wall ruptures beside us. We shield ourselves as a pipe bursts, spraying water into the hall.

Lixue's eyes leap to mine. Doug's already up top. If he evacuated, he must know this place is ready to implode.

"It's Doug," I shout across the gap. "He can't stop this. The more power he takes on, the less control he has. Forget the freed Seasons. They chose their own fates. And they're safer out there on their own than the ones you're holding prisoner down here!" I wait for her to hurl fire at me. But she just looks at us, her fists clenching and unclenching at her sides as the walls shake. "If you don't let us fix it, we're all going to die. I know how to stop this."

"I can't let you go!" She shakes her head as if she's trying to convince herself.

"Then at least let *them* go!" I point toward the dormitories above us. There must be hundreds of Seasons trapped in their rooms. "There's still time to save them."

Lixue gnaws her lip as the Guards wait for her command. They duck as a chunk of ceiling collapses behind them. The auxiliary power flashes and dies. Alarms blast and sprinklers explode to life, raining over our heads.

She shields herself with an arm. "There are too many of them! We'll never be able to get them all out!"

"Is there a way to disable the locks to all the dormitories from the Control Room?" Chill asks.

Lixue nods.

"Do it," I tell her. "There's an emergency tunnel at the cardinal point of each wing. They lead out through the catacombs." I take Lyon's map from my pocket and tear it into four sections, one for each wing. I give Winter to Chill and Poppy, Autumn to Amber and Marie, and Summer to Julio. They tuck the pieces under their shirts. I hold out the last piece of the map to Lixue. She hesitates.

"Take it," I say, shoving it into her hand. "Evacuate everyone from the east wing. Tell them all to find a partner, or better yet, a group of Seasons, as soon as they reach the surface. Tell them to lie low until the quake stops. We'll find a way to broadcast a message when it's safe to come back."

Lixue and the Guards give me one last look as they turn to leave, dodging debris as they race toward the Crux.

50

A CRASH OF WOOD

<u>FLEUR</u>

Doug adjusts the rearview mirror, angling it away from him. He looks ridiculous in the driver's seat of the tiny Volkswagen Golf, with his blond hair nearly brushing the roof and his legs bent to fit so his thighs touch the steering wheel.

"Where are we going?"

Doug ignores me, flipping through station after station of static.

I hunch into Gaia's sopping coat, crammed against the passenger-side door of the boy's car, as far from Doug as possible. The shiver fighting its way to my surface has nothing to do with the cold. Remnants of Gaia's magic are still warm inside me, like embers waiting to die. Like they could reignite and burn me alive if they're allowed enough air, and I hate myself for it.

What Doug did to that boy—and the small part I played in it—was nothing Gaia would ever have done. She would never have taken an innocent life. Would never have forced anyone's hand. Live or die—she always gave us the choice.

And I took that boy's choice. Because Doug had taken mine.

The crackle of static breaks. . . . *wind speeds more than one hundred fifty kilometers per hour off the Isle of Wight . . . Man died in Hampshire when a tree fell on his car . . . Several critically injured after lightning strikes in Winchester . . . Flights now also grounded at Gatwick and Heathrow . . . More than four hundred thousand without power . . .*

I reach and switch off the radio.

"You didn't have to steal his car," I snap, angry that there's no punishment I can inflict on Doug without suffering it myself. Maybe I deserve it. "His family might have needed it."

He looks over at me, his mouth twisted with disgust. "Don't be such a hypocrite, Fleur. Since when have you or your friends ever cared about taking things that don't belong to you?"

"That's not the same thing."

"You're right. It's not. I gave the kid a transmitter and sent him home. Which is more than I can say about you." A fleeting image of Denver darts through his thoughts, and I turn toward the window. Doug turns south, taking us back toward the park.

"If we're going back to the Observatory, we could have walked," I argue. "We didn't need a car."

"You're cold and wet and tired. You and I have a lot of work to do, and you're no good to me if you're passed out." He switches on the heater, manhandling the dials and shoving the fins on the vents so they're pointed toward me. But I don't need his charity. Or his attitude. I don't want to think about what kind of work Doug means. I just want to get back down to the Observatory. Back to Jack.

The car slows. Doug eases to a stop along the brick perimeter fence around Greenwich Park. The wipers slap back and forth, ticking off seconds as we sit in the middle of the empty road, rain and sleet bouncing off the hood. I glance up, eyes narrowed through the windshield to see why we've stopped.

A couple runs through the park, hands locked together, their pace too quick, their faces drawn. They don't bother to slow as they step into the crosswalk. She glances back over her shoulders as he pulls her across the street. Even from a distance, I can see their fear.

Doug cracks his window, his crystal eye trained on them as he draws in a breath. I smell it too.

A Summer. An Autumn. Running together.

Doug revs the engine. The couple looks up, their eyes widening as Doug slams the car into gear. His foot comes down hard on the accelerator and the car lurches under me. I grip the door, one hand braced on the dashboard as the car squeals toward them.

"What are you doing?" The car straddles the center lines as the couple nears the middle of the road, directly in our path.

"Teaching a lesson," he says, upshifting as the engine screams.

The boy pulls the girl by the hand and they sprint for a side street.

The tires throw up plumes of sleet and water as we fishtail on the icy road. Doug shifts, turns, and suddenly we're right behind them. Chasing them down.

"Stop it!" Gripping the door, I press back into my seat. "You're going to kill them!"

"You're catching on quick." He jerks the wheel, turning sharply as they double back down the next street, back toward the park. It's their only chance of outrunning us.

"Don't do this," I plead with him. "It's only the two of them. There's no harm in letting them live their own lives. Let them go!"

"And then what?" His bumper is dangerously tight on their heels. "Who takes the regions they've abandoned? Who keeps everything from spiraling out of control? You?" He darts a sharp look at my face, returning his gaze to the road—to his target—as the car's tires smack into a pothole. "When hundreds of others start getting the same idea, are you going to come with me and find new Seasons to replace them? Are you going to help me turn them? Train them? Hope they all don't defect and abandon their posts?" His laugh is scornful when I don't answer. "I didn't think so."

The car skids again, chasing them through a turn as they sprint hand in hand for the brick wall, toward the entrance to the park. We're too close. Moving too fast. There's no way they'll make it.

"These two can serve as a lesson to the others. Trust me," Doug says, leaning into the accelerator. "It's better this way."

The car surges, feet from the couple's legs. I reach across Doug and grab the wheel, twisting it hard with both hands. Doug slams on the brakes. The car careens off the road, the girl's sweater a bright blue blur in the passenger-side window as we glide past her toward the bricks.

There's a metallic crunch and the splintering of glass as my body's thrown forward. A splitting pain pierces my forehead as the seat belt digs into my neck. I lift my head, blinking through the dizziness, catching a splash of blue through the opening in the gate, before my head falls limp against my chest.

51

TO PERISH TWICE

JACK

We all take off at a sprint for the Crux, following Lixue and her team up a locked stairwell normally restricted to the Guards. When we reach the dormitory level, I stick close to Julio as we break off into groups. Lixue raises her voice over the ringing alarms and falling debris, shouting orders into her transmitter.

"I said open the doors in every wing! All of them!" She looks back once over her shoulder as she whips out her key card. But the one Fleur gave me is already in my hand. I give the one I stole from the Guard outside Doug's apartment to Julio, and we both get busy opening the other ports as Lixue and her team disappear behind the ivy-shrouded gate into the east wing.

Amber and Marie shout a quick "good luck" as they race through the Autumn port.

My feet root in place as I watch Chill and Poppy dash into the Winter wing.

*I'm pretty sure your guard dog—*and *your magic—just turned up in a stasis chamber in the gymnasium in the north wing.*

Julio pauses, waiting for me at the Summer port. "Come on, Sommers! Let's go before this whole place caves in."

Before this whole place caves in, burying the eye with it. Without it, our whole plan to save Fleur, stop Doug, and avoid a global catastrophe goes up in smoke.

I start toward the north gate.

"Jack!" Julio shouts across the Crux.

I turn, jogging backward toward the plexiglass port. "Get everyone in the south wing to the mouth of the tunnel. If I'm not there in forty minutes, then get to the surface and find the others."

"But Fleur . . ." Julio's eyes say everything. Our plan to extract her through the ley lines is no longer an option. The reserve power systems are already starting to fail, and every stasis chamber in this place will be buried under thirty stories of rubble within the next few hours. But I know what she'd say. Behind Julio, through the steamy plexiglass port, Summers pour out of their dorms. Handlers with panicked faces carry their sleeping Seasons on their shoulders. Others rush from room to room, helping to evacuate those too weak to save themselves.

"She'd tell us to help them. No matter the cost. Go," I tell him. "Get them out and find the others."

Julio nods once, a tight snap of his head, as if there are words he's holding back. He darts through the port and starts shouting out orders. A moment later, a train of Summers follow him down the hall and out of sight.

I jog through the north gate. Chill's already got the Winters organized, forming a line into the passage in the closet, the one Kai and I used to sneak up from the catacombs. As I rush past him toward the gymnasium, he calls out to me, "Jack, where the hell are you going?"

"I'm going after the eye."

The low rumble grows louder, as if the earth is preparing to scream. As if the entire place is ready to devour itself. I cut through the back halls of the Winter wing, dodging debris and shielding my face from the sparks that shower from dangling wires.

I round the last turn to the gym. The doors are jammed shut, and I shoulder them open, wedging myself inside. The air is thick with fumes. The gymnasium is filled with rows of stasis chambers on wheeled platforms, their lids open and dark, the room already evacuated. A generator sputters on the far side of the room, low on fuel. A single domed lid is still closed in the far corner, bright inside, the ventilator humming.

I weave through the rows of stasis chambers toward it, spotting Kai's crown of short, dark spikes through the fogged glass. Her face is peaceful behind a layer of frost. The Guards evacuated everyone but Kai—the *deserter*, Lixue called her. They probably deemed her unworthy of rescuing.

"Come on, come on, come on!" Frantic, I push buttons on the display, but the lid won't open. I fall as another tremor rocks the room, huddling under Kai's chamber as a chunk of ceiling collapses. When I look up, the red emergency release lever is right in front of me. I flip it. The lid of the dome rises with a rush of fog, exposing Kai's naked body. Her right hand's clenched in a fist. I pry the eye free and zip it into my pocket.

Torn, I stand beside her chamber. She tried to kill me. She tried to kill Amber. Still, I can't leave her here to die.

I shrug off my jacket and wrap it around her. A stitch tears in my shoulder as I grab her arm and pull her upright. With a groan, I sling her over my good shoulder and haul her to the exit.

"Just so we're clear, we're even after this," I mutter, wondering if part of her can hear me. If any part of her will wake up and remember this.

"Not that it matters, but I was actually starting not to hate you." Emergency sprinklers flare to life above my head, dousing us as I head for the maintenance closet. The shelves are still pulled away from the wall, the vent we crawled through still hanging open.

"And I'm sorry." I pant as I descend into the tunnels. The stone walls mute the shriek of the alarms. "You're right, I should've said something sooner, but I knew you'd be pissed, and I was afraid you wouldn't give me time to explain," I say through a wheeze as we reach the bottom. I snap my lighter on and wave the flame in front of us, blinking away dust. "I tried to talk to Névé. Tried to get her to listen or just let us walk away, but Chronos was offering a bounty for our deaths, and Névé wanted the prize. Fleur tried to hold her back, but when Névé went for the kill, Amber had no choice but to defend herself. Névé's death was an accident. But taking her magic to save Amber, Julio, and Fleur . . . that was my decision, and I take full responsibility for that." It feels better, like a burden's been lifted, to say it out loud, even if she can't hear me. "So there you have it," I say, adjusting her weight as I carry her deeper into the catacombs. "I'm an asshole for not telling you before, and I'm sorry."

A crow swoops over my head and I follow it, almost certain I'm headed south. The bird flaps hard, darting back and forth across the blocked tunnel ahead, its wings beating in a blind panic.

I hold the lighter higher, illuminating an impassable wall of fallen rocks.

"No!" Sweat drips in my eyes as I strain under Kai's weight. A cave-in.

A smaze tumbles back and forth, searching for an opening before disappearing through a paper-thin gap between two fallen stones. There has to be another way out.

I turn around, careful not to hit Kai's head on the narrow walls as a tremor shakes the tunnel. Stones fall from the ceiling, pelting Kai's back and my shoulder. I duck, dropping the lighter as a shower of rock crashes down in front of us. The tunnel goes black, the air thick with dust.

Easing Kai to the dirt, I feel around me for the lighter.

My hand closes over it, and with a *snick*, the cave warms with dusty light. The flame stays steady, not a single waver, as I hold it aloft. My stomach turns as I realize why.

No air.

The tunnel is completely blocked on both sides of us.

"Oh, shit," I murmur.

The rumbling quiets, giving way to a soft trickling sound. I angle the light one way and then the other, my heart climbing higher in my throat as I trace the sound to its source. Water pours from a crack in the stone, spilling down the wall and spreading over the floor, the soles of my shoes slowly disappearing under the shimmering black surface of it.

The water rushes under Kai's outstretched legs, lapping at her cheek where it lies against the tunnel floor. I take her shoulders and prop her upright against the wall. By the time I get her steady, the water's already up to my ankles.

I sluice through it toward the blocked opening, tearing at the fallen stones with one hand and holding the lighter high with the other. The stones plunk down, one by one. But for every rock I manage to move, another's waiting behind it.

This is it. We're going to drown down here. Maybe it's karma. Nature balancing out my fate for the shitty things I've done.

Another rock splashes free. The water's so cold I can hardly feel my legs anymore. My fingers bleed, nails breaking as I scrape at the edges of the stones.

When I turn to check on Kai, the water's reached her chest. I wade through it, my shoulder burning as I haul her over it once more and carry her back to the wall.

"I guess this is Ananke's idea of poetic justice," I mutter as the water laps at my waist. "My punishment for trying to drown you in my damn infinity pool." I hold Kai around her waist as I kick at a stone, desperate to loosen a path for the water to escape through, but the pressure's too strong. "What I wouldn't pay to be a Summer right now."

"Exactly how much are you willing to part with?" comes a muffled voice through the stone.

"Julio?" I yelp with joy. "How the hell did you find me?"

"You haven't showered in a week, asshole. How do you think?"

"A little help here?" I shout back.

For a moment, there's only silence from the other side of the wall. I rock forward, tightening my grip on Kai as the water pulls at my ankles.

It rushes backward over my legs, the water level falling, exposing the pile of stones in front of us. Behind us, a wall of water roils and froths, held back by some invisible barrier.

"Stand back!" Julio's shout is labored, his voice strained. The wall of water inches closer, creeping toward us.

"Hurry!"

The loose stone I'd been working to free wobbles and shakes. With a last kick, Julio knocks it clear, and the rest of the barrier tumbles down around it. Julio and I rush to move the stones away until we can see each other over the top. His eyes narrow on Kai as he digs.

"You're a goddamn saint. Or a fucking idiot," he says through a grunt as he strains to hold the water in check. "I can't decide." He hauls the last stone from the pile, opening a space big enough for me to pass through as another rumble builds in the walls. "Let's get out of here."

He shoves me down the tunnel as his dam bursts, and the water chases us toward daylight.

52

HIS BESETTING FEARS

<u>DOUG</u>

There's something stuck in my eye. Something's pulling me. Tugging me. An arm around my waist. Lilies in my face. And smoke. A shrill voice, yelling at me.

"Doug, get up! You have to get up!"

Gaia. She's there. Upside down.

No. I'm upside down. Hanging from my seat belt. Blood spatters the roof of the car. Firelight catches on a broken bottle. The smell of spilled liquor and smoke fills the air.

Gaia leans in the broken window, reaching for me. She's beautiful. The most beautiful woman I've ever seen, her silver hair reflected in the fuel slick on the pavement, her voice like an angel's. "Come with me now and live forever by my rules. Or die tonight."

One eye opens, the other stubborn, refusing. I blink away something viscous and red, swearing quietly when the back of my hand cuts my face. My coat sleeve shimmers.

Glass. I'm covered in it.

Orange flames dance through the cracks in the windshield. Black clouds billow from the crushed hood of an unfamiliar car.

The car I stole . . . The kid's key ring dangles from the ignition.

"Come with me now, or we're both going to die!" Fleur tugs at my seat belt, struggling to unhook it. Blood drips down her temple from a cut on her head, staining the ends of her hair.

"Damn it, Doug! Get up!"

My hands are clumsy as I grope for the latch. It's stuck.

"There's a knife . . . in my pocket," I mutter, hardly able to form a coherent thought. She reaches for the pocket closest to her. "Left. The left pocket."

With a muttered swear, she wedges herself between me and the steering wheel. I lift my arm, giving her room, groaning as pain explodes behind my rib. Fleur winces, sucking in a sharp breath as if she feels it, too. She flips open the blade, sawing through the thick fabric of the seat belt. When it finally snaps free, she grabs my arm and hauls me out, both of us screaming as my rib shifts.

The fire crackles and pops, hissing as it makes contact with the rain. Fleur chokes on the thick smoke as she wraps my arm around her shoulders and guides me through the gate into the park. I feel her inside my head, prodding the edges of my mind for soft spots. Not spying. Checking for damage, I realize. I wonder how much of that memory she saw before I woke up. If she saw everything that happened that night. If she saw my argument with my mom. If she saw my dad walk out or heard what he said. If she saw me polish off that fifth of cheap booze in my car just before the wreck. I shake off her arm and push the memory somewhere deep.

There's a deafening explosion behind us. Propelled by a blast of heat, we land facedown in the grass. Fleur pushes up on her hands, twisting to see the car engulfed in flames. Rain streams down her face, soot and blood trailing over her cheeks as she stares across the park at a blue speck in the distance.

The ground seems to shake. I can't tell if it's my tweaked sense of balance or if it's actually moving. Fleur looks down at her hands where they dig into the grass. Her eyes become glassy and distant. I feel the tug of her magic as it reaches out from her body, spiraling into the ground. My own chases it, painfully slow.

Our eyes lock.

Tremors.

Deep.

"Come on," she says, nearly dragging me to my feet. "We have to get back. The north portal is close."

Arm thrown over her shoulder, we hobble north. Halfway across the long stretch of green, Fleur pauses, her hand digging painfully into my rib.

She tips her head toward the heavy rumble of footsteps we both sense vibrating through the ground. I follow her gaze as a swarm of bodies spills into the gate from Park Row. Winters. Dozens. No. *Hundreds* of them. Fleur whirls, gasping as a wave of Seasons thunders toward the center of the green.

Springs, Autumns, Summers . . . they crest the rolling hills toward us. They're all running, exploding from every cardinal direction, converging in the center of the park. Among them, I spot the khaki uniforms of Guards—*my* Guards—breaking up the Seasons and dividing them into groups as they arrive, directing them in clusters toward the portals on each end of the park.

"Lixue," I mutter, "what the hell are you doing?"

"What's happening?" Fleur asks, searching the distant faces of the Seasons on the green. "They're evacuating. Something's wrong." She starts toward them, but they're headed right for us. For the north portal behind us.

I grab Fleur, turning and tugging her by the hand as the throng surges closer. She nearly trips, craning her neck to see over her shoulder, probably looking for her friends in the mob. I pull her across the street and up the steps to the row house.

Water streams down my face as I bang on the door. A Guard peers through the sidelight, her eyes widening when she sees us. Muffled voices shout as the locks slide open and the door swings inward. I drag Fleur across the threshold. She runs straight to the parlor window, hands pressed to the glass.

"Lock the portal down," I shout back to the Guard. "No one gets inside. Am I understood?" I storm into the parlor and snap the drapes closed. There are too many of them. My head's splitting. I can't think.

"You can't just leave them out there," Fleur cries. "They need help. They're your Seasons. You're supposed to protect them!"

"They abandoned the Observatory. They know the rules."

"What about that boy? The one you murdered and turned just now? Did you bother explaining the rules to him?" She follows me to the kitchen, close on my heels. "You felt that quake. Those Seasons had no choice but to run!"

I feel them coming. Feel their feet on the street before they even reach the front porch. They pound on the door, their faces pressed to the sidelights, shouting my name.

"There's always a choice." I take Fleur by the arm and shove her to the cellar door. "No one gets in!" I call over my shoulder, slamming the door behind us.

I shut my eye, listening to the muted thumps of fists against the portal door, the muffled pleas. Fleur paces at the foot of the stairs, her fear and adrenaline rioting inside me.

I shrug off my wet coat, biting back a groan of pain as I peel off the sleeves and sit down on the top step. My side throbs, and I tip my head back against the door. *This is it. The end of the Observatory. The end of everything.* Lyon is probably laughing in his grave. And Michael . . . I hope wherever he is, he isn't witnessing my failure.

I bury my bleeding head in my hands.

"Chronos?" the Guard asks through the door. "There's someone trying to make radio contact. He says Jack Sommers is asking for you."

53

TO SEIZE THE EARTH BY THE POLE

JACK

Auggie opens his door just after midnight, drawing his ratty robe closed around his flannel pajamas. The wind roars, sheets of rain lashing our clothes and blowing across his threshold as we stand there, drenched and shivering. I'm pretty sure he's going to slam his door on all of us, until he sees the body slung over Julio's shoulder. Kai's dripping hair is the only part of her that isn't covered by the blanket we found in the back of the van we stole to get here, but it must be enough. Auggie's dark eyes dart past us to the alley behind his row house, then he ushers us inside.

The door closes, muffling the howling wind outside. Poppy and Marie exchange skeptical looks once we're all stuffed in the cluttered parlor. The fly I saw last time I was here buzzes curiously around us. Amber sniffs and wrinkles her nose.

Auggie pushes the blanket back from Kai's face. He pulls a penlight from his shirt pocket and pries open one of her eyelids, studying her pupil as he passes the beam in front of the frosty swirls in her iris. "Let me guess," he says dryly, "you finally got around to telling her about her sister."

"You knew?" I ask. He was less than welcoming to me when we met. I thought he, like many, only knew about me because of the rebellion. If he knew about my involvement in Névé's death, why didn't he tell Kai then and there?

His nod is tight. He points to a rumpled sofa against the far wall. Julio drops Kai into it, wrapping the blanket snugly around her, tucking her arms securely against her sides, probably afraid she'll wake up and come after him with a shiv of ice.

"Daniel Lyon paid me a visit about a week before you two showed up here. He said Kai might come seeking my help, and she might bring a surprising guest with her." Auggie blows out a weary sigh, watching her sleep. "Didn't seem right to keep that kind of secret from her, and I didn't want any part of whatever Lyon thought was coming. But he said it was critical not to distract her from whatever mission she was on. He said she would discover the truth on her own, at the right time." He turns to me, frowning at my wet clothes. "There's a closet upstairs. Get some towels for you and your friends. You're tracking water everywhere."

The others huddle in the parlor as I ascend the rickety wooden steps. Just like the lower floors, the hall upstairs is littered with old junk. Sagging cardboard boxes line the walls, and I'm forced to wedge myself sideways to open the first door I come to. Flipping on a light switch, I gape at the contents of a cluttered bedroom. The room smells old, like the basement of the boys' home where I lived when I was human. It's filled with vintage things: A sewing machine with a huge metal pedal.

An old Hoover vacuum cleaner with giant wheels and a placard that says 1912. A radio with actual dials. And a turntable for vinyl records I'd bet Amber would kill to get her hands on.

The floor creaks as I step inside, reaching for a reel-to-reel film projector like the one my mother used to play old home movies on.

"Don't touch anything with those wet hands." Auggie's voice rises up the stairs. "I spent years rebuilding everything in that room. Every piece of it is worth more to me than you are."

I back out of the room, turning off the light and closing the door behind me to search for towels. I find them in a closet farther down the hall and pile them into my arms before descending the stairs.

"I assume you're here because you need help cleaning up this mess." Auggie gestures loosely to a huge console television as I distribute the towels to my friends. The TV is older than I am. Maybe even older than Amber. Auggie adjusts the rabbit ears on top, bringing the images into focus. The muted black-and-white weather report casts gray light over Kai's face as she sleeps. Her breathing's shallow, her face ghostly pale.

"We had nowhere else to go," I explain. "Doug's lost control of his magic. The entire place was coming down. We evacuated as many Seasons as we could through the tunnels."

"And Doug?" he asks. "Where is the staff?"

"He got out. I assume he has the staff with him." And Fleur. But I doubt Auggie cares much about that.

He lifts his chin, studying me down the length of his hawkish nose as if he's forming some opinion of me. "And you thought I could help you find him."

"No, I . . ."

Auggie turns for the door to the cellar. I rush after him, remembering all the tools and gear and equipment he has hidden down there. "Wait, *can* you?"

"No." He snaps the chain hanging from the ceiling. A lightbulb flickers on, illuminating the narrow turn in the creaking steps as he descends them. "Too many Seasons running amok. Too many storms. Too many power outages. . . . Finding Doug will be next to impossible unless he wants to be found."

I follow him into the cellar. "What if I have something he wants?" The crystal is a warm weight against my side. I draw it from my pocket and hold it between us.

Auggie's pupils flash. "Where did you get that?"

The others tread down the stairs. I ignore their hushed whispers as they take in Auggie's collection of weapons. Auggie reaches for the eye. I close my fingers around it. This is the only play I have left. "How do I draw him out?" I ask.

Auggie sucks his teeth, scratching at a patch of stubble on his jaw. He gestures for me to follow him to a shelf in the corner, where he whips a bedsheet off an old VHF radio, throwing up a cloud of dust.

"Whoa," I say as Auggie lugs it from the shelf. "I haven't seen one of these since I was in high school." And even then, they were old. Auggie sets it on an antique desk, then drags a chair across the room and sits in front of it. "Does it even work?"

Auggie grunts, his glasses low on the bridge of his nose as he switches on the radio. The fly circles him once before alighting on his shoulder.

Curious, Amber comes to look, too. "I don't understand. How's a radio going to help us get a message to Doug?"

Auggie's smile is slight, and maybe a little smug. "The Observatory's always listening."

"The Observatory's empty," I say. "The Control Room is probably buried by now."

"Only the parts below ground." Auggie frowns as he tunes the dials. "Tell your friend that blade is sharp."

I turn to see Julio messing around with some kind of katana. I draw a finger across my throat and point at the shelf where it came from. He puts it back in its sheath with an exaggerated sigh.

Auggie switches on the mic. "North Portal . . . North Portal . . . Do you read me?"

Marie, Chill, and Poppy hover close, listening as Auggie adjusts the knobs. I rub my eyes, fighting frustration and fatigue. The radio is a dinosaur. There's no way this is going to work.

A hiss breaks the silence. "This is North Portal. Identify yourself."

The hair on the back of my neck stands on end. The damn thing actually works. My gaze flicks to the beaded curtain at the entrance to the back room. If Auggie managed to get all that stuff upstairs working, what else is he capable of fixing?

"This is . . . Black Fly." Auggie clicks off the mic, his eyes twinkling with mischief. "I've been listening to the Control Room's communications over these lines for years. You know, a fly on the wall." He waves his hand, gesturing at all of us. "Or now, apparently, a fly in their ointment."

"This is a private frequency," the staticky voice says. "You do not have authority to transmit."

"To hell with your authority," he grumbles before switching on the mic. "I have a message for Chronos. Do you copy?"

I hold my breath through an extended pause.

"Who is this?"

"Patch me through to Douglas Lausks."

"I'm afraid that won't be poss—"

"Tell him Jack Sommers wants to speak with him."

Auggie gets up from his chair, motioning for me to take his seat. The leather creaks as I ease into it. He turns the mic toward me.

We hold our collective breath through a series of clicks.

"I assume you made it out alive." Doug's voice is gruff—impatient and hostile. If I close my eyes, I'll see him walking beside me down the hallway to the Crux, slamming my back into the wall and shoving a flame in my face. With every fiber of my being, I want to kill him. I want to rip Fleur out of his mind and run him through with Lyon's scythe.

"Disappointed?" I bite out.

"Not at all. You and I have unfinished business."

My eyes slide back to the beaded curtain. "I'm ready to settle up. Name the time and place."

The length of his pause makes my skin crawl. "The bandstand. Greenwich Park. One hour from now. You come alone."

"You come with Fleur." I tug my damp hair, worried I've said too much. I can't afford for Doug to suspect this is a setup. "I want proof that she's alive and safe. Then you can do whatever you want with me."

Static crackles like frost. "One hour," he says. "Don't make me wait."

Auggie switches off the radio. "Why didn't you tell him about the crystal? You could have used it to negotiate for the girl."

"I'm not negotiating with anyone."

"There's no way he'll give her to you."

"That's why I'm going to take her." I get up from the chair and round the desk, pushing aside the beaded curtain to Auggie's back room.

"What are you doing?" Auggie asks.

I stoop beside the old stasis chamber I saw when I was last here, examining the buttons and dials. The dome of the chamber is real glass. Not plexi. No plastic parts. It's all brass and bronze and silver. All gears and big glass bulbs with fine curls of steel filament. "What would you need to make this thing work?"

Auggie's brow crumples. "Just power. The machine is simple, but it's—"

Chill whistles low, examining the dials at the foot of the chamber. "This thing is incredible. I've never seen one this old."

"Please . . . don't touch those. They're very delicate," Auggie says, hovering over Chill.

"Is there a transmitter?" I ask.

"Of a sort," he says hesitantly. "I mean, all the parts are there, but—"

"That console TV upstairs, the radio, the old reel-to-reel, and the turntable in the bedroom . . . You got those working, didn't you?"

Understanding dawns on his face. "You can't be serious."

"What are you thinking, Jack?" I turn to see Amber behind me, giving me that same wary look she wore the day I first told her I wanted to break us all out of the Observatory.

"I'm going to get Fleur back through the ley lines, just like we planned. It's the only shot we have at getting her away from Doug."

"Jack, this stasis chamber looks like it belongs in a museum," she sputters. "What if it doesn't work?"

"Do we have any other choice?" The others filter into the small room behind her. I look at each one of them, begging them to trust me the way they did before. "It's the same plan, just a little farther to run. We can do this. I know we can. I'll meet Doug in Greenwich Park and get the transmitter to Fleur. Poppy will pull Fleur through the ley lines. While Doug's distracted, I'll grab the staff, then I'll lead him back to Auggie's. We'll take Doug down here, exactly the way we talked about."

Auggie's eyebrows shoot up. The thin wire rims of his glasses slide down the knot on his nose as he gapes at me. "Absolutely not! I've kept this place a secret from the Control Room for decades."

I sweep an arm around the room. "All the more reason to confront him here. He won't know what he's walking into. We have all the weapons we need to fortify this place and set a trap." I can already see it playing out in my mind. Marie and Poppy can pick off his Guards from the windows upstairs when they get close, and Julio and Amber can ambush Doug once he makes it inside. If Fleur's already here, then each of the gods' magic will have a host. Chaos averted. "Can you get it working?" I ask Auggie in a low voice. This chamber is my entire plan to save her. We have no other options.

Auggie clears his throat softly. He moves to a tiny engraved box on a shelf on the wall. Reaching inside, he takes out a circlet of silver, copper, and gold and places it in my hand. "Fleur will have to be wearing this."

The bracelet is bulky—a wide braid of shiny metals. "It's too big. How am I going to get it to Fleur without Doug noticing?" It's going to be hard enough just getting close enough to put it on her.

"That won't be your only challenge. The bracelet is only a conductor. In addition to wearing this, she'll need to be near enough to a ley line to be drawn through it." Auggie takes a map from the shelf and unrolls it, then straps a magnifying light to his forehead.

"What is it?" I ask, leaning over his shoulder to read the faded ink.

"A map of the ley lines. When this chamber was in use, this was the only way to channel a Season home." He traces a finger over the page, pointing to his house on the map, slowly dragging it north, his gaze intent, searching for something.

"Finding a ley line is easy," Chill says, pointing to the center of the map. "The Prime Meridian passes right through Greenwich Park. If Fleur's at the bandstand, she'll practically be standing on one."

"It's not that simple," Auggie says, squinting through his glasses. "This isn't Wi-Fi. The device has to be located on a line as well. There," he says, tapping the map. "We can move the stasis chamber to Burgess Park." I lean closer to the map. The park is due west from the intersection of two ley lines.

"How far is it?" I ask.

"Not far," Auggie says, rolling up the map. "The van parked in the alley . . . it's yours?" Julio gives a noncommittal nod. "Good. We can use it to move the stasis chamber. If we hurry, there's still time to get the chamber to Burgess Park."

Burgess Park is at least four miles from the bandstand. I'm fast. But with an injured leg, and on little food or sleep, four miles will feel like I'm prepping for a marathon. Or a gauntlet.

I had imagined slipping a transmitter into Fleur's hand. Had imagined Poppy's voice riding along in her ear, keeping her safe. Suddenly, the plan feels like too much of a long shot. What if Doug sees the bracelet and catches on? What if the chamber fails and she ends up in the wind? What if I never make it back to Auggie's with the staff?

Chill claps my shoulder. Giving it a reassuring shake, he says, "She'll be okay. We'll bring her home. I swear."

"I know." If anyone can bring her home, he and Poppy can. But there's small comfort in that when the entire future of the world is riding on my ability to get her to the ley line and deliver the staff to my friends.

"Take this," Auggie says, fitting a wireless headset around my ear. It looks like some kind of transmitter. I reach up to touch it, wondering how old it is. The corner of Auggie's mouth turns up as he adjusts it. "Don't worry. It's new technology. Your Winter friend here will be able to track your location. He'll be able to hear you, and you will hear him."

"We'll take care of Fleur," Chill says quietly. "Better get moving. You've got less than an hour to make it to the bandstand."

I turn for the stairs, expecting Julio and Amber to try to stop me. Expecting someone to voice out loud all the what-ifs clamoring inside my head.

Julio raises his palm to me, grabbing my hand when I slap his and dragging me in for a hug. He smacks my back, careful to avoid my stitches. "Don't let the asshole get close enough to mess up your hair," he says, pulling a reluctant smile out of me. "Let's go. I'll give you a lift to the park."

Amber nudges him out of the way. She wraps her arms around me, squeezing me hard. "Be safe," she whispers. "We've got your back."

54

BOW AND ACCEPT THE END

Jack's up to something. He'd never be foolish enough to agree to this. Gnawing my thumbnail, I pace the edge of the bandstand, staring out into the park. Rain pours in sheets over the lip of the octagonal roof, spattering the flagstones below it. The tall towers in the financial district are eerily invisible, the horizon wrapped in a thick black haze, washed out by churning storm clouds. Entire swaths of the city are unlit, without power.

It's easy to see why Doug picked this place. He paces the perimeter of the bandstand, his eyes bright as they swing like a searchlight over the park. The bandstand is high ground, offering clean lines of sight in every direction, the tall trees spread out in a wide ring around the iron structure like giant guards. This whole thing reeks of a trap. And I don't like how slippery Doug's mind feels when I try to see what's happening inside it.

Doug stops moving. He stiffens as Jack appears in the distance, like a smaze through the mist. I run to the rail, but Doug's mind grabs hold of me before I reach the steps.

The shirt under Jack's jacket is stained, traces of red bleeding through the wet fabric. There's an odd lean in his step, as if he's favoring his right leg, and a ragged hole in his jeans becomes visible as he approaches. The rain amplifies the tang of blood in the air.

Jack pauses just inside the ring of trees. His eyes flick to me, careful not to stray long from Doug and his scythe. If Jack's injured under all that blood—if he's in pain—he's trying hard not to show it. Still, I'm surprised he didn't conceal his injuries, knowing Doug will undoubtedly try to exploit them.

Or maybe that's all part of Jack's plan. To make himself into easy prey. To sacrifice himself in some stupid, selfless way to save me, like he did in Cuernavaca.

My voice breaks when I call out to him. "You shouldn't have come."

"He *needed* to come. Didn't you, Sommers? To prove yourself. To prove to *her* that you're not some has-been, washed-up, impotent fuck-up with low self-esteem and mortality issues."

To his credit, Jack doesn't flinch.

I jerk hard on my magic. Doug shakes it off with a dark laugh. He's trying to look careless, but I know better. His fingers burn around the staff and his head is pounding. His cracked rib aches every time he draws a breath. Just like Jack, he's refusing to show it.

"Just to be clear," Doug shouts, "you're here to submit yourself to me. Or you can fight me, if you'd rather die a hero." Doug points at me with the end of his staff. "But you should know that anything you do to harm me will harm her equally." He scratches the cut on his forehead with the tip of his finger, making sure Jack sees it. Jack's gaze skips to the matching gash on mine. His eyes dance between us.

I told Jack that Doug would never hurt me. That Doug *couldn't* hurt me. But I didn't tell Jack this. I knew if I did, it could cost Jack his life. That he would hesitate to protect himself against Doug to avoid harming *me*.

I can see the wheels in his head turning, changing direction. Whatever he had planned, he hadn't accounted for this.

"Don't worry about me. I'll be okay." I clutch the ache in my side, wishing Jack could read my thoughts. That he could understand this small clue—this weakness of Doug's I'm trying to project to him. That he could know how badly I wish he would turn around and run from this.

Rain slices down his face. "I want to see her first," he shouts.

"You've seen her."

"Just let me say goodbye to her. Then you can have me."

Doug's laugh booms across the green. "How stupid do you think I am? That's as close as you're getting. On your knees, Sommers." The ground heaves. Grass tears as a root erupts behind Jack, grabbing his ankle and dragging him down. He splashes down on his hands and knees in the mud.

My clenched fists shake at my sides. Doug's figured it all out. How to wield the earth magic. How to use me to make Seasons. He has everything he wants. And now he has Jack. Doug's last remaining weakness is me. "Stop it! If you kill him, it will destroy me. The pain of it will haunt you. *I* will haunt you."

"You already do." He adjusts his grip on the scythe, his eye burning with hatred as he smiles at Jack. "You have no idea how long I've waited for this." He takes a step toward the stairs, but I'm faster. If he's going to cut Jack down, he'll have to go through me.

I leap down the bandstand steps, my mind already fighting to loosen the root from Jack's ankle. "Get up!" I shout to him. Jack shakes out of the root's grip, and my mind slips free of the plant as Jack kicks it away from him. I'm running to him, only feet away from his outstretched hands when my legs lock up. My body jolts to a stop, the momentum nearly toppling me forward into Jack's arms as Doug slides like a serpent into the deepest recesses of my thoughts. I feel him stretch, taking up every last corner of space, pulling me back to him. A tear slides down my cheek. "Run, Jack! Go!"

Jack's eyes open wide with shock as I drop to my knees. As Doug's magic drags me down like a stone. "I'm not leaving you," Jack says, kneeling in front of me. He takes me by my shoulders. They're shaking with the effort of resisting Doug's will.

"Listen," Jack says urgently, his hands framing my face. "I know I made you a promise at the villa before they took you. I know I told you I'd never leash us to this place again. But I also promised you I would come up with a way to fix this and get us out of here. And to do that, I need you to trust me." Jack's hand slides into his pocket. "Whatever happens next, forgive me."

Something cold circles my wrist. A coil of braided metals. I feel Doug stumble off the bandstand toward us. The heavy thump of his staff against the grass. Jack's fingers slide into a patch of dirt between us.

"I'm sorry, Fleur. I'm so sorry!" His hands fly up, scattering mud in my eyes.

I cry out, clawing at my face.

I can't see. Can't open my eyelids.

Behind me, Doug screams. I fall forward into Jack's arms as Doug loses his grip on my mind.

"Run, Fleur!" Jack hauls me to my feet. He runs, dragging me behind him, breathing apologies, begging me to move faster. I trip, but he doesn't slow. I anchor my thoughts into the ground, feeling out ahead of me with my mind, anticipating the shallow dips and hills. Every blink stings, bringing thick, hot tears to my eyes. The landscape is a painful blur in front of me.

"I know it hurts. But if you're hurting, he's hurting, too. Keep him out of your head!" Jack rasps, pulling me faster. "Don't open your eyes. Don't let him see through you."

I feel Doug recovering. Feel him rising to his feet. I feel his magic lashing outward, tracing our connection, listening to the ground, searching for me.

My shoe catches in a rut and my ankle turns. Jack slows when I suck in a sharp breath. "Keep running!" I say, forcing myself to keep up.

I don't know how far we've gone. Or where we are. My shoe slaps down on a hard surface—a sidewalk or a street. Jack picks up speed. Eyes shut, I let my magic guide me, determined to keep pace with him.

Finally, he drags me to a stop. Breathing hard, he takes my face in his hands, brushing away dirt and rain. "Can you see?"

Blinking my eyes brings on a fresh wave of pain. I catch a flash of my surroundings before I'm forced to close them again. The white face of the Shepherd Gate Clock ticks behind Jack's head.

"Do you know where we are?" he asks.

I nod. "What are we doing here?" I say, frantic when I feel my connection to Doug getting stronger. "He's coming, Jack. We should keep going. You should run, please!"

Jack turns my face back to his. "Listen to me carefully. You have to get to the Meridian. You know where it is."

"But the fence." There's a brick wall behind him. A high iron gate. The Meridian is on the other side of it. I feel its faint *tick* pulsing through the bricks.

"There's a tree above us, just over the fence. Find it."

"I feel it."

"Can you feel the ley line?"

I nod.

"Get over the fence," he says quickly, tightening the coil of metals around my wrist. "Stand as close as you can to the Meridian. Call out to me the second you're there. Chill and Poppy will take care of you."

I grip his hand before he can let go. "But what about you?"

"Don't worry about me. I have a plan."

"Jack, no—"

"Go, Fleur! Now!"

Jack ducks and taps my leg, presumably to hoist me toward the tree. I grab his head and pull him upright, bringing his face to mine. I reach out with my mind, tracing my connection back to Doug's, grabbing hold of my magic and reeling it toward me. Gaia's magic clings to me as I drag a small finger of her power inside me, then through me, until a tiny flicker of it warms the breath inside my lungs.

Hands tangled in Jack's hair, I press my mouth to his. I think about our kiss at the pond. The snow. The ice. The winter scent of his breath and the frost on his skin. I remember the way that kiss tasted as I seal

"We should stay and rest for a while," she suggests. "Maybe your smaze will come."

I answer around a mouthful of chocolate. "We've been down here for more than a day already, and it hasn't bothered to show itself."

"Maybe we're moving too fast. Like, remember when you were little and your mom would tell you if you ever got lost, just stay put so it'd be easier for her to find you?"

I choke on a dry laugh. "I stayed put for years waiting for my mother. I promise, she never came looking for me."

"Oh," Kai says quietly. I hate the undercurrent of pity in it. The last thing I need or deserve is Kai's sympathy. "Either way, it wouldn't hurt to rest," she suggests. "Aside from that nap in the catacombs, you haven't slept since we left Cuernavaca. And you lost a lot of blood."

I pace the room. If I sit down, I might not get up again. "We don't have time to rest. We need to find my smaze. And then I need to find Fleur and Chill."

She stares into the bag of chips, searching for a whole one in the crumbs. "Relax. He won't kill them. Not yet, anyway," she amends. "He'll wait until he finds you."

I watch her face, wondering what kind of relationship she and Doug had for the short time they were here, planning their escape. She talks as if she knows him intimately. And I can't reconcile that with the person Lyon trusted with those maps.

I pluck the second Twix from the wrapper and chase it with a bottled water. Thirst slaked and hunger momentarily sated, fatigue finally digs in its claws. I slip off my jacket and holster, the air too thin and warm in the powerless room.

"Looks like someone beat us here," she says. Piles of loose papers and files are scattered around her. Our ratty old couch is flipped upside down, the hard drive's dismantled, and the glass top of Chill's desk is cracked. My stasis chamber is gone, its wiry guts dangling from the wall.

I kick aside Chill's keyboard, a sudden heaviness settling in my chest. The room still smells faintly like him. Like Dorito cheese and contraband beef jerky. With a pang, I bend to pick up the remains of his plush polar bear. Its seams are ripped open, the stuffing spilling out. I carry it into our old bunk room and set it back on his bed. My closet doors hang open and my old rolled-up sketches of the Observatory are gone. And the footlocker where I kept Fleur's ornaments . . .

I slam the closet door and drag my hands through my hair. I should have paid Boreas to pack them up and store them. Should have asked Lyon to ship it all to our home in Cuernavaca. And now Doug's taken them. I can guess why he'd want the maps, but why her ornaments?

Rubbing my eyes, I lumber back to the front room. Kai's righted Chill's desk chair. She plops down into it, tearing open a bag of chips. She holds one out to me. "I found them in a drawer. Candy bars, too," she says. "And there are some bottled waters in the mini-fridge under the window—"

"I know where my own mini-fridge is," I say irritably, ripping the bag from her hand. "These are Chill's."

With a scowl, she snatches it back, tucking a chip forcefully into her mouth. "In case you haven't noticed, we haven't had anything to eat besides bread and water since we got to London. I don't care *whose* chips they are. I'm hungry. And you should eat, too." She pitches a Twix at me, and my stomach grumbles like a damn traitor for it. With an infuriated sigh, I tear into the wrapper, jamming a whole candy bar in my mouth.

I cry out, clawing at my face.

I can't see. Can't open my eyelids.

Behind me, Doug screams. I fall forward into Jack's arms as Doug loses his grip on my mind.

"Run, Fleur!" Jack hauls me to my feet. He runs, dragging me behind him, breathing apologies, begging me to move faster. I trip, but he doesn't slow. I anchor my thoughts into the ground, feeling out ahead of me with my mind, anticipating the shallow dips and hills. Every blink stings, bringing thick, hot tears to my eyes. The landscape is a painful blur in front of me.

"I know it hurts. But if you're hurting, he's hurting, too. Keep him out of your head!" Jack rasps, pulling me faster. "Don't open your eyes. Don't let him see through you."

I feel Doug recovering. Feel him rising to his feet. I feel his magic lashing outward, tracing our connection, listening to the ground, searching for me.

My shoe catches in a rut and my ankle turns. Jack slows when I suck in a sharp breath. "Keep running!" I say, forcing myself to keep up.

I don't know how far we've gone. Or where we are. My shoe slaps down on a hard surface—a sidewalk or a street. Jack picks up speed. Eyes shut, I let my magic guide me, determined to keep pace with him.

Finally, he drags me to a stop. Breathing hard, he takes my face in his hands, brushing away dirt and rain. "Can you see?"

Blinking my eyes brings on a fresh wave of pain. I catch a flash of my surroundings before I'm forced to close them again. The white face of the Shepherd Gate Clock ticks behind Jack's head.

"Do you know where we are?" he asks.

I nod. "What are we doing here?" I say, frantic when I feel my connection to Doug getting stronger. "He's coming, Jack. We should keep going. You should run, please!"

Jack turns my face back to his. "Listen to me carefully. You have to get to the Meridian. You know where it is."

"But the fence." There's a brick wall behind him. A high iron gate. The Meridian is on the other side of it. I feel its faint *tick* pulsing through the bricks.

"There's a tree above us, just over the fence. Find it."

"I feel it."

"Can you feel the ley line?"

I nod.

"Get over the fence," he says quickly, tightening the coil of metals around my wrist. "Stand as close as you can to the Meridian. Call out to me the second you're there. Chill and Poppy will take care of you."

I grip his hand before he can let go. "But what about you?"

"Don't worry about me. I have a plan."

"Jack, no—"

"Go, Fleur! Now."

Jack ducks and taps my leg, presumably to hoist me toward the tree. I grab his head and pull him upright, bringing his face to mine. I reach out with my mind, tracing my connection back to Doug's, grabbing hold of my magic and reeling it toward me. Gaia's magic clings to me as I drag a small finger of her power inside me, then through me, until a tiny flicker of it warms the breath inside my lungs.

Hands tangled in Jack's hair, I press my mouth to his. I think about our kiss at the pond. The snow. The ice. The winter scent of his breath and the frost on his skin. I remember the way that kiss tasted as I seal electrons around an atom. Fleur cries out and a lance of pain drives through my head. I drop the staff, cupping my eye. A beam of light burns through it, radiating between my fingers.

Fleur's magic pulls away from me, tugging itself toward the Meridian. My mind clamps down on her, desperate to hold her inside me as she's ripped away.

A swarm of sparks breaks free of my body and soars over the fence. I rock back on my knees, shielding my face from the white-hot flash as Fleur absorbs it, and like a bolt of golden lightning, she's sucked down into the earth.

The sudden absence of her magic leaves the park darker than it was. Colder.

The scratching burn is gone from my eye. But something feels . . . wrong. My heart begins to pound and my pulse quickens.

You are now, and will always be, alone.

I clutch my chest. Pain explodes behind it as Gaia's magic begins to rage.

Jack turns to face me. There's hope in his eyes. Fear in his sweat.

"Where is she?" I bellow.

His smile is triumphant. "You don't know, do you? You can't feel her anymore."

I charge at him.

Jack ducks my swing. He drives a punch into my cracked rib, as if he knew the injury was there. The hit doubles me over. When I look up, he strikes the blind side of my face. His fist snaps against my cheek. I shake it off, the sting paling in comparison to the riot happening inside me.

Jack leaps for the scythe.

I tackle him, catching him by the back of his jacket and hauling him over. I throw a punch to his jaw. Another to his gut. He expels a fogged, cold breath that smells faintly like Fleur. Like magic . . .

I stare down at him, my fist frozen as I try to make sense of it. Jack pivots out from under me, swiveling onto his side. He scrabbles for the end of the staff, but I'm taller, my arms longer. I leap over him, my fingers reaching it first.

Jack rolls to his feet as I get to mine. We circle each other, panting steam, dripping rain. He inches away, backing toward the footpath.

"I can help you, Doug. But we don't have much time."

"I am Time! I control it!" I swing the scythe. It hisses past his midsection, kissing the side of his coat.

"If you were in control, the world wouldn't be coming apart. Admit it, you're in over your head. You need help."

"I don't need a damn thing from you."

Jack widens the circle, increasing the space between us. His eyes are hungry on the staff, like he's torn between running and fighting for it. A thick cloud of fog passes between us. Jack sprints, disappearing inside it.

"No!" With a flash of my scythe, I stop time. The pain takes me to my knees. The smell of blood overwhelms every other scent as a thick, hot stream of it flows from my nose.

I stagger upright. Jack's surrounded by mist, frozen midstride. Positioning myself in front of him, I release my hold on my magic. Jack hurtles toward me, his eyes flying wide as he skids to a halt. He falls at my feet, scrambling away from me, leaping back to avoid the scythe as it swings.

"How did you do that?" he pants.

"Where is she?" I spit blood, wiping my nose on my sleeve.

"Listen to me." He holds out his hands as we circle each other, as if I'm some kind of feral creature he's trying to cage. "That pain you're feeling is the magic. It's going to fight its way out, and when it does, it's going to kill you. And if you don't give up some of the power, it will probably destroy all of us. The Observatory. The Seasons. Everyone."

I laugh at his assumption that I care. "If I'm going down, Sommers, you're all coming with me."

I swing the scythe again, and this time, Jack runs.

56

TATTERED AND SWIFT

JACK

I haul ass into a patch of thick fog. Stitches pulling, muscles screaming, lungs on fire, my feet fly down the sloping path toward the northwest side of the park. Doug must be screwing with time. It's the only explanation for the way he appeared right in front of me. No one can move that fast. But to do it again, he'll have to spot me first. I stick to the dense white ribbons of mist, changing trajectory every few yards. The staff is heavy. It'll only weigh him down. I just have to stay far enough ahead of him.

Doug screams my name. I don't look back.

"Jack?" Chill's voice in my ear is a light in the dark.

"I'm here," I say in the short space between breaths. Fog and rain weave a heavy blanket over the park, obscuring the path ahead of me. I don't know where the hell I'm going. With any luck, maybe Doug doesn't, either.

"Did you get the staff?"

"No."

The length of his pause makes me want to turn around. To go back and fix my mistake.

"Keep going," Chill says. "It doesn't matter. You're doing great."

But it does matter. Our whole plan depended on me taking the staff.

"Fleur?" I pant. "Where is she?"

"She's here. She made it."

The relief almost brings me to my knees. I hit flat terrain at the bottom of the hill and push myself faster. "Bring me home, Chill."

"I've got you."

"Jack!" I turn over my shoulder, nearly tripping at the nearness of Doug's voice. The fog parts. Through it, I catch a flash of silver.

I lengthen my stride. "Doug's right behind me."

"How far?"

"A hundred yards, maybe." I thought the staff would slow him down. That the fog would hide me. I've got to get off the path. Someplace he can't see me so easily.

A stitch in my leg tears as I hurtle into a cluster of trees.

"No. Stay on the path. I need you in the open." Chill sounds more confident about this than I feel.

"He's too close." I hop fallen branches, splashing through wet grass. "I won't make it."

"You'll make it. Trust me."

Fuck.

I veer back onto the path, feeling far too exposed, even in the dark. "I hope you're right about this."

"Have I ever steered you wrong?"

"Don't get me started."

He barks out a laugh. "Bear left at the fork ahead of you."

"What fork?" The city around the park is completely dark, not a light in sight, as if the entire power grid's down. Suddenly, the path splits ahead of me. I veer left, my pace slowing as a cramp grips my side.

"Keep going, Jack. You can do this. Breathe through it. You've got a few miles left in you. You're not home yet."

"Sommers!" The wind carries Doug's voice. It cracks on my name, tight with pain and rage, breathless from running. "I'm going to kill you!"

The wind bites my face, pushing me back by the shoulders. I shake rain from my eyes and see lights flickering at the edge of the park.

Not lights.

Flames.

"Do you see lights ahead of you?" Chill asks.

"Yes."

"Head straight for them. Whatever you do, don't stop."

I force myself into a sprint, shoes slapping puddles as I race toward the flickering fires ahead of me. Behind me, Doug's footfalls grow louder.

Shapes emerge from the darkness, holding flames in their palms. Each time I pass one, another ignites in the distance.

My breath is loud in my ears.

"Keep going," Chill says. "They've got you."

"Who?" I breathe. "Who's got me?"

A figure appears through the mist in front of me. I stumble as the shape of the scythe cuts through the fog.

"Shit, he's in front of me!"

"Get down, Jack!" Amber shouts, somewhere ahead, to my left.

I duck at the telltale *whoosh* of a fireball soaring. An orange light hisses through the air like a comet. Doug dives left to avoid it, and I veer right, following the path and picking up speed. A crack spreads across the walkway in front of me. As I leap over it, the ground explodes in a spray of dirt. I look back when I don't hear Doug's feet behind me. Roots lash at his legs, holding him back. He roars, propelling a blast of wind toward the Seasons crouching in the trees.

The force of the gale blows me off the path. I risk another glance over my shoulder, but I don't see Doug anywhere.

"Chill?"

"Keep moving! Look for the lights."

I run toward the flashes of firelight ahead of me, skidding in the muddy grass as Doug emerges out of the fog.

His face is haggard. He's breathing hard. Blood streams from his nose, staining his bared teeth. He starts toward me. I duck as a bolt of lightning streaks across the sky. Doug turns at the deafening crack as a tree collapses, knocking him down.

A voice shouts from the woods, "Move it, Jack!"

I break into a sprint. My feet find the path. A gate materializes through the fog ahead of me. Too high to jump. No way around it. I slam on the brakes, but my momentum's too strong, and I brace for the inevitable impact. A tree groans to my left. A branch wraps around my waist, and I'm yanked off my feet, swooping upward as I'm tossed over the gate.

I fall on my face on the other side. An unfamiliar voice shouts through the fog, "Run, Sommers! I'll buy you time."

I push myself up and keep running, crossing a street.

"Where am I?" I ask, sucking wind.

"Just passed Crooms Hill," Chill says. "You're doing great. Only three miles to go."

My chest feels like it's going to explode. "Three miles? I can't—"

"Don't slow down, Jack. Just keep going. Follow the fires."

They flash like runway lights in front of me. "Who are they?"

"A few Seasons we evacuated from the Observatory. We arranged an escort service for you. We thought you might need a little help."

"Yeah," I wheeze. "Help is good. Thanks."

He gives a low chuckle. "Stick to the lights. They'll guide you to the tracks."

"What tracks?"

"They're just ahead of you. Follow them west. Doug's moving faster than we thought. You need to make it across Deptford Creek. If you can get across the bridge, I can slow him down."

"The bridge? Sprinting across wet railroad ties in the dark? This is your plan?"

"It's our best shot. You're going to lure him into a bottleneck." Chill stifles his microphone, muting his conversation with someone else. Sweat trails down my sides and my footsteps feel heavy. Everything feels too heavy. I slow, clumsily unzipping my jacket as I jog. My shoulder aches as I peel it off. Fishing the eye from its zipper, I tuck it into the pocket of my soaked jeans and toss the sopping jacket away from me.

The last flame gutters out as I reach the tracks.

The rails are dark, the shape of the raised ties hard to make out. The toe of my shoe catches on one and I pitch forward, my hands and knees coming down hard on icy metal.

"Jack?" Chill asks, a rising tension in his voice. "What happened? Why'd you stop?"

"I can't . . ." I pant, the words caught in my raw throat. "I can't run anymore."

There's a shuffle in my ear. The tense cadence of familiar voices. I bow my head, my chest heaving, my hands braced on the tracks. Rain streams over my neck and off the edge of my nose.

"Get up," a voice says.

I lift my head, scanning the blackness in front of me, but the voice I heard wasn't out there. It was inside me. In my ear. "Fleur?"

"If you love me, you will get up and get across that bridge. Now, Jack!"

I scramble to my feet, negotiating the tracks with careful heavy steps.

"You can do this," she says. "Just focus on what's ahead of you, and don't look back."

I anchor myself to the sound of her voice as I stumble over the ties. I want to tell her I love her. That if I don't make it, I died trying. But I can't catch enough air to utter the words. Every breath burns.

Rain slashes sideways across my face. Behind me, fire hisses through the air. A gale throws me off-balance, and I hold out my arms to steady myself.

I look down. "I'm on the bridge."

"Don't stop. No matter what happens, keep going." Every word sounds tinged with worry.

"Sommers!" Doug's voice booms behind me. I push myself faster, using my outstretched arms for balance to counter the wind. I hardly feel it where it cuts across my body. Rain forms a layer of ice on my skin. Maybe I'm too cold to feel anything. Maybe I'm already in shock. Doug won't have a chance to kill me. Hypothermia will.

The track shakes. Despite Fleur's warning, I look back. Doug. He's on the bridge.

There are no trees to haul me over the creek. No fireballs to buy me time here.

"I'm not going to make it. Fleur, I—"

"Don't you dare stop! Doug's tired and he's hurting. He's using too much magic and he's wearing himself down. Just get to the other side of the bridge. We'll handle the rest."

The wind stutters. I duck my head, pushing against it. My ice-crusted hair slaps against my cheek as the wind shifts, building momentum. The black surface of the water peels back from the side of the bridge, the wave receding to reveal the shadowy creek bottom underneath. A familiar howl reaches my ears . . . a funnel forming.

"Move your ass, Jack! Shit's about to get ugly!" Julio. Behind me. Somewhere on shore.

I run, tripping over the ties. I don't look back as the waterspout spins over the side of the bridge. The force of it pulls me, dragging me backward into its path. I lean forward, pressing ahead to get clear of it. Doug's shouts are muffled in the roar. When I can't resist the pull anymore, I throw myself down on the tracks, grab the rails, and hold on.

The spout rattles the track. I turn to look over my shoulder, certain I'm about to be crushed by a train. The funnel twists across the bridge, tearing up ties. I can't see Doug behind it.

"Now, Jack! You have to move now!" Fleur's voice is hard to hear over the crack of shattering wood. I push myself to my knees, then to my feet, my head bowed against the wind. A fire flickers in the distance.

I'm close.

The creek bed disappears. There's a warehouse to my right. An access road to my left. The wind slows as the funnel disperses.

"Sommers!" Doug's voice feels farther away. Beaten. Exhausted. Angrier than before.

I stumble off the tracks, following the light, veering left over the edge of the rail onto the narrow road that runs parallel to it. I tell myself to run, but my body won't listen. I stagger through the deep puddles, clutching the cramp in my side, every labored breath burning.

A pair of blinding white headlights cut sharply toward me. I raise my arms, shielding my eyes as a car skids to a stop. The window rolls down.

"Get in." Lixue grips the steering wheel, frowning at the train tracks. Her wipers slap at the rain, flinging water at me. "What do you need? An engraved invitation? Get in the damn car!"

"It's okay," Fleur assures me. "She'll take you to Auggie's. We're on our way. I have to go. I'll meet you there."

My earpiece goes silent as the connection shuts down. I gape through the rain at Lixue. Her knuckles are white around the wheel.

"Last chance," she says, inclining her head toward the bridge.

With a muttered swear, I slide into the seat behind her, glaring at her in the rearview mirror as I slam the door. Maybe she'll think twice before she gets any bright ideas about killing me and dumping my body.

She throws the car in reverse, wet tires squealing as she backs down the access road. Her headlights cut through the fog. Doug parts it like a curtain, watching us from the end of the bridge as we speed toward Auggie's house.

57

HE MUST SEEK ME

DOUG

Lixue and I lock eyes through the open window as Jack ducks into the back seat of her car. I manage a few steps toward it before her car peels out. Dropping to my knees at the edge of the storm-beaten bridge, I clutch my side, watching her taillights shrink to the west.

"Stop," I say, staggering off the tracks into the street. I shout to the sky, "Stop, stop. Stop!"

The silence of the wind is sudden and shocking.

Raindrops hang like crystals in the air, the sunrise brightening the sky behind them, silhouetting the trees. Their branches are frozen in place, bent by the storm. The churning creek is motionless under what's left of the bridge, the white-capped waves still as stone.

Nothing moves but me.

I lumber through the rain, breathing through the crippling tightness in my chest. The more I use my magic, the worse it hurts. Every time I called on an element to fend off an attack, it only seemed to stoke a battle inside me. I glance inside a burn hole in my coat, wincing at the blistered flesh. My leg bleeds freely where a falling branch cut me, and there's dirt in my eye, kicked up by the winds.

My insides feel battered as I walk toward Lixue's car. I should have known. Should have sensed she'd already turned when she begged me to open the portals for the Seasons she'd led out of the Observatory.

Hissing with every step, I lean heavily on the staff. I don't know how much longer I can hold time back.

If you were in control, the world wouldn't be coming apart. . . . Admit it, you're in over your head.

I shake myself as I approach Lixue's car, determined to keep it together. I still have the staff. I still have the magic.

Jack's face is a mask in the rear window. Lixue's windshield wipers are frozen midstroke, the rain spraying up from her tires suspended in midair. I kick the side of her car, but my foot passes through it like a ghost.

I throw down my staff, pacing in front of her headlights and tearing at my hair.

I can freeze time, and for what? What good is the most powerful magic in the world if I feel powerless when I wield it?

I draw a heavy breath, surprised to find so many smells still hanging in the air: the exhaust from Lixue's car, Verano's cloying reek, the smoky moldering odor of his Autumn girlfriend . . . and something else . . . that brisk cold glimmer that had ridden the air at the clock.

It had come from Jack.

But how?

I close my eyes, tracking them by scent. Julio Verano is already a quarter mile away, headed west. Amber Chase isn't far behind him.

Lixue and Jack, Julio and Amber . . . they're all heading west. And I can guess exactly where they're going—to find Fleur.

She must have changed directions inside the ley lines. If the others are heading west, she must have been diverted off the Meridian. And that's a trail I can trace. There are only a handful of ley lines in all of London.

What I wouldn't give to see the look on Jack's face when he finds her, and me already there, waiting beside whatever stasis chamber they've managed to steal, holding her plug.

Clutching my side, I bend to recover my staff from the road and head west, my magic attuned for the electric hum underground. My cracked rib stabs my side with every step, and there's a void—a strange stinging absence in my mind. I knew it the moment Fleur disappeared. Her magic tore itself from mine like a Band-Aid ripping free, leaving a raw, angry wound in its place.

I roam the frozen streets of Greenwich. I don't know where I'm going. Only that I'm following the hum of a ley line. Blowing trash hangs in the air, mid-tumble. A fork of lightning glows in the sky. There's not a soul in sight. Not a light shining on any porch or in any windows. And I wonder if this is what the world will feel like when it ends. If I'll be the only one left.

The ley line converges with Julio's and Amber's scents. The farther west I go, the more the trajectories of their paths seem to align. I follow them through the empty streets toward . . . Peckham.

My feet go still as a conversation I had with Lixue just days ago comes barreling to the front of my mind.

. . . got a hit on a street cam in Peckham . . . She got off a bus there an hour ago.

58

NOT ONE WAS LEFT TO CONQUER

JACK

My door's already open when Lixue swings the car into the alley behind Auggie's place. The van's nowhere in sight. I tap the speaker in my ear, but the connection is still down.

"Fleur?" I call her name as I tear through the puddles toward Auggie's door. "Where is everyone?"

Lixue gets out behind me without bothering to shut off the car. "I don't know. They should be here by now. They were supposed to meet us . . ." Lixue's next words hang unfinished. There's a soft snap behind me, and something heavy thumps to the ground.

I turn, stumbling backward from the car. The driver's side door hangs open, the windshield wipers slapping rain over the side. Lixue lies in the middle of the street, her head bent at an unnatural angle. Sparks of her magic mix with clouds of exhaust.

Doug stands over her, blood streaming from his nose. A deep violet bruise darkens his cheek and burn marks checker his coat. He doesn't spare Lixue a glance as he treads over a puddle of her ashes.

How the hell did he find us? I have the eye; he couldn't have known where we were going. And there's no way he made it here this quickly on foot.

I look past him, expecting to see a car full of Guards, but he's alone.

"Haven't you learned by now?" he asks, limping closer. "There's no point in running. You can't stop what's coming. You can't hide from Inevitability."

I back away from him, one slow step at a time. "I can stop it. I can change it. We both can. It's not too late to make the right—"

"Don't you dare finish that sentence. You and Lyon can both go to hell." He lumbers toward me, gripping his scythe with both hands. Nostrils flared, he lurches to a stop halfway down the alley. His head tips toward the sound of a door creaking open behind me.

"What a surprise," Doug says, baring his teeth. "You look like shit, Kai."

I stiffen at the familiar sound of an arrow being drawn from a quiver. I turn slowly over my shoulder. Rain drips from the short dark ends of Kai's hair. Her hands shake with stasis tremors around her bow. Her arrow's already nocked and ready, the wicked retractable barbs aimed somewhere between me and Doug.

"What can I say? I'm full of surprises." Her voice is raspy and low as if she's just woken up. An oversize flannel shirt hangs lopsided on her shoulders, the buttons misaligned, as if she rushed to fasten them. The pajama pants she wears are far too big, trailing the ground so only her toes stick out.

Doug spits blood on the pavement. "Glad to see you made it out of the Observatory."

"Are you?" Her bare feet drag through the puddles, slow and cautious, her narrowed eyes darting between us as she creeps steadily closer. "I was under the impression you didn't care. Maybe I was dreaming, but I could have sworn I heard the Guards call you on the radio when the evacuations started. If I remember correctly, I believe your exact words were, 'Let her rot down there.'"

Doug's laugh is harsh. "You remember that, do you?"

"I remember a lot of things you never meant for me to hear."

His smile crumbles. A muscle works in his jaw as they exchange a long look. Thunder rolls, ominously close.

"How'd you get out?" he asks.

"Someone carried me." The point of her arrow shifts slowly to me. She licks rain from her lips, drawing a steadying breath as if she's preparing to shoot. "Sommers has the eye. He took it from me."

Instinct makes me raise my hands. "Can we talk about this?" I ask in a low voice. "Please."

"You've already said all I needed to hear." Her gaze leaps to mine, pointed and piercing. As if she's trying to shoot a message straight through me. She slinks sideways into the middle of the alley, trapping me between her and Doug.

His face slackens with surprise and his eye rakes over me. "You have the eye? Let me see it."

"Show me your back, Winter," Kai says quietly.

I blink against the rain, searching the alley for a way out. There's a wall behind me, a building in front of me. Kai to my right. Doug to my left. I consider taking my chances and running. Better to go down fighting, right?

But something in Kai's words . . . and in her eyes when she said them . . . makes me hesitate.

She's staring at me with that same determined laser focus she had while we were in the cavern, right before she doused the torch and we ran.

No more jokes about keeping my arrows where you can see them. . . . When are you going to start trusting me?

Rain beads down her face. She doesn't blink. Her nostrils flare. Is this some kind of a test?

Show me your back . . . Winter.

I look down at my hands, certain I'm imagining the way they shimmer in the icy rain. They're not even shivering.

I raise them, slowly turning my back to Kai. She comes up behind me and frisks my wet jeans. Her free hand dips into my pocket. She holds the crystal up where Doug can see it. She's standing close enough for an elbow to the ribs.

Her gaze flicks up to mine. A warning.

Doug's palm is blistered with frostbite, the cracks red and seeping, as he reaches out expectantly. "Toss it to me."

Kai shakes her head. She slips the eye in her pocket, retreating a few steps behind me, putting me smack between them. "Don't move," she says. A chill skates through me and I brace for an arrow. I'm not sure which one of us she's speaking to.

Doug's eye twitches. "Give me the crystal, Kai."

Headlights slash across the mouth of the alley behind him. Tires squeal as the van skids to a stop.

Fleur throws open the passenger door, hurling herself out the van, her bare feet tripping on a pair of borrowed sweatpants that could only be Auggie's. Her pink hair sticks to her face, darkened by the rain. My breath stills at the sight of her.

"Doug, stop this!" she shouts.

Julio, Chill, and Amber rush into the alley behind her. I look between them, silently begging them not to interfere. The plan we made in the catacombs is moot. There's only one way this ends. They should run while they can.

Doug doesn't bother to turn around. He closes his eye, lips parted as if he can taste the others in the air. "Do you know why, Fleur? Why I didn't kill him that day I left you in my office?" he asks, the words taut with emotion. "I could have found him. The same way I found you that day in the catacombs. I could have searched every tunnel and appeared right in front of him. I could have ended him then. Do you know why I didn't?" His voice shakes, rage straining the cords in his neck. "Because I could *feel* what it would do to you. I knew it would tear the world out from under you. And I didn't want to subject myself to that kind of pain again. But now?" He wipes his nose, paling at the thick smear of blood as the rain washes it from the back of his hand. "I'll gladly kill both of you."

Fleur rushes forward.

Kai's bowstring creaks behind me. "Stay back, or I'll shoot him!"

Fleur trips to a halt. Julio, Chill, and Amber pause beside her, their eyes darting back and forth between Fleur and me as if they're not sure whether they should charge ahead with her or hold her back.

415

I give a slight shake of my head, hoping like hell I'm not wrong about this. Poppy and Marie watch through the rain-beaded windows of the van, their hands pressed to the glass.

"Doug, please," Fleur begs. "It doesn't have to end like this."

"You're in no position to ask me for anything," he seethes, turning to face her. "You had your chance. You had a choice between saving Sommers and saving the world. And here we are," he says, throwing up his hands. "The Observatory's gone. The sky is fucking falling. Tell me how it ends, Fleur!"

"I can't," she cries.

"I can," Kai calls out. Doug turns to her. A trickle of blood flows from his ear. "You want Inevitability?" she asks him. "You want to see how this ends? Fine, you can have it. But I want your assurance first."

Doubt rides the crest of his brow. "Assurance of what?"

"That Sommers will get what he deserves."

He laughs. "And you want to be the one to give it to him?"

"It's only fair."

This is what he's wanted all along, isn't it? To watch me die. That my end should be at the hands of someone I thought was loyal to me.

Fleur's fist twitches at her side. I give another tight shake of my head, willing her to trust me.

Doug's desperate gaze drops to Kai's pocket. His hands flex around the staff, his palm slick with blood where he holds it. Pain contorts his features and he sucks in a ragged breath. "And in exchange, Inevitability will be mine?"

"Make your choice," Kai snaps.

"Fine," he snarls. "Be done with it."

Fleur cries my name. My breath hitches with the sound of the bow's release. The arrow hisses past my ear, soaring through the head of the staff—a clean shot into the empty hole where the eye should be.

The arrow's barbs flare with a *snick*. A trailing line of thick, clear filament falls across my shoulder. Kai jerks the line with a grunt, winding it toward her. The staff slips from Doug's blood-slicked fingers, and I grab the handle as it rushes toward me.

Shock slackens Doug's face. He stumbles, arms outstretched. Time seems to move in slow motion. His shout is feral as he charges toward me.

I draw the handle back and swing. The scythe buries itself deep in Doug's chest. He drops to his knees in front of me.

Amber, Julio, Chill, and Fleur jolt to a stop.

"Oh no," Julio whispers as a hot wind whips through the alley.

Static hisses in the air. We all duck at a sudden deafening *crack* as lightning strikes a streetlight, showering the alley with glass.

Doug's body starts to glow. Beams of light radiate from his eye. Bolts of electricity surge from his chest through the blade, burning cold as they pass into me.

Amber, Julio, and Chill lift their heads, shouting my name. Fleur pushes to her knees, fighting wind, crawling on hands and knees to get to me. Another fork of lightning splits the sky. I cry out as the bolt strikes Fleur, and behind me, Kai screams.

59

THROUGH THE THIN FROST

FLEUR

I blink awake to a dim gray sky. My clothes are soaked through and my cheek is pressed against cold, wet pavement. Soft rolls of thunder rumble quietly in the distance. A trail of ash-colored water trickles over the street.

My head feels foggy. The moments before the lightning strike are a blur as I roll onto my side, staring at a patch of scorched pavement. The staff rests on the ground beside it, the handle loose in Jack's outstretched hand.

"Jack!" I scramble to his side. The van door slides open behind me. Feet slap the puddles, pounding through the alley as I reach him. Jack's skin is ice cold, his face slack, unresponsive, when I take him by the cheeks and gently shake him. "Jack, can you hear me?"

Auggie kneels, nudging me aside to pry open Jack's lids. Amber, Julio, and Chill rush toward us, hovering over Auggie's shoulder. Marie and Poppy shove in close to see.

Jack's irises are solid white. Frosted mist curls from his mouth with his shallow breaths.

"Jack's eyes are doing that creepy Winter thing. And he smells like one. How is that even possible?" Amber asks, her own eyes welling.

My breath catches. It worked. Those tiny sparks of magic I pulled from Doug and breathed into Jack before I left him at the clock . . . they survived. I *feel* them stirring inside him now, like an extension of myself.

That breath of Winter stayed with him, though the park, through the run and the storm on the bridge. It was inside him when he held the staff and killed Doug. But that would mean . . .

Julio bends down, gently prying the staff from Jack's hand. No sooner than he picks it up, Julio drops it with a swear. The staff clatters to the ground. He shakes out his fingers, steam rising from his handprint where he touched the handle. "Shit, that's cold!"

I take Jack's hand, peeling back his limp fingers. His palm is fine— the calloused skin frigid, but unblemished where he held the scythe.

"I kissed him," I whisper. "I kissed him at the clock before you pulled me into the ley lines. I gave him a breath of Gaia's magic." I had reached through my connection, into Doug, where Gaia's magic was still clinging to me. I had pulled a few sparks of her magic into myself, the same way Doug had pushed it into me before I resuscitated the boy he killed. Only instead of concentrating on the fiery heat of them, I'd focused all my thoughts on the cold. On Jack. On the way his magic had felt when he'd first kissed me.

I gave him *Winter* magic.

"I wasn't even sure I could. I wasn't sure it even worked. Jack

419

probably didn't even know. But the magic must have been inside him when he took the staff. If Jack wasn't entirely human when he killed Doug, then Chronos's magic . . ." I turn, looking up at them. "It must have passed to Jack."

Julio goes perfectly still. He looks at me like he's seeing a ghost.

"What's wrong?" I ask, holding tighter to Jack. Julio takes a step back from me. Poppy, Amber, Chill, and Marie . . . even Auggie . . . they're all staring at me.

"Your eyes, Fleur," Amber says, "they look like Gaia's."

I blink, touching the skin around them. I don't see any differently. But as I look at each of their stunned faces, I *feel* different. I feel *them*. Each of them. As if I could reach out with my mind and touch their magic. I feel Amber's heat. The ebb and flow of Julio's breath. I feel the wind in Chill's soul. I feel Marie's and Poppy's worry, and Jack's pain. And something else . . . a magic I can't quite place.

I turn as a low groan rises down the street. Kai curls on her side, her face pinched with pain. Auggie runs to her, his hands moving over her as he checks her for injuries. He pries open her eyelids. "We should get them inside. Hurry," he says, sliding an arm under Kai.

Kai's eyes flutter open as Auggie hefts her to her feet. There's a collective gasp as she lifts her head. Her eyes meet mine, glittering like two pale diamonds under her heavy lids.

Kai touches one of them with her free hand, her face a mask of disbelief as she prods the skin around it. She pats her pocket, as if she's lost something and can't remember where it is.

"Jack's plan worked," Poppy says, cringing as she watches Kai hobble toward the door. "Sort of."

During the short ride in the van, Poppy and Chill had explained Jack's plan. Jack, assuming he was human and incapable of taking the magic, was supposed to give the staff to Julio. Amber was supposed to take the eye. And hopefully, when Julio struck Doug with the scythe, the magic would split apart and bind itself to whoever was holding the object it was tied to. Julio would take Chronos's magic, Amber would take Ananke's, and presumably, Gaia's magic would be drawn to me.

Jack's plan still worked, just not exactly the way he imagined.

Auggie tries to move Kai inside. Her face twists with pain and she slides from his arms, planting her feet on the ground. She looks down at me, piercing me with a strange, almost bottomless gaze. It's like placing two mirrors face-to-face and staring into them. Like you could see infinity in their reflection. She blinks, shaking her head as if she's trying to make sense of what she's seeing. "The Winter magic," she rasps. "You have to take it back from us."

I hold tightly to Jack's hand. "We'll wait. When Jack wakes up, he'll make his own decision. I won't make it for him." Jack had swung that scythe out of desperation, in self-defense. He couldn't have known this would happen. He planned for Julio to become Chronos. That's what they'd all agreed to. He should be allowed to choose his own magic—his own fate.

I hover protectively over Jack, brushing back the iced locks of his hair. His forehead's freezing, his skin glazed in frost. Ever since he died and lost his magic at the lake, this is all he's wanted—to come back and claim his magic, to become a Winter again. It feels wrong to make this choice for him without asking. I can't do that to him. Not again.

"Then he'll die." Kai's shaking, sweating and unsteady as she leans into Auggie's side. But her eyes never leave mine. They're clear and fever-bright. Her proclamation doesn't feel like an empty threat. It feels like a statement of fact. As if she's already seen it happen in her mind.

"You don't know him. You don't know how strong he—"

Kai steps out from under Auggie's arm, bracing her hands against the ground as she kneels in front of me, putting us eye to eye. An image reveals itself in the diamondlike facets. A woman leaning over Jack, taking his magic. I suck in a sharp breath as I recognize the woman's face. It's not Gaia. Not Jack's past I'm seeing. It's me. Our future . . .

Kai blinks and the image is gone. "He won't wake up from this. He's injured and exhausted. The magic you gave him was barely enough to ensure his survival through what he just endured. If he'd been human, he'd already be gone. But he doesn't have enough power to fight this for long. And his body isn't strong enough to sustain this kind of pain. There are only two possible outcomes. He cannot be both. And the only way to rid Jack of the burden of Time is for one of you to kill him and take it for yourself, the same way he took it from Doug." Her gaze slides to Julio, Amber, and Chill.

Julio steps away from Jack. None of the others move.

"Or Fleur can take the Winter magic," Kai says, letting Auggie lift her to her feet.

"But I—"

"You have Gaia's power now. You're the only one who can."

I touch my chest, thinking back to the moment I lay dying in the children's hospital. I'd heard Gaia's voice inside me—heard the choice she offered me. And even though I wasn't conscious, she knew my answer, as if she *felt* my heart's desire. The day Jack died at the lake,

Gaia had known his answer, too.

Calling on my new magic, I reach out to Jack's body. The process is as familiar to me as breathing, as familiar and easy as using my earth magic. Jack's heartbeat is wild and arrhythmic, his pain overwhelming. The deeper inside him my magic travels, the more chaotic his body feels. I remember Lyon's face when he took Michael's magic . . . what Gaia told him.

You cannot be both a Season and Time. One draws its magic from chaos, the other from order. They are diametrically opposed. It would tear you to pieces.

Jack's Winter magic screams out to mine, twisting inside him like an icy gale. I can feel it, fighting for space. Fighting for control. Can feel him suffering as the magic shears away his strength from the inside.

I stroke his cheek. *What should I do, Jack?*

The answer whispers inside me: *I trust you.*

A tear slides down my face as I glance up at Kai. She leans on Auggie's arm, a hand clasped to her chest, her suffering written in the lines of her face.

Our friends all look to me, waiting.

But I know . . . I have to make the choice Jack would want me to make for him. Same as I did that day at the lake. Same as Jack did when he made the choice to pull me through the ley lines. Because in his heart, he knew I trusted him to make the right choice for all of us.

I turn to our friends, certain this is right. That this is what he would want for them. "Help me get him inside."

60

AND LO, IT IS ENDED

FLEUR

Weak afternoon light filters around the drapes in Auggie's spare bedroom. An antique clock ticks incessantly in the corner. Jack's hardly stirred through the hourly chimes. I sit in a folding chair at his bedside, my hand on his chest and my forehead resting on his bare shoulder, fighting the urge to sleep.

Kai and Julio are bickering downstairs. Mostly about Jack. Julio's scared Jack's been asleep too long. That something's wrong with him. Kai insists she's seen Jack's future and he'll be fine—that he just needs time to rest and recover from the trauma and all his injuries. Julio was quick to remind her she inflicted the worst of them, making her an unreliable authority on the matter. I hesitated to leave them in the same room together, but Kai seemed certain Julio wouldn't kill her, and I didn't see much sense in arguing those odds with her. Apparently, Ananke's magic has given her the gift of unerring foresight, a fact that she subtly enjoys rubbing in Julio's face whenever he annoys her.

To appease my worry, Auggie and the others agreed to remain downstairs and keep the peace so I could stay up here with Jack.

I bury my head in his shoulder. The dull ache in my chest is becoming harder to ignore, the anxiety making it harder to breathe. My palm rests against his heart. This is all going to be new for both of us. I'm not even sure of the extent and scope of our power, or how it will work together. Kai says that when Jack wakes, he'll be able to see the past clearly, that he'll see all my memories and choices in my eyes—and that he'll understand. For now, touching him doesn't relieve the pain and pressure I'm carrying, and I can't manipulate time. All I can do is be here when he wakes up and hope I made the right decision.

"Your hands are cold," he murmurs.

I lift my head. His hand slides over mine, clammy and warm, but slightly less feverish, and a small smile teases the edge of his lips.

Suddenly, his chest stills.

His smile falls. My heart sinks as his eyes dart back and forth under their lids, and I know by the sudden spike of his heart rate that he's remembering.

His head turns on the pillow. I force myself to meet his gaze as his lids flutter open. He reaches for me, his thumb brushing the skin under my eye.

"They're weird, I know." My face warms the longer he stares at them. I try to turn away, but he cups my cheek, gently turning me back to him.

"No, it's just . . . I need a minute," he says, coaxing my chin up. "I wasn't sure I'd ever see you again. I just want to look at you." His gray eyes dart back and forth between mine, as if he's watching scenes from a movie play out in them.

"You gave me the magic," he says. "The ice on my skin while I was on the bridge . . . It had nothing to do with the storm. When we kissed at the clock . . . you breathed it into me."

I nod into his hand. "Kai knew there was magic in you. She smelled it in the alley, when she came out of Auggie's house."

"She called me 'Winter.' But that means . . ." He frowns as if he's struggling to piece together what happened next.

I hold his hand to my cheek. His eyes lock on mine as I let my memories fill in the gaps for him, beginning with the moment I materialized in the stasis chamber in the back of the van. I show him how Julio and Amber had rallied the evacuated Seasons to aid his escape. How Lixue had been among them and offered to help when we weren't sure he would make it past the bridge.

He swallows at my memory of his sleeping face, covered in frost, as blindingly beautiful as sunlight on snow in those moments before the extraction. Silent tears stream down my face as I remember it for him. How he'd bucked and cried out in his sleep as I'd drawn out his Winter magic. How he'd fallen silent after and didn't wake up.

Kai had been awake during her own extraction. The smaze I drew from her lungs into mine had held a glimmer of Jack, but also pieces of Kai and her sister, and when I'd breathed it into a glass jar Auggie had brought for me, Kai had stopped me before I could seal the lid. She asked me to let it go. Together, we set it free.

But Jack's . . .

"You held on to it," he says, wiping a tear from my cheek.

It had only been a handful of sparks. But the weight of that decision had felt far greater. "I'm sorry," I say through a shuddering breath. In the span of hours, I gave him his deepest desire and ripped it away again. "I had to take it from you. Kai said it would kill you if we didn't. But I couldn't release it yet. Not without asking you."

He brushes a lock of hair from my eyes. "I've let it go. You should, too."

"Are you sure?"

He nods, taking my hand. I draw a slow breath and let go. A silver tendril of magic spirals up from my lungs. The smaze is small, translucent and thin, having only lived in Jack for a short while, and I wonder if this one was any easier for him to part with. It hovers, circling the bed before dashing under the door.

The chatter ceases abruptly on the lower floor. Feet pound up the stairs, a flurry of movement and frantic voices. The bedroom door flies open.

Julio bursts in, carrying the staff in a ratty old oven mitt. "We saw the smaze. Is he awake?" Amber, Chill, Poppy, and Marie rush in after him.

Jack gives them a weary smile. "I'm awake."

"It's about time," Julio sighs. "For Gaia's sake, Sommers, we thought you were dying."

"I told you he'd be fine." Kai lingers in the hall, her crystalline eyes unreadable as they land on Jack.

Jack gestures to her face. "No patch? How'd you manage that?"

"I guess Ananke was happy to have her eye back. No more curse," she says with a shy shrug.

There's a simmering tension between Kai and . . . well, everyone. If we hadn't all seen what she did—saving Jack's life, giving him the staff, standing stubbornly by his side through the extraction of his magic—I'm not sure any of us would have been inclined to let her stay. But something tells me the tension has nothing to do with us, and everything to do with her newfound sight. As much as she boasted about her power with Julio, she's wary of looking at us. Careful when she speaks. As if she's afraid to get too close or say too much. Even to Auggie.

Julio chucks Jack's sore shoulder, making him wince, before holding out the staff to him. "Just for the record, Sommers, I'm not calling you His Majesty, Chronos, His Excellency, or Dad. So don't let this thing go to your head, or I might be forced to remind you of your humble roots."

Jack's laugh relieves the last of the pressure I've been holding. "Got it," he says. "No honorifics." His brows grow heavy as he looks at the scythe. He starts to reach for it, then changes his mind. "Put it in the umbrella stand over there for me, will you?"

Julio frowns. "Sure, okay." The others exchange concerned looks as Julio sets the staff in the stand and strips off the oven mitt. The scythe looks a little like a stage prop, and yet not completely out of place in this room full of antiques.

Auggie edges his way inside the room. "Not to be the bearer of bad news, but there is quite a lot of work to do—Seasons to rehome, storms to settle, an Observatory to salvage—so as soon as you feel up to it, we should probably all discuss how to proceed."

"Gaia, Chronos, and Ananke," Jack whispers. "I don't even know where to start." He rubs his eyes, already looking overwhelmed.

"I sent out a radio transmission to the four portals this morning, informing the Guards there's a new Chronos," Auggie explains.

"How did they take the news?" Jack asks.

"Remarkably well. It seems Doug didn't earn much loyalty during his short tenure. They're relieved, I think, that their new Chronos is someone Lyon chose—and trusted—to be his successor."

Jack's throat bobs at that. I rest my hand on his, giving it a reassuring squeeze. I'm not sure if it's grief over Lyon's death or worry over the professor's enormous expectations of him that seems to be stuck in Jack's throat. His voice is thick when he asks, "What about the evacuated Seasons?"

"The portals have been directed to provide shelter to as many displaced Seasons as they can find here in the city, and they're to send global updates through any open, secure channels to those abroad. They're soliciting volunteers and relocating willing Seasons to storm-ravaged areas and regions in need. They're awaiting further instructions from you . . . Chronos," he adds delicately.

Jack starts to sit up. I push him back down by the shoulders, saying, "We'll be down in a few minutes, Auggie." I give them all a pointed look. One by one, they slip from the room. Kai's the last to go.

"How much time do we have?" I whisper to her as she leaves.

"Fifteen minutes won't harm anything." Kai's smile is wry as she pulls the door shut.

I can already see Jack's mind working. Worrying. Bits and pieces of complex plans falling into place. "Relax," I say, climbing onto the bed. I rest my head on my hand and stretch out alongside him. "Kai says it's all going to be fine."

"How?" His frown is riddled with doubt.

"She won't tell me. But there's no sense arguing with Inevitability. Or with me." I curl into his side and lay my head on his chest.

His laugh rumbles under me as I trace lazy, lacy patterns over his skin. It's warm, the lingering scent of Winter so faint I have to breathe deeply to find it. "Are you okay?" I ask, wondering if he misses the cold. If his new magic will ever feel like a fit. The beat of his heart is steady and strong, keeping time with the clock in the corner.

"I'm okay." He tips up my chin. "I'm more worried about you."

I know what he's asking. In my eyes a moment ago, he didn't just see the memories I showed him. He saw everything. Every fight, every conversation, every trauma I sustained while I was Doug's prisoner.

"I'm okay."

"You couldn't have saved him," he says quietly. "It was never your responsibility to fix him. He made his own choices. He knew the cost."

"I know." And yet, I still feel his loss in ways I don't think I entirely grasp yet.

"Fleur, I know . . ." He pauses, choosing his words carefully. "I know you never intended to come back to the Observatory. That you probably never would have if Doug hadn't forced you to come. I know you wanted things to stay like they were, but . . ."

"You don't have to say it," I say, resting my chin on his chest. "Things are different now. We have a responsibility." To the Observatory. To all the displaced Seasons. To our friends. We can't go back to the villa. Not now. Not yet. Maybe not ever.

I lift my head and look him in the eyes, so he can see that I'd made this choice already on my own. Before I knew Gaia and Lyon intended this exact outcome for us. Before the power was ever ours, when everything seemed hopeless. I knew I would take Gaia's magic even if it meant losing my freedom. "Someone had to rise up and take responsibility for the future. It might as well be us."

He cups my cheek, pressing a soft, reverent kiss to my lips. "You're amazing, you know that?"

"We should go," I say, tempted to deepen it and stay hidden in the crook of his arm for the rest of our immortal lives. "We have a world to save." The thought is more than a little terrifying.

"We have time."

"Says who?" I tease.

He grins against my lips. Rolls me over him and pins me to the bed, trailing kisses down my neck. "Says me."

I erupt in a fit of giggles. "I think the power's already going to your head."

"Only because you gave it to me."

We both start at a persistent thump, like a broom handle pounding against the ceiling downstairs. Julio's voice booms through the floor. "Get down here, asshole. We've already got a million fires to put out."

Jack plants a kiss on the tip of my nose. With a sigh, he sits up and reaches for the staff in the umbrella stand.

61

ALL THE DIFFERENCE

One Month Later

JACK

Glass clinks, a pile of glittering shards collecting in the dustpan as I sweep them from the rug. Some are thick and curved, remnants of the orb Lyon smashed when he freed my smaze. Others are thin and flat, pieces of the framed poster I shattered to find Lyon's last letter.

Amber offered to send a custodial crew to handle it for me. But the thought of sending a cleaning crew, or even using a vacuum in this room, seemed wrong—the noise, the speed, the distant efficiency of it—like something Lyon wouldn't do. Lyon believed in doing the work. He believed in quietly and thoughtfully sweeping your problems toward you. That the simple act of kneeling to scoop up your own mess and discarding the broken pieces could be a lesson in itself. Everything was a lesson to Lyon. And even after a month as Chronos, I still have so much to learn.

It was hard to unlock his office door and step into this space a month ago. Seeing it this way, remembering Lyon was gone for good, had cracked something inside me all over again. But as I turn over a chair and set it on its feet, sliding the drawers back inside his desk and straightening his blotter, I'm not surprised to realize he's right. The simple act of picking up his office sweeps the dust and sharp edges from my memories of him, making the space he takes up inside me feel less broken and easier to spend time in.

I drop slowly into his office chair, taking in the view from this side of the desk and wishing I didn't have to. I would give anything to sit opposite him one more time, to tell him what all his lessons—even the painful ones—meant to me. If my new role has taught me anything, it's that there is no going back. All we can do is remember our lessons, try to learn from them, and move forward.

I check my watch. The broad platinum band and face match the color and finish of the Staff of Time from which it was made. Not long after I'd inherited it, I hired a retired Summer to melt it down. A watch-maker's apprentice in his former human life, he molded the ore and built the wristwatch precisely to my specifications. The image of a lion is etched on the back. A small diamond rests on the tip of the hour hand, another on the minute hand, and icons representing each of the four Seasons are embedded at the four cardinal points of the dial.

The rest of the staff was melted down for placards memorializing friends we've lost along the way: one for Lyon and Gaia, one for Woody, one for Noelle, and even ones for Lixue, Boreas, and Névé.

I scoop Lyon's scattered books from the floor and lay them on the desk, pausing over his tattered copy of *Aesop's Fables*. The illustrations bring a smile to my face as I remember the first time I saw him carrying it, when he found me breaking into the Hall of Records, searching for a way to save Fleur.

I turn to the last page, surprised to find an ornate iron key taped to the inside cover. It's rustic and old, with complex filigree around the handle and large square teeth. I pry it from the tape and set the book down to study the key more closely. The patterns aren't any ordinary filigree . . . they're the tangled roots of a tree. The shape matches the carving on the ironwood doors to the Hall of Records downstairs—the Tree of Knowledge.

And I know, without a doubt, Lyon left this key for me.

I finish tidying up. As I look back at his office, I send up a wish for Lyon and Gaia, that they're together out there in the universe somewhere. I turn off the lights and pull the door closed, locking the office behind me.

Seasons, Handlers, and staff pause in their work to greet me as I walk by. I don't correct them when they call me Chronos anymore. The effort to blend in was pointless. Even though I don't wear a suit or carry a scythe, they all refuse to call me Jack. If anything, Fleur says the absence of the scythe and my willingness to swing a hammer alongside them has earned their respect, and this is simply how they show it. But if anything, I look up to *them*. Fleur and I had little choice but to stay. And there were plenty of Seasons, Handlers, and staff who decided not to, choosing instead to forge their own paths.

I slap hands with a familiar Winter as I pass through the open port into the Crux. The plexiglass barriers were the first demolition project we tackled. The completion of the task was celebrated with music, dancing, torchlight, and cake, and the party lasted for hours. When we woke the next day, we started our first addition to the Observatory—a memorial wall encircling the Crux, listing the names of every Season, Handler, and staff member who perished in the storms and quakes.

I take the elevator down to the Admin level. The doors open to the ever-present drone of drills, saws, and hammers, but the place is coming together day by day. Auggie's row house has been converted into a construction management office, where he facilitates our external processes with human vendors, bankers, and shipping companies. We've depended on our retired staff members—who look old enough to pass as contractors—to handle our supply runs, rent construction equipment, and sign off on deliveries to our warehouses up top, while Fleur and I are coordinating the restoration efforts down here.

I weave around a set of tall ladders in the gallery. Craning my neck, I find a team of Seasons and Handlers repainting the fresco that was damaged in the quake. I can't help but notice that the faces of Chronos, Ananke, and Gaia look a little like me, Kai, and Fleur. The Seasons on the ladders grin mischievously down at me, paint smeared on their smocks and their faces. I shake my head and smile back at them. I'm going to have a hell of a time convincing Julio this wasn't my idea.

Maybe he won't notice. He and Marie spend most of their time supervising the training and orientation program for new Seasons. Handlers who lost their Seasons during the storms have been given the option to become Seasons and be assigned regions of their own. Marie was reluctant about the idea at first, but Chill was adamant that it could work. Already familiar with our world and their roles, the new Seasons were quick to adapt and eager for the opportunity to live part of the year up top.

Meanwhile, Amber's taken charge of the new Guard, whose

primary responsibility is the health and welfare of Seasons and Handlers worldwide. Poppy manages Season Relations, and Chill's become acting director of IT. Together with Amber, they track the flow of Seasons in and out of the Observatory, scheduling peaceful handoffs between them and arranging transport home when their time is up. Chill's team monitors the freed Seasons who chose to live up top, deploying an emergency response team to handle compliance issues as they arise.

It's not all sunshine and roses. There are squabbles from time to time, and even with all our collective magic, we can't avoid every storm. But we face them down together, as a community. As a family. Cleaning up our own aftermath is all part of the growth.

No one argued when Fleur and I gave Poppy and Chill the keys to Doug's suite. Amber, Julio, and Marie were happy to knock out a few walls between a couple of dorm rooms, which they've converted into a two-bedroom apartment. Fleur and I offered to help Kai do the same, but she was content to move quietly into her old dorm room. With the exception of a few classes she teaches for Julio, she spends most of her time looking into the future, identifying humans who will eventually choose to become Seasons. Poppy uses the information to organize Fleur's travel itinerary, making sure she arrives at the precise moment of the human's untimely demise, and then arranging for the new Season to be escorted safely home.

Fleur and I settled into Gaia's old apartment; Fleur couldn't bring herself to move into Doug's. She doesn't talk much about what happened between them, but occasionally, when she needs to share the burden of things that are too difficult to say out loud, she'll show me flickers of her memories. One in particular haunts her more than the others—the face of a boy Doug killed who Fleur had tried to save by turning him into a Season. We managed to find his stasis chamber, buried below the rubble. Abandoned during the evacuation, the chamber had lost power. The boy hadn't survived, and his magic escaped through a crack in the dome.

The walls around me narrow to torchlit tunnels as I descend them into the ancient passages below the west wing. The hum of a generator grows louder ahead, until I'm standing in front of the doors to the Hall of Records. The security panel beside it is dark. The key card system was disabled—the second demolition project after we dismantled the gates in the Crux.

I pull open the Tree of Knowledge and am greeted by a rush of musty memories. Motion sensors trigger the lights. They roll on, room by room, letting me know I'm alone as I walk by the glass display cases of ancient scrolls and leather-bound tomes. I pause in front of a heavy steel door.

The iron clanks quietly as I slide Lyon's key into the lock. The hinges creak, and a chain of lights flickers on as I push the door open. I draw in a surprised breath at the size of this room. The restricted section, containing the history books Michael forbid us to read, was off-limits to Seasons when I lived here before. There doesn't seem to be an end to the rows of dust-coated manuals and texts. No end to the shelves and display cases containing antique machines and ancient inventions.

I tip my head, reading the spines of the books, too afraid to touch them for fear of degrading the delicate parchment. The entire library seems to be ordered chronologically, and I find the volume—the very same volume I was searching for when Lyon caught me sneaking through the stacks in the main room of the Hall.

The History of Natural Order Volume 121 stands out a bit from the other volumes, misaligned from the other neatly shelved spines, as if it was put back in haste. As I pluck it from the shelf, a folded letter slips from its pages. My throat tightens as I recognize Lyon's familiar loopy scrawl.

Jack,

I hope that the fact that you're reading this letter means the worst has already passed and you and Fleur are both recovering from your ordeal.

You once sought this particular volume, if memory serves me. At the time, I could not share it with you. For great leaders do not come to greatness by traversing an easy path. They forge it themselves, suffering losses, pain, and triumphs along the way. You have earned the title. It was an honor and a privilege to hold the mantle for a short time, until you were ready to take it.

You are no longer a thief of knowledge here. You hold the key. You own this knowledge now, and with it, the power to grant or deny access to it. A leader who rises on footholds of ignorance never climbs very far. I trust you and Fleur will make thoughtful, balanced choices.

By now, you are probably wondering, what is the power of Chronos? The heart of Chronos's power doesn't lie in the blade of the scythe. It lies in the sharpness of the minds of those who wield it. The power lies in the wisdom it grants you, not to see the future and find the easy path, but in the lessons learned in hindsight. You alone have the power to stop time, not because it grants you control over others, but so you may hold control over yourself. The magic grants you time to think—detached from the actions and influences of others—before making the difficult choices you're responsible for making now.

The magic of Time may feel insignificant when held up to others, but it's more powerful than you may yet realize. You possess the gift of life lived in the moment, the power to pause and see the beauty and wonder all around you, so you may better remember who you serve and why. And in those frozen solitary moments, it serves to remind you that even the greatest of rulers can only truly move forward and effect change in the world in synchronicity with those around us. This lesson—the lesson of companionship and trust—I derived great joy in watching you master. It is, perhaps, the greatest gift I could have given you. And it is the reason I felt ready to hand over my staff to you, by way of Doug, and to move forward into the next cycle of my life. We are both only changed from one form to another. . . .

With this key and my blessings, I leave you to your kingdom, and to Fleur. May you serve it well together.

With pride in all I've seen in you—both past and future,

Daniel Lyon

PS—This room has been neglected and would benefit from a full-time curator. I believe you may already know a person well-suited for the job.

A smile chases away the lump in my throat. I pull my phone from my pocket and click through my contacts. Auggie's voice mail picks up.

"Hey, Auggie, It's Jack. Give me a call when you get a chance. I've got a project I could use an expert's help with." As I disconnect, I can't help admiring how perfectly Lyon's plans always seem to fall into place, even in his absence.

I tuck the book under my arm, leaving the door to the restricted room wide open when I leave. The lights turn off on their own as I exit the room, the same way they'll turn on again for the next Season who comes here looking for answers.

62

AND WE MOVED ON

FLEUR

Jack's late for dinner. Kai assures me he's on his way and will be here before the evening's entertainment is over. Like every night, the dining hall is full to the brim, every Season, Handler, and staff member packed into one room, the clatter of trays and silverware and chatter almost deafening. A snowball soars over our table, catching Julio in the shoulder as he stuffs the last of his garlic bread into his mouth. His head snaps up, a scowl on his face, until the chanting starts.

"Ju-li-*oh*! Ju-li-*oh*! Ju-li-*oh*!" Soon, everyone in the room is shouting his name, pounding their forks on the tables. A blush burns his cheeks as he reaches for his new guitar—a shiny, full-bodied acoustic Amber bought him a few weeks after they settled in here.

The hall goes wild, clapping and shouting his name. A group of Autumns in the back wave tiny flames above their heads. Among them, I recognize the couple Doug nearly ran over with the car. Coral, the

Summer girl who'd been wearing the blue sweater, curls under Rusty's arm, laughing as he waves a flame above her head. A few Springs, Winters, and Summers join in with lighters. Holly, the Observatory's oldest and most beloved cafeteria attendant, dims every overhead light but one.

Julio tunes his strings as he walks to a stool set under the spotlight. Poppy elbows Amber in the ribs as Julio teases out the opening chords to one of her favorite songs. Marie cups a hand over her mouth and shouts for Julio to get on with the damn show already, her lighter held high over her head.

My gaze keeps returning to the door. I hate that Jack's missing this. After the long days of hard work—after the calluses and sawdust, the aching muscles and paint-splotched clothes—we all look forward to the hour after dinner. It's a lesson the seven of us have carried with us since our time on the run: a little laughter, a song, a hot meal shared with friends—it's the best medicine for a battle-weary soul.

Funny, if you'd asked me a year ago if I could ever imagine myself returning here, I'd have told you I'd rather die. Now I can't imagine living anyplace else. Not because of where we are, but because of the people I share this new life with. I feel them—every soul inside this room is part of me, connected to me, means something to me. They are all a piece of me, and I of them, and I know now what I was never entirely certain of when I made the decision to remain here—that I would lay down my life for every single one of them. In their faces, I see the seven of us as we were. I see who they are yet to become. And that vision of the future sustains me.

A draft blows past my neck and circles my ankles. I turn to see Jack ducking in the door, hoping to go unnoticed.

Julio uses a break between songs to take a sip from his water bottle.

He spots Jack slipping stealthily past the tables, and his eyes twinkle with mischief when he shouts, "Give it up for your Chronos, everybody!"

Seasons call out and wave to Jack, beckoning him to their tables. He smiles, waves, and makes a beeline straight for the shelter of the food line. Julio steals back the spotlight, strumming the intro to one of his favorite tunes, encouraging everyone to sing along.

Halfway through the song, Jack appears beside me carrying a tray full of salad and pasta. He plants a kiss on my cheek and takes a seat across from Kai. As he settles, he catches her eye. They exchange a prolonged glance that steals the smile from Jack's face, and she promptly turns away.

I rest my hand on his knee, raising an eyebrow. He gives my hand a squeeze, as if to say he'll explain later. I don't push, content to let him tear into a mound of spaghetti while the rest of us celebrate the end of another day.

Just another meal at home with close friends and found families.

JACK

Kai emerges from the Blackheath tunnel just south of Greenwich Park right after dinner. She gives me a crooked smile, the silver aviator sunglasses she wears to conceal her eyes reflecting mine.

"I thought you couldn't read the future," she says.

"I can't." The evening is balmy and cool as the sun slips lower in the dusky sky. I tuck my hands in my pockets, matching her leisurely stride toward the duck pond.

"Then how'd you know I'd be here?" she asks, raising a skeptical eyebrow.

"You made the decision to leave days ago." The grass is still damp, littered with fallen limbs. The persistent storms finally cleared last week, and cleanup has been ongoing throughout London. "And don't pretend you're surprised to see me."

She grins at that. "Were you spying on me?" She hitches her backpack higher on her shoulder as I trail her through the park. It's strange to see her carrying something other than her bow on her back. But I guess it's hard to board an airplane with one.

"I wasn't spying," I say defensively. It's mostly true, but I haven't gotten the knack of my sight yet, and sometimes I see things I don't intend to. Like when I saw Kai at dinner an hour ago. She'd glanced up as I sat down at the cafeteria table opposite her and in her eyes, I saw the plane ticket she purchased online last week. One way, to New Zealand, departing tonight. "You don't have to leave, you know. We all want you to stay. Even Julio," I tease her.

"I know," she says, one side of her mouth quirking up. "He doesn't know it yet, but he's going to miss me when I'm gone. You can tell him I said so." We walk in companionable silence past the pond.

"I left you all the names and dates, enough to keep Fleur busy for a few months," she says. "You'll be fine without me for a while." Her lips purse, as if she's holding something back. I know better than to ask her why. Kai's guarded with her sight, careful not to overshare. If she doesn't want to elaborate, she has her reasons. And I've decided we're all probably better off not knowing our futures. Which makes me wonder if this is why she's chosen to leave.

I take her gently by the elbow, pulling her up short. "Look. Before you go, there's something I need to—"

"I already know," she says, her sigh heavy, her smile a little melancholy.

"Right." I rest my hands on my hips, squinting against the low sun as I stare out at the park, trying to figure out what to say. It's hard to look Inevitability in the eyes and ask it for a second chance.

"I've already forgiven you," she says. "And you've already forgiven me. You know that."

"Still, I should have told you about Névé. We both should have. Lyon and I had no right to keep that from you." Maybe Kai has forgiven me, but I still haven't forgiven myself for that.

"Maybe." She shrugs. "Maybe Lyon should have told me when I woke up. But then what? Would I have gone to Mexico to help you or to kill you? Or maybe you should have told me in the tunnels when you figured out who Ruby was. If you had, what would I have done?" She arches an eyebrow. "I think now maybe I understand why he didn't always tell us everything."

She pushes her sunglasses higher on her nose, looking past me at the long stretches of grass as if she's trying to figure out how to explain. "I can't stay, Jack. Lyon was right to cover the eye. To separate it from the staff. You and Fleur are better off not knowing the future. You deserve to live in the moment and make your own choices without that burden."

"Does this have anything to do with the agreement you made with Lyon to protect me?" I'd seen that, too. And it had hurt to watch, knowing she made that promise to him out of guilt over what she had done to me in Cuernavaca, when all the while, Lyon had never told her what I'd done to Névé. "This is your home, too, Kai. You don't have to leave to protect me or to spare my feelings."

"This has nothing to do with you or Lyon. I've already honored my promise to him. I just . . ." She rakes back her short hair with a heavy sigh. "I just need to find myself, Jack. I need to figure out who I am apart from Ruby. Apart from this place. I might already know how my story's going to end, but I still want the experience of living it. I want to make my own decisions for a while."

I frown at my reflection in her sunglasses. I can't imagine what it must be like to know your own fate. It's one thing to look in someone's eyes and see their past. Or to look in the mirror and have to face your own. It's entirely another to see the consequences of a lifetime of choices you haven't had the chance to make yet.

Kai puts a finger to the bridge of her glasses. She smiles, pulling them down just enough for me to see the glimmer in her eyes. In them, I see Kai—glimpses of her future. Rock climbing, kayaking, hiking a glacier. Camping in the mountains. A kiss on a beach. It relieves me of some of my guilt. And if I'm being honest, eases a little of my worry—it's good to see a future where the world is still here. But it doesn't diminish the loss. Our brief partnership hasn't been without its challenges, but there have been moments when she felt like a friend. I know she wants me to say goodbye, to turn around and walk away. But that doesn't make it any easier.

I glance at my watch, wondering how much time I can steal from her. Maybe I can convince her to miss her flight. She pushes her glasses back in place.

"You'll be okay," she says, throwing a soft punch at my shoulder. "And so will I. You and Fleur are going to finish rebuilding the Observatory. You're going to be loved by everyone and make beautiful Seasons together," she says, wagging her eyebrows suggestively. "And I have it on good authority you and I will see each other again in the not-too-distant future. I promise," she adds, claiming it as a choice and not leaving it to fate.

"I'm counting on it." Thumbs hitched in the pockets of my jeans, I wait for her to be the first to leave.

"Show me your back, Chronos," she says, dragging a laugh out of me as she walks backward toward the bus stop. I'll never get used to people calling me that.

I give her a salute before turning away, hoping she's right. About everything.

EPILOGUE

Six Months Later

<u>JACK</u>

I nearly trip on Fleur's heels as we navigate down the steep wooded hillside, my hands covering her eyes.

"Where are we going?" She chokes on a breathy laugh as I bump into her back. She knows exactly where we are. Her consciousness is attuned to every branch and blade of grass on this mountain, but she's doing a good job of playing along for my benefit.

"Just keep your eyes closed." I pick up the pace as the hillside levels out and the boarding school comes into sight.

The soles of our shoes stick in the cold mud as I lead her to the edge of the pond. It feels like just yesterday that I was holding her hand, dragging her out on its surface, asking her to trust me, promising her I wouldn't let her fall under as I froze the water beneath her feet.

I take my hands from her eyes. "Open them," I whisper, wrapping my arms around her waist.

She bites her lip with a nostalgic smile. "Are you okay?" she asks, leaning against me, her head tucked under my chin.

My grandfather's cabin is gone. I spent the morning sitting on a boulder, staring at the black ring of ash where it had stood. "Yeah, I'm okay."

She turns in my arms. There's soot on her cheek and I brush it away. "We can rebuild it," she says. "I know a few good contractors." We laugh and I pull her into me, holding her as I watch the sun begin to dip below the trees.

"I'd like that," I say into her hair. She smells exquisitely familiar, but different now. More than lilies, more than Spring. She's the ancient oaks in Greenwich Park and the salt mist of the Thames. She's the woodsmoke at my grandfather's cabin, the creosote in the canyon, and the crashing surf in La Jolla Cove, wild and lovely, reflecting every elemental magic inside her.

"Come on," she says, taking my hand and tugging me toward the water's edge, a dangerous glint in the facets of her eyes.

I dig in my heels and consider pausing the timer on the world just to keep from getting wet. "Fleur, what are you doing? I can't take you skating."

"Who said anything about you taking me?" She steps onto the pond, raising a cocky eyebrow as the water freezes under her. She pulls me along with her, the shelf of ice growing until it's wide enough for both of us, spreading all the way to the opposite shore until the entire pond is ours. She's far more powerful than I ever was.

"Show-off," I tease her, but she catches my subtle flinch. This place is full of memories. Not all of them beautiful. Most of them painful.

"We can go back," she says, her face falling. Guilt shimmers in her eyes.

"No," I say, pushing out with one foot. I know better. There's no going back. Only moving forward in time. It's how we heal. How we rebuild and start over. I may not be a Winter anymore. But I'm someone new. Someone stronger. Not just because I'm Chronos, but because of who I was before that—the man I became when I accepted that my magic was gone and I faced my fears anyway. "I want you to take me skating," I tell her. "And then I want you to throw me down on the ground and kiss me like you did before."

Her mouth falls open in mock indignation as she guides me backward across the ice. "I didn't kiss you. You kissed me."

I stop abruptly in the middle of the pond, tug her into my arms and hold her against me, searching for that specific memory in her eyes. I don't have to look far. Fleur reveals that kiss to me, along with a few others that raise my body temp by degrees.

"Be careful," I murmur. "The ice is thin."

"I won't let you fall a second time."

"Too late," I say, threading my fingers through her hair. "I already did."

Time stands still as she reaches up on her toes to kiss me. Our lips meet somewhere in the middle, and we both linger after it's over, our chilled breaths mingling. Lyon was right about the power. About the magic of living in the moment. About the importance of pausing every once in a while to appreciate what's right in front of me. I trace Fleur's lip with my thumb, memorizing the contour of her smile, my reflection in her eyes. Not because I'm afraid of what tomorrow brings. But because she's here with me now.

I take her hand and let her lead me in lazy circles around the pond. For tonight. Tomorrow. Forever. This is enough.

ACKNOWLEDGMENTS

This duology has been both a labor of love and a source of incredible joy for me. I adored writing these characters and their remarkable journey, and I'm eternally grateful to everyone who helped make these books a reality.

My stories would all be collecting dust and cobwebs in my head if not for my agent and Handler, Sarah Davies, who has guided me through every book with infinite wisdom and care. February 15, 2011, I made the decision to enter the Greenhouse. I am grateful beyond measure, Sarah, for the decade I've spent making books with you.

Thank you to the team at Rights People for your enthusiasm for Jack and Fleur, and for bringing my Seasons to other parts of the world.

I'm so, so lucky to have such a supportive publishing team. Tara Weikum, thank you for taking my books under your wing. My stories shine brighter for the wisdom and advice you, Sarah Homer, and

Caitlin Lonning bring to every read. And this cover! Where do I begin? Designer Jessie Gang and Garrigosa Studio, you've captured the imagery of this world so beautifully, and I must be the luckiest author in the world to have a cover created by you. Ivy McFadden and Bethany Reis, thank you for the time and care you take with my words and my voice. It means the world. Gillian Wise, you are a magical being with extraordinary gifts, and I'm in awe of you. I owe my successful launch to you (and my UPS driver). Seriously, you're amazing and I so, so appreciate you. And a million thanks to Shannon Cox, Sam Benson, and the entire team at HarperTeen.

The chapter titles for this book were borrowed from lines of poetry by Robert Frost, whose verses always manage to remind me of Jack. And the lovely line of poetry in Chapter 19 is taken from John Donne's "The Sun Rising."

I couldn't do this job without Megan Miranda and Ashley Elston. Thanks for refilling my well, making me laugh, and keeping me balanced. I'd be in the wind without you.

Thanks to the keen eyes and generous hearts of the very talented critique partners who braved this wild, messy sequel with me: Christina Farley, Chelsea Pitcher, and Tessa Elwood—I'm so grateful for each of you.

For the talented folks who create bookish art—your work brings me so much joy. I'm so inspired by you. Many thanks to Jessica Khoury, mapmaker extraordinaire, for plucking the Observatory from my imagination and rendering it so exquisitely. Salome Totladze (@morgana0anagrom), you are magical! Thank you for making my Seasons so perfectly real! And Marissa at Burning Bright Candle

Company, thank you for capturing each of my Season's unique scents. How lucky I am to enjoy art created by each of you!

To One More Page Books in Northern Virginia, who generously hosted my launch event.

To my parents—for your endless support.

To my husband, Tony, who makes it all possible.

To my children, who one day may recognize bits and pieces of themselves in my books. Nick and Connor, whether you read them or not, every story I write is for you.

And finally, thank you to my readers. To the bookstagrammers (omg, those amazing pics!), bloggers, and reviewers. To the booksellers who support me. To the educators and librarians who put my stories in the minds and hands of those who need them. To the book box companies—The Bookish Box, Fae Crate, Totally Booked Crate, and Beacon Book Box—who embraced *Seasons of the Storm* in the middle of a pandemic and helped make the launch month a huge success—you all are amazing! To those who've been there since my very first books and to those who are only now finding them. My imaginary worlds, and this wonderful sandbox of creativity I get to play in, wouldn't be nearly as much fun without you.